WAITING TO INHALE

PAWS ON THE KEYBOARD

WAITING TO INHALE

WICK SHORTS
BOOK ONE

Published by Paws on the Keyboard
www.pawsonthekeyboard.com

ISBN 978-1-952763-00-7

Printed in the United States of America

WAITING TO INHALE

MAX THOMPSON
with K.A. THOMPSON

WAITING TO INHALE

WICK SHORTS BOOK ONE

A DAY IN THE LIFE

Hyrum's room was best described as ordered chaos. He kept it tidy in the same way that 3 ½-year-old Rhys and his younger brother and sister kept their playroom tidy: toys technically put away yet stacked unevenly, looking as if a hard sneeze would blow them over. Hyrum's treasured print books were on the shelf above his toy box, some placed with consideration, spines out so he could see the titles, others stacked in different directions with pieces of drawing paper between them, edges folded down, corners slightly torn. His clothes were placed in his dresser, the drawers only half-closed, legs of jeans draped over the side, with socks jutting out the top.

No one said anything to him about the state of his room. He made an effort in putting things away, and it was his private space. His sister sometimes twitched when she passed his open door, resisting the impulse to step in and straighten things, but she respected that he had things arranged the way he wanted and suspected that his misstacking of some of the items were intentional. Were a toddler to sneak into his room with the intent of absconding with one of his toys, the noise would draw an adult down the hall.

He owned only one fragile thing—a nanoglobe that Drew had given him—and he placed it out of easy reach. He was afraid it would break, and was especially afraid that if it were accessible, a toddler would grab hold, shattering the glass, and cutting themselves. He either didn't notice or didn't care that he was never gifted things that were easily breakable, nor that he was gently persuaded to not purchase those things for himself.

"What fun can it be if it breaks easy?" Drew asked him on those rare occasions he was tempted. "You can't really play with it, and who wants a toy they can't play with? It's not even about the kids. You work hard for your money, and if it were me, I'd want something I could really use."

Hyrum Charles Munson, 48 going on 7, sometimes 10 on a good day, sometimes 5 on a bad one, more than anything wanted to be good. Part of being good was rising before the sun, a habit left from a childhood that demanded it from him. He woke a little after four in the morning and quietly got dressed; from age seven on he crawled out of bed before dawn to help his mother get everything ready for breakfast, making sure the kitchen was spotless as she cooked, double-checking to be sure his father wouldn't find a speck of anything on the table that didn't belong there.

Life was better if Levi Munson left the house without anger. It wasn't wonderful and it wasn't happy, but it was better.

Now he could sleep as late as he wanted, but the habit was ingrained. He also knew if he were up by four-thirty, he would have a quiet half-hour alone with his brother-in-law. They sat together at the kitchen table while Jax sipped at his coffee and tried to wake up enough to go for a run with the Emperor, or while Jax mentally prepared himself for a long day of royal duties.

On days that Jax ran with Will, Hyrum made the coffee and when Jax was ready, he often went outside with him and sat on the steps at Union Square, where he cheered them on with each lap. On days Jax had a schedule that precluded running, Hyrum made breakfast for him. Jax had given up telling Hyrum that it wasn't necessary; he was capable of getting his own food and didn't want to impose, but Hyrum insisted.

He wanted to help; he wanted to be good.

This morning, I was curled up at the foot of Hyrum's bed, watching as he stretched and yawned, waiting for that deep breath he often took before sitting up. When it came, I carefully stepped up the side of the bed to greet him, rubbing my head against his arm, gently so that I didn't scare him.

"Wick, hi." He lifted me up and nuzzled his face to the top of my head. "Did you sleep with me all night? I didn't kick you or anything, did I?"

I spent a few hours here. You barely moved.

"I had a dream about my daddy." He grunted as he got up, then shuffled toward his bathroom. "Or maybe it wasn't really him. It was like when we were at Shivan's, and Jax wanted to shoot my daddy. That wasn't really him. I don't think, anyway."

It wasn't. But I understand your confusion since he wore your father's face.

"In my dream he was yelling at my mom because I didn't know how to tie my shoes and it was her fault that I'm stupid. But I know how to tie my shoes, Wick." He finished up in the bathroom and slipped his jeans on, then grabbed his shoes. "Look. I'll show you."

I've seen you tie your shoes. You're not stupid. Even if you couldn't, that doesn't make you stupid.

"I learned how when I was eight, I think. Red taught me. Mom thought it was a pain and it took too long, so she used to tie them for me. But Red knew I would learn. He didn't think I was stupid."

Not knowing how to do something just means you haven't learned it yet. That's all.

"Anyway, at least I didn't set Daddy's hair on fire in the dream. Sometimes I do. I always put it out, on account of that's the right thing to do."

I followed him down the hall to the kitchen and waited on the breakfast bar while he started a pot of coffee. He never drank any; he didn't like the taste, and *really* didn't like what it did to his bowels. He loved the smell, though, and was inhaling deeply when Jax shuffled into the kitchen.

Jax greeted him with a kiss on the top of his head. It wasn't likely that he would do more than grunt until he'd had a few sips of his coffee. Hyrum knew this; it had bothered him when he first came to live with Jax and Aubrey, worried that he was upsetting Jax, but after a week or so he understood that Jax just wasn't quite awake and he was getting up earlier than he needed to, for no reason other than he wanted that quiet time with Hyrum.

After Jax had enough of the coffee and the last bits of sleep lifted, Hyrum asked if this was a running day or a workday.

"Work," Jax grunted. When Hyrum started to get up, Jax gestured for him to sit back down. "Breakfast meeting. There will be coffee and donuts. Don't tell Aubrey."

Hyrum giggled, which turned into a snicker when he heard Aubrey coming down the hall, wanting to know what was being withheld from her.

"You're up early," Hyrum said, trying to keep Jax's sugar-laden-breakfast secret. "Is today a babysitting day?"

"Wick has an early checkup today, and there are a few things I'd like to get done around here before we go," she answered, reaching across the breakfast bar to rub my head. "You have therapy right after. I thought we could go together if you'd like some company."

She also had appointments throughout the morning and would be taking a car. Hyrum scrunched his nose at the idea of sitting in the back seat while someone else drove them around; he might have agreed if he was the driver, but these were official appointments, requiring a formal escort from the guard.

That also meant he would have to wear a dress shirt, which he absolutely did not want to do.

"I can take Wick to his appointment," Hyrum offered. "I'll put the basket on my bike, and he can ride there, and then he can go to my doctor with me."

"Is that safe?" she wondered.

"Drew made me a new basket. It has a special top and everything, so Wick can't fall out. But he can still see everything if he wants and even if I fell, Drew says he would be okay. I'll be careful."

"How about it, Wick?" Jax asked. "Who gets to take you to get poked and prodded this year?"

I jumped from the breakfast bar to the table and went to Hyrum. It wasn't that I didn't want to go with Aubrey; it was more that Hyrum looked hopeful.

"I'd say my feelings are hurt, but you'll have more fun with Hy."

"Why isn't Will taking him?" Jax asked.

Will had three toddlers to wrangle all morning and didn't want to drag them to the vet. Instead, he was taking them to the Ozoo complex, where they had a playroom connected to his office and frequent interlopers coming in to visit with them.

I wasn't sick; had I been, Will would have asked Jay to watch the kids and taken me himself. This was just a checkup, something Hyrum could handle on his own. As soon as we left the building, Aubrey would be on the phone to let the vet's office know who was bringing me, making sure the doctor knew to withhold any upsetting information, should there be any.

Riding his bike was, hands and paws down, Hyrum's favorite thing to do. He rode it everywhere he could, exploring San Francisco in a way he'd never been allowed when he was younger and living with his parents in Florida. He avoided sections of the city where cars were allowed, though sometimes he braved the lighter traffic near Golden Gate Park; none of the hills bothered him, and he now knew the city as well the natives did.

I sat on the guard's desk near the door while he retrieved his red bicycle from under the stairs and clipped the basket on. He chatted happily with the guard on duty—it didn't matter who was at the desk; Hyrum rarely left without at least saying hello and often had conversations with the younger guards about comics he'd read or a TV show they were both interested in.

He'd added "TV" to the lexicon in the royal house, from the King down to the newest guards. There was confusion at first—what does he mean, he watched TV?—but it was easier to adopt his terms instead of convincing him that what he engaged in was the viewing of entertainment videos, or vids. Drew joked that it was only a matter of time before it filtered to the public, and soon everyone would use centuries-old words to describe current tech.

"Well, they already do in Florida," Jax reminded him. "Hell, we do. Look at cell phones. Cellular tech vanished three hundred years ago, but the term held on."

As Hyrum clipped me into the basket, making sure the stiff mesh bubble top was secure, the guard reminded him to be careful on his ride. That used to bother him, as if he wasn't careful and needed to be told, until Will explained that they weren't hinting that he wasn't careful enough. They were telling him they cared about him and didn't want him to be hurt.

"Is that like when Drew tells me to have fun when I go somewhere?" Hyrum asked. "Aubrey says it means 'I love you.'"

"Indeed."

The guard outside held the door open so that Hyrum could easily get his bike out, and he called back, "Thanks, I will be!"

I had no doubt.

That was why I was willing to get in the basket.

He thought like a child a good part of the time, but he would never do anything to get me hurt and would pay closer attention to make sure I was safe.

~

What I didn't expect was how nervous Hyrum would be, sitting in the waiting room at the vet. He held me on his lap, bouncing on his toes, whispering to me that it would be okay. He took Lazybones to the vet when he was little, and it was always okay. "They might do things you don't like, but you have to let them because it's the doctor."

I know. There's a lot of unnecessary touching involved.

"Lazybones hated it on account of he always got a shot, and he always got a temperature thing shoved up his butt. But it doesn't hurt. The temperature thing, I mean. The shot might, but just a little. I don't like shots. Not at all. Last time when I needed one, Red and Joe had to hold me down on account of I tried to run away. And then I kicked the doctor in his privates. But he wasn't mad. I said sorry."

There would be no piercing of my feline flesh with a needle and no invasion of my nether regions. Hyrum had little experience with medicine in Pacifica; he watched, quietly, as the vet looked in my eyes and then prodded my belly, and he bit back a whine when told it was time for my vaccinations.

The vet took a long swab on a stick from his assistant, swiped it in my left ear, then got another to do the same for my right, and was done.

"That's it?" Hyrum asked. "No needles?"

The vet blinked, trying to think of a reason why he needed to use needles, and coming up with nothing, said, "No needles. I need to pry his mouth open and get a good look, so don't be upset if he fights me a bit. Cats generally don't like this."

Hyrum scrunched his nose. "Just ask him to open his mouth. You don't have to make him do it."

"It doesn't work—"

Hyrum bent over and looked at me. "Wick, can you open your mouth for him? He needs to see your teeth and stuff. Maybe even all the way down to your tummy."

"Really, he won't—"

I sat on the table, tilted my head back, and opened my mouth as wide as I could.

"See? If you ask him nicely, he'll do it."

No one ever asked me before, I said when the vet was done trying to look down my throat. *That was a nice change.*

I was proclaimed healthy though still a bit underweight, which was said in a manner suggesting that every time he'd told Will to feed me more, the advice had been ignored. Hyrum picked up on it, and as he scooped me off the table said, "Wick gets to eat a lot, whenever he wants. But he runs around a lot, too, like up and down the stairs and stuff, so he's never gonna be fat. He's just little, that's all."

"I know. He's always been small, but—"

"I eat a lot, too, and I'm small and skinny except for my legs. Some of us are littler than others."

He's not wrong, you know.

The vet caved; I was fine, I was healthy, Hyrum was absolutely right. He hovered behind the front counter while Hyrum asked how much the visit was and if he could use a cash card because he didn't have any "real" money—there was no charge, the Emperor had set up an account with them—and on the way out the door I heard the vet whisper, "Oh, of course, I forgot he's from Florida."

Hyrum heard it, too.

"Well, that's not my fault. I'm glad you didn't get any shots, Wick. I hate shots. One time when I had shots, Daddy said I was a wimp because I cried. But it *hurt*. It hurt a lot."

Well, sure, you got stabbed. I'd cry, too.

He held me close as we crossed the street, even when people waved and said hello to him. He jutted his chin in response, something he'd picked up from Drew, and his mood lifted as people asked how he was, but he didn't ease his grip on me until we were in the waiting room of his therapist's office.

I'd been to the building before, once, when Will waited there for Aubrey and Hyrum. The video monitor had been on and he suffered through children's programming, blurting an expletive at an anthropomorphic cartoon elephant just as Hyrum and Aubrey exited the office.

I didn't mind being here. There was no sterile, antiseptic fog hanging in the air, stinging my nose and eyes. The waiting room was bright and cheery, with each wall painted a different color, and a toddler-sized whiteboard took up considerable real estate on the back wall. Dozens of markers scattered about, and as many names as there were markers had been spelled on the board in new-writer scrawl.

Jacob.

Ethan.

Charlotte.

Hyrum glanced at the board but didn't add his name, whether from disinterest or a want of not having the world know that he saw a therapist once a week, sometimes twice if he'd had a particularly upsetting day. This was one of those weeks; he'd been here three days earlier and asked Aubrey to make him another appointment.

She didn't ask why; she got up and made the call, refusing to pry. If he wanted to talk, he would. It might be her, it might be Jax, or it might be Eli, but it wouldn't happen until after he'd been here and sorted through his thoughts.

Dennis.

Parker.

LaCretia.

In tiny letters near the bottom, someone older, perhaps thirteen or fourteen, had written in block letters *are loved*.

I wondered if any of the children who had written their names had ever seen that.

I wondered if Hyrum had.

Dr. Graham Cheshire was younger than I expected. I'd had a mental image of Hyrum's therapist as a wizened older man with a lock of gray hair flopping down in his eyes, wearing a suit a size too big, his dress shoes scuffed and worn. The man who had been tending to Hyrum's issues for the past six years was younger than he was. His hair was dark and neatly trimmed, and he wore jeans with a blazer thrown over a t-shirt. He was young enough that I wondered why Aubrey had picked him, not only for Hyrum but for Oz as well.

The room Hyrum carried me to resembled someone's living room, not a doctor's office. There were comfy chairs and a sofa, toys on the floor, and a kid-sized table that nestled under the window, complete with tiny chairs. What it lacked was a coffee table, and when Hyrum bounced onto the sofa, he wasn't sure where I should be. At home, he would have set me on the coffee table and let me decide for myself where I wanted to be. Here, the protocol was unclear.

Dr. Cheshire reached for one of the tiny chairs and set it near the sofa. "You must be Wick," he said as Hyrum set me on it, thanking him at the same time. "I've heard a lot about you."

Of course, you have. I'm awesome.

"Hyrum tells me you're a very good listener." He held out a hand, letting me sniff his fingers before touching me. Most of the time when people did that, I rubbed my face on them so they would know I welcomed a well-placed head skritch, but this time I opened my mouth and gently closed my teeth around his middle finger, much to Hyrum's horror.

"Wick, that's mean! Don't bite him."

Dr. Cheshire understood. "He's not biting me, Hyrum. It's a warning."

I felt Hyrum's fingers tapping my back. "Wick, you have to let go! You're gonna get in trouble."

I wasn't, and I knew it. I looked up at Dr. Cheshire and noted how his mouth twitched at the corners, holding back a grin.

"It's fine," he said. "I think Wick wants me to understand that he's very protective of you, and I appreciate that."

I let his finger go.

"I'm really sorry," Hyrum said, voice shaking. "He's never done that before."

I'd bitten quite a few people in the past, violently even, but he didn't need to know that. Dr. Cheshire repeated that it was fine, and then asked me if he could pet me.

This time, I rubbed up against his hand.

After that, I did not exist, which I was fine with. Hyrum cut right to it, and the therapist sat back in his chair and listened to Hyrum describe the dreams that were bothering him, waking him night after night, all revolving around his father. He'd hit his breaking point and couldn't take it anymore.

"When did the dreams begin?"

"Around my birthday. Maybe before. Or maybe after. I don't know why."

Tobias.

Hyrum grunted. "There was this man named Tobias. Maybe he's why."

The doctor waited, giving Hyrum time to think. I waited, too, because I didn't see a way that he could explain having met his dead father in Saint Francis, nor the realization that Jax wanted to kill him all over again. I wasn't even sure Hyrum understood that we were in a simulation and that none of the people he'd met were real.

"He looked just like my daddy," Hyrum finally said. "But I know it wasn't really him."

"Because your father is dead."

"No, that's not why. I think Jesus would let me see my daddy if it was important enough. But I know Tobias wasn't my daddy because he said I was a good man. And he said I was loved. Daddy would have never said that on account of he thought I was bad, and he never loved me."

"And following that, the dreams began."

He listened as Hyrum described the dreams in detail, dreams that sounded more like the nocturnal tauntings of a madman. These were all things the doctor had heard before, tales of abuse that Aubrey had also listened to. The doctor kept his composure and talked Hyrum through the ugly facts of his life, while Aubrey fought to stay quiet and tried desperately not to cry.

"I know Daddy can't ever hurt me again," Hyrum said as he wound down. "And I know Aubrey and Jax and Will and Aisha and Oz and Drew and Zed and Jay and Eli love me, and they want me here, but I don't know why I still dream about my daddy."

"Have you spoken to your mother lately?"

Hyrum nodded and seemed to deflate. "I didn't tell her about the dreams. She would just say it's nonsense and to stop thinking bad things about him on account of he's dead. Jesus wouldn't like that."

"What did you talk about?"

"Stuff." Hyrum shrugged. "She decided she wants to live in her own house again, so Red and Joe and Spencer fixed it up for her. I think maybe his wife told her to get out. She's kind of nosy and pushy."

"Spencer's wife, or your mother?"

"Both." He giggled. "That's mean. I'm sorry."

"It's the truth of your experience. And it might explain your dreams. On top of meeting a man who looks like your father, suddenly your mother has plans of her own. Does it bother you that those plans don't include you?"

Softly, "I'm scared that they do."

~

We rode the rest of the way down California Street—his therapist was two blocks up—looped around at Market and having built some speed, he reversed direction and began the long climb up a street so steep that Jax nearly killed himself barreling down it when he was a teenager. I heard the gears on his bike grind, and then Hyrum chuckled. His guards were behind us and one uttered, "Holy fucking god," as he crested the first intersection.

"Watch, Wick," he said, pumping harder. "They hate this."

He pulled away from the two guards behind him, nearly cackling with glee, and when he reached the third intersection, I heard the familiar whine of an air bike coming from Sansome Street. It waited until we passed and then slipped in behind us, following close, but not too close, allowing him the illusion of riding alone.

Usually, he turned onto Grant, cutting through Chinatown on his way home, but this time he turned onto Kearney and headed for Columbus, which prompted the guard to speed up and settle beside him.

"Slow down and let them catch up." The guard was as amused as Hyrum. "It won't go over well if one of them has a heart attack."

"I'm just going to the chocolate place," Hyrum said. "Can they catch up there?"

The guard nodded and fell back into place and let Hyrum ride as fast as he wanted. By the time he was done at Ghirardelli, the others would be waiting, probably breathless and very liking wanting to vomit, and the guard riding the air bike would be gone.

"Jax said if they wanna keep their jobs, they have to keep up," Hyrum said, changing gears. "Is it okay, Wick? Should I take you home first?"

It's okay.

"I think you're okay. I wish I could understand you like Will and Drew. I don't want to make you mad."

You hear words sometimes. We'll get there.

He slowed down when we reached the street in front of Ghirardelli Square, but instead of getting off and locking up his bike, he let out a tiny squeal and said, "It's Denny!" He rolled across the road and pulled up next to the bright red bike taxi and the driver who had given Hyrum his first ride in one not long after he came to San Francisco.

Denny lifted his hand for a high-five. "Hyrum, my man. How's it hanging?"

"I dunno. Should I look?"

Denny barked out a laugh. "I was just heading back to Market. Up for a fast ride?"

Hyrum glanced over his shoulder at the guards who had just arrived. "You might miss people who want to pay you for a ride."

"I get better fares when I start at the Ferry Building. How about it?"

If they can't keep up, they can get another assignment.

"Loser buys a root beer!" Hyrum squealed, taking off.

His laughter trailed behind us, and I wanted to know which guard would throw up first.

~

He did not lose. He edged Denny out by the length of a tire and then waved off the root beer when Denny was approached by a tired tourist who just wanted to get to Pier 39 and had no idea how to do that without taking a walk for which he no longer had the energy. Instead of collecting on the bet, Hyrum locked his bike up—using two locks, the way Aubrey asked him to, even though the guards would never let anyone steal it—and we headed into the Ferry Building. There were cheeseburgers there, he told me, and since he'd ridden all the way up California, he'd had enough exercise that he could also have a milkshake.

Have a root beer if you want.

Root beer sounded good, he said, though really to himself and not me, had too much sugar. The milkshake had milk, which made it healthy. It was the same mental gymnastics routine he often did to justify what he wanted. Pizza was purchased by the slice because getting a whole pizza would be greedy; he ignored the fact that the slices were 8 inches long and the personal-sized pizza was only 6 inches around. Donuts were bought two at a time, but only one ever had chocolate glaze because getting it on both was decadent and probably a sin.

Sin was something he avoided; if he wasn't sure about something, he asked Drew or Will. He thought he should ask Aubrey, but there were some things a brother should not ask his sister, and besides, she might tell him it was a sin, while Drew would tell him it wasn't, and Will would say it didn't matter. Greed, however, he knew was a sin; it didn't apply only to money or things, but to food as well, and he tried hard to not be greedy.

Unless he was extra hungry. Jesus would understand that.

He loved chocolate shakes, but not with whipped cream, and he asked three times to be sure he wouldn't get any.

His server knew him from his several dozen other lunch visits, knew he never wanted the whipped cream because it was "icky," but humored him anyway and didn't mention the repeat requests. He also knew who I was—I had a vague notion that his name was Braxton and I'd been there before, but it was a long time ago and I was uncertain—and asked Hyrum if I wanted steak or shrimp today; they had both, and he would be happy to get some for me.

"Both," Hyrum said. "He loves both. That would make his day."

You know me so well.

"Oh! Can you ask for it to be cut into tiny pieces, so he doesn't choke? I'd be in trouble if he choked."

No one would blame you. But I'll try to not gobble it so fast that it's an issue.

He turned to look out the door, down the long hall that led to ferry exits. At the very end, far enough that we really couldn't see it, was Sophia's new café.

"I hope I can still eat here when Sophia opens up," he said with a sigh. "I don't want to hurt her feelings by coming here, but she's not gonna have cheeseburgers."

When Sophia's café, *Sof y Z*, opened, the menu would consist mostly of fusion foods with an emphasis on Mexican. She wouldn't be offended if Hyrum kept going to his favorite burger place, though she might tease him if he didn't stop in for dessert. I made a mental note to tell Will; he could pass it along to her, just to make sure she knew Hyrum had thought about it and didn't want to be impolite.

We sat at a table near a window with a view of the dock, and beyond that, the bay. Hyrum watched ferries slip past, waving at people who wandered by on their way home. More than half recognized him and returned his wave, and half of the rest at least smiled at him.

"I really like this place, Wick. They make burgers like my mom does. Not skinny but not so big I can't bite into it. And they put butter on it when they cook it. Mom did that, too. She said the butter made it juicier, but Red thought she did it to give Daddy that extra kick toward the heart attack she wanted him to have."

That doesn't sound like Red.

"I think he was joking, but maybe not. Daddy always ate three of them, on account of how good they were. He was mean a lot, but he also told Mom lots of times that she was probably the best cook on the planet, and he was surprised he wasn't fat because of it."

She had to be a good cook. Anything less and he would have been upset.

"I dunno. I don't think Mom hated him like she wants me to think. She coulda done things to stop him, you know. And she didn't. Maybe that means she liked him a little. Or didn't like me at all."

People do stupid things all the time without meaning to. It's not always personal.

"Well," he said around a bite of burger, "I get to live here now. Aubrey and Jax love me, and I love them. And I get to ride my bike and eat burgers. So maybe I should stop thinking so much, even though I have dreams about Daddy."

When he paid the bill, he calculated the tip carefully, muttering under his breath about percentages being too much like fractions, even though they weren't minuses and fractions *were* minuses and he was *done* with that. Aubrey could try all she wanted, but he graduated from school and that meant no more fractions.

He didn't mind her history lessons; those gave him things to talk to Jax about. He loved spelling and grammar and was learning about poetry. He enjoyed adding and subtracting and he was adamant that things like half cups and quarter cups in baking didn't count. He refused to learn fractions or admit that he had even a tenuous grasp on them. I watched as he ticked numbers off on his fingers, and then head-butted him when he asked if he'd gotten the number right.

Close enough. You might be on the high end, even.

I rode through the Ferry Building in the crook of his arm. He stopped a dozen times to greet people, mostly those running small stores and spots where tourists and ferry riders could grab quick bites, and when we were almost to the end, where Sophia's café was under construction, he dug into his pocket for his wallet to make one more purchase. Outside, he searched the Embarcadero as I perched on his shoulder, bouncing on his toes as he looked toward the Bay Bridge, anxiety building with each push off his toes.

I'm gonna fall, dude. If I don't fall, it'll be because I used my claws, and neither of us wants that.

He slowed, giving me a chance to re-center myself before he twitched hard at the sound of his name coming from the back of a pack of tourists.

"Hi, Hy! Hi, Hy! Hi, Hy!"

I was nearly launched airborne when he jumped up, trying to spot his friend. "Ash! Hi!" He raised the bag he'd been clutching in his other hand. "I got you some lunch!"

Ash, someone I had never heard of much less seen, skipped around the group he'd been following and was reaching out before he was close enough to take the bag.

"It's egg salad, the way you like it with mustard on the bread," Hyrum told him. "And there's chips and a drink."

Ash opened the bag and sniffed, inhaling as if he were taking in the aroma of the best meal he would ever have. "Weren't expecting you today, Hy. Dumb luck I was trailing them people."

"No stealing. You promised."

"No stealing. But I can ask. If I'm nice, people will give me munchies and drinks. Or beer. One old guy, he bought me a beer last week. Another guy, he tried to give me happy pills. Nope, nope, nope. That's what I said. Nope, nope, nope. Ash don't do that. Those make you slow and stupid. I said that. Thanks, but no thanks. Go make someone else slow and stupid."

We followed Ash to a bench near the pier entry and Hyrum sat down, leaving space between him and his friend. "Don't be mean, okay? Why don't you go ask the shelter for help? I know they would. Will says they help anyone who wants it, and it's free."

"Don't wanna work," Ash said around the huge bite he'd taken from his sandwich. "Don't wanna live inside."

"But they would give you food. You wouldn't have to ask people every day."

"Make me live inside. Nope, nope, nope. I get food outside, and when I stink, I shower at the beach. Lots of places to poop. I like outside."

Hyrum knew it was not an argument he would win. I pieced it together as they talked while Ash wolfed down his food. He was good at convincing people to feed him—clearly, Hyrum was buying lunch for him at least once a week—and he'd learned where he could trade his dirty clothes for clean ones. I suspected wherever he went for that, it was connected to the shelter system, but even if Hyrum could understand me, I wouldn't have said so.

My ear twitched at the sound of someone sitting on the ground nearby; one of Hyrum's guards had pressed close while another walked past, making sure Hyrum knew where he was. Ash seemed oblivious to the men who looked like tourists, his concentration on Hyrum and his food, and not necessarily in that order. They were pushing closer to make sure they could hear; Hyrum had freedom to roam, but not freedom to overly extend himself.

I had the feeling that they were comfortable with Ash, that this had been going on long enough that it was nothing more than Hyrum helping someone in need, but no one was taking a chance. I eyed the distance Hyrum had placed between himself and Ash; he wasn't taking a chance, either.

When the last bite was gone and Ash had drained the drink cup, Hyrum asked if he'd gotten enough. If not, he could go get him another sandwich.

"I'm good. Thanks. Lots of thanks, Hy. You're a good guy."

"Where are you gonna go today?"

"Up to the beach. Take a shower. Throw rocks into the ocean. Someone's gotta keep 'em off the beach. Little kids, they can get hurt, you know?"

Ash left, and we wandered down the pier to watch ferries come in while Hyrum let his lunch settle. He'd learned the hard way, he said as he tucked me close. If you eat a burger and fries *and* have a milkshake, then when you ride your bike home, your tummy starts to rumble. When that happens, you have to stop at the place that sells cookies and cupcakes and four kinds of milk to use their restroom, and they'll let you because they're nice, but you really should buy something, on account of that's polite.

For the record, it had happened to him three times, and each time he bought little bottles of chocolate milk to share with Rhys and Marco. It was before Alex and Charlie were old enough to drink chocolate milk, otherwise he would have gotten them some, too. Jonathan wasn't even born then, and neither was baby Eli.

He promised that as the babies got older, he would buy more chocolate milk to share.

"I like the name Eli, but they shoulda given him a different name than his great-grandpa," Hyrum said, sighing. "How's he gonna know if we're talking to him or not?"

You always call him baby Eli.

"Maybe they'll give him a nickname, like Red's got. No one calls him Redmond except Mom when she's mad."

Kinda hard to truncate a three-letter name, but okay. I suppose we can just call him E. Get three or four people yelling down the hall for him at once, and it'll sound like a torture chamber.

Eeeeee. Eeeee. Eeeee.

Or maybe crows.

Or bats in the belfry.

We'll think of something.

Half an hour later, after giving up on renaming Oz and Drew's infant son, and after waving at three incoming ferries, he decided his lunch was settled enough, and we went back for the bicycle. As we passed his guards, one sighed, "I swear, if we go back up California, I'm asking for a new assignment," and the other laughed and said, "No, you won't. You've never had this much fun at work."

For certain, he'd never had this much exercise.

~

Mrs. Strauss, owner of the shop that sold cookies and cupcakes and four kinds of milk—regular, chocolate, strawberry, and watery ick milk, I was informed—was crossing Market Street carrying boxes that obscured her view, causing her to tilt her head to one side just to see where she was going. With every third step, the top box shifted, she paused, and once she seemingly had things under control, it happened again.

Hyrum pedaled faster, and when we were near the shop, he stopped the bike and then ran to help her. He left me in the basket with the top closed and darted into the street, and despite the vehicular traffic ban, he looked both ways first.

"Always look, Hyrum," Will reminded him on a day when he'd moved to run across Geary Street. "Personal cars aren't permitted downtown, but there are still delivery vans, taxis, and air bikes to keep an eye for."

He didn't want to be squished, because squishing hurts; even if it was a cursory glance, he made sure to check for something coming at him. If there had been, he still might have jumped out just to grab Mrs. Strauss, though I'm not sure what he would have done about her boxes, which had started to slide again by the time he reached her. He took two and would have taken the third if she'd let him, but truthfully, Hyrum was quite a bit shorter than she was, and his view was almost as blocked by just the two.

She extended her gratitude to him with an offer for a free cupcake. Hyrum beamed but politely declined since he had just had lunch and didn't want to throw up while riding his bike, and eating a cupcake might do that since he was full. Besides, he had me, and he already felt bad about leaving me in the basket.

You handled that nicely. I know you wanted the cupcake.

"I really am full," he said to me as he mounted the bike. "Also, I want to ride a little more. I can take you home if you want. Just meow and I'll take you home."

I did not meow.

The basket was not entirely comfortable, especially when he rolled over the cable car rails or the small round things in the street intended to separate the red bike lanes from the green bike lanes. The red, he explained as he crossed lanes to get into the correct one, were meant for people like Denny who rode bikes for work, like taxis or delivering food. The green lanes were for people like him, who were just riding around for the fun of riding around.

"But Denny can use the green lanes if he wants, on account of sometimes there are slower people in the red ones. Drew says the law says I have to be in the green but crossing the red is okay. And the law says Denny can ride in the green even though he has the red one. I think that's okay."

The riding lanes were newish, installed soon after the surge in bicycle ownership that followed after the royal offspring and their Uncle Hyrum took to the streets with brand new bikes several years earlier. There were the curmudgeonly few who mocked them for using such antiquated transportation, but so many more saw the joy in Hyrum as he raced Drew down the Embarcadero or his giggle-laden laps around Union Square, and they wanted to try it for themselves.

Bicycle rental kiosks popped up, followed by specialty retail stores, then repair shops. Riding became popular downtown, where there was no competition with traffic for safe street space, but plans had been made to extend the bike lanes around the city. It all stemmed from Hyrum's desire to learn how to ride a bike, something that had been forbidden to him when he was a boy.

Riding had become fluid motion for him; he switched gears effortlessly and tackled the city hills as if he'd been born to them. He could also easily jump the curb, but only did it once with me and was quick to apologize when my head slammed into the top of the protective mesh on the basket.

"Maybe we need to put some squishy stuff on top. That way if you hit your head again, it won't hurt."

Or airbags. An airbag would be nice.

"Oh! Maybe Drew can make a little helmet for you. And tiny sunglasses. Then you'd look like people in books that ride those loud bikes Will likes."

I'd be awesome in a helmet and leather jacket. We could form a bike gang. Wick's Wild Wizards. You'd need goggles, I think.

He stopped again. Just outside the Paper Hut, a man on his knees was sweeping a scattered mess of dropped pens with his hands, trying to get them into a little pile, and Hyrum wanted to help pick them up. He greeted the man by name, a cheery "Hi, Mr. Hoover," as he dropped the kickstand and then squatted to begin scooping up the pens. "What happened?"

"I sneezed, that's what happened. I sneezed, and everything went flying. Hyrum, if you're holding a hundred ink pens in an old, flimsy bag, don't sneeze."

"Okay. I won't."

"How's the new drawing paper? Liking it?"

"I like it a lot. But I feel bad because I'm kind of hiding it from the babies. I let them use the other paper, though. The stuff Jay gave me. I've been selfish with the new paper."

The last of the pens had been stacked on the ripped bag, which Mr. Hoover began rolling around them. "Ah, don't feel guilty. They're happy with the paper you let them use, right? And I bet your friend Jay doesn't let anyone else use his professional art supplies. Sometimes, you need to keep something nice for yourself."

"I know, but I still feel bad. I should share."

"They're happy to draw pictures on the other paper, I promise. Now," he grunted as he got up, "thank you for helping me. I'm too old to be on my knees like that."

"Maybe next time you should carry them in a box, in case you sneeze again."

Mr. Hoover wasn't much older than Hyrum, so I'm not sure why he was too old to get down on his knees while it didn't bother Hyrum at all. Then again, Hyrum often sat in a deep squat while he played with Rhys, and Jax couldn't fathom how anyone over six could still manage that.

Why doesn't Mr. Hoover call you Mr. Munson? He knows you're about the same age, right?

I might never know.

~

It seemed like Hyrum was taking the long way to get back to Ghirardelli, where he'd abandoned the chocolate in favor of riding with Denny. There was no getting around a hill or two, but none were as long or as steep as California—well, there were bigger and steeper hills in the city, but not between Hyrum and the chocolate—so the guards had less to whine about.

I was certain that's where he was headed, until he made a sharp turn and reversed direction to head up Taylor Street (which was a bit of a climb, though I didn't hear anything from the Queen's bad word list coming from behind us.) He stopped at Grace Cathedral and locked the bike to a utility pole near the front steps, and then stood on the sidewalk and stared up at the centuries-old church.

Oz and Drew got married here.

Oh, remind me later to tell you about their reception.

There was a fly...

"I'm not Catholic," he said, mostly to himself. "But I see people going in all the time and I think they're tourists. Would it be okay?"

It's okay. It's open all the time so anyone can go in.

"I like the churches here." He set me in the crook of his arm and started up the steps, slowly, still unsure. "They're really pretty. Back home, church is just a place like a store with pews. Daddy said we're not supposed to decorate them too nice, because then everyone is looking at the walls and not thinking about the Lord."

And yet he built a bunch of super expensive and ornately decorated temples.

Hyrum had never seen the inside of a temple. His own

father deemed him unworthy and ripe with sin, denying him the most sacred rites of their religion, the things that would guarantee him a spot in the highest level of heaven.

Once inside, he sucked in a deep breath. "Oh. Oh. Wick, this is *really* pretty."

He took tiny steps up the aisle and stopped near the center, dazzled by the stained glass border between the ceiling and the walls. Without meaning to, he pressed me to his chest, and I could feel the increasing beat of his heart and how quickly he was breathing. He turned around and around; this was more than he could absorb in a minute or two, but it rapidly overwhelmed him and he needed to sit down.

"Will anyone get mad if I sit here?" he whispered to me.

Sound carries in the cathedral. A deep voice came from the tiny room where Oz and Aubrey had waited before the wedding, "Please sit. Enjoy yourself."

Hyrum turned sharply, feeling as if he'd been caught doing something he shouldn't. There was another sharp breath as the priest approached, but he relaxed when the priest held his hand out to Hyrum and introduced himself as Father Dan.

"I'm Hyrum. This is Wick."

"I know Wick," he said, touching the top of my head. "And I haven't met you, but I do know your sister. Please, feel free to explore the church if you like."

"I just want to sit for a minute. This is so pretty. It makes my stomach hurt."

Father Dan gestured to the closest pew. "Wick is allowed on the pew or the ground. Don't worry about whether it will upset anyone." He sat next to Hyrum. "Wick's a bit famous here. He was the highlight of the Princess's wedding."

I was, wasn't I?

"I didn't get to see that. But my mom did, on TV. She told me about it later."

You were too busy walking across the country when they got married.

"I missed a lot of things," Hyrum went on. "Is it a sin if I say I don't miss my church? It would be a lie if I said I did."

"Church is a place to connect with God," Father Dan said, carefully. "Do you miss God?"

"Nuh. I talk to him every day. Aubrey says he hears me and he's always with me, no matter what my daddy said. But I don't go to church anymore, and that makes my mom mad."

"Would you like to go back?"

"To Florida?" Hyrum flinched. "Nuh."

"I meant to church."

"Oh. I didn't really like it on account of it always made me feel bad. But I like bible stories and talking to Jesus, and my sister helps me read her bible. I can read the kid's bible that Will bought for me, but hers is hard. It has really old words and they don't make sense to me."

"There's nothing wrong with a children's bible, Hyrum. Whichever brings you joy and touches your heart, that's the one you read."

Hyrum enjoyed both, and he cherished the time spent cuddled up with his sister on the sofa, reciting the bible verses his father used to force upon him. The difference was that she didn't require him to memorize them, and if he tried and got them wrong, she didn't anger.

Aubrey loved his take on most of the bible verses he recited. He understood the spirit, even if he tripped over the words.

"Did Aubrey tell you about me?" he asked after a while, half an hour into a conversation that Father Dan steered into shallow waters meant to make Hyrum feel safe. "That I'm not smart?"

"We've spoken about you. I believe her exact words were that you're warm and wonderful, and you deserve as much happiness as you wish for."

"I'm happy. I like living here."

"But?" he prompted.

"I'm scared that God is mad at me. I'm not sad that my Daddy is dead, and I don't miss my mom. And I have bad dreams about my daddy. I think God is trying to talk to me in my dreams."

Tread carefully, Padre. I'll bite a priest if I have to.

"God is not mad, Hyrum. I promise. He understands why you don't grieve. And he understands that men grow up and live apart from their mothers. Most men don't long to be with them again."

Softly, "But I'm not honoring them."

"I think you are. You have a relationship with the Lord, and you speak with him daily. You work hard and think about others first—your sister is certainly proud of you."

"She doesn't go to church, either. That makes Mom mad, too."

Father Dan nodded. "Her attendance would make services difficult for others, and she doesn't want to interrupt their worship for the sake of her own. She has spiritual advisors and speaks with them often."

"People like you?"

He nodded. "She listens to people of many faiths and gives each of us equal consideration."

"She met me a rabbi last week," Hyrum mused. "I liked her. But she kept asking me to turn on lights and then turn them off. I did it but she coulda done that herself. I'm pretty sure she had all her fingers and stuff."

"It was her sabbath," Father Dan explained. "Part of her religious law is to leave untouched the trappings of modern life that require work. She employs someone to do that for her, lights and cooking, things like that."

"Oh. Okay. It's a God thing."

"It's a God thing."

"I'm not Catholic."

"I know," Father Dan said. "Faith is built on many layers, and none of them look the same, but they're all equally important. Everyone is welcome here, and there are weekly multi-faith services."

Hyrum's nose scrunched as he considered what he wanted to ask. "Do you do blessings here? The last blessing I got was from my brother Red, and it was a long time ago. But it's okay if you don't or I can't get one because I'm not Catholic. I don't know what I am."

"You," Father Dan said as he rose from the pew, "are one of God's children. That's all that matters."

He placed a hand on Hyrum's head and bowed his own, which made me think I should get a good hard look at the floor, too. I listened to the blessing, which was private so I won't say anything about it, and then as they prayed together—Father Dan went along with Hyrum's off-the-cuff, conversation-with-Jesus type of prayer—and didn't look up until I heard him say "amen."

Brace yourself, padre. The hug of all hugs is coming.

I was not wrong.

Hyrum threw his arms around Father Dan as he thanked him and then asked if he could come back someday.

"Come back, we'll explore the church together. There's more to see than this."

"That's the biggest church I've ever seen," he said as he secured me in the basket. "The prettiest, too. And I like Father Dan. It feels like his blessing was a really good one, and I think Red would have liked it. My mom would have wet herself." He let slip a tiny giggle. "Mom peed herself a tiny little bit in church once, but she was really pregnant, so it was okay. Daddy got mad, anyway. But he was always mad, so it doesn't count."

He glanced over his shoulder, looking for the closest guard, and with another amused giggle, took off down California. He didn't pursue the same death-defying ride Jax had at 17; Hyrum slowed for intersections and kept a sharp eye out for people. But the guards were not as attuned to the steep downhill, and when one shot past him, Hyrum yelled, "Don't ride your brakes, you'll wear them out!"

This particular guard was Catholic, as evidenced by him crossing himself when he reached the flat part of the street.

Hyrum coasted toward the plaza, still laughing, and he stopped near the fountain. A cluster of small children played nearby, watched closely by mothers who sat on the steps to talk, and Hyrum waved at them. One small boy roughly Rhys's age broke away from his friends and ran over, excitedly asking Hyrum if he could play today.

"I can't today, Brian," he said. "I have Wick and it's not fair to make him sit and wait for me that long."

"Aw. He can play, too."

"I'm sorry. We're just gonna sit for a minute today. Maybe I can play next week."

Brian shuffled back.

I have a request, if I can make you understand.

"You want out? Okay, but I really am only staying for a minute so the guards can catch their breath."

I need something to drink, Hyrum. I'm getting thirsty.

He set me on the flat edge of the fountain. The water was tempting, but if I stretched to get a drink, I might fall in, and I wasn't sure it was safe, anyway.

Thirsty.

Please hear that.

Thirsty.

"Sometimes I stop and play with them," he said, gesturing to the kids. "One day I was sitting here, and their ball rolled at me and I rolled it back, and they kept doing it. I made sure their moms were okay with it, on account of they might think I was weird or something. But they didn't."

Spiffy.

I pawed at his arm, trying to get him to hear me.

I haven't had water since this morning, dude.

"It's only gonna take them a minute until they can ride again."

The last thing I wanted to do was make Hyrum feel bad, but I'd reached the point where going for a swim seemed like a good idea. I backed up a step, opened my mouth, and started panting.

That got him to his feet. "What's wrong, Wick? Are you okay?"

Oz would have understood. Jax would have. But Hyrum had no idea what a panting cat might need, and he went from mild concern to panic so fast that I felt awful about it. I turned and stretched to see if I could reach the water in the fountain, risking that it was loaded with not-cat-friendly chemicals.

He snatched me up before I fell in.

"No, Wick! That might make you sick. Little kids *pee* in there!" Then the realization hit him. "Oh no. Oh no. Oh no. You're thirsty. I'm sorry, Wick. I'm really sorry."

He pressed me to his chest and ran, leaving his bike to the mercies of whoever might want to take it and headed for the small coffee shop near the old Hilton. He was near tears when he reached the door and thundered inside, yelling for Mrs. Welby. She was behind the counter and, I guessed, knew him well enough to take him seriously when he shouted across the room, "Wick needs water before he dies!"

Mrs. Welby, a woman his mother's age, didn't rise to his level of panic and calmly grabbed a glass and filled it, and told him to bring me over. She set it on a booth table and told Hyrum it was all right to set me on it; she would disinfect the tabletop when I was done. I stuck my face in and began lapping the cold water, hoping that Hyrum would calm down by the time I could tear myself away from it.

"I coulda killed Wick," he sobbed. "I never got him a drink today. It didn't think about it."

She rubbed his shoulder. "He's all right, Hyrum. It's not a hot day, and surely he had something to drink earlier."

"But not when he was with me, and we've been bike riding all day. I got him lunch but forgot to get him a drink. He started doing this" —he mimicked my panting— "and it was really scary."

"Cats do that sometimes. My Tinker does it when she's hot or upset."

"It's not hot out," he sniffed.

"Then all he needed was a drink. That's what he was trying to tell you."

I sat back on my haunches, water dripping from my chin. He looked terrified, like he was waiting for me to shrivel like a raisin, which made me realize I'd gone too far with the panting.

I rubbed against his arm.

Thank you. I feel better now.

"Take another drink, Wick. Please. I gotta be sure."

I did as he said and lapped up a bit more water, as much as I could without getting my head stuck in the glass. He sighed, satisfied that I wasn't going to curl up and die, and then remembered he'd left his bike near the fountain.

"Oh. I hope it's still there."

You have guards. They won't let anyone take it.

"It's okay if it means you got a drink," he said, though I knew he'd be crushed if it were stolen. "I'm really sorry. I should take you home. Maybe we're done riding bikes today."

I'm fine, I promise.

His bike was waiting right outside the coffee shop, an arm's length away from the guard who had whined the most yet had thought to move it closer, right where Hyrum would see it as he exited the coffee shop. He gave Hyrum a thumb's up and went back to his usual position, mounting his black bike, and they waited to see where Hyrum wanted to go. His mood had taken a turn; he was slow to secure the mesh basket cover and slower to get on his bike.

He decided against taking the guards up California again, choosing to head down Market instead. It proved to be a good decision; otherwise, a woman might have been gored by a tree limb, right there on the sidewalk outside the drugstore.

~

Partly because teenaged Jax was an idiot who had ridden down California on an old bicycle, not stopping, not slowing down, cars had been banned from the downtown area. There were exceptions: taxis could drop people off and pick people up if called—no loitering for fares—and delivery vans could come into the area to unload. Air bikes were permitted, with speed restrictions. Vehicles for the differently-abled were allowed. But personal air cars, personal land rovers, and buses were not.

There was ample parking on the outskirts of the restricted area, and the city was walkable if one could ignore the many hills. Locals had long gotten over their anger about the ban, and tourists quickly learned how they could get their trinkets and souvenirs delivered to their hotels, eliminating the need to carry everything around. The initial outcry over the ban and the grumbling regarding the need to rent parking nearby faded quickly; subway traffic increased, street-level public transport decreased, and crime plummeted.

There were no buses to jump on, no taxis to hail, and muggers couldn't outrun the numerous security drones. Downtown San Francisco was safe to roam, owed to the testosterone-fueled stupidity of a sixteen-year-old prince.

Mid-afternoon was generally quiet along Market Street. The lunch rush was over, and people who worked downtown were mostly inside. Tourists were closer to Union Square or wandering around Fisherman's Wharf and Per Thirty-Nine. Market was a major avenue that ran down the center of the city, so there were nearly always a few people out and about, but there could be a block or two between groups of people.

The important thing here, though, is that because there were few vehicles on the street at any given time, the trees had been allowed to grow and weren't trimmed as often as they once had been. Without the worry of impeding traffic or damaging cars, city planners made the decision to allow for some natural growth. The trees along Market were taller than in other parts of the city, with thick canopies that stretched over the street and sidewalks.

They were also very old.

Hyrum pedaled slowly, still upset, and he was quiet. He'd spoken to me all day as we wandered, but now he fell silent, and I let him be. He only rarely heard a word I said, and I didn't think talking nonstop, hoping he would catch something, would be helpful. I watched him instead of looking at where we were headed and saw his eyes go wide a fraction of a second after I heard the first crack.

The bike was still in motion when he jumped off, letting it fall to its side. I went down with it, protected by the mesh, and I bounced, but not painfully. I was able to turn as the bike landed on its side and skidded forward a few feet and watched as he sprinted to the sidewalk. His voice was loud and abrupt as he shouted, "Watch out!" at a woman who had not heard what he had, and certainly had no idea that she was a breath and a half and only one or two heartbeats away from having a tree limb as big around as Hyrum land on her head.

He grabbed her by the arm and yanked her, ignoring her shriek to let go, into the alcove of the drug store doorway, using his own body to shield her from the little twigs and leaves that tipped the fringes of the broken limb. He only let go when he was sure they were safe, when his guards—their own bikes left in the street—began shouting for him, ordering him to speak out, as they tugged on the branch to pull it off the sidewalk.

"I'm sorry I touched you," Hyrum said as he stepped back. "I didn't want you to get squished."

Her indignity over being grabbed vaporized and she clutched at his arm, trying to pull him back. She pressed one hand to her chest, trying to catch her breath, trying to thank him without being able to speak, trying to do anything other than melt down. Hyrum promised her she was all right and that one of his guards would make sure she got home okay, but he had to check on me, on account of he let his bike drop and I might be scared.

I was not scared.

I was, however, contemplating the possibility of divine intervention. Something propelled him off the bike, and I didn't think it was the initial sound of wood cracking.

Good job, dude. I don't think even Will could have moved so fast.

But he is getting old, so there's that.

"I'm sorry, Wick," he said as he carefully picked his bike up. "I didn't have time to think. I hope you're okay."

You did good.

And I mean that literally.

"But now we can tell Drew that the basket works. Oh! Maybe we shouldn't tell Aubrey. She'll just get upset and then she'll make you show her that you're okay." He leaned toward the basket and whispered, "Sometimes that ends in a bath, and you wouldn't like that."

No. I would not.

He pedaled a bit quicker the rest of the way home, a bit lighter, and after he stored the bike, he sat on the stairs with me, staring out the front door.

Hyrum's mood was better, but there was a bubble of anxiety forming around him, but I couldn't fathom why. He'd saved a woman's life; he should be flying high on the adrenaline rush.

There was no reason to be nervous.

I followed his gaze and realized Will was coming down the steps from Union Square.

Before Will stepped inside, Hyrum was on his feet and began speaking before Will had both feet inside. "I made a big mistake with Wick and I didn't know he needed water and he did this" —he panted for a few seconds— "and I'm really sorry and if you're mad that's okay."

"I'm not mad." Will reached down and tucked a finger under my chin. "You don't look any worse for the wear."

It was my mistake. I should have found a better way to let him know I wanted a drink. I wasn't that bad off.

"Wick only wanted to convey the idea that he was thirsty, Hyrum. The mistake was his."

"Was not," Hyrum grumbled. "I shoulda known. We had lunch and I didn't get him a drink. He had steak and shrimp, and that needs a drink."

"Clearly, he's fine. We'll come up with a signal he can give you in the future, so he doesn't alarm you again."

"I'm still allowed to take him for rides?"

"Did he enjoy it?"

I did.

"Then you're allowed."

Visibly relieved, he followed Will up the stairs. At some point, he'd brought the kids home, and they were in Aubrey and Jax's living room with Marco, stacking wood blocks as high as they could before throwing stuffed animals at them. Aubrey was at the table where she could keep an eye on them, thumbing through a cookbook, and she smiled when she saw him.

"You've been gone a while."

"We did stuff. Wick's checkup was good, and he doesn't have to go back for another year. But he needs more food."

She didn't ask about his appointment; if he wanted to talk about it, he would, and she knew that. Aubrey glanced at her watch and said, "That was a few hours ago. Plenty of time to get into some mischief."

"Nuh. I was good."
"You're always good. What did the two of you do all day?"
Hyrum set me on the table and then shrugged.
"Nothing special. Just a bike ride. What's for dinner?"

THE SEEDS

Late at night, there's a hint of music in the air. If I sit at the head of the stairs and listen carefully, I can hear it drifting like tiny dust motes made from song, and the tune is different depending on where I look. If I turn my head a tiny bit to the left, I hear Aubrey's gentle laughter tumbling down the hallway, or Jax's whispers that are meant only for her. If I turn a bit to the right, I hear baby Eli suckling in his sleep while his parents watch and marvel at the tiny perfect human they've created, and their certainty that they will somehow screw him up. I often hear Hyrum tendering his thanks for a day well lived, or his giggling over a new book or something he's drawn with the colorful, tooth-mark-pocked pencils that Jay gifted him.

I listen for Hyrum often, because if I hear him sniffing or struggling to hold back tears, I know I need to go to him.

If I move to the other side of the stairs and cock my ear toward the floor above, I hear soft feet gliding across the tile and gentle music wrapping around Will and Aisha. Sometimes they dance, often they simply sit in the quiet and talk, but this is when they can relax and just be. Their babies are tucked in and asleep, and their song is pure joy.

When I move back to the balcony-side of the staircase, I hear King Eli snore softly, and chances are he's asleep in a chair in the living room. Across the hall from him, Jay and Navi are quiet; she studies while he sketches, neither of them ever quite far from their work.

It's from that spot near the stairs I decide where I need to be. On this night, with the music of home life broken by sour notes of pain, I knew I couldn't do anything for them myself, so I headed upstairs to get the person who could hear me, understand me, and interfere without being overbearing.

~

Will was awake. He'd been in bed for an hour, choosing to stay there rather than move and risk waking Aisha, but she was as deeply asleep as she was going to get, so I didn't worry about jostling the bed. I crawled up Will's side of the mattress and patted his arm with my paw to get his attention.

He followed me into the living room. Before Aisha—and sometimes even after—I would have told him what I wanted while he was still in bed, but after having three kids and not getting nearly as much sleep as she wanted, Will had asked me to rouse him quietly when needed. Unless it was an emergency, whatever I wanted could wait until he was in the living room with the bedroom door closed. In an emergency, I was free to scream like someone had stepped on my tail.

I'd done that once, years before. His heart rate had probably recovered by now.

My reports generally centered around distressed toddlers. Rhys was a light sleeper, and he was often afraid of getting up in the dark. If he was too distressed to go to the bathroom but needed to, I got Will. If Charlie was awake and had peeled off his diaper to chuck across the room, I got Will. If Alex's legs were through the crib slats, I got Will. I rarely got him because of my needs or boredom; I got him, sometimes woke him, because of his kids.

He never complained. The kids were half of why his heart kept beating.

This was no different.

Jay is on the balcony and he's sad.

"Jay's sad," he repeated, sounding annoyed by the reason for my intrusion. "He's a big boy, Wick. I think he can handle being a little sad."

Not a little sad. It's a big sad. A great big sad. I think he and Navi and breaking up.

That got his attention. Navi was Jay's Aisha, the woman he would do anything for, the one for whom he would save his last breath. Before Jay asked her to marry him, Will and Aisha mused that if he didn't propose soon, they would have to adopt her to make sure she didn't get away. She had been proclaimed *One of Us* before she moved into Drew's old apartment with Jay; she'd been trusted with the family's secrets.

A range of emotions exploded on Will's face: sorrow, regret, mourning, and then protective determination. He loved Navi, but Jay came first.

Biology was irrelevant; Jay was his son.

"Do you know what the issue is?" he asked me.

I do.

"And?"

It's not mine to tell.

"Of course not." He let out a tired sigh. "You could save me some time with him by giving me a hint."

I could, but then I'd be telling, and I won't.

Jay stood at the balcony railing, glass in hand. He didn't turn when Will opened the door, but I saw his ear twitch and he knew someone was joining him but didn't care enough to see who. Pain rooted him in place; the effort to turn was too much. I jumped onto the chair behind him while Will leaned against the rail, looking down onto Union Square.

The air around Jay was thick with the aroma of cheap cinnamon whiskey.

"Is that Navi? It's a little late to be wandering around downtown."

Jay didn't look up. "Study group before they start their shift at five," he said. "They're working with a bio-printer today. Mass wants them to figure out why we can print every organ except the brain and reproductive system."

"As an exercise?" Will asked. "He already knows why."

So did Jay. "I guess. Navi knows. Or I assume she knows. We talked about it a long time ago, when she was asking me about my surgery and everything that led up to it. She said then it sucked that we couldn't just order a dick off the Internet. Well, a functional one. Apparently, you can totally get one that, like, glues on."

Jay had sparked her interest in gender medicine while they were dating, and he was why she headed straight for Brian Massimo after graduating with her nursing degree. There was nothing about the process that bothered her, and she harbored zero judgment about the people who came to him for help; she wanted to be an advocate for younger patients whose parents were hesitant to allow their children to transition.

"It's not a reassignment," she said, bristling at the antiquated but still used terminology. "It's confirmation. The only reassignment is mental, people who need to wrap their head around it and get used to using the correct pronouns."

She was good at what she did, quickly becoming a gentle, effective advocate. Mass fostered her skills and suggested she could do more. He turned her focus to medical school, and a decision had been placed at her feet: study here, in this When, or leap forward and study in Mass's birth-When, where her education would be significantly more comprehensive and could put her skills on equal footing with his colleagues.

"All right. So she's headed for work. Why are you still up?"

"Why are you?"

"I have life-long sleep issues. You, on the other hand, have been known to nod off with toddlers screaming not five feet from your head."

"Yeah, well." He gave a half shrug. "I'm awake. It is what it is."

"You're not a drinker," Will said with a nod toward the glass Jay clutched. He sniffed and added, "Drew's preferred poison?"

Jay nodded.

"Drunk?"

"Little bit, yeah," Jay said, which made Will snort.

Tell him if he doesn't start talking, I will.

Will did not tell him that. He focused on the Square, though by now Navi was surely past his sightline and it wasn't likely that there was anyone else down there to snoop on. Even the pigeons were probably asleep somewhere, dreaming about all the ways they could torment me. There might have been an inebriated person or two, staggering home after being shown the door at Fuzzy's or Kaluto's, but I didn't hear any drunken chatter or high-pitched laughter rising from the street.

They stood in silence for a good five minutes, staring at an empty Square. Jay sipped at his drink but didn't offer Will any, and Will didn't ask.

The night was pitted by quiet, the air filled with little more than the sighs of human breath and the drumbeat of hearts. Will could wait for as long as Jay needed him to, and he could stand still, not moving, barely blinking, until Jay was ready to speak.

I'd seen him stand guard over the royal offspring for hours at a time during state dinners; he had the eerie ability to see everything around him when he didn't appear to be looking. Waiting through Jay's silence was physically easy, even if it was emotionally difficult.

He only twitched when Jay sucked in a deep breath.

"She doesn't want kids," Jay finally said.

"What?" That made Will move. "I thought you'd discussed that."

"We did, early on. She knew I wanted at least one. She said she wanted one, but just one. But now?"

Will turned the outside heater on and gestured to the chair next to me. "What changed?"

Jay's voice tangled around the words. Everything had changed; life had changed. Medical school was no longer a concept but a reality and with it the decision about where to study. "And now she's spent time with all the kids. She'd never really been around little kids before and doesn't think she would be able to give a baby or a toddler the amount of time it deserves. She refuses to shortchange a child because of the things she wants to do, and she won't consider doing anything else. And no, I didn't ask her to change her mind about school. She needs to be a doctor in the same way I need to paint and draw."

He'd pointed out that he could be the primary parent, a mostly stay-at-home dad, the way Will was. His work was fluid, and there was no reason he couldn't cart a kid to his studio. He could find space at home to create, and if not, he would get a bigger studio to work from. He also wasn't in a hurry; if she wanted to finish school first, he could wait that long.

"But then she pointed out that graduating was just the start of everything for her. She had a residence and a fellowship to get through, and at the end of the day, she doubted she wanted to come home to a child who would need more attention than she could give. And I get it, it all sounds perfectly reasonable, and her major concerns are for this kid we don't even have, but…"

"But you want to be a father," Will said.

"I can't imagine my life without her, but damn. And before you say it, no, having little brothers and a little sister is not enough. It's not the same."

"I understand." If anyone did, it was Will. He'd cared for Oz and Zed from their first weeks until they were old enough to not need a babysitter, but they weren't his own, though it was all he thought he would ever have.

"God. The night before my surgery, after you left? I couldn't sleep. Hell, Mom didn't even suggest I try. She knew I wouldn't."

The night before his seventeenth birthday, after Will had gone home and the birthday cake Aubrey had made for him was properly destroyed—he'd sucked down half of it by the time Aisha reminded him he couldn't eat anything else, and covered the few slices that were left, storing it on top of the refrigerator—he sat in the darkened living room, staring out the big picture window. While Aisha tossed and turned in her bed, he kept an eye on the park across the street, the playground bathed in soft light from a nearby lamp post. The night was still; there were low pockets of fog and no breeze. He'd glanced at the trees to be sure; they weren't moving at all, the very tops hidden in the mist.

There was no one in his line of sight. No people, no cats or birds, no runaway dogs cutting through the park.

He'd never played on that playground. Aisha moved him from Las Vegas to San Francisco when he was eleven years old, into the apartment that his father had purchased for them. He'd watched younger kids play but had never spent more than a few minutes there, and when he had, it had been while he sat on a bench or perched on top of the border wall, usually waiting for his father or stepfather, and sometimes Zed.

He'd been tempted to use the swing set. It was a long, tall six-seater, practically an invitation for a pre-teen to attempt to get the swing to go over the top. He was small and light but had legs strong enough to pump that hard. That night he stared at it and played with the idea that he could go outside and give it a whirl, though he realized a full rotation would never happen.

Still, he could get higher than any of the little kids who frequented the park.

It might be fun. It was time to inject fun into his life. He deserved it.

He didn't move from the sofa. Instead, he stared at the swings, wondering if he would ever use them, if after the surgery he would still feel too old to play, too afraid that somehow, if he let his guard down long enough to enjoy a few minutes of mindless fun, that someone would discover his secret.

He was not the only transgender teenager in San Francisco, but he had only shared his truths with Zed, and Zed would never tell.

In the stillness of the night, he caught a breath of movement. The middle swing jiggled; he thought a breeze had picked up, and he looked to the trees to see how much of one there was.

The trees were still.

The other swings were still.

The lone swing moved back and forth, in tiny increments, until it was swinging a foot in either direction. He felt a sharp surge of warmth spread throughout his belly, and his breath caught in his throat when the thought wove through his brain: *I can have children. A kid of my own. When this is done, it will be real, and I have that.* If he had waited until his mid-twenties to have surgery in this When, as George wanted, he would look fully male but would be sterile. By letting Will take him to his birth When and having surgery there, he would be fully, genetically male, and would be fertile.

He'd always thought that if he had children, it would be with a surrogate or through the use of an artificial womb. If he was lucky enough to find a woman who loved him enough to spend her life with him, they would never be able to procreate the way the rest of humanity did. He accepted that. He was fine with that.

But Will changed everything.

He saw the swing move and felt the presence of a child not yet born, a child who waited for him, who wanted to be his.

"It hit me hard. This meant I could have children of my own, and I wept. I mean, I didn't just cry, Will. I *wept.* The floodgates opened. Tiny but brave Jay, crying his eyes out over a kid that didn't exist. But I felt that kid waiting, and I wanted him even then. I still feel him. I don't just want to be a father. I *need* to be."

Will understood. "I grieved through many nights, crying over children I would never have. But then life changed, and now I have four."

"What if Mom had said she didn't want another one? That I was all she needed. Would you have been okay with that? Could you have lived with it?"

He's not asking about you, not really.

"Our circumstances were different than yours," Will said. "When we married, we weren't sure if we wanted one together or not, though she did tell me she was open to the idea. Still, I went into this marriage wanting only her. I'd had nearly twenty-five years to miss her, and a life with her was all that I longed for and felt like having that would be more than enough."

That was Jay's problem; he wanted Navi to be enough. His gut screamed that she *should* be enough, but his heart was yelling right along with it. She'd known he wanted kids. She'd told him she did, too. He dove deeper into the relationship believing they would one day have a child together, and to take that away felt unfair. "And yet life without her?"

Will had no idea what to tell him and said so. "But I am always willing to listen, even if only to have someone to vent to."

"And if I decide that this is a deal-breaker?"

Will nodded. "I will always be on your side."

"I was going to call you Dad," Jay said, softly. "Whatever happened to that?"

"The name belongs to your father," Will said. "And I understand."

Jay got up, then bent over to give Will a kiss. "I love you like a dad, you know."

"I know. You *are* my son, Jay. The love I have for you is no different than what I feel for your brothers and sister."

"Fuck all that you can't tell me what to do." Jay opened the door and stepped inside, hesitated, but then let it close behind him.

Now do you get why I didn't tell you?

"I get it, Wick. Now tell me how to unbreak his heart."

You can't. Because either way, if he stays with her or lets her go, it's gonna be in a lot of little pieces, and he might not ever find them all.

~

There was nothing Will could do. He wanted to do *something*, chase after Navi and lecture some common sense into her, beg or bribe her, but he recognized that he was tired and the issue was not constructed from common sense. It was—aside from being a sounding board for Jay—none of his business. He checked on his three small children and then settled onto the sofa with a book, and I headed downstairs.

I couldn't help Will read until he was sleepy, but I could keep Jay company.

His apartment smelled vaguely of acrylic and oil paint, though his art studio was now down the street roughly a block away. He'd had one upstairs for a few years, but that was now the toddler's playroom. After I wiggled through the cat flap, I looked around; there was a new painting hanging on the wall over the sofa. There was almost always a new painting hanging on one of his walls. He let the work settle with him for a few weeks before submitting things to galleries, and they sold well.

I recognized this painting. I'd seen it hanging in a museum, nearly two hundred years in the future, in a room dedicated to the artwork of James Okuda, Junior. It was filled with brightly colored raindrops dancing above the happily curious face of a young man whose reddened eyes glistened with tears. The man vaguely resembled teenaged Zed, his green eyes and deep black hair, the mixture of curiosity and overwhelming joy that often tugged at the corners of his mouth in an unbridled grin. There was also deep sorrow and pain, and as I stood looking at it, I wondered if Jay had a sense of impending doom, if he knew that Zed's soul might one day be so battered and bruised that his family would fear he would lose himself to it.

Jay was on the sofa, staring at a late-night news broadcast, not really seeing or hearing anything about the ongoing efforts to rebuild Chicago. I listened for a moment; it had taken years to clear rubble from a war that went on only for a few months, but Prime Minister Shazia Van Hoff—Drew's mother—was certain that the majority of the work was behind them, and tourists were welcome and encouraged to visit to see the new city for themselves.

It sounded like politispeak, even though I knew she was sincere. She'd worked hard, and what she offered the world was a shiny and new city to play in, all while making sure the rest of Midlam prospered as well.

You should visit Chicago, dude. Someone needs to paint their new skyline.

"I'm all right, Wick. If Will sent you to check on me, tell him I'm fine."

No, I'm just here because I'm nosy.

He sucked in a deep breath and leaned forward so that he could see me. His arms rested on his legs, hands dangling between his knees, and when he exhaled, I felt his breath brush across my fur, the whiskey fumes stinging my eyes and nose.

"You enjoy getting into shit, don't you?" It was a question and not an accusation.

Sometimes. What did you have in mind?

"I need to talk to someone who isn't necessarily on my side. And there *are* sides to this, Wick. I can see both. But everyone here will be on my side, and Navi will suffer the fallout and feel most of the pressure. That's not exactly fair."

Sophia might not be on your side. She's still not happy about being pregnant for her entire married life.

"There's only one person I can think of who might understand how I feel. And I need you to take me to him."

I waited.

"I feel bad for even asking you to do this, but I have no idea how to find him and I suspect you do."

He's not in this When, is he?

"Jesus, this would be easier if you and I could speak. Look, I want you to take me through the portal down on the Square."

You have a transponder. You can go without me.

"I know *when* I can find him, just not...how. I want to find myself in, like, thirty years or so. I need to speak to him, I just need—"

Will had lifted his unofficial and unenforceable ban on going forward. He'd taken Jax and Aubrey to meet themselves. He took Oz and Drew to do the same. He spent days with his parents in the future, and they'd become the kids' grandparents as much as their actual grandparents were. I sometimes went through the small portal in Oz's closet to visit Lux, Jo's cat. I played with Hyrum and carried on long conversations about his life there and his counterpart's life here.

If Jay wanted to go talk to himself and needed me to accomplish that, I didn't see a reason not to.

"I just have a gut feeling you can help me connect there," he went on. "But I won't force you. If you're willing, jump in my lap. If not...no hard feelings. I swear. I'd—"

I jumped onto his lap before he could finish the thought.

I don't know how I'll communicate there unless old Hyrum is around, but having me with you might be proof you are who you say you are. And you need that since you don't look like how the other you probably did at your age. They know me. And I don't exist there anymore, so it's not like they would confuse me with myself.

He threw on a sweatshirt and tucked me to his side. On the way out, he nodded at the desk guard but didn't say anything to her, and once we were at the Square's steps, he picked up his pace, eager to get through.

"You're in control here," he said to me. "You pick the date and time. I have no idea what day to shoot for, but I figure you'll know when and where we can find someone."

I had an inkling. Old Drew and Zed had fallen into a pattern not unlike Will and Jax; they often met at the bakery in the morning, though for them it was a quiet time away from work and kids and not a spot to begin a morning run. Will and I ran into them frequently on our way to see his parents, and they were almost always alone.

I timed it so that we arrived on a day soon after the last one I knew of that Will had been there. It was just before Drew's sixtieth birthday, a late October morning absent of fog, when it was cold but the day's warmth was a certain promise that inched through the city. Zed would be there, grabbing coffee before heading to Alcatraz or Blackshear Academy. Drew would be there drinking hot chocolate before heading to Ozoo.

As soon as we were through the portal, I wiggled to get out of Jay's grasp. They were right where I expected them, at a table not far from the bakery door, and they needed to see me before they saw Jay so that there would be no question about his identity. I landed gently and scrambled across the cool concrete and then leaped onto the table before they'd even realized I was nearby.

It took a few seconds for them to fully recognize me. Usually, I snuck in through the bedroom portal and went straight to Lux. Any other time, I was with Will. Drew realized who I was first, but I interrupted his surprised greeting.

Look. At the portal. This is Jay.

You know Jay. He used to be Jimmy.

Look.

They finally looked to where my nose pointed, and Jay approached, almost shyly.

Zed got to his feet. "Holy shit, you're going to catch so much crap from the Emperor for this," he said, laughing. "Damn, you got *big*."

"You recognize me?"

"You're a hell of a lot taller than yourself and not nearly as skinny as I remember, but yeah." He sniffed. "Damn, how much have you been drinking? And for breakfast?"

"It was night when I left home, and I'm quickly sobering up." Jay sat in the chair Zed pointed to. "The Emperor will get over it. Are you and I still friends? That sounded like you haven't seen him in a while."

"He's still my bro, and we see each other damn near every day," Zed said. He looked at Drew and added, "This one goes by Jay. Less confusing for us, I imagine."

"You anointed me with the name. You didn't for him?"

"Tried to. We went through a few. Triple-J. Jimbo. Jimmers. Even Jay. It just didn't stick. His stepfather was such an asshole about it."

Jay snorted. "I suppose George still calls him Jaime?"

Zed nodded. "Slips up now and then. But he prefers Jimmy and was damned insistent about it." He took a moment and then added, "They're cool with each other if that helps. He was a dick about it for a long time, but when it came down to it, he paid for everything."

"Yeah, he was a total dick with me and damned near died because of it. In my When, anyway. Supposedly I'll still get the funds as a trust when I turn twenty-five. But...I don't really care."

"You'll care when you see how much," Zed chuckled.

Drew scrunched his nose. "You're not twenty-five yet? Yeah, no, you don't look twenty-five. Hm."

"Neither do you and yet the last time I saw you, like, yesterday, you were. Did I really wait until then for all the surgeries? How much suckage did that entail?"

Jimmy had waited until his twenty-fifth year to get the most significant of his surgical procedures. With George standing in his way until his eighteenth and then having the money dangled in front of him, he opted to wait for no reason other than it lifted the financial burden from his mother and father.

"He began hormone therapy the day he turned eighteen but was willing to wait for the rest to make their lives easier," Zed explained. "And his wife was willing to wait. He knows you were able to get rolling sooner, and he's genuinely happy for you. Happier still for your mom. His has been alone far too long."

"That he knows of," Drew chortled.

"His wife," Jay said dully.

Zed reached across the table for Jay's left hand and tugged at his ring finger. "Ah. All right. Where are you in life? Still in school? Dating? Engaged? Or did you embrace another direction? Gay? Swinger? Celibate? Or—"

"Stop," Jay said, chuckling. "But I'm glad you're still willing to give me shit."

"Always."

"But…that's why I'm here. Where I am in life. I feel like I need to talk to myself about a major decision I have to make."

"That'll certainly annoy the Emperor," Drew mused. He turned to Zed and said, "This means we're required to help. I do enjoy annoying him."

Jay wasn't sure how to take that. "Don't like him?"

"Oh, hell, I love the bastard," Drew said. "We picked up right where we left off, before he died. Although it breaks my brain a bit, seeing him so much younger than I am."

"Well," Jay mused. "You are kind of old. Like, you could be my father. Except he's not that old, either."

"Eh, bite me. You want help or not?"

Jay didn't answer but looked at Zed. "Hell, for that matter, same goes for you. What are you now, like, seventy?"

"Ha. You're so funny. I can still take you, you know. Well, if you hadn't gotten so much bigger than I am. And the muscles. But if you were still Jimmy? I could totally take you."

"So could Aubrey," Drew snorted. "Do you really want to see him? The Emperor might not be wrong about creating expectations about your life. The only reason he brought your Oz and Drew here to see us was for their benefit in understanding what happened politically when we ended the monarchy. They still know very little about our personal lives. Nothing about our children or what Oz did once she became a private citizen."

"I need to know what kind of heartbreak I'm headed for," Jay said. "Because as far as I can see, that's all there is ahead of me."

"Ah, Navi," Zed murmured.

"Then I'm not wrong. He knew her, he loved her, and left her?"

Sucking in a deep breath, Zed sat back in his chair and considered it. "Do you really want to know? Fundamentally, do you need to know?"

Jay explained his dilemma. They listened carefully, especially to the things he wasn't saying. Jay waxed poetically about their love and how excited he had been to start a life together, knowing that she loved the man he was and had no issue with the gender he'd been assigned at birth. She wanted to help others like him, so much so that she was willing to live centuries away from her own life to make it happen.

"So yeah," he said as he wound down. "I need to know."

"I'm not sure how much to tell you," Zed said.

Drew gave a slight shrug. "They're not trotting along the same path, Zed. Just tell him."

"The Emperor—"

"—can suck his own dick if it upsets him. And I'm sure he's bendy enough he could do it."

"Gross," Jay muttered.

"Well, I'm not wrong, am I?"

"Do you want to contemplate what freaky things your dad can do?" Jay asked.

"Huh. I forgot. He's your stepfather."

"Note he didn't apologize," Zed said. "But about Navi."

Jay waited.

With a deep sigh, Zed went on. "They met in college, before Jimmy had surgery but after he'd begun hormone therapy. He was honest, and it didn't matter to her. They dated a while, married before his surgery, and they spent a couple fairly incredible years getting to know each other all over again. I'd honestly never seen him so happy."

"But?"

"But. Right around the third anniversary of his surgery, Jimmy realized he wanted to start a family. He didn't care how— any option was one he was willing to consider. She slammed the brakes, hard. The idea of a baby had once appealed to her, but the reality? She was working long shifts and didn't want to sandwich kids into a brutal schedule."

The Navi of this When had also gone into gender medicine, specializing in research to improve surgical technique. She trained under Brian Massimo, Jimmy's surgeon, and was just as dedicated to her career as her mentor, if not more so.

"Kids were that important to him?" Jay asked. "Enough to end a marriage over?"

"Not at first. But he grew to resent it, and she felt it. But the worst of it was his hurt over how easily she extricated herself from their marriage. She told him she understood she had two choices, either ease up on her career and have a child or stay the course and lose him. She walked away. She made a surgically precise incision that amputated their relationship from her life, and once she walked out the door, that was it. They never spoke again."

"Never?" Jay's voice cracked as he spoke. "As in *never?*"

Navi sent friends for her belongings and a lawyer in her stead to sign the final divorce papers. Zed believed she considered that to be a kindness to Jimmy, and her absence would make it easier. "But it damn near killed him."

"There's a bright side," Drew said. "He married an old girlfriend a few years later. He's happy."

"Kids?" Jay asked.

"Not yet," Zed answered. "But his wife still says it's not off the table. His itch for a family was soothed over by her sister's large family and all her nieces and nephews."

"There are what," Drew mused, "twelve?"

"Something like that," Zed said. "Lots of tiny people running around. They spent most days off with her family, watching the youngest of the tribe. He loved it. But now that they're older, that itch is begging to be scratched, and she's definitely not opposed."

"The idea of old people having babies would gross me out if my mom hadn't had Rhys and the twins," Jay said. "You guys are up there, aren't you?"

"I have grandchildren," Zed said with a laugh. "My kids are...prolific."

"Their mom?" Jay ventured.

Don't tell him. Just don't.

Carefully, Zed said, "There hasn't been a day gone by that I haven't loved their mother. I wouldn't trade a single moment of our life together."

I stepped across the table to rub my head against Zed's arm, purring when he began tickling my chin. Jay watched, and the realization hit him. In a small, sad voice, he said, "Don't tell me anything else. I won't repeat this."

Zed leaned forward. "Your Emperor knows my life, Jay. Trust him. He's not afraid to change the future, and he won't let your Zed shatter."

"Because he knows it can't be changed for us," Drew said. "But, no worries. He won't let the worst happen. Your timeline will diverge. Hell, it already has. The fucker's alive."

That made Jay laugh. "And here I assumed having been King would have cured you from picking up my bad habits. Zed's mother is always on my ass about my language."

"If anything, that job made it worse. I have no idea how Oz stuck with it as long as she did. It was bad enough during the war, but after? Dealing with the people in charge of the rest of the world brought out Jimmy-level language I'd never thought I was capable of."

"And my mother still yells at him for it," Zed said. "Wait. You knew she's still alive, right?"

He knew. "Visiting your parents is a highlight for mine. I don't get many details, but it's clear that they love your mom and dad here as much as they do at home."

Zed's attention diverted. "Still want to meet yourself?"

Jay shrugged. "I'm not sure I need to anymore. I—"

"Too late." He pointed behind Jay. "Here you come."

Jay turned and watched a decades-older version of himself, a much shorter and slighter version, stroll across the Square. Jimmy stopped when he realized who he saw at the table, and he grinned. "It's a little *me!*" he squealed. When Jay stood up, Jimmy hesitated again. "Well, now. Not so little. You are me, right?"

"The improved you," Zed said. "Taller, heavier, and *so* much better looking."

"Fuck off, Zealand," Jimmy said as he grabbed a chair.

He sat next to Jay, and the difference between them became apparent. Jay was over six feet tall, and his reluctant following of Will's advice to keep active and work out was evident in his broad shoulders and tight biceps. Jimmy was thin and slight, the product of long days spent painting and drawing and little else. They looked more like father and son than the same person; Jimmy kept sneaking glances at Jay, making me wonder if he regretted waiting so long to become himself.

They made small talk—how's mom, is dad still a slut, hey did you know mom met the Emperor right about here and sucked his tonsils out, oh yeah, and back home he told her about it, and she was actually happy—until Jimmy leaned back in his chair, cocked his head a touch, and asked, "So, how'd your dick turn out?"

Zed howled. Jay inched his chair back and muttered, "What the fuck, dude?"

"Just curious. You had surgery so much earlier than I did. I'm wondering if it made a difference or not."

"Your dick is normal," Zed sighed, which seemed like it was the hundredth time they'd discussed it. "Stop."

"You two compared?" Jay asked.

"He needed to know," Zed said. "Only real difference is he's circumcised, and I'm not."

"Oh." Jay shifted uncomfortably. "Yeah. Well. Hm. I'm not."

"Spill it then," Jimmy said. "Massimo couldn't create a functioning foreskin. I was damned lucky he was stellar at creating the glans. And he wasn't half bad at coaxing inches and girth."

"Aren't you glad you came?" Drew asked Jay. "You have a dilemma, and they want to discuss your genitals."

"Puberty, too," Jimmy said. "The whole kit and kaboodle. I've always wondered how life would have been if I hadn't waited until my mid-twenties to start everything. Are you done? I don't think I had my last surgery until I was twenty-seven. That was a fucking long time to wait for good sex."

"Long done," Jay said. He turned to Drew and asked, "Your call. How much can I say about the difference having Will in my life made? Especially if it involves his When."

"He knows when the Emperor was from," Drew said. "He knows about the portals and knows we use them now and then. Hell, he's been through a couple of times. Tell him anything you want."

Jay took a moment to consider. "I only had one surgery, on my seventeenth birthday. Mass is from Will's When, and they took me forward to have it done there. It was one procedure, took like four days of floating in a tank with nanobot-riddled goo, and when I came out, it was all done. And now there isn't a test in existence that would show I was ever anything but male."

Jimmy twitched and turned his chair to face Jay. "Tell me about it. All of it."

While Jay told Jimmy the tale of his transition, Drew quietly got up and fetched fresh coffee and hot chocolate, bringing the latter to both Jimmy and Jay—extra chocolate, no whipped cream—counting on them having the same tastes. While Jay explained about the nanobots and how surgery would function in almost two hundred years, Drew listened carefully, taking mental notes.

I knew it was one of the things he was working on, developing sub-micro nanobot technology specifically for medical use, but I couldn't tell Jay to cut back on the details. I considered sitting upright and placing my paw over his mouth, but he'd already given Drew ideas, and for all I knew, that was how Drew got them in the first place.

"I had a few miserable months of late puberty and went through growing-pain hell, but the surgery itself? Just the one thing. I was sedated through the whole thing, and when I woke up, I had the body of a thirteen-year-old boy. By the end of summer, my body caught up with my age."

"I'll be damned," Jimmy breathed. "I'd be lying if I said I wasn't jealous."

"And you could have avoided that whole thing with Blake," Zed said, laughing. "Gone straight for the thing you really wanted."

"Blake wasn't a mistake," Jimmy said. "He scratched an itch and was happy to oblige. If he hadn't met Rob, who knows? It might have gone on longer."

"Do I want to know?" Jay asked. "Who's Blake?"

Blake, Jimmy explained, was a friend he'd met the summer before starting college. He was effervescent and, as he described himself, fabulous as fuck and gloriously gay. He took a liking to Jimmy and was one of the first—other than Zed—to whom Jimmy admitted the truth.

"No lie, I had a bit of a man-crush on him. We got a little drunk one night, and I told him straight up I was curious as hell about sex and would kill to just play with a penis. If I couldn't play with my own, I wanted to play with someone else's. He was down for it. There wasn't a damn straight thing about him, but his brain said I was male and fuck it, why not give a vagina a try for once?"

"Once," Zed scoffed. "You two banged like bunnies for nearly a year."

"Seriously?" Jay asked.

"Seriously," Jimmy said. "No lie, the sex was great, but there was never a time when I thought, hey, I'll keep the junk I was born with and stay with him. He was in it for the orgasms and because he liked me. I turned a blind eye to his other hookups because I got it. He wasn't getting anything from screwing me. I wanted a male body to play with, that was it. He was more interested after the surgery, but by then I was married. Hell, so was he."

"Holy shit," Jay uttered. "There was never a Blake in my life. I'm not sure I'd have gone that route."

Jimmy had no regrets. "It made me fucking fantastic in bed," he said, amused. "I know what it's like from both sides of the mattress. My first wife appreciated it. The women who followed appreciated it. But I would trade that for having been able to go about it the way you did."

"Your first wife," Jay groaned.

"Jay has a conundrum," Zed said. "And it has everything to do with Navi." He explained why Jay was there and how much he already knew.

"I don't know if I can give you an honest answer," Jimmy said. "I mean, yeah, my marriage ended horribly, but it was still one filled with love. And the reason she left? I suppose if she saw me now, she'd be mad as hell. I still haven't had kids. She left me so that I could have one. I just wish she'd done it better."

"She made a choice," Jay said. "A valid choice. But I need to know how you felt. Like, if she'd told you sooner, before you married, would it have made a difference? Have you ever thought about it?"

"Kid, I thought about that a million times. I don't know. Sometimes I think I would have married her anyway, but most of the time I resent that I didn't know before we made the commitment. I resented her reasons. I would have given up everything to be a father, like, fuck the career, you know? If I could go back now and choose between my career and kids, I'd choose kids. And I've had an *amazing* career."

"No details," Drew warned.

"Pick your battles," Jimmy said to Jay. "But…your heartache will be real, and she won't change her mind. She also has a remarkable career ahead of her, and it was probably the right decision for her."

"In my shoes, you'd end it now."

"Knowing what I know, yeah, I'd end it. That doesn't mean you have to. My Navi was an amazing woman, Jay. She was everything I could have hoped for and then some. I loved her as much as I think I was capable of, and I don't regret that part of it at all. If she'd wanted a baby but couldn't have one, I'd have lived with it. If she couldn't have stomached the idea of hiring a surrogate, I'd have lived with it. It was the absolute declaration that broke me. If she hadn't left, I would have, eventually. That doesn't mean you have to."

It wasn't the clear answer Jay had hoped for. He wanted to hear that they'd gotten their happily ever after, that she'd changed her mind along the way, or he had. He wanted to hear there were no regrets. He also wanted to pry about the turn Jimmy's life took; he was married, but to whom? He had an amazing career, but how?

Drew nudged the conversation back to the Emperor, and that he needed to be there for Drew's birthday. He'd been given an eighty-year-old bottle of scotch, and he wanted to share it with Jax and the Emperor, his brothers, and in memory of Carter, who in this When was long gone.

Jay humored them and promised he would make sure Will was there for his birthday. When he scooped me up to leave, he whispered that he was sorry, but he wasn't quite ready to go home.

"Take me back further than home," he said. "I want to be there on the day when Will breaks my mother's heart. I won't interfere. I just need to see it."

I couldn't fathom why, but as we stepped through, I thought about the day I waited in Will's apartment, and how broken he was when he came home.

~

Union Square was littered with people. An art display at the center of the Square had drawn tourists, and they strolled between the displays, soaking in the warmth of the sun and the bright spring day. The easels would have been great to hide behind, peeking around the edges to snoop while also checking out the drawings and paintings that normally would have captured his attention. Instead, Jay picked a spot on the edge of a cement planter not far from the one where King Jackson declared his mother irrevocably wed to the Emperor, and we waited.

They picked that spot to marry upon, to accept and embrace the King's Royal Decree, because it was where he had run from her, and they wanted to reclaim it.

There were enough people around that Jay didn't look out of place, and if I tucked myself close to his leg, I wasn't noticeable. Even if young Will looked over at us, I was just someone's tiny cat, one that resembled his Wick. Jay would not be on his radar; he wasn't someone Will would recognize as being from his future.

Aisha was there already. She was impossibly young, staring in the direction of Will's apartment, nervous and filled with hope. She lifted onto her toes, looking for him over the heads of people passing by, and her breath hitched. Jay's gaze was fixed on her, and I wanted to ask him what he was thinking, did he realize how young she was? Was she as beautiful as he expected?

I'd always thought she was beautiful, but I thought anyone willing to sneak bites of dead and delicious things to me was stunning.

I kept quiet, though, not wanting my voice to carry and for her attention to drift our way, even for a moment. I watched her as intently as Jay did and felt a pang of regret when her eyes lit up. She'd spotted Will down the street and was so happy to see him. I knew what was coming, and my stomach did a slow, burning churn.

Someone sat beside us; I noted the movement but didn't look, not until he spoke.

"This was brutal." Will kept his voice low. "Try not to react. She's not your mother, after all."

Jay turned his head sharply. "How?"

"Gut feeling. After Wick left, I couldn't concentrate on the book I had in hand. I had a suspicion and looked out the window in time to see you disappear into the portal."

"But how did you find us? This wasn't our first stop."

"I stepped into the portal thinking in terms of Wick's last known location. Had that not worked, I could have checked the portal logs. It's not difficult to find someone, at least not where they entered and when they headed to."

"So, no privacy in traveling."

"When children have access, it's a necessary invasion."

"Why *do* children have access?" Jay asked.

The heir to the throne would always have a transponder. It was a safety hatch, and it gave them a way to escape if necessary. "Jax was given one when he was small, and Eli taught him to use it in an emergency. Oz was given one when she was an infant. I imagine baby Eli will get one soon."

So why did we head for the safe house in Denver when Levi went after Drew?

"Because we knew it might be for months, and Zed would not have had an anchor if we'd hidden in another When."

I looked up at Jay. *He just didn't think of it, not until later.*

The young Emperor headed up the stairs, looking every bit as hopeful as Aisha did.

"I wanted a kiss for my birthday," Will said softly. "I had no idea I was about to hurt her, nor that I would run off, devastated. Right now, his heart is beating so hard he can feel it in his throat. His hands are twitching because he so badly wants to reach out and touch her."

Young Will was conflicted, something Jay empathized with. He was still conflicted about Navi, and while Aisha poured her heart out to the Emperor, he explained his visit with Jimmy, and how it hadn't brought anything into focus. He was just as confused and torn as he'd been, when what he needed was an answer.

"And this?" Will asked, not looking away from the young couple. "How will this help?"

"It was the end of something amazing. I hoped it would give me perspective."

The younger Will sucked in a small, tight breath when Aisha reached for the string on the Emperor's hooded sweatshirt. That simple movement, touching without touching him, brought him back to reality and to the realization that what he wanted could never happen. If he didn't break her heart, she would be stuck in a romantic limbo with him.

He snatched the string out of her hand. I thought Will would turn away, unable to witness this, but he continued to watch until the Emperor turned and ran. He didn't look to see where the Emperor went; he knew that he had ripped the sweatshirt off and dropped it, and then ran until he physically could not.

He'd never seen the aftermath and couldn't take his eyes off Aisha.

Tears streamed down her face, and her breath came in great gulps, and slowly, hands pressed to her mouth, she sank to her knees.

"No," he whispered to Jay, who twitched as if he wanted to go to her. "This had to happen."

Her heart wasn't just broken; it exploded. She went to her knees and sat back on her heels, gasping for air, her face wet with tears and snot, and when it seemed as if she might choke on her anguish, a woman ran up from behind her, and crouched, slipping her arms around Aisha.

It wasn't Aubrey.

I didn't recognize her.

"Yolanda," Will said, mostly to himself. "Her roommate."

"Yolo?" Jay asked.

Will nodded. "The same."

"She was in Vegas. I didn't know she'd lived here, too. Hell, she's talked about moving here because she misses mom."

"For your mother's sake, I would welcome that. But she hates me."

"Well." Jay chuckled. "This might be why."

Yolanda hated him before this moment, though he was never clear why and she had never joined them for studying or picnics in the park. Jay, on the other hand, had warm memories of her. She'd been like an aunt to him when he was little, and she still sent him birthday cards. She might not like Will, but she loved Aisha.

"Did you know that she was the one who helped mom after you left?" Jay asked.

He'd suspected. "But seeing it? I thought it had been hard for me, but this…"

"Because you loved her. And this way, she had a life."

"The life she wanted." Will finally turned away from her. She was on her feet, and Yolanda was guiding her away. "Part of what she confessed to me this day was an expectation of family. She was willing to wait for years if I needed her to, but one day she saw us together, with children. She looked forward to it. She couldn't imagine life without a family. I knew that could never happen."

What if you'd known you could learn to touch her and not hear inside her head?

"That might have made a huge difference, Wick. But that wasn't a skill I learned until after my father's work was completed. It's a skill that young man might never learn—"

"He's you," Jay said. "He's not the Emperor before you. He

is you. He'll live, Will. He'll live and he'll grow up and marry that girl and have three little weirdos with her. One brainiac, one nudist, and one drama queen."

"But first, she'll have you." Will leaned over and kissed Jay at his temple. "And that's why it's imperative that this plays out. I will not risk a world without you in it."

Oh, ask Jay about Jimmy and his love life.

"Jimmy Okuda's love life is none of my business."

Jay chuckled. "Maybe not, but you'd be interested."

Will picked me up, and we headed for the portal on Market Street, where they could slip through it without being noticed. Jay told him about Jimmy and Blake, and what might have been had he not had Will to help him. Will was amused and reminded Jay there might be a Blake out there for him, still.

"I'm not sure I'd go that way," Jay said. "But it seems like something Jimmy needed."

We paused near the portal. "He wants children of his own?"

Jay nodded. "I get the feeling he does."

"You could give that to him."

"What, me and a turkey baster? No thanks. If there's a kid out there I'm responsible for, I want it."

"No," Will said with a chuckle. "I meant he could meet Mass in my birth When and spend a day or two in the tank. I believe Mass would be amenable to the notion."

"You'd change that."

"I would."

Check with old Drew first, make sure time really is a wad of spaghetti.

"Yeah, I don't know what that means," Jay said when Will repeated it, "but listen to the cat. If Drew thinks it's worth changing the timeline, I'd be happy to take Jimmy there."

"And the direction of your own life?" Will asked.

Jay didn't know.

"Suggestion?"

Jay nodded.

"Take your time. Give Navi's news a chance to settle a bit longer. But don't marry her until you're sure you can live with it."

"I know. And I won't try to talk her into it, either. I know better." He sucked in a deep breath. "I can't imagine life without kids, Will. And I don't want to. I know what's going to happen when she comes home."

"You're sure."

Jay nodded.

"I am truly sorry, Jay."

Jay inhaled deeply, shakily. "Yeah, me too. And I'm sorry your heart got broken here. It wasn't just Mom. But goddamn, I'm glad you found your way back to her."

After making sure Jay was all right, Will lifted me onto his shoulder. "Head home. Wick and I have another stop to make."

"To see Drew?"

"To see me. To help myself. I'll be home later in the day."

Jay slipped into the portal, vanishing like fog.

What are you up to?

"The same thing he was. The search for a sliver of hope. Only this time, I wish to dispense a bit of it."

Before you talk to Drew.

"I'm not changing anything. Just...giving myself something to hold onto."

Just have me home in time for snack o'clock.

I understand there's shrimp to be had, and if I miss it, you're totally taking me to the Ferry Building for more.

~

As Jay made his way through the portal for home, the young Emperor sprinted toward the Bay Bridge, and Will pondered his next move. He'd had a notion, one that turned into a whim, and then a task he felt tempted to tackle, but the precise date and location hadn't yet settled into his brain.

Are we playing tourist for a while?

"Contemplating," he said. "Jay has unknowingly given me license to do something I probably should not, and I'm trying to decide if I should do it, or just go home and leave well enough alone."

What are we doing? Maybe I can help.

"We are doing," he said, glancing at the transporter bracelet on his wrist, "exactly what I've discouraged the kids from doing. Forbidden them, even."

Big kids or little kids?

"Big."

Sweet. We're going on a snooping expedition.

"Something like that," he chuckled.

There was a specific week tickling the recesses of his brain; he knew it had occurred before he left Aisha a blubbering mess on Union Square, but after he had decided that his birthday wish would be for a single kiss. I waited on his shoulder, straining forward to see what he tapped onto the bracelet's screen. I didn't fully understand how the transporter worked, but I recognized the month and year we were heading for. He was nineteen, on the cusp of turning twenty, looking forward to while also dreading the birthday party Aubrey insisted on.

It was a party that popped before the first balloon had been inflated, and he wouldn't have another until he turned forty-three.

Why are we—

We jumped from Market Street to half a block from the parklet where he spent long afternoons with Aisha, Jax, and Aubrey.

—going there? Well, here now. What's here?

"Hell week." He looked in the direction of the parklet and then checked his watch. "We should be there right now. Sit on my left shoulder, Wick. We're just going to walk past."

I crawled over his head, moving to his left shoulder.

If you walk that direction, they'll see me here.

"To Jax and Aubrey, I'll simply be a man walking around with his cat on his shoulder. They might think you resemble Wick, but I don't think we'll garner more than cursory consideration."

What about the Emperor? He'll pay attention.

"I'm counting on it."

They were at the picnic table. Aubrey and Jax sat on opposing sides of the table, their noses buried in study notes but little fingers tapping against each other. Will had a tablet in front of him and seemed to be asking Aisha questions, but he caught sight of us as we passed the first of Jax's guards, and until I could no longer see him, he continued to watch.

Okay. What was that for?

"I just want him to know we're around."

You're stalking yourself. That's kind of creepy.

"We simply passed by. That isn't stalking."

Are we done?

"No."

Then you're stalking him.

~

We jumped six times, to places he thought he had been that week, and found the young Emperor five times. There was no need for Will to remember exactly where he'd been on any given day; he knew that he'd started most mornings at the coffee shop where Aubrey worked and that he crossed the plaza at six o'clock. He ran the Embarcadero after that, while Jax and Aubrey headed to school, and he spent a considerable amount of time in the city library. His days at the shelter were typically on Monday, Wednesday, and Friday, making him easy to find; he left at roughly 1 p.m. to grab lunch and then meet everyone else at the parklet.

The young Emperor was a creature of habit, and from six in the morning until six in the evening, he stuck to his routine.

When did you change that? You're not as rigid with your days anymore.

"When it occurred to me that following the same patterns day after day made me vulnerable. Once I became someone other than a young man that the Prince spent time with and my name was known, I understood that it was in my best interest, and Jax's, to vary my routine."

Like your name was known then.

"You know what I mean."

They made fun of you on the news, you know. Or maybe it

was making fun of Finn and Jo. What kind of parents name their son 'Emperor?'

"I am aware."

Will never approached the young Emperor but made sure he'd noted our presence before wandering out of sight to jump again. On the last jump, he plucked me off his shoulder and held me to his chest, and said, "You don't need to be quiet anymore. Once we land, tell him hello. Loudly."

I blinked, and we were in the middle of his teenage apartment. The Emperor lounged in the oversized bean bag, staring at a video monitor, a game controller in hand. On the screen, a soldier exploded in a mass of computer-generated blood and guts that was a bit too realistic but matched the odor hanging in the air a bit too well.

Dude. It stinks in here. When was the last time you bathed?

He paused his game, not at all surprised that Will had magically appeared in his living room.

"That was not hello," Will admonished.

Yeah, well, he'll get over it.

The Emperor set the controller aside but didn't get up. "I wondered if you planned on speaking with me. Do I get to know how you got here?"

"Absolutely not."

"All right." He rolled off the bean bag and stood, gesturing to the tiny table shoved against the far wall of the makeshift kitchen. "At least it wasn't one of the royal offspring following me around this time. Nosy little shits. Beer?"

"Scotch." Will gestured to the refrigerator. "And not the swill you give to Jax. The bottle just inside the freezer, behind the container of meatloaf Donna pressed you to accept. And yes, they are nosy, but they mean well."

He took the bottle out of the freezer. "Still taking it on ice? Or will I outgrow that?"

"Depends on the scotch." Will looked at the bottle and said, "Straight up is fine. And sip at it, don't guzzle. This deserves to be savored."

How did you even get it? You're not legal.

"No one asks for my ID," the Emperor said. "It's a perk."

"Also, he brought this from home," Will said. "And there are, what, nine more bottles hidden behind the towels in the linen cabinet?"

"You remember how many?" He set a glass in front of Will, along with the bottle.

"Indeed. And you know why."

The Emperor nodded. "Savor everything you can when you have an expiration date. I keep repeating things to myself, hoping they'll stick in my memory. I'm not sure why, though. It's not like I'll have much use for the little things in twenty-two years."

Little things add up to big things.

He reached across the table to rub between my ears. "Says the biggest little thing there is."

"He remembers your youth now," Will said. "He's gradually regaining things lost to the years he rarely saw you."

That made the Emperor smile.

Should we tell him stuff like that?

"That seems like a safe thing to share," the Emperor said. "I know my future. Why are you here? I wasn't surprised to see you around the city but was far less certain we'd meet. Certainly not in my apartment."

Which still smells.

He sniffed. "I don't smell anything."

"It smells," Will said. "Open the windows every now and then."

"You sound like Aubrey." He got up again and opened the refrigerator, and after a minute of digging, brought a fruit platter and cheese to the table. "Soft cheddar," he said to me as he shredded pieces from the block. "The Queen doesn't like it when we give you this, but we won't tell her."

Aubrey gives me cheese.

"She's not Queen yet. I meant Donna. She worries about your dental health because this sticks to your teeth, and you won't let her brush them."

"He still won't," Will said. "But it's fine. I'll give him a dental chew later."

"I miss caring for you," the Emperor said as I ate. "You've been a good friend to Jax, but I'd be lying if I didn't admit I would prefer you lived with me."

"Be careful what you wish," Will said with a chuckle.

"I wish many things. But you know that." He gave me more cheese, which I knew I shouldn't eat but did anyway because I'm polite. "Right now, that wish is to know why you're here in the middle of the night."

"You have the good scotch."

"I have decidedly mediocre scotch, which passes for good when you're sharing it with a nearly twenty-year-old prince. Though I stole a bottle of Dad's better stock. He hides his good stuff. Hid."

Will sipped at the scotch, watching his younger self pick at fruit that had seen better days. "There really isn't anything keeping you from visiting your parents. Only a timeline written about in the Old Mint, one to which Finn had an unreasonable attachment. It's already happened to him. Visiting your parents won't change what will occur later."

The Emperor shrugged. "Staying here is what I was told to do. It was easier for everyone. I'll wait for him and fix his ship when he gets here, then send him on his merry way. Over and over and over, until time stops repeating itself. Why are you here, old me?"

I'd like to know, too.

"You've not slept this week," Will said. "I can help."

"You remember not sleeping this particular week."

Will nodded. "Like you said, savor everything. That includes the pain."

"I have the feeling there will be a lot of that. Am I ever getting this under control?"

You can't tell him that.

"I can tell him, Wick. And no, I'm sorry. You're going to have issues with sleep for the rest of your life."

But—

"There will be long periods where you'll sleep well enough," Will went on. "But that won't be for many years. But this time, because it's been horrific, I can help."

"I'm certain I've tried it all. Even a drunken stupor doesn't help."

"This requires no pharmaceuticals. Send Jax a message and ask him to pass the word along that you think you'll be able to sleep for a good ten hours and ask that no one disturb you. Then get ready for bed."

"Get ready for bed," the Emperor repeated. "And then you'll what, tuck me in?"

"Indeed."

The young Emperor chuckled. After he fished his phone from his pocket, he slid it across the table. "I'll go brush my teeth like a good boy if you'll text him."

"Shower," Will said as he tapped at the phone's screen. "Wick's not wrong about the odors in here, and I suspect the source might be human."

"Eh." The Emperor grunted. "Suck my balls, old man."

Will didn't look up. "I'm not that bendy."

While we waited for the Emperor to remove a small fraction of the smell in the apartment—most of the odor was owed to never-opened windows, the startling pile of sweat-encrusted socks in a laundry basket near the door, and lingering cooking aroma drifting from the family downstairs—Will did something he never did while waiting in someone else's home.

He snooped.

He examined books piled upon an unlevel shelf the Emperor had nailed to the wall between two windows, he glanced at papers scattered on a cheap plastic end table next to the bean bag chair, and then he picked up the game controller and un-paused the game the Emperor had been playing.

In five minutes, he racked up thousands of points, making sure he saved his position when the sound of the shower cut off.

Is that even fair? It was his game.

"He keeps getting stuck there. I just got him over the hump."

He'll be mad when he realizes.

"And he'll get over it."

You looked at his personal stuff, too.

"It's my personal stuff, too, Wick. There's nothing here that

I'm unaware of. He wouldn't consider it an invasion."

Well, it is.

"One cannot invade their own privacy."

Right now, you're different people. It doesn't matter if he's you when you're not here. You are. If he ate a hot dog, you wouldn't feel full. You're not the same.

"Point taken. But I am certain he would not consider it an invasion of his privacy."

He came out of the bedroom with a towel wrapped around his waist. "Whose privacy are you invading?"

"Yours, according to Wick."

He snooped. He looked at your books and some papers over there.

"He's already seen all of this," the Emperor said. "Besides, I keep the hard-core porn well hidden."

"You have no porn." Will gestured to the bedroom. "Go to bed."

He turned around and went back into the bedroom, tossing the towel aside. "Fine. I'll go to bed. Just what is it you have in mind?" He slipped under the sheet. "You're me. So what would this be? Masturbation? Incest? Simply weird and uncomfortable?"

"I don't recall being quite so crass," Will said.

You were a demented hornball, just like Jax. The only difference is that you used bigger words and had no clue about sex.

"Still no clue, I presume," the Emperor said. "You've got to be close to the end."

"Hm."

"How's that feel? Worse than it does for me now? I should be looking forward to my birthday this year, but truthfully, it's just another milestone to be ticked off on my march toward forty-two. I can't imagine how it will be in twenty years."

"The closer you get to forty, the more accepting you'll be. The years in between will be wonderful, Emperor. I can promise you that."

"William," he said softly. "Please. I haven't heard my own name since I left home."

Will nodded and sat on the edge of the bed. "William. As difficult as it is not to, focusing on your forty-second year won't help. Don't miss all the days in between because of a date that might never come."

He knew history; he was acutely aware of his own. This was more than information stored in the Old Mint. His life had been written about in dozens of books, and his legacy was worthy of a place in history texts and was taught to young children. He'd known the Emperor's life in startling detail before he had any notion that he was the Emperor.

There was no escaping that ending.

"Everything you're doing here," Will reminded him. "This is all to change the one thing that not only ended your life but the world. History might not be on your side, but that doesn't mean your future won't change."

Time is spaghetti.

"You've seen the data in the Old Mint. You know how many time loops there are in which Dad has tried and failed."

"It will only take one victory."

No sauce, though. Old Hyrum told us that much.

Oh, wait. You'll meet Hyrum later.

"The odds are against it, old me. He can try in a million loops of time, but if the end is what's meant to be—"

"You don't believe in Kismet."

"I believe in the data. Look, I know my role. Stay here, fix the damned ship when Dad gets here and has no clue who he is. I'll spend nearly twenty-five years waiting, just to repair some burned out plasma battery cells. A five-year-old could do it."

"And yet, he trusted you with it."

"Only because I wanted to leave home," the Emperor said, nearly pouting. "He could have asked Mom to just show up with her ship bearing extra batteries, and then take him home."

He wouldn't recognize her. His brain was Swiss cheese. Which probably isn't very tasty on top of spaghetti.

"There was more to his reasoning than simply repairing the ship. You're cultivating a relationship with the future King and Queen, people upon whom Finn will rely. He understood that by allowing you to leave, he was gifting you with family. Something you didn't have as a child."

"I have cousins—"

"You were brutally alone, and you know it. Your parents understood that sending you here meant two decades of love and companionship and the end of your isolation. No matter how it feels, know that they didn't let you leave to get rid of you. Letting you go was the most difficult thing they ever did, and they miss you horribly."

"We'll never really know that, though, will we? Because once they show up here, together, the clock starts ticking. There won't be enough time to wade through the reasons I wanted to leave home."

"There will be. I can promise you that much, William."

"Don't promise—" He twitched forward. "Is that a wedding ring?"

I crawled onto his legs. *People wear rings, dude.*

"But I don't," he murmured. "I don't care for how they feel."

Will held his hand up for the Emperor to get a better look. "All it takes is a single victory."

"How old are you?" He stopped staring at the ring and looked into Will's eyes. "Please. The truth."

"Forty-nine."

"That's—"

"Six years and a few months past my expiration date. I was happy before, William. Truly happy. In the years to come, your relationship with Jax and Aubrey will only become stronger, and you'll be a significant presence in the lives of their children."

"Australia and Zealand," the Emperor said.

"Oz and Zed."

He'll be significant until they hit twelve or thirteen.

"What happens then?"

"Puberty," Will chuckled. "A necessary evil. But between their births and then, you'll be able to touch them. The hugs and kisses alone will be worth it."

"Wait. You're married. How?" His eyes went wide. "You've had sex!"

That made Will laugh.

Dude. Focus.

He focused, but not on what I thought he should.

"Come on. What's it feel like? I mean, not the climax, but… it. I mean—"

Use your big boy words, William.

Will knew what he was fishing for. "Rub your finger along the inside of your cheek. Not exact, but similar."

The Emperor stuck his finger into his mouth.

Great. We traveled how far to teach him what a woman almost feels like?

"He's twenty, Wick. I recall being insanely curious. I also recall being willing to settle for a kiss. Just one."

"A quick one." The Emperor spoke around his index finger before realizing how it looked. "Short enough that I won't hear her thoughts, nor she mine."

"I remember."

"Is Aisha the one? Your wife?"

Will nodded.

"Kids?"

He nodded again.

I wanted to know why he was telling his younger self anything, but I stayed quiet. He answered every question the Emperor asked of him—how many kids, when were they born, why did he wait so long to have them? Will sat there patiently and answered every question, only pausing when the Emperor asked him why he hadn't married Aisha when he was younger.

Will showed him a picture on his phone. "This is Jay. And trust me when I say that you don't want to do anything that will prevent him from being born."

"I don't understand."

"I didn't learn to control what happens when I touch someone until after Finn succeeded. Being with her wasn't possible until then."

"So she left you," he guessed. "But she came back?"

"She left because I broke her heart. And so will you."

"Never."

"She deserves a life with someone who can do more than love her. She shouldn't have to wait over twenty years to get that."

"I know, but I can't just break her heart."

"William, you have to. If you don't, she won't leave San Francisco. She won't meet James, and then won't have Jay. I wouldn't trade him for those years, I swear." He took the phone back and looked at the picture. "Truthfully, neither of us were ready for a commitment so intense, even if we were meant to be together. I needed the distance to mature. She needed the distance to find the things she needed most."

She needed to be a mom, dude. Before she hit her forties.

"She loves you," Will said. "That will never change. But yes, you will need to break her heart in order to have this life when it's time."

There were tears in the Emperor's eyes. "When?"

"Soon."

"Do I get that kiss?"

Bigger picture, William. You get the girl later, when it matters most.

"So, no, I don't."

"Listen to Wick," Will said. "Bigger picture. The moment will come when it's time."

"The wait was worth it?"

"More than I can adequately express."

You're gonna fall off a few times, but you'll get the hang of it.

"Wick," Will sighed.

The Emperor picked me up and held me close to his face. "I'm glad you get your snark back. You haven't been nearly as sarcastic as you were when you lived with me. I miss you."

You'll get me back. Most of the time, at three in the morning.

"I did say to be careful what you wish for," Will said. "Lie back. The point was to help you get to sleep."

He did as Will said. "Wait. Why did you tell me all this? Dad would explode if he knew."

"Then don't tell him," Will whispered. He touched the Emperor's forehead, and he was instantly asleep.

I sat on his chest, riding up and down with every breath he took.

Is this why we came? To give him hope?

"I came to help him sleep," Will said. "However, I do have another agenda."

We waited quietly, until Will was sure the Emperor was as deeply asleep as possible. He moved me to his own lap, and then set his hand on the Emperor's forehead, closing his eyes as he went to work. I waited for an hour, as he sifted and probed for the things he needed and didn't speak until we left the bedroom.

You took his memory of tonight, didn't you?

"There will be a vague feeling of a dream, and the suggestion of possibilities. I left him with hope, Wick. Something he desperately needed."

What else?

"What else might there be?"

You sat there for a long time. I've seen you play with memories. It doesn't take that long.

"I left him with a few suggestions. Ideas that, over time, will percolate from the recesses of his mind."

In a few years, the Emperor would gift a tablet filled with novels to Prince Andrew, on his eighth birthday. He would continue to curate Drew's love of science fiction and would quietly—while continuing to foster a shadow of fear in the boy—cultivate Drew's thirst for science and finding new things to do with existing technology.

In two decades, the Emperor would find himself at odds with the broken pieces of his father's egg-shaped time machine, unable to repair the batteries he had learned to work with when he was a child. In the midst of his frustration, he would look to my backup transponder as a way to send Finn home. He would build the gate that Finn would then use to thwart the meteor headed for Earth.

The most important ghost that would linger in the Emperor's mind was the notion that he should be the one to step through the portal when the time came; it wasn't fair to expect his childhood friend, his cat, to give up his life simply to see if the world had ended. If it had, his own life was over. It made more sense to go himself and risk stepping out on the other side into nothing.

You created an insurance policy.

"Something like that."

Those aren't free. There are premiums for that.

"And he'll pay them with pieces of his heart, Wick. It will be worth it. I promised him."

I don't suppose you planted the suggestion that he clean up around here and get rid of the funk.

His mouth twitched, the corners tugging upward.

You did, didn't you?

He answered with a tap on the jump bracelet, and we landed at home, just outside the open apartment door. There was fresh air, and sudden, jarring noise.

Rhys was yelling at Charlie to put his pants back on.

Charlie was yelling that he didn't have to.

Alex was yelling just to yell.

Just beyond the noise of a little boy about to turn four and the rantings of toddlers asserting themselves, I heard Aisha and Aubrey laugh, and then felt Will sigh.

He didn't lie to himself.

It was totally worth it.

BECOMING BLACKSHEAR

You're going to get in trouble. I didn't tattle, but they're gonna know.

Hyrum sat on the floor of Jax's office, using the ornate wood desk as a backrest, and he tapped on the screen of his tablet with his pointy finger. Rhys was next to him, and when the video on Hyrum's tablet appeared on the giant monitor, he squealed. "You did it! We can watch it here without the babies!"

They'd wanted to watch a cartoon Hyrum downloaded to his tablet while they were upstairs, in the living room, but Alex and Charlie were being Alex and Charlie, which meant hearing it would be next to impossible with the overlay of screaming toddler chatter, and every few seconds one of the twins was sure to do something in an attempt to get Hyrum's attention. Normally he didn't mind that the penalty for their affection was frequent interruptions, but this time he did. He and Rhys wanted quiet, and currently there was only high-pitched giggling, yelling, and the slamming together of toys.

Hyrum asked Aubrey if he could take Rhys upstairs, promising he would be extra careful, and they wouldn't touch anything except the TV.

Will and Aisha's door would not be locked; Aubrey knew that. They had the same open-door policy she did: if you live in the building, you're family and our home is your home. The only exception, times the door was locked, was because Alex and Charlie were Alex and Charlie, and if they were home there needed to be a barrier between them and the stairs. There was always a guard somewhere near the door or the stairs, but the new rule was that if only one parent was home with them, the door needed to be locked.

Aubrey told Hyrum that they could go, but to be back for lunch. Tacos were on the menu, and she knew he wouldn't want to miss that.

I followed because I wanted to be where it was quiet, too. That state of quiet was relative to the volume at which Hyrum would turn the cartoon on—he had the same taste in sound that Rhys did, complicated by minor age-related hearing loss—but it still seemed like a better type of noise than Alex's shrieking. But instead of heading upstairs, Hyrum hesitated and then headed down to Jax's third-floor office. He peeked down the stairwell for snooping guards, and finding none, gently wiggled the doorknob to see if it was locked.

The door opened with a soft click.

"Don't touch Jax's things," he told Rhys. "We're only gonna watch the cartoon, okay?"

I sat between them and the monitor, hoping Hyrum would hear me.

You opened the door. There's a silent alarm. It turns on the security cameras.

They already know you're in here. Not only will someone be here soon, they're gonna tell on you.

"Wick, hush," Hyrum said. "Turn around and watch. It's really funny."

But what's going to happen in about three minutes won't be.

Hyrum snatched me from my spot on the floor and set me between his crossed legs, admonishing me again for talking, because he and Rhys *really* wanted to watch this cartoon. It was about a superhero with his own red dragon, one that looked like Jeff, and they didn't want to miss it because of loud babies or jabbering kitties.

Fine.

I heard footsteps on the stairs and wondered who it was. There was a chance it was Vicat, Rhys's personal guard; if she'd seen him on camera, she would rush to protect him from the other guards who might not appreciate how sweet and sensitive he could be. It might be the teenaged backup desk guard, who would puff out his chest to look as intimidating as possible, and then growl at them—or worse, he would yell. If he yelled, Hyrum would cry, and if Hyrum cried, so would Rhys, which would annoy Will, and no one wanted to annoy Will.

Hyrum was old enough to be the desk guards' father, but it wouldn't matter. He was where he was not supposed to be, and this wasn't like riding his bike in places he knew Aubrey didn't want him to go. This was the King's office; the only one allowed there without explicit, previous permission was the Emperor.

I listened closely.

Dress shoes. Two pair.

One person was dragging his feet along, the other had a specific cadence. One did not take the stairs as often as he should, the other ran them for sport.

Another smaller set of feet started up from the near the front door, but I wasn't worried about that. She would not say or do anything to upset Rhys and Hyrum unless directed to.

I relaxed a bit.

Blood would not be shed today.

I'm not gonna say I told you so, but...

Jax and Will stood in the doorway. The volume on the cartoon was unnecessarily loud, and both Hyrum and Rhys were transfixed. They didn't realize they weren't alone until Jax cleared his throat; Hyrum twitched with surprise and regret, but Rhys smiled.

"Daddy! Look, Hyrum made the cartoon play *really* big!"

Will crossed his arms. "Where is it you're supposed to be?"

Rhys frowned. "Watching cartoons."

"Here?"

"I don't know." He wasn't sure where to look. Will had his serious face on and Hyrum seemed scared, and Jax wasn't giving anything away. "Aunt Aubrey said we could."

"Hyrum?" Jax prompted.

He sighed hard and turned the cartoon off. "I told her

we were going upstairs to watch Will's TV. I'm sorry. But we didn't touch anything except the TV. I didn't use the computer, I promise. Drew showed me how to make shows on my tablet play on the TV, and—"

"At any point, did you ask permission to use my office?" Jax asked.

"Are you mad?" Rhys asked, voice small.

"Well, I'm not happy." He continued to focus on Hyrum. "My office is not a playroom, and I expect permission to be asked before so much as touching the doorknob."

Will gestured for Rhys to get up and then signaled for Vicat to come in. "You're going upstairs, and you will apologize to your aunt for lying to her about where you intended to be."

"But that was me!" Hyrum protested. "He never said nothing!"

"Rhys, did you hear him say you would go upstairs?"

He nodded.

"Then you owe her an apology. Going somewhere else was wrong, and you know that."

Hyrum got to his feet. He held his hands near his chest, shaking them, and tears sprung to his eyes. "It was me. He shouldn't get spanked. It was me. Spank me."

"Daddy, am I gonna get spanked?" Rhys asked though he didn't seem to be upset by the notion.

"No," Will said. "We don't do that."

"What's spanked mean?"

"Go," Will said. "We'll discuss this later."

Hyrum was still in tears. I jumped onto the desk so that Will could see I was there, hoping he would listen.

He didn't do anything except turn the monitor on.

"That's not the issue, Wick."

I know. But he thinks it is. Did anyone ever tell him the office was off-limits? Because you know he wouldn't have come here if they had.

"Why here?" Will asked Hyrum. "The monitor upstairs is perfectly functional. For that matter, you have access to several between your living room and mine. Drew would have gladly allowed you to use his."

"This one's big," Hyrum answered, sniffing. "I never watched one that big. It's even bigger than yours."

"Did you know you weren't allowed to enter the office without permission?" Will asked. "Did Jax ever tell you it was off-limits?"

Hyrum's hands pressed to his stomach, and he barely managed to squeak out, "No."

"All right then." Jax plucked the remote for the monitor from the top of his desk. "It's my fault."

"No," Will said, "they said they were going upstairs. That matters."

Hyrum bounced on his toes, clutching at his shirt. "But I didn't think of it until we were in the hall and I didn't think about telling Aubrey. I'm really sorry."

"And you'll apologize to her." Jax held the remote up. "From now on, use this when you turn the monitor on. I'll leave it on the arm of the chair. But first, check the upper right corner. If it's safe to use, the light in the corner will be green. If the system is in use somewhere else in the building, the light will be red, and you absolutely cannot turn it on."

Don't tell him about the blood and guts he might see.

Or your freaky porn collection.

He had Hyrum turn it on and off and asked him to point out the lights. They went over the things in the office Hyrum wasn't allowed to touch—nothing on the desk, nothing in the desk, in fact, nothing from the desk to the wall—and assured him it was fine to pull the chairs away from the other wall to sit in.

"We knew you were in here because you didn't use an access code to open the door," Jax went on. "When that happens, the security cameras in here activate, and the guards can see who's in here. You were lucky. If the desk guard had been new and unfamiliar with you, they would have burst in with arms drawn."

"I don't know what that means."

"Guns. They would have been prepared to shoot," Will said.

"Oh. That's not good."

Jax gave Hyrum permission to use the office monitor unless he was working; he had to promise to tell Aubrey where he was going and to stay away from the desk, but if what he wanted was to watch TV, that was fine. He could play video games, as well, but only if he connected his tablet to the monitor.

You have a game console right there. Teach him how to use it.

"Don't bring Charlie or Alex in here," Will said. "Rhys will listen to the rules, but they will not."

"They came here to get away from the little monsters," Jax said.

"They're not monsters," Hyrum sniffed. "They're just babies but they're loud."

"And they take toys you don't intend to share, and lately they argue for the sake of arguing," Will said. "We do understand."

"You can bring toys here, too," Jax said, "but the same rules apply, all right? Now go tell your sister you're sorry for lying to her. And if she's angry, you'll just have to deal with it."

"Okay."

"Hyrum." Jax stopped him at the door. "No one in this house gets spanked. Ever."

"You promised no spanking *me*. But I didn't know about the little ones."

"Never," Will agreed.

"Okay."

"No one gets spanked?" Jax asked when Hyrum was halfway up the stairs. "Not even a tiny bit?"

"What are you suggesting, Jax?"

He wants to know what freaky things you and Aisha are into.

"Ah. No."

She slapped your butt once.

"That doesn't count, Wick."

"Do I want to know?" Jax asked.

"Probably. Wick, go upstairs and make sure no one is too upset."

Purr therapy?

"If needed."

Jax bent over, hands on knees. "Wick, is he avoiding the question? There's shrimp in it for you. Just meow if he's avoiding it."

I let slip a tiny meow and then ran for the stairs before Will could refute or Jax could renege.

~

As expected, Hyrum was in the kitchen with Aubrey. With his hands plastered to his chest and stomach, he bounced lightly on his toes, cheeks wet. Aubrey made him wait; he'd apologized, but she wanted him to understand that violating Jax's office wasn't a little thing and that it could have turned out badly.

No one would have shot him, but without the security cameras, he and Rhys would have been frightened half out of their minds by the guards bursting in, yelling. I might have peed on the plush red carpet, someone might have jumped up and broken things on Jax's desk and the minor infraction would have become a Big Thing.

"You were lucky that Jax and Will were in the building." The stern tone she hoped for hid in the shadows of the amusement that dripped behind her words. After all, Oz and Zed had done the same thing when they were little, sneaking into the office to watch a movie they had been denied permission to see. She'd expected this sooner or later. When he bounced harder, his heels striking the floor, she gave him the tiniest blip of a smile. "I accept your apology, Hyrum. I know you didn't mean to do anything wrong."

"Rhys didn't get in trouble, did he? On account of it was my fault."

"He apologized and is washing his hands. Lunch will be ready soon."

Alex and Charlie were in the bathroom with him, which meant there would be a mess to clean up when they were done. Soap would coat the vanity with water puddled on the floor; chances were high that Rhys would dribble on the floor, and in an attempt to mimic his big brother, Charlie would pee all over the back of the toilet. Before he could finish, Alex would run down the hall, yelling that her brothers were making a mess.

I didn't need to go watch them to know the result of three toddlers in a bathroom.

It happened at least three times a week. Aubrey never complained, but instead praised Charlie for his efforts, and thanked Rhys for helping to potty train him.

She told Hyrum to wash his hands, too, but didn't add that he'd been wiping his nose with the back of his hand and snot was not on the lunch menu. "Oh, and your computer pinged. I think you have a call."

He checked before going into the bathroom. It was his mother, and he shrugged it off. "I'm not calling back, Wick. I always feel bad when I call her."

No skin off my nose, dude. She whines a lot. But you know she'll call back later.

"Maybe I'll feel like talking to her later. After tacos."

He did not feel like talking to her after tacos. After the tacos were gone and all that remained were splatters of beef and cheese with crumbles of tortilla shells, while he helped clear the table, Aubrey told him she'd had a nice talk with their mother before lunch.

Hyrum was nearly always polite and listened to his sister carefully, but this time he grunted. He didn't want to hear Valerie's latest gossip, didn't care if Spencer's wife was the devil wrapped in a frumpy hand-sewn skirt that she didn't need because Spencer earned decent money and could buy her anything she wanted, didn't care if Elle was disobeying her husband by taking a part-time job even if it was in a daycare center. Or rather, he cared, but not the way she wanted him to, with judgment and disapproval.

If Spencer's wife was proud of her sewing skills, he was happy for her.

If Elle wanted to work and it made her feel good, he was happy for her.

He didn't want to judge anyone for the choices they made. And deep down, he approved. There was no agreeing with his mother on some things.

"She's coming the day after tomorrow for a visit."

Hyrum dropped the handful of seasoned ground beef he'd intended for the trash onto the table. "Why?"

"Because she hasn't seen you in a while, and she'd like to. It will only be for two or three days."

"If I call her back, will she stay home?"

"This is a big deal for her, Hyrum. Shuttles frighten her, and she's coming alone."

He sighed hard. "Then she should take her broom."

~

Eli would like to go for a walk. Take Hyrum.

Drew looked up from his computer and glanced at his newborn, who was sound asleep in the bassinette next to the desk. "Eli wants to go out," he repeated with a twist of a sigh. "Where does he want to go? Fuzzy's for his first bender?"

He thinks the fresh air would do him some good. He'll sleep better after.

"Ah. And I suppose taking Hyrum was his idea, too?"

It would have been if he could form a clearer concept of Hyrum. Right now, he's just Snuggly Dude and Giver of Kisses.

"Well, Hy is a champion snuggler. What am I?"

Happy Man, full of warm touches and soft voices.

"And Oz?"

Boobs.

She's his favorite, but don't take that personally.

Where is she?

"Downstairs in her grandfather's apartment. She has a conference call and needed someplace quiet while she rips one of her contractors a new one."

Get Hyrum. I'll warm up the stroller.

We lapped Union Square, keeping to the sidewalk, in case Oz finished verbally destroying the contractor who dropped a ball or two or ten and delayed the opening of a major hotel at the Wastelands by a month or more and then wanted to join us. Guards trailed behind and watched from Union Square, though to anyone looking, they all seemed like tourists taking in the cool night air. I tried to mark where every one of them were; Hyrum had two guards following and Drew had two, but there were four keeping a careful eye on people who so much as glanced at the royal heir.

If Hyrum or Drew met with an unfortunate end, it would be sad. But Eli was second in line to the throne, and if something went wrong, he would be the most protected. He was bundled up in the stroller, wearing a heavy pair of footed pajamas with a light blanket over him, and he was only half awake, with no clue that he was the most important person on or near Union Square that night.

To be fair, he wasn't quite aware that he was a person at all. I sometimes peeked at his dreams, and he viewed life in terms of how satisfied he was. Boobs fed him and told him how wonderful he was and how loved he always would be. Happy Man soothed him when he felt cranky. Snuggly guy comforted him even when there was nothing wrong. He had no concrete opinion about his cousins, but Aubrey was Warm and Squishy and Jax was Too Loud. Will was Strong but Soft Man and Aisha was Smells Nice. But Grandpa Eli, he was Everything but the Boobs, and little Eli looked for him constantly.

Right now, he was trying to get a fix on Hyrum, who had been unusually quiet all through dinner, and though he agreed to go outside with Drew, he wasn't happy about it. Drew tried to pull conversation out of him but was met with shrugs and sighs and the occasional grunt.

Buy him hot chocolate and a donut. Trust me.

Drew trusted me. We headed onto the Square for a snack at the bakery, and after Hyrum had licked all the chocolate from his donut and taken a large bite, Drew asked him what was bothering him.

"You know Jax isn't really mad about his office," Drew said. "You're not in trouble."

"I know."

"Rhys isn't in trouble, either."

"I know."

"Then what's bothering you? You've been quiet all evening."

Hyrum took another bite. "My mom's coming to see me."

"Oh. Yeah, okay, I get it."

"Every time she calls, she says something about me coming home, and now she's moving out of the little house in Spencer's back yard, and she's going back home, and she says there's a big room for me with a new window and everything, but I don't want to go."

"Then don't."

"But she's my *mom*. I have to do what she says."

Careful.

"Hy, you're a ward of the King. He's the only one who gets to say where you live. And he'll say you get to live where *you* want to, not where she wants you to."

He knew that. He understood that there were official papers signed by a Supreme Court judge that named Jax his legal guardian, and that he would never make Hyrum go where he didn't say he wanted to go. But he also knew his mother. "She's gonna talk a lot and say things and then she'll make me feel bad about how much I like it here and then make me feel like I *have* to move and I'm a bad son if I don't. But I don't want to. If I go back there, my life is over."

He wasn't being dramatic. Life as he had come to love would end, and he would wallow in the misery of the ghost his father had left behind.

"Look." Drew shoved his cup aside and set his crossed arms on the table. "You can't leave now, anyway. We're knee-deep in the nano-suit project at work, and I need you for that. Literally, my life is at stake here. We're fine-tuning what I'll wear when I go to Elysium, and your input is critical."

"She won't believe that."

"Doesn't matter what she believes. You see things no one else does. You have ideas no one else does. I need that."

Hyrum was a lot like Drew in that respect. Drew had big ideas that popped out at the right moment; Hyrum had smaller ideas and needed context—like being in the room with the spacesuit Ozoo Enterprises was designing—but they tended to be as important as Drew's. Just before Christmas, when Drew was working on the gel that kept Elysium's computers at a safe operating temperature, Hyrum coughed up the answer Drew had been searching for, a way to raise the temperature of the environment around the computer without sacrificing heat dispersion and function of the computer systems. It was a simple ratio alteration, fewer nanobots and more gel, and additional liquid to thin the gel just a tiny bit. Literally a microscopic bit, yet it made all the difference.

He didn't understand the principle of resistance, but he knew it was easier to swim through water than it was through syrup and thought that the nanobots would find it easier if the gel were thinner. "You don't get as hot when it's easier to move."

Drew listened to Hyrum; other people in the lab were all highly educated and *of course* they knew better than Hyrum. But Drew thought it was worth a shot, and it worked. He made several micro-adjustments and the operating temperature dropped a full degree. Tests suggested the room temperature could be raised as much as 7 degrees. It was also why Drew was headed for Elysium and why a new suit was being designed. He was testing not only the new gel but the temperature of the pod it would be used in, necessitating new suits for the humans who managed the routine maintenance. His life truly did hinge on Hyrum's idea.

His voice was barely above a whisper. "She's gonna make me go, Drew."

"That's not going to happen. Your home is here. She can't make you do anything."

Hyrum said he knew that, but for the first time, I think he was lying.

~

I curled up on Hyrum's bed and listened to him cry. He was on his side with his knees drawn as tightly to his stomach as he could manage, and twice he slid out of bed to throw up. I'd intended to peek at his dreams, to see if there was anything he wasn't saying, if there was anything I could tell Drew or Will that would help, but he never made it past the drifting stage of slumber, where a person hovers in that gray area between sleep and being awake.

He didn't get up to make coffee for Jax or to sit at the table with him. He waited until Jax had left for the day, until Aubrey was getting ready for Will to bring Rhys and the twins downstairs, and then waited a bit longer to make sure they'd had breakfast. His stomach rumbled and the smell of waffles almost nudged him out of bed, but he didn't move until Aubrey knocked quietly on his door and then opened it when he didn't answer.

"I'm okay," he said thickly. "I didn't sleep good, that's all."

"I just wanted to make sure you're all right, sweetheart," she said before she closed the door again.

"What am I gonna do, Wick?" Sitting at the edge of the bed, he looked like he had a hangover and held his head in his hands as if it hurt like one. "I don't know what to do."

Tell her no.

Remind her Jax is the head of your family, and you listen to the head of the family.

"I know my daddy isn't there anymore and he can't ever punish me again, but I don't want to live with my mom. I want to stay here."

Go take a shower. Maybe hot water pouring over your head will help clear it a little.

His breath hiccupped. "Aubrey lets me have toys." He barely spoke above a whisper. "I have blocks and cars and even a doll. Mom would make me leave them here. There's nothing to play with there. She threw away all my toys."

Shower.

Shower.

Shower.

"She would make me leave my pencils and markers here, too, on account of I used to eat them. But Aubrey lets me have as many as I want, and she doesn't yell when I forget and stick one in my mouth. She just says, 'Sweetie, don't eat it, all right? If you eat it, you won't have the pencil anymore.' One time, when I was thirty, I bit a pencil in half and Mom got so mad that she hit me and said that was stupid. I love drawing pictures, Wick. I'll never get to do that again."

Go stand in the shower. It helps you think. Even Will thinks so.

Shower.

I waited on the bed while he showered, listening in case of a meltdown. If he sat down and started wailing, I could run and get Drew. Or Aubrey. She would understand if I bolted from the cat flap near his door and started howling at her. She would at least follow me to see what the problem was.

He didn't sit in the shower and cry. When he came out of the bathroom, his eyes were brighter, and he was an entirely new level of happy.

What did you think of? The shower helped, didn't it?

"Are the babies done eating?" He cocked his head to listen. Loud giggling drifted from the living room, and Charlie loudly proclaimed he was wearing pants today. "Good."

It's always good when he wears pants.

He probably means a diaper, but that's something.

He was named for you, you know. You and Finn. At least you two keep your shorts on.

For the most part, Hyrum kept his pants on. He limited his nudity to his bedroom, on nights he felt a tiny bit naughty and wanted to sleep naked, and occasionally he wandered to the guest bathroom across the hall to grab a clean towel without getting dressed. No one cared; Zed had a history of stomping through the entire apartment naked, before he married Sophia and moved downstairs.

Around the toddlers, however, he was careful. I waited while he dressed, and then followed him out. All three of them jumped up from where they were playing in the living room and ran to hug his legs, and then demanded he bend over so he could collect his good morning kisses.

"I thinked you was sleeping all day," Alex said after she kissed his cheek.

"I have pants!" Charlie proclaimed.

He was, indeed, wearing actual pants, a toddler-sized pair of jeans that were a half size too big. He lacked a shirt and had removed a sock and a shoe, but he was wearing more than he normally did.

"For all day?" Hyrum asked.

Charlie shrugged. He knew better than to commit.

Hyrum waved off Aubrey's offer to make breakfast for him because he was capable of making his own, and it wasn't fair for him to expect her to do it. He poured batter onto the waffle machine and then watched the kids play while he ate, and after he finished, he quietly washed the dishes. Aubrey slipped past him to get to the coffee and kissed the top of his head, asking whether he worked today or not.

"Only if Zed calls me. I work for Drew in a couple days. We made new air tubes and we have to test them."

"Any plans for today?"

He shrugged. "I'll play with the babies for a while. And maybe when they take naps, I'll go for a bike ride. Is it okay if I go to Pier Thirty Nine and watch the birds bug people? It's really funny."

"You wouldn't be planning on tossing a little food around to help that happen, would you?"

His "no" was wrapped around a giggle.

"Go have fun, but be nice."

The rest of the morning was a blur of building blocks and games invented by toddlers and an almost-four-year-old. Hyrum led them in a march up and down the hall and around the living room, going fast enough that they had to jog to keep up with him. Aubrey asked him if there was a reason, aside from pretending to be the pied piper, and he leaned in to whisper to her, "If they're tired, they'll take good naps and I won't feel bad about leaving for a bike ride."

He often took rides while they slept, but she nodded and thanked him for it because his attention to them now meant she could get a few chores done, and that meant she could sit down and read while they napped. After giving them a snack, Hyrum tucked them in and told them a story about Lazybones, the cat he'd had when he was younger.

Lazybones, who was not nearly as lazy as his name suggested, had once caught a baby squirrel and brought it into the house. He hadn't killed it; Hyrum thought he wanted a pet of his own, and he let it loose in the living room while Levi Munson met with elders from the church. Lazybones, being a cat, allowed his prey to run halfway across the room before he gave chase. He scrambled over chairs and laps, leaping over the head of a High Priest, and he ran across the bishop's shoulders before pouncing on the terrified little squirrel, which he then deposited at the feet of First Minister Munson.

"Levi," the bishop said dryly, "that cat believes you to have inferior hunting skills. I suggest you accept his offering with praise and thank him for the bounty you are about to enjoy."

The squirrel shot off again, missing Levi's ire-laden, "Fuck off, Brother Hamilton." He bent over and jabbed a pointy finger at Lazybones and warned him to catch the vermin and take it outside, or else wind up with his lazy bones on the outside of his fur.

Valerie Munson heard the commotion from the kitchen, and when the tiny brown streak headed straight for her, she opened the back door and shooed it outside with a broom, slamming it closed it before Lazybones could follow.

The impressive thing, Hyrum said, was that Levi didn't get mad. "Daddy told that story about Lazybones and the squirrel in church even. He said it was proof that God uses even his smallest creatures to teach us things and take care of us."

"Like Wick takes care of us?" Rhys asked, yawning.

"Yeah, like that. Wick takes care of everyone here. I hope my mom knows that, so she doesn't get mad when he gets on the table when she's here."

She has been informed.

Charlie and Alex were already asleep. Hyrum kissed Rhys on his forehead and told him to have a good nap, but he didn't tell him he would see him after he woke up.

He always said he would see them. Sometimes he warned them he might not be home, but he would be back before dinner. Sometimes he said he would be in his room reading, or that he had to go to work to help Drew think about things, but he never sent them to sleep without promising he would be there later.

What are you up to?

I followed him into his bedroom. He grabbed his red and blue zebra-striped backpack and shoved clean underwear and a fresh t-shirt into it; when I pawed at the zipper, he whispered, "I'm running away, Wick. Not forever. Just until my mom goes home."

If you run away, she won't go home. She'll stay here until they find you.

Aubrey was picking up toys and had her back to the hall and the stairs, and didn't turn as he called out, "I'm going for my bike ride now." She called back, "Have fun," but her hands were full of plastic blocks, and he was down the first flight of stairs before she could look.

I'll go and keep an eye on him.

I ran after him, and when he pulled his bicycle out from under the stairs, I jumped into the basket.

"You can't go, Wick. Not this time."

Wanna bet?

"You need to stay home." He slipped the backpack on and then tried to pick me up. For the first time, I leaned back and let slip a tiny growl. Not enough to scare him, but enough to let him know I meant business. "Wick, I'm not gonna—"

You need to let me come with you.

"Oh. You can tattle on me," he said as the realization settled. "If you go with me you can't tell."

Bingo.

He grabbed the protective mesh cover for the basket and clipped it in place, and then rolled the bike out the door. We headed for the Embarcadero, but this time he didn't stop at the Ferry Building for a cheeseburger. He sped by the red kiosk that had the best hot dogs he'd ever tasted, and that included the ones Aubrey made for lunch on rare occasions. He kept pedaling until we were past Marina Green and at the edge of Crissy Fields and then stopped to consider where he wanted to go. If we kept heading west, we would wind up at Fort Point, which wasn't a good place for running away unless one wanted to sleep nestled in a brick alcove, which we did not. He had the rest of the city to consider, even places he hadn't yet explored, but he turned around and headed the way we came, going past Ghirardelli Square and back to the Embarcadero. He stopped near the intersection of Jefferson and Hyde, considered what he could do, and turned in the direction of Alcatraz.

He knew how to get there—Zed's skiffs were parked close by, and he was allowed use of them to get to work—but it wouldn't be a good destination for someone running away. Zed was there and would tell Aubrey where he'd gone.

"I don't know where to go," he finally admitted.

Turn around. There's a hotel behind you.

"I could find Ash. He knows places to hide."

That's not a good idea. Ash sleeps on the beach.

"Maybe I could sneak into the Ozoo building. There are lots of places to hide there."

And security guards who would notice you. Just turn around. Turn around.

Turn around.

"Maybe I'll just ride for a while and think about it." He mounted the bike and turned to ride toward the Ferry Building, but only went ten feet before he stopped again. "That's a hotel, Wick."

No. Really?

"I can stay there as long as I want."

Theoretically.

He hesitated at the entry.

You're allowed inside.

"Can I take my bike inside?" he asked the doorman. "And the cat? If I pay for a room?"

The doorman beckoned to the guy whose job was to open car doors for customers. "Our valet will secure your bicycle," he said. "And yes, your cat is welcome to stay."

Yeah, they know who you are. They're not gonna tell you no.

"It's my only bike." Hyrum wasn't quite willing to give it up. "If I lose it, I'm gonna get in trouble."

No, you won't.

"Sir, if we misplace your bicycle, we will offer compensation," the valet said. "If there are issues, I will personally address them."

It's fine, dude.

"I don't know what that means."

"If something happens to your bicycle while under our care, we'll pay for a new one."

He didn't want a new one; he had an attachment to this bike because it was a gift from Santa and it was red, his favorite color, but agreed because no one would say that unless they planned on being super-duper careful, and super-duper was better than regular careful.

Once in the lobby, he clutched me to his chest. "Wick, this is nice. It's not as pretty as Father Dan's church, but I like it. Daddy would say it looks like a place for people with their heads up their butts. I think he probably stayed here before. Aubrey said he was in San Francisco once and she saw him, but no one was happy about it. I bet she told him to stay here."

Hyrum made no special requests but was taken to a spacious room with a sweeping view of the bay. There was no balcony; instead, there was a massive window that ran nearly floor to ceiling, and it opened to an iron safety gate. Placed in front of it were two comfy chairs and a tiny table made from chunks of colorful glass. Someone could sit with their coffee and enjoy the early morning or a beer while watching the restaurants come to life at night.

He settled onto the oversized bed to search for something to watch on the big-screen entertainment monitor. He pulled his shoes off—taking care to set them neatly on the floor, side by side—and then piled all the pillows behind his back and pulled me onto his stomach. "We'll go get some food after I watch some TV," he said. "But if you get really hungry before then, just crawl onto my lap and poke me. Okay?"

Don't count on it.

He scrolled through the available videos and broadcast shows and decided that he needed to keep up with the news while he was away from home. Will and Jax often talked about things going on in the world during dinner, but if he wasn't going to be there to listen, it seemed like something he should do. Cartoons could wait until he was home again.

"Sometimes I see Red on the news," he said absently. "He doesn't run Florida anymore, but they talk like he does."

Reporters in Florida are biased. The Prime Minister is a woman, and they'll never give her credit for the progress she makes.

"He made a new rule that girls are allowed to wear nice pants in church instead of dresses all the time if they want to. Boy, people got mad about that. *That* was even in the news."

I'm not sure why it matters what people wear, but okay.

"Oh, and he made a church law that says ladies can teach high school seminary. People got super-*duper* mad about that. But girls have to take it just like boys, so they know all about the Bible and the other books, so I don't know why it's a big deal. Used to be they had to take it even if they didn't go to high school."

I thought teaching was one job women were allowed there, at least teaching small children.

"I didn't get to take seminary on account of I didn't go to school, even when the girls got to. But Red and Joe and Spencer made sure I learned the same stuff. Daddy didn't even mind."

He didn't mind as long as you memorized everything.

You don't quote the Bible like you used to. I kind of miss that. I wonder what it says about running away.

"Maybe someday girls can be priests, just like—"

He twitched at a knock on the door, but he didn't get up to see who it was.

That's a mistake. You need to answer it.

"Be really quiet," he whispered.

The TV is on. He can hear it.

He ignored it twice more, even when I warned him that not answering wouldn't do any good. I slid off his chest because I was pretty sure about what came next, and I was right.

The lock made a clicking sound as a key card was tapped onto the entry pad, and Hyrum jumped up as the door opened.

"Relax," Will said as he entered. "I wanted to make sure that you're all right."

Hyrum was off the bed, clutching his hands at his chest. "How did you find me?"

"Your guard alerted me."

Shirt clenched in a tight fist, he bounced on his toes. "That's not fair! They're not supposed to tell! You said so!"

"No one called Aubrey or Jax." Will kept his voice even and spoke calmly. "The guard was merely concerned for your wellbeing and was also worried because you seemed uncertain before entering the hotel. There was a question regarding whether you entered on your own, or because someone else had directed you to."

Liar.

"That's still telling."

This time, Will assured him, it was necessary. They would have also informed him if it had been Oz or Zed, if they felt that something was not right. "When there's a question, they notify me first, Hyrum. I decide whether Jax and Aubrey are informed, and I promise you, I was called on many occasions when they were younger. When Rhys is older, Drew will be informed if there's a question."

"But I'm not little like Rhys. I get to go where I want."

"Indeed." Will sat in one of the chairs by the window and gestured for Hyrum to sit in the other. "If Rhys had left the building, Vicat would have physically restrained him and then brought him home. No one is stopping you, Hyrum. They were only concerned and didn't wish to intrude."

Hyrum let go of his shirt and crossed his arms. "I'm not going home."

The corners of Will's mouth twitched up, just a tiny bit. "I'm not here to take you home. You have every right to be here. There's nothing wrong with wanting a night to yourself. There's nothing wrong with wanting your own space. You could get your own apartment if you chose, though I think that would break everyone's hearts."

"I don't want an apartment. I just—I'm not going home until my mom is gone."

"Ah. I see. She certainly chooses to ignore that you're not a little boy anymore."

"I'm a man now," Hyrum murmured, uncertain.

"But you are still *her* little boy," Will said. "We will always be our mothers' little boys, Hyrum. Yours simply has difficulty understanding where the line is drawn, and why she should not step over it."

Will should know. His mom tried to draw a line between him and Aisha.

The fog of stubbornness faded, and Hyrum sat on the bed with a sigh. "She's always talking about her house that got fixed up and a room she has just for me. A really big room with a new window that no one ever threw me out of. She wants me to go with her and live. I'm not gonna."

"No one—"

"If I have to go back, she's gonna treat me like a baby. I won't have a job, and I won't be able to ride my bicycle on account of I might get hurt or lost. She would make me leave my toys here. I don't want that anymore. I want to take baths alone or showers if I want. I get to take showers here."

"Wait. She was still bathing you?"

Hyrum shrugged. "I could wash myself, but someone had to be in the bathroom with me on account of I might drown. But I've never drowned, Will, not even a little bit. Aubrey only ever helped me when I first got here, right after you found me. And she lets me go places. I have friends here. I don't have friends in Florida." He grabbed at his shirt again, clutching the fabric with both hands. "Mom makes me sleep with the bedroom door open so she can hear what's going on and make sure there's no shenanigans. I don't even know what that means, but I like sleeping with the door closed."

He'd never be able to sleep naked again.

It's a new thing, Will. It makes him feel adult.

"All right." Will reached for a notebook that had been placed on the little table. "We'll make excuses for your absence. Do you know how to order room service? This is the menu."

He carefully explained how to order food, how to tip without cash, and where to place his tray when he was done eating. When he was certain Hyrum could place an order for the cheeseburger, fries, shake, and the root beer he would surely want, he demonstrated how Hyrum could order a movie that didn't appear in the monitor's menu.

Warn him about the movies in red. He won't want to watch kissing things.

"Are you gonna tell Aubrey?" Hyrum asked before Will left.

"She deserves to know where you are. When you fail to show for dinner, she'll be worried."

"She's gonna come get me."

"I promise, she won't."

"But mom—"

"She'll have time with Aubrey," Will said. "I imagine she hasn't had time alone with her since she was a very small girl."

Or ever.

"Wick?" Will asked. "Are you staying with Hyrum?"

It's my vacation, too.

"I'll inquire at the desk about having a litter box sent up, then."

I can use the facilities. No worries.

He reminded me to aim better than usual, told Hyrum to have a good night, and left. Hyrum pressed his hands to his stomach and then swallowed hard.

"He's not mad."

Of course not.

Relief poured over him. "We get to stay!"

His grin reminded me of his first Christmas here, when he saw the bicycles Santa had left for everyone.

Dude, if your mom shows up and tries to make you leave, I'll fight her. Like, teeth and claws. Or just a deep growl. People don't like a deep growl.

He turned to look out the window, searching for the first thing he wanted to do. I hoped it included something dead and delicious, but if not, something to make him giggle and smile.

"What's something I never done before, Wick?"

Well, this, for starters.

"I told Aubrey I was gonna go to the pier and watch the birds bug people. We should do that so that it wasn't a lie."

I'm not a fan of pigeons.

"If I find a bench to sit on, you have to get on my lap, okay? That way I know you're okay. People like you, and I don't want someone to try to take you."

The guards would stop that, but okay.

"I know my guards are still following me but if a bunch of people got between them and me, they might not be able to stop someone really fast. Like I saw a man on TV, he runs so fast that he can jump over things and other people running still can't catch him. I bet he can even run faster than Will."

Well, to be fair, Will is pushing fifty and isn't as fast as he used to be.

He decided against getting his bike from the valet. He walked toward the pier with me trying to balance on his shoulder—he was getting better with me there but still didn't have the hang of it—and stopped short of Pier 39 to buy a bag of popcorn. I knew it wasn't his snack. This was a bag filled with pigeon magnets. Hundreds, if not thousands, of buttery little pigeon magnets.

The long bench halfway down the pier was vacant. He bought a soft drink from the hot dog cart and sat down, reminding me to get on his lap, and he waited. There was munching of the magnets, of course, because it's impossible for a person to hold a bag of warm, buttery popcorn and not eat some. That would be like setting a plate filled with real live fresh dead shrimp in front of me and expecting me to not at least sample it.

I don't care if you tell me no. Turn your back, and I'm stealing a bite.

We sat directly across from a popular fish restaurant, one with al fresco dining for the people-watching tourists that frequented Fisherman's Wharf. He nibbled on the popcorn and leaned back as if he were soaking up the sun, though he was searching for the birds that often lurked on the second level railing. When he'd spotted half a dozen, he flicked a kernel that had fallen onto his knee and giggled as they descended on it.

Hyrum was careful to not launch any popcorn near the tables where people were eating. He carefully flicked pieces to his right and his left, and the only ones bothered by it were people trying to walk past without being bombarded by hungry pigeons. When a dozen birds were pecking at popcorn pieces, a server from the restaurant stomped to the railing, mouth open to complain.

One of the guards strolled past, muttering as if talking to himself, and moved on. The waiter sighed and went back to work; Hyrum was a nuisance, but he wasn't breaking any laws, and none of the birds had landed on the patio. Yelling at the Queen's little brother for something that was merely annoying was not worth the potential fallout.

Jax and Aubrey would have sided with the server, but he had no way of knowing that.

Hyrum giggled again and lifted me to his shoulder, declaring the shenanigans almost complete. He headed for the end of the pier, where there was a view of the bay, a dozen birds hopping behind him. He casually dropped pieces of popcorn along the way, and when we reached the pier railing, making sure no one was standing nearby, he upended the bag and with a swiping flourish, sent the remainder flying.

People watched from the periphery. It didn't seem to bother anyone; they were too amused by Hyrum's gleeful laughter to do be annoyed. He bounced on his toes, hands pressed to his chest, and giggled wildly as more birds flocked to his buttery bounty.

This time, a guard stepped up to him.

"Hyrum, you're too close to the rail. Wick might fall off your shoulder and into the water."

He stopped bouncing. "Oh. I'm sorry, Wick."

I could have jumped in the other direction if I thought I was about to be launched. No worries.

The guard was not done. "One question. Do we need to call for bicycles? All but one went back with the last shift."

"Nuh. I'm gonna walk the rest of today. I might go to the marina grassy place and then the sand. I think Wick will like the sand."

"You need anything, Wick?" the guard asked. "Food or water?"

He asked as a reminder to Hyrum, lest we repeat the panting incident.

"Oh, I bet he wants something to drink. Do you think the fish place will give me a little cup with water in it?"

The guard reached into the cargo pocket on his pants and pulled out a collapsible cup. "Take this. It'll fit in your pocket, and you can fill it at water fountains." He demonstrated how to open and close it, and then handed it to Hyrum. "It's okay, I have another one. Please take it."

The cup was not standard issue, and I wondered if Hyrum's guards carried them now, just in case.

He offered me water on the pier, again when we reached the aquatic park, and yet again when we reached Crissy Field.

I would have preferred food at that point, but he was happy playing in the sand, and he mentioned getting lunch at the Italian place across from the hotel.

"Drew says they have really good pizza. I like the place we usually go but I want to try it. He says the pepperoni bites back."

I wasn't sure a restaurant was a good idea, given that he was digging in the sand, and by the time he was done he'd jammed most of it under his nails. He brushed it from his pants, though, and went into the restroom where he thoroughly washed his hands and arms, digging out the detritus from under his nails.

"You need to go potty?" he asked as he dried his hands. "Oh, no. I'm sorry. You're not one of the babies. But if you gotta go, meow at me. I'll help."

Given the volume of water you've offered me, that's not a bad idea.

He made sure I didn't fall in, checked to be sure I hadn't missed, and for good measure washed his hands again. Before we left, he asked if I needed another drink—just meow—and I head-butted his cheek to let him know I was fine.

~

He hesitated outside Piazza's; some restaurants allowed me inside, some allowed me on the patio if they had one, and others—unless I was with Will or Jax—wouldn't let me in at all. Hyrum didn't want to cause a fuss and realized that if he said he was Aubrey's brother that they would let me in no matter what the rules were, but he didn't want to use that.

"Oz says it's rude, and it's not fair to other people. If you can't eat here, I'll go somewhere else. I can get pizza another day."

Or order it to go.

Still, his hand lingered on the door handle, uncertain. He was about to turn around and find another place to eat, but the door popped opened and Sean McAllister stuck his head out.

"Hyrum! Long time no see!"

Sean was a former reporter for the university newspaper and had once scored an interview with the King. The interview turned into a short adventure in Will's birth When where he learned about time travel, anti-gravity playgrounds, Will's beloved motorcycle, and that was followed by several days in a holographic simulation of Saint Francis. He'd learned too many of the family secrets and was a potential liability, but neither Will nor Jax was worried he would tell anyone.

There was little reason to worry.

No one would believe him.

Sean wasn't interested in discovering what the penalty would be if he blabbed to the world that the royal family not only traveled in time, but each of them had—in his words—superpowers. He'd seen Hyrum and Rhys play with electricity. He knew Will and Drew could communicate with me. By the time we left Saint Francis, I was certain he had no intention of blabbing to anyone, but it was not because he was afraid.

Sean McAllister was loyal, and he wouldn't put any of the family at risk for the things they could do.

Hyrum hadn't seen him since they'd parted ways in Finn's lab, but he'd read the editorial piece Sean wrote at the end of the school year, and blurted out, "I liked your story about Jax! It was really good!"

Grinning, Sean ushered him inside. "Thanks. Did Mr. Blackshear like it?"

Hyrum nodded enthusiastically. "He says he thinks you should be a writer when you grow up, but not a reporter on account of you're not mean enough."

"Yeah, I don't like pestering people."

"But you can write stories about them! How come you're here? You look like a waiter now."

"I am a waiter now. This is my grandfather's restaurant. I work here every summer and sometimes on holidays. Is this your first time here?"

"Uh-huh. Drew says you got really good pizza here and I wanted to try it." He slid into the booth Sean gestured to. "Is it okay for Wick to be here? I don't want to get in trouble if he's not allowed. I can come back."

"He's fine. I know the owner, and he kinda likes me." Sean

sat on the other side of the table. "Hey, want to split a pizza? I'm due for a break and I'm hungry, too."

Hyrum nodded again. "I like pepperoni. What do you like? We can have different things on the same pizza. Drew showed me how to do that one time when I wanted pepperoni and he wanted stupid stuff. But then he added pepperoni to the stupid stuff, so I don't know why he didn't just get pepperoni by itself."

"Drew's weird," Sean said, chuckling. "He and Oz come here every now and then." He leaned forward and whispered, "One time, he got ravioli with *spinach* in it."

"Ugh."

"So how come you're here by yourself?" Sean asked as he tapped their order into a tablet.

Hyrum giggled. "I ran away."

Sean's finger hesitated over the tablet. "Should I text Drew and tell him that you're all right?"

"Nuh. Will knows where I am. He said it was okay if I wanted to stay in a hotel while I run away."

"Does he know you have Wick?"

"Uh-huh. Wick said he wants to stay with me, so we're gonna do adventures. Today we tossed popcorn at pigeons and then went to the sand and played in it, but I washed my hands so I won't get any on the pizza." He held his hands up and checked his fingernails. "Maybe there's a tiny bit left."

Sean assured him the few grains of sand still under his thumbnail wouldn't leap out and attack the pizza. When another server brought their drinks to the table and they smiled at each other, Hyrum leaned across the table and whispered loudly, "Is she your girlfriend?"

Sean's eyes widened. "Um, we haven't talked—"

She grinned and said, "Yes, I am. Introduce me to your friend, Sean."

Hyrum jumped up and held his hand out to her. "I'm Hyrum. You're pretty."

"Thank you. And I'm Kit."

"Like a kitty?"

"Something like that."

"Wanna have pizza with us? We got a big one so there's gonna be lots." He looked at Sean. "Are you gonna marry her?"

"Oh my god, Hyrum. We've only been dating—"

She laughed and let go of Hyrum's hand. "I'm not on my break, but thank you for asking."

"Okay."

She leaned toward Hyrum and whispered, "We just might get married someday, but he doesn't know it yet. Don't tell him."

"Kit smells nice," Hyrum said as he sat down.

"What about you?" Sean pressed. "Any girlfriends?"

"No, no, no, I don't want a girlfriend."

"Sure about that? They're kind of fun to be with."

I thought you could barely talk to women. That's what you told Jax.

"Ah, Wick speaks. I'm just teasing him. I know he's too busy for a relationship right now."

"I'm not too busy," Hyrum countered. "I just don't want to. Girlfriends want to hold hands and kiss and do other kissing things."

"Never met a girl you liked that much?"

Hyrum considered it. "There was a girl in school who wanted to kiss me, but I said no because you only kiss your girlfriends and I didn't want one. But she was nice. Her name was Maddy and that was short for Madison, and even if I wanted a girlfriend she was only seventeen so I said to her, 'I'm old enough to be your daddy,' and she said, 'Nuh-uh you're in school too,' so I told her I was forty-four on account of I was then, and then she said 'Oh, you're super old.' So then I met her to Barry, and she liked him and he was only eighteen and new in our class, but he said he liked kissing things. I made him promise to be nice and not kiss her until she said it was okay."

Somehow, Sean followed Hyrum's train of thought. "Well, it's probably a good thing in that case. She wasn't old enough to give consent if you had wanted to kiss her."

"Uh-huh. Will said if I ever want to kiss a girl, I need to ask him or Drew if she's old enough and then to make sure I have consent, even though I don't know what that means. I said I would ask Aubrey, but Will says she might cry on account of she doesn't want me to move away and if I start kissing girls I might want to. Oh! You kiss a girl now! Did you move out of your mom's house?"

Sean had, in fact, moved into his own apartment. While they ate, they discussed what independence felt like, and Hyrum admitted that even though he lived with his sister, that was a big part of why he didn't ever want to go back to Florida. Here, he was independent. There, he was a child.

"That's why I ran away. My mom is coming tomorrow, and she might make me move back there. So I'm gonna stay in the hotel until she goes home."

"I get it. I love my mom, but I don't think I'll ever want to live with her again. Look, a hotel will get expensive. If you need a place to crash for a few days, I have a spare room. No bed, but I can pick up an inflatable. I have a pretty good entertainment system with tons of video games, and there's a playground close by. It could be fun."

Hyrum thought the hotel would be just fine; his mother was only going to be there a few days, and it's not an adventure if you stay with someone else. Then it's just visiting. Sean put his number and address into Hyrum's phone just in case and made him promise that he'd call if he needed company or just wanted someone to hang with.

"We can run around on Ocean Beach with play swords and pretend we're the Lost Boys," Sean said.

Hyrum agreed that sounded fun, but the light in his eyes changed.

~

After wandering around the Wharf for another hour, he decided that stretching out on the bed sounded like a good idea. We watched cartoons until he was hungry again, and he carefully planned out his meal before calling room service. Before he picked up the phone, he muttered the directions to himself: "Will said say 'hello' when someone answers and then to ask for room service, and then wait for another person to answer, and then say 'hello' again and my name and my room number. Then I get to say I want a cheeseburger and fries and chocolate milkshake. Be sure to say thank you."

He followed Will's instructions exactly, until after he'd given them his order when he blurted out that he needed cat food, too, and did they have the kind in the can with the red stripes and the little kitten face on the front?

"Wick!" he gushed when he hung up. "They have your favorite kind of food, and they're bringing two cans! One's beef and one's fish and shrimp, so you can pick."

Imagine that.

"I never heard of a hotel having cat food, but I asked because just in case, and they have it."

There may have been interference on my behalf. But it's still nice.

He celebrated this little victory by jumping on the bed. "It's not an adventure if you're not a little naughty." He bounced for several minutes, giggling, and when he stopped, he said, "Okay, I won't do it anymore. But that was fun. I never got to do that before."

I don't think anyone minds.

Worse things have happened on that bed.

After we ate, he carefully stacked the dishes just outside the door, the way Will instructed. He watched the news—he did not see Red, which disappointed him though he expected as much—and then another cartoon before taking a shower and helping me in the bathroom. Before he turned out the lights, he knelt by the bed to say his prayers, remembering to ask for good things for all the people he loved, and he gave thanks for the fun day he'd had. After a quiet "amen," he reached into his backpack and grabbed Chuckles, the stuffed rabbit he slept with. He left the curtain open so he could watch starlight bounce off the water while he fell asleep, and I curled up on the bed next to him.

"That's so pretty," he whispered. "I wish we lived near the water. I'd like to see it every night."

He was quiet for a long time, but he didn't close his eyes. I waited; I didn't want to fall asleep until he did.

"If we lived near the water, we could play on the beach every day. Bike rides would be a lot funner, too."

The kids would enjoy it, for sure.

"Maybe sometimes I can sleep in Will's office. He can see the water from there."

Drew has a bay view, too. He'd let you stay there every now and then.

There was another long stretch of quiet, and he blinked slowly, slow enough I thought he was drifting off.

"I'm not a lost boy, Wick," he finally said. "I'm not lost."

I know.

He rolled onto his back.

"I'm not a boy, either."

I know that, too.

"I know Will and Drew think I'm a man, but I still don't feel like one."

I don't feel like I'm over four hundred years old, but here we are.

"How come I have to be like this? Why can't I be normal?"

You are normal.

"My daddy did this to me. It's not fair."

No, it's not. But we wouldn't have you any other way, dude. You're what we need, you know.

"Joe said Daddy did mean things to Mom on account of he thought I was gonna be a girl. But Joe didn't know why that was a bad thing. He said girls are really nice and sweet, and he wanted a bunch of daughters because boys give you headaches and they eat boogers." His breath hiccupped, and he wiped his arm across his nose. "If he didn't want a girl so bad, he coulda taken Mom to one of those doctors. Joe said that was against the law, but people do it anyway. He says it shouldn't be against the law because sometimes people get scared and do stupid things on account of not having safe doctors or safe homes, but I don't know what stupid things."

I don't know, dude. I'm glad he didn't.

"Maybe because it's a sin? Daddy cared about sin and what the church thought, except for when he punished us. And a doctor coulda told them I was a boy. Like Oz and Drew found out

Eli was a boy when he was still just a tiny thing in her tummy. Is that a sin, too? Finding out?"

Religion was not my strong suit. Hyrum and Aubrey were the only ones I knew who held onto faith as a matter of fact and not hope-filled belief. Still, I'd heard enough from Hyrum over the years he'd lived with us to have an idea which direction he would always head, and that was wherever he thought God and Jesus were.

The only thing your dad feared was Jesus. He probably didn't do it because no matter what, the things he believed told him that Jesus wanted you to be there. Beating on your mom was just an outlet for his rage. He had a lot of that.

"Jesus loves everyone," Hyrum sniffed. "But all the things Daddy did, it probably made Jesus cry."

I'd ask what about God, but I was there when your dad told the world he was *God.*

"Why didn't Jesus fix me?"

Because you're not broken.

"I know what I don't know, Wick. And I'll never learn things like Drew does. The only time I ever felt a little bit smart was when Aubrey and Jax sent me to school. I already knew how to do most of the things we were supposed to learn. I even wanted to quit because I knew that stuff, but the teacher asked me to stay, on account of the other people in my class could see how I did things and then they would know that if they really wanted, they could do them, too."

Here's a thought for you—Drew will never learn things like you do. He sees things other people don't, but you see things he doesn't. He loves that about you.

"Drew got to go to real school, not life skills. And he got an extra degree when he graduated. *And* he's gonna be a doctor, but not the kind that gives you shots."

That doesn't make him better than you.

"He's loads better than me. He's not afraid of anything, not even kissing things."

Dude. I jumped onto his chest so that I could see his face. *How much of what I'm saying are you grasping?*

"Can I tell you a secret, Wick?"

Always.

"I won't ever do kissing things because it hurts. I don't think it hurts men when they're doing it with women, but I think it hurts women. It hurt when Daddy did it to me."

It doesn't hurt them. If it did, they'd just go around kicking random men in the junk until all men stop trying.

"Daddy hurt me so much. That's why I did the thing and set his hair on fire. I didn't mean to, but he was gonna punish my little sister, and—"

He pulled Chuckles in tight and gulped for air.

He deserved it. And you put the fire out before it did any real damage. That was a kindness you didn't have to extend to him.

"Why didn't Mom stop him, Wick? She knew he was doing it. She heard me crying, I know she did. She didn't stop him from doing it to Aubrey or our little sisters. And she cleaned the room under the stairs on account of he didn't want to punish anyone in a dirty room. Why didn't she do anything? She could have stopped him. I know she could."

He would have beaten her so badly that she would have died, Hyrum. I don't think she knew how to stop him.

"She knew how to stop him. Or she could have called the police. Or told Grandpa. Grandpa Jake would have made him stop. He hated Daddy. If she had told him before he died, he would have made it all stop."

Your dad was the head of the church and the country. I'm not sure he could have done anything. Levi would have killed him, most likely.

"I think Daddy got someone to kill him, anyway. Grandpa knew Daddy hit Mom and they had words about it. I heard him say that it made him sad that he ever made her marry Daddy, and if he could ever find a way to undo it, he would. And then he was dead a couple days later. I guess it doesn't matter now. Even if Daddy never punished me, I'd still be stupid."

Listen to me.

Hear me. Please hear me.

You're not stupid. You just don't know things you've never been taught, same as anyone. You learn at your own pace. That's fine.

"Rhys knows things I don't, Wick. He reads really big books and he can do fractions. He's not even four years old yet."

Rhys is like Will was at that age. He's an anomaly. Look at Charlie and Alex. Rhys was reading when he was their age, but Charlie can't even keep his pants on, and Alex thinks Grandpa Eli ate the last living unicorn in the world.

Hyrum grunted.

Jax told her that unicorns have rainbow blood, and after Eli ate it, he sold all the blood, and that's how they make rainbow cotton candy.

"Charlie just likes being naked, that's all. I bet if he wanted, he could learn to read like Rhys does. Will tries to teach him, but Charlie runs off on account of he thinks Rhys can do all the reading for him. I wonder why they're so different."

He'd stopped crying, and his breathing evened out; I wanted to keep him from ramping up again.

Maybe Rhys was conceived in Will's birth When. I know kids there read and write earlier than kids here do.

"Can Isaac read?" Isaac was Jay's little brother. Technically, he was George's clone—Jay's other stepfather—but Jay considered him to be his brother as much as he did Rhys and Charlie. He was created in Will's birth When and lived there part of the time. "If it's a time thing, he should be able to read."

He and Rhys trade books every now and then. And Aisha has been teaching him math when he visits. They like to play school together.

Isaac and Rhys, I mean. Not Isaac and Aisha. I suppose Aisha likes it, too.

"I like Isaac. He's pretty quiet, though."

I think he doesn't feel well a lot of the time. George is afraid he's getting time-sick, but Jay says he mostly feels bad before he has to go back to the other When, and he's always afraid it's time to go back.

"Maybe he's nervous."

Or just sad that he has to go. But he has to because George needs to go home to reset every now and then. Otherwise, he'll get time-sick, and that won't do Isaac any good.

"If I had a thingy in my head like Rhys does, I could have run away to Will's When. That would have been the best adventure."

Rhys only has one as a safeguard, in case he gets separated from Will and Aisha. Oz got hers when she was little, too.

"Or maybe I would have gone to see Shivan and Jeff and Fluffy. I'd like to ride on Jeff someday if he'll let me."

He'll let you. Tell him he's pretty. He digs that.

"I hope we go back soon."

I'll make sure of it.

"We have to take Rhys, so he can play with Quinn."

We will. You sound sleepy now.

"Yeah."

He closed his eyes, and I waited until his breathing slowed before sliding onto the mattress. I curled up on the other pillow and was almost asleep when he said, voice thick, "I have to go home tomorrow, Wick. Real men don't run away from stuff like this. I have to go tell my mom I won't move no matter what."

~

The ride home was quiet. Hyrum was too nervous to carry on even a one-sided conversation; I listened to the sound of his pedaling instead, the smooth cadence, the clicking when he switched gears, and I heard confidence in his effort. He no longer had to think about what he was doing, and no longer had second thoughts about riding up steep streets or worried about losing control on significant downgrades.

The bike slowed as we approached Union Square. Hyrum shifted gears and rode the brakes until he was barely rolling along. I heard swearing from one of the guards behind us, a particular grumbling that grew louder as he neared, and then faded as he shot past us. He stood on his pedals, trying to regain control, but he was almost to the cable car turnaround before he was able to stop.

I don't think he's been riding very long.

Hyrum glanced over his shoulder when he heard an air bike approaching.

"You all right?" the guard asked. "Gut feeling. Is something wrong? Someone bothering you?"

"My mom's coming today."

"All right. I understand. I can direct you to Alcatraz. Surely Prince Zealand has work for you today. Would you like me to call?"

Hyrum allowed himself a tiny grin. His guards knew how he felt about his mother; this guard had listened to Hyrum complain about her before, one who embraced the new rules about interacting with the royal family. He often engaged in real conversation with Hyrum and didn't simply tolerate the wild ride his train of thought could take.

"I have to go home. My real home. Not Florida."

"Let me know if there's anything I can do," the guard said.

There wasn't anything any of the guards could do unless Valerie Munson attacked her son, and verbally didn't count.

Securing the bike under the stairs, which required no actual locking of the bike but instead making sure it would not fall over and block the way down, took twice as long as usual, and then he trudged up the stairs, pressing me to his chest. He passed Vicat halfway up—she'd probably been checking Rhys's schedule for the day—but she was clearly in a hurry and only had time to say hello. Once at the landing in front of the entry, he hesitated again. Aubrey was in the living room, picking up toys left by the small sticky people; he sighed and then stepped in, asking if she needed help.

"Sweetie." She smiled and dropped the metal truck she'd picked up into a basket. "I didn't expect to see you so soon. How was your night out?"

"It was fun. I had pizza with Sean. Did you know his grandpa owns the restaurant across from the hotel?" When she shook her head, he went on. "It's really good and he has a girlfriend now and she works there with him. And he has his own apartment. I think he moved on account of kissing things."

"Probably," she chuckled.

"Anyway, I was good, and I made my bed this morning, and I took a shower last night and said my prayers. I didn't leave a mess for anyone to clean up. Will showed me where to put my dirty dishes."

She had no doubt that he'd behaved, though he pointedly did not mention jumping on the bed.

"I'm glad you had fun, Hyrum. But next time, please tell me before you decide to stay out all night, all right?"

"You're not mad?"

"Of course not. But if Will hadn't told me where you were, I would have worried—the same way I worry when Oz and Drew stay out and don't tell me they're going to be late."

He promised to let her know, though I felt a disappointed breath escape him.

He wasn't sure there would be a next time.

"When's Mom coming? I woulda stayed out longer but that woulda been rude."

She glanced at the clock. "Half an hour. Would you like to go with me to pick her up? She took the shuttle to Oakland and is coming across in the ferry."

His eyes lit up. "She's really riding on the boat?"

"She said you made the ferry sound fun."

"It is! Drew took me to Sausalito lotsa times and we got lunch and cupcakes, and he made me tell Oz we ate all the cupcakes over there. But he was teasing, and he brought her some. I think she really likes them."

"Ask Oz to tell you about the time she ran away. She rode the ferry there to look for cupcakes when she was six years old."

"By herself?" His eyes went wide. "You let her?"

"Oh, no. She never asked permission. But Will saw her slip out, and he followed her to make sure she was safe."

He peppered her with questions all the way to the Ferry Building; by the time we reached the pier, he didn't need to ask Oz anything because he'd heard the entire story twice. I thought Will was the one he needed to ask; he had a much better take on Oz's runaway story, though it probably had less impact without the details of why he'd followed her.

It was a lesson in the effects of changing time; Will learned that the memories go with you, and you remember the things you change. He lived with the agony of having seen six-year-old Oz's lifeless body pulled from the water and felt every horrible minute of it despite having altered her personal narrative.

He didn't want to examine it too closely; he knew he could change things and live in the new reality, yet if he went back more than a week or two and changed something, nothing in his own timeline changed. He was less certain about what might happen if he went back several years and changed a major event; he might be able to get home, but he thought it was equally likely that he wouldn't be able to.

Aisha thought Old Drew, the one they frequently visited thirty-five years in the future, could explain it, but Will wasn't sure he wanted to know. Knowing might lead to temptation, and some things were better left alone.

Hyrum's dread over his mother's visit faded in his excitement over seeing her ferry slide up to the dock, and he bounced excitedly on his toes as she made her way down the ramp. There was no hiding where he and Aubrey waited—they were surrounded by uniformed guards, and other people were kept at a fair distance—but he still waved his arm in a wide sweep and called out, "Mom! Mom! We're over here!"

Valerie Munson moved slowly, leaning heavily on a cane she gripped tightly in one hand while trying to carry a small suitcase in the other. She smiled when she saw Hyrum jumping up and down and was visibly relieved when one of the guards ran up the ramp and took the bag from her and then offered his arm.

He gave a short bow when they'd made it to where Aubrey waited. "Your Majesty," he said before turning to Valerie. "Ma'am."

"Thank you, Graden!" Hyrum blurted. "She mighta fallen without you."

The guard managed to keep the grin from his face. "Hyrum. Wick."

"Oh," Hyrum breathed out as Guard Graden turned and went back to his post. "He's working in a uniform. He won't get into trouble on account of me talking to him, will he?"

Aubrey promised he would not as she bent forward to kiss her mother's cheek. "You're allowed to converse with the guards, Hyrum."

"But Will said when they have uniforms on—"

"I promise, it's fine. Mom, how are you? How was the trip?"

Valerie lifted her cane and tapped it on the ground. "Too fast. You barely have time to open a book, and already the shuttle is landing." She leaned into Hyrum as he hugged her. "The ferry was fun, Hyrum. Much more enjoyable than your brother's boat."

"Who has a boat?" Hyrum asked. "Joe? Spencer?"

"Joe," she said with a heavy sigh. "He speeds around the lake like a damned fool. Can you imagine?"

Hyrum could imagine, and it made him giggle.

She reached up and touched my chin. "And how are you, Wick?"

Ready to bite your finger off if you take Hyrum away from me.

"Wick," Hyrum giggled.

You heard that, didn't you? You're hearing me more and more. I like that.

Any conversation I might have been tempted to have with him needed to wait. Aubrey had arranged for lunch at *Sofy Z's*; it was not officially ready for customers, but Sophia was eager for a soft opening and jumped at the chance to serve the Queen and her mother.

Granted, to Sophia Aubrey was less the Queen and more like her own mother, but this was a ready-made photo op suggested by the Queen herself and could be used in launch advertising. No one asked Valerie what she thought about it; like it or not, she was having her picture taken a few hundred times while dining on enchiladas and freshly made tortilla chips.

Sophia hovered in the background, directing two photographers who kept their distance as they shot pictures, and she allowed her employees to interact with Aubrey instead of hovering over them herself. If not for the other vacant tables, it would have seemed like a typical lunch out for three people eager to catch up with one another.

Hyrum held the chair for his mother before he did for his sister, ignoring protocol that demanded Aubrey be seated first. He understood it was the way things were supposed to be done in public; he simply didn't care. His personal hierarchy suggested that mothers come before sisters, at least when being a gentleman mattered, and he was damn well holding his mother's seat first.

When they were comfortable, he pulled a highchair from a spot near the host's stand and covered it with a large dish towel procured from a busboy. I didn't argue; I hated highchairs on principle, but he was showing that he was still a gentleman, considerate with the women around him, and careful with Sophia's brand-new café furnishings.

He helped Valerie navigate the menu, steering her away from the spicier things he knew she wouldn't like, pronouncing names of foods she was unfamiliar with. I kept an eye on Aubrey as the words rolled from his tongue as if it were his native language; she had a half-smile playing about her mouth, and her eyes glittered with pride. When Hyrum had first arrived in Pacifica, dirty, disheveled, with a matted beard and hair that had been cut at odd angles, he couldn't have done much more than point to pictures of the foods he liked most, and would have eaten crayons if given a chance.

"The green sauce is really hot," he told Valerie when she asked him about the enchiladas. "Sophia likes smoke to come out of her nose when she eats it. But the red sauce is good and not too hot. Just ask for the red sauce without the little pepper next to it. That won't burn your tongue."

She handed the menu to him and asked that he order for her. Aubrey did the same, and when the server stepped up, Hyrum sat up straighter and spoke confidently as he asked for three orders of shredded beef enchiladas with red sauce, two without the red pepper next to it and one with, and then asked for chopped shrimp for me.

"Sophia said she would have shrimp for Wick anytime he wanted to eat here," he said when the server headed for the kitchen. "He can't have the steak on account of it soaks in things that would make him sick. Onions, I think. She also said if he ate the steak it would make flames shoot out his a...butt."

She also said there was fish I could eat. But I'm happy to have the shrimp.

He was mostly quiet while Valerie talked about the things going on at home, allowing Aubrey to have a conversation with their mother. He laughed when Valerie expressed surprise that Bree was playing basketball—*basketball! There are girls' teams all over the place now!*—and when she told Aubrey that Red expected his youngest daughter to get a part-time job over the summer.

"Imagine that. A young girl with a job. I can't fathom why he wants her to, but he expects it. She's not even given a choice in the matter."

"Her world is different than yours was," Aubrey reminded her. "Red is trying to set an example for the church. Women in Pacifica typically work, and Florida is now part of Pacifica."

"Well. If they just find the right men, they won't have to."

"That's not the point," Aubrey said, lightly as to not start an argument.

"Do people like me get to work now?" Hyrum asked. "Daddy said we weren't allowed to before. Did Red say it was okay? Can everyone work?"

Valerie scrunched her nose. "Why would they want to? Their families should support—"

"I have *two* jobs," Hyrum said. "People here don't treat me like a baby. I go to work like everyone else."

She reached over and patted his hand. "I'm glad you have something to keep yourself busy. But if you were at home, you could still do volunteer work."

Hyrum opened his mouth to protest—that's not home anymore—but Aubrey bristled at the implied criticism of his work.

"Hyrum's jobs aren't busywork, Mom. The things he does at Ozoo require incredible patience and concentration, as well as attention to detail that most people simply don't have." She gestured in the direction of the space station. "Look at Elysium.

There are essential operations that wouldn't function if not for Hyrum's work, and he takes a tremendous load off Drew's shoulders."

"I keep track of lots of things," Hyrum muttered.

"And his work with Zed brings a spiritual edge to how the dead are cared for. Zed needs him to provide comfort with a bit of religious spark to family members coming to the island to see their deceased one last time. Hyrum prays with them all, and his strength in spirit, never breaking down in the face of such sorrow, is what they need most. There's no one else who can do it as well as he can."

"I pray with the people who want me to. Sometimes people don't. And I read stories and sing to the little ones," Hyrum said. "Zed says it matters on account of their spirits might still be hanging around for a little bit, and it might help them feel better."

Valerie blanched. "You sing to dead children?"

"Sometimes. Sometimes I tell them about Jesus and that he's going to help them. Father Dan said to be sure I know their moms and dads are okay with that, though."

"Father Dan," she repeated.

"I met him when I went into his church to see what it looked like. It's the prettiest church ever."

"Dan is one of my spiritual advisors," Aubrey said. "Hyrum has been speaking with him quite a bit lately."

"He's Catholic?" she asked, not expecting an answer. "Hyrum, no. We do *not* offer praises to the Pope."

"I've met the Pope," Aubrey said. "He's a wonderful gentleman. But before you get upset, Father Dan is very respectful of Hyrum's beliefs, and he's well educated on the doctrine of the Church of Florida."

"He knows Red, too," Hyrum offered. "They met a couple times when he was here for meetings and stuff and talked about churches and history. Red told me about it. Father Dan is gonna help people from Florida start a piece of the church here if they want."

"I don't want you associating with Catholics," Valerie hissed, glaring at Hyrum.

"How do you feel about the Jewish?" Aubrey intentionally poked at her. "Hyrum has met with Rabbi Joan a few times, as well."

The mention of the rabbi caused Hyrum to brighten and bounce once in his seat. "She's really nice. She said if I wanted, I could be a helper on the Jewish sabbath, doing stuff like turning on light switches. I can't remember what it's called."

"A Sabbat goy," Aubrey offered. "She currently has one, but he's heading to college soon, and Hyrum may take his place."

"You're going to help a Jew turn on her lights," Valerie sighed.

"Jesus would want me to," Hyrum said. "And Red said it was okay. He said, 'Hyrum, the Christian thing to do is to offer help to those who need it no matter what they believe in.' And he said that even on the Sabbath, people need light. Like, maybe they want to read the old testament and pray. I probably have to turn on her stove, too, so she can cook dinner. She has little kids and they gotta eat. Or I could cook something for them. Like grilled cheese."

We were spared a religious rant by the arrival of food. The conversation shifted to grandchildren and the kind of parents Oz and Zed were turning into, though Valerie thought it was far too soon to know anything about Oz's mothering skills. Eli wasn't even old enough to get on his hands and knees to rock back and forth; save the declaration of her skills for when he became mobile and was into everything.

"You," she said to Hyrum. "You were into everything and then some. I'd never seen a baby so fast on his knees. One minute you were asleep on a blanket by my feet; the next, you were in the kitchen licking the floor."

Hyrum snorted. "I never licked the floor."

"Hyrum, you licked everything."

"Including the Bishop's shoes," Aubrey said lightly. "He was amused. Dad, not as much."

"I don't think there was a square inch of that house you didn't lick," Valerie said. "Even the outlets. Though we had no idea then that electricity wouldn't hurt you."

Bet he didn't lick the ceiling.

"Will says we all have gifts. We just have to find them and then learn to use them."

"The Emperor says a lot, Hyrum. Not all of it is true."

"Speaking of the house," Aubrey said, changing the subject before Hyrum felt personally attacked, "why are you moving back into it? I thought you were happy living with Spencer."

"Oh, I was. But his mother-in-law is ill, and she needs to be close by. It's better if she takes the cottage out back."

Red and his brothers remodeled the family home to suit her tastes and needs, expecting that one day she might want to return. Spencer's mother-in-law sped up the decision when it was clear she needed help after having a stroke. Valerie swore she didn't mind; they'd gotten rid of that awful space under the stairs, and there was now a bedroom off the living room, which meant she wouldn't have to worry about climbing the stairs as she aged.

"There's a room upstairs for you," she said to Hyrum. "It even has its own bathroom."

"Any room upstairs has its own bathroom if no one else lives there," he said. "But I like the room I got here. My toys are here. And I have lots of books. And a computer tablet and it has lots of books on it, too. I get to read by myself every day."

"What else did they do to the house?" Aubrey asked.

There was a new kitchen, new floors, new everything. Her boys had removed every trace of Levi, replacing his cheap plastic cabinets with stained wood, trading out thin windows for triple-pane wood-trimmed wonders. There was new, bright paint on every wall, inside and out. She had never imagined the house could be as beautiful as it was; she'd argued against the expense until Red reminded her it was an investment, and if she chose to sell the house one day, they would recoup everything.

Yeah, when she dies, they get their money back.

"Please tell me you'll visit and see it," Valerie said.

Aubrey promised she would, but Hyrum eyed his mother warily.

You have jobs, dude.

"I might come," he finally said. "I might not be able to get time off."

"Surely, you can get a few days."

He shrugged. "Drew is getting ready to go to Elysium, and we're working on a new spacesuit for him. There's a lot of work we gotta do on account of Oz said if he dies in space, she's gonna kill him."

~

"I'm worried about you, Hyrum." Valerie took the dish he'd rinsed off and put it in the dishwasher. It didn't matter how many times he tried to tell her Aubrey preferred dishes done by hand. That was nonsense, there was a perfectly good dishwasher, and they were going to use it. He grunted a few times and tried to explain how it wasted water, but caved in. Aubrey, he reasoned, wouldn't mind just this once if it kept the peace. "Do you know why?"

"I'm okay."

"Are you? You've changed. You're…cavorting…with people you know better."

"I don't know what that means but I don't think so."

"People who aren't good for your eternity," she whispered, as if she were uttering a four-letter bomb ripped right off the top of Aubrey's bad word list. "People who might influence you and keep you from the celestial—."

He scrunched his nose. "My friends are nice."

She waved it off. "Nice isn't the issue."

"Besides, I mostly go to work or play with the babies. I talk to lots of people, though."

"You're getting too close to people who might pull you away from the Lord."

"Nuh." He shook his head. "I say my prayers every day and I read my bible stories. I even teach the stories to the babies on account of Aubrey says it's good for them and Will and Aisha say it will help Rhys and Alex and Charlie be better people."

That, she claimed, was good, and she was proud of him for being willing to bring faith to atheists. But there was more to it, and she feared for what would happen to him in the next life. She wasn't comfortable with the way life was in Pacifica, the way people mixed faith and things better left to stand alone.

He had no idea what she was hinting at. Valerie spoke in hushed tones, trying to keep those in the living room from overhearing her plunge into a swampish pool of bigotry. "We taught you, Hyrum. When we reach the celestial—"

"Everyone will be made white and pure," he sighed, reciting lessons taught in the Church of Florida's Sunday school. "But that's not true. I read some old church history that Red gave me. It says we get to stay the way we were when we were alive, but if we lost arms and legs and stuff, we'd get them back. Good people don't turn white in heaven."

She leaned in close. "Good people are already white *here*, Hyrum. I don't want you risking your eternity—"

Abruptly, Hyrum said, "You need to talk to Red."

"And you need to listen to me. If our family is going to be whole, you need to toe the line here. You know that."

He slapped the water off. "We're not going to be together in heaven even if that is true. You know Daddy won't be there. David won't be there on account of he'll die in jail here and wake up in jail there. And if I have to say Aisha and Sophia and Jay and the babies aren't good people, then I won't be there on account of it's not true."

"They're good people for *here*," she said. "That won't get them *there*. They'll be stuck on the lowest level—"

"Jesus isn't like that," he argued. "Red said—"

"You should be more concerned with what the Lord says."

He took a step back, eyebrows knotted. "Red is the prophet. He talks for God. What Red says is the truth, even if we don't like it, and Red says skin doesn't matter. People matter and I can love anyone I feel like. And I love Aisha and Sophia, and their babies, and Jay, too." He leaned toward her, just a bit. "Red even said I could love a *boy* if I wanted."

Her hand shot up, but she stopped short of slapping him. "Don't you dare."

Do I need to get help? I can go get Will or Drew.

Really, I can.

"It's okay, Wick. Me and Drew have to work tomorrow. I should go to bed. Drew wants me to drive so he can read some papers on the way."

Drew wants you to drive because Drew is still afraid of driving.

"I'll pray for you tonight, Mom. I think you need it."

He left Valerie in the kitchen, alone, with several dishes still waiting to be loaded into the rarely used dishwasher. She slowly lowered her hand and then stared at it, as if she wondered why she hadn't been able to hit him.

He's not a little boy, and you know it. You can't bully him anymore.

I just wished Hyrum was as certain of that.

~

Hyrum rolled out of bed at four-thirty to spend time with Jax; he shuffled down the hall in shorts and a t-shirt, making sure the door to the guest room was still closed. He turned the coffee maker on and sat at the table, half asleep, one wary eye on the hallway. He didn't want to start his morning arguing with his mother; he didn't want to spend any part of his day arguing with her. Before going to bed, he slipped into Oz and Drew's room, and when he came out, he was visibly relieved.

Drew needed him at work; there was no getting out of it and he refused to give Hyrum the day off. Valerie could get as upset as she wanted, but they were too close to the finish of the spacesuit design, and there were things Drew wanted Hyrum to look at.

"Tell her to blame me," he told Hyrum. "You can't have a day off, not until we're done with the suit."

It wasn't a lie; Drew hadn't stretched the truth. He needed that suit to be in the manufacturing phase within two weeks. He always had Hyrum look at new products before finalizing the design because Hyrum truly did see things others didn't. He was a lot like Drew in that respect, but his brain wasn't cluttered with all the science fiction Drew had absorbed as a child, and he had no preconceived ideas about how things should look or how they should function. Drew wanted things to look cool and futuristic; Hyrum wanted things to work.

"You're here early, Wick," he said to me when I jumped up to the breakfast bar.

Will didn't need me last night.

In fact, I'm sure he didn't want me there. I kept an eye on you instead.

"Did you sit on my head last night? Or did I dream that?"

I was on your pillow, peeking at your dreams. You probably felt my paw on your forehead.

"You were in a dream. We were riding my bike and when we stopped to have lunch, you said you would bite my mom's finger off if she poked it at me again."

Awesome. You can totally understand me when I sneak into your dreams. Next time I'll tell you to talk to Will when you wake up. He can explain what I'm doing.

"I don't think your teeth are strong enough to bite a finger off all the way. I don't even think I could do that."

You'd be surprised.

"I bet fingers taste bad, anyway."

You're not wrong. I've bitten a few over the years. Fingers, toes...faces. It's not pleasant.

Jax came out of the bedroom at five, wearing a dress shirt and tie, coat slung over one arm. Hyrum mused that he wasn't running with Will this morning and told him to sit down, and he would make breakfast. Jax knew better than to argue; unless he had a breakfast meeting, Hyrum wouldn't let him head for work without eating. I lounged on the breakfast bar while he cooked—Jax had finally given up trying to get me to stay off it— and jumped to a chair when bacon was offered.

I stayed there and peeked over the edge of the table while they ate and was still there when Jax kissed the top of Hyrum's head before he left for work, and I waited there while Hyrum headed off to shower. I was still there when Aubrey came out—she was surprised by the pile of bacon Hyrum had left for everyone—and when Valerie came out at six-thirty.

The house was waking up. Eli was crying—the infant, not the old King, though it was entirely possible that he was downstairs sobbing, too—and Drew was in the shower, singing about feeling like a natural woman. Oz cooed to her baby, trying to soothe him, probably from the horror of his father singing about being a natural woman. And from upstairs came the sound of tiny feet thundering down the hall, which would be followed, I presumed, by squealing and at least one adult yelling at Charlie to get down from whatever he was climbing, and to put some pants on.

Baby gates no longer held them. Will had considered building one across the stairs, but Charlie could scramble, and if he made it to the top, the fall would be horrific. The door was often closed and locked, but no one trusted that they couldn't figure it out. Vicat suggested a guard be posted near the stairs, outside the apartment door. It was either that or secure their front door with the same biometric lock that had been put on the balcony door, opened only by handprint, and too high up for a toddler to reach.

Aisha declared that idea to be a pain in the ass; if she had a kid on each hip and stuff in her hands, unlocking the door would become work.

There was now a rotation of younger guards at night and during part of the day. The kids learned their names and often took cookies and drinks to them—something that never happened when Oz and Zed were children—and they'd become fond of the men and women who sat in a chair outside their door.

When it was time to come downstairs to stay with their Aunt Aubrey, the guard would follow and wait in a chair near the balcony.

Valerie was unhappy that the family apartment had no door, and she glanced up the stairs before coming to the table. "You can't even walk around in your robe," she complained to Aubrey. "There's always someone looking."

"I can, and I do," Aubrey said. "You get used to it."

"I could never."

"The guards are respectful. Unless there's a good reason,

they don't even peek into the apartment on their way down. If they need something, they knock on the wall first."

"But if you and Jax just want private time, sitting on the sofa watching TV—"

"Mom, the kids are all over this building. We have an open-door policy. If we want to sit and watch the news, we do it and yell when they get too loud. If we want privacy?" She pointed down the hall to the bedroom. "We've been known to go in and close the door, just to talk."

Valerie couldn't imagine sitting down to have a simple conversation with her husband. "I don't think the man ever asked my opinion on anything. Yet I've heard Jax take your advice a dozen times."

"He wasn't raised to think men were superior beings," she reminded Valerie.

"How did he deal with the things Levi did to you?" Valerie asked, her voice hushed. "Did you tell him before you married?"

"I told him very early on. And he was extremely patient with me. He spoke with my therapist—"

"You saw one of those doctors?"

"Of course, I did. I think I was sixteen when I found the one I was sure I could trust."

"But why? The Lord—"

"Because prayer wasn't enough," Aubrey said bluntly. "I saw girls my age with boys and realized I wanted a social life. I would never have that if I didn't learn to trust them. Therapy helped me get to the place where holding someone's hand wouldn't leave me a sobbing mess."

Valerie's hand went to her mouth. "You didn't—"

Aubrey raised an eyebrow. "Jax is the only man I've slept with, if that's what you're getting at. But no, we did not wait for marriage."

"Oh, Aubrey..."

"Mom, the virginity ship sailed when I was still a little girl. I wouldn't have married Jax without knowing that I could *be* with him. That wouldn't have been fair to him."

Valerie swallowed her argument. "You should talk to Red, just in case—"

"Red knows, Mom. You don't think I would have had him back in my life and not asked him for a blessing, do you? My big brother is the *Prophet*. He knows my worst secrets, and he's blessed me despite them. Red is very good at offering comfort, you know."

"All those years with your father when he was Prophet, and I still have trouble remembering that Red heads the General Authority now. He still feels like my—" She stopped when Hyrum wandered from his room, heading for the table. His neatly combed hair was still wet from his shower, and he'd trimmed his beard. He was dressed in new black jeans, his first pair made by Mrs. Kovlov, and his bright pink t-shirt was tucked in. "Hyrum Munson, you march back into your room and change into something presentable."

He glanced down, unsure what the problem was. "I'm allowed to wear jeans to work. Sometimes we get dirty, and—"

"You are *not* a little girl. Go change that shirt."

"Mom," Aubrey sighed. "Take a breath. Hy, did you eat with Jax this morning?"

He nodded. "I made him eggs. I can make you eggs, too, if you want."

He didn't wait for an answer and practically hopped into the kitchen. Whether they wanted eggs or not, they were getting a heap of scrambled eggs with cream cheese melted into them. I knew what he was doing; he was very careful to melt the cheese slowly, which took time. Time he wouldn't endure being criticized.

"What's on your work schedule today?" Aubrey asked, even though she already knew.

"We gotta make sure the new suit fits Drew super snug but also gives him room to turn on the tights if he needs it."

The tights were tightly woven with nanobots; they activated with a single thought from his upgraded transponder—he'd gotten a second one, not willing to risk losing his ability to understand me—and would protect him if the outer suit tore or was hit by something. He would be the first person to wear the nano-suit in space; others had tested prototypes in the lab, but his trip would be the first active trial.

"Hyrum," Aubrey told Valerie, "has been studying quite a bit of science and history lately. I think it's fair to say that he knows more about nanobots than I ever will."

Valerie had no idea what they were.

"Tiny, tiny robots," Hyrum said. "So tiny, you can't really seem them unless there are loads of them together or you look with a special microscope." He considered it for a moment and added, "That's like a sciencey magnifying glass."

"You're still teaching him? Valerie asked. "I thought he was done. He has his diploma."

"On his days off from work, we cover the things he's most interested in. Will helps him with science, and Aisha has taken over math. When he tells us he's done, then we'll stop."

"Drew says people should never be done learning," Hyrum said. "That's why he's still going to school again even though he's already got an important job. He's gonna be a doctor, but not the kind that gives you shots."

"What's left for you to teach him?" Valerie asked. "He can already read."

"There are lots of big words I don't know," Hyrum said.

"We've been delving into history lately," Aubrey said.

"I wanted to learn that on account of Jax used to be a history teacher and now we can talk about stuff like that."

"Hyrum has also been tackling bigger books, things he can read to the children. And he's developed a love of poetry."

"I like to read them and figure out what the stories are," Hyrum said as he scooped the eggs out onto plates. "That's kinda hard sometimes. Poems say one thing but mean something else. I need help figuring it out."

"Metaphors," Aubrey said. "Plenty of people have difficulty with them, Hyrum."

"Hm." He set the plates down and then sat in the chair next to me. "One time I read a poem, and it said the sky was on fire. That didn't make any sense on account of you can't set fire to the sky. Eli said it was talking about the sunset. Sometimes the sky turns red when the sun sets. It's really pretty when it's foggy and the sun sets. Maybe I'll write a poem about that."

"You write poetry now?" Valerie asked.

He nodded enthusiastically. "Aubrey said it would help me understand them better. I wrote one last week, but it needs a little work."

"I'm sure it's fine," Valerie said.

"Do we get to hear it?" Aubrey asked.

Hyrum closed his eyes, biting his bottom lip as he tried to remember it.

"Sandberg says Karl comes on little cat feet.
But I see Karl and you can bet
That cats don't like him
On account of he gets you wet
But I like Karl because he kisses my chin
And he has cold arms that tickle my skin
I ride my bike with Karl up hills and down
And he makes me smile but never frown
Karl comes and then he goes
He hugs the bridges, he touches my nose
When he goes away, I am not sad
He'll come back tomorrow
And that makes me glad."

Aubrey opened her mouth to offer praise—he'd worked on that poem for nearly a week, and it was the first time she'd heard it—but Valerie sucked in a tight, horrified breath and nearly growled when she looked at Aubrey. "*That's* the perversion you're teaching him?"

Aubrey didn't have a chance to answer. Valerie turned on Hyrum and kept right on going. "You can*not* write about another man like that. It's not normal. It's not natural. I don't care what Red has told you. I won't have it. And look at you, dressing like a little girl, and you're writing love poems to *men*."

"For God's sake, Mom," Aubrey sighed.

"No. Enough is enough. I won't have him—"

Drew threw the bedroom door open and hissed at Valerie to keep it down. The baby was just falling asleep again, and he'd had a hard night. Her jaw dropped. Not because Drew had snapped at her, but because he was wearing a neon pink dress shirt and an even pinker tie.

"*This* is what I'm talking about. The example—"

Drew didn't care. "What the hell?"

"Hyrum wrote a poem about Karl," Aubrey explained. "She took offense."

Drew's ire faded. "Karl? Sweet. Hyrum, can I hear it?"

"Stop encouraging his perversion!"

Hyrum stood up, tears in his eyes, and he ran past Drew, slapping his half-closed bedroom door open.

"How the hell is a poem about *fog* perverted?" Drew asked. "That's what you scared my son over? Fog?"

Breakfast was over, whether Valerie was done eating or not. Aubrey grabbed the plates and put them, none too gently, into the sink. "It could have been a poem about a friend. Why would you think it was anything more?"

"Karl," Valerie started.

"Locals named the fog Karl centuries ago. He was *so* happy when he learned about it. It led to a discussion with Will and Jax about life here in the twentieth century and made him understand that there's a link between literature and history." She stopped when Hyrum stomped out of his room, paper in hand, tears streaming down his face.

He thrust it toward Aubrey. "What's wrong with it?"

Aubrey kissed his forehead gently. "Nothing. It's a wonderful poem, sweetheart."

Drew took the paper from her and read it. "Hy, this is amazing. You totally got it, how everyone who lives here thinks of the fog as a treasured friend. I'm proud of you. This took a lot of work."

"I don't write about bad things," Hyrum said to his mother. "Even if I wrote about another boy, that's not bad. You should know that by now. I'm not bad. I'm not."

There were careful footsteps on the stairs, and I looked past Drew. Eli slipped into the living room and sat on the far end of the sofa, lost in shadows. He saw that I'd noted him and held a finger to his lips.

Don't tell.

Valerie jabbed her pointy finger at Hyrum. "Enough is enough is enough. You're going home with me."

"What?" Horrified, Hyrum looked to Aubrey.

"Don't look at her," Valerie ordered. "I'm your mother, Hyrum. She's your sister."

Hyrum's hands went to his chest, fingers knotted together. He wound and unwound them, repeatedly, choking on tears until he managed, "Are you really? My mother?"

Valerie flinched. "Of course, I am. What are you thinking?"

"I see other mothers, how they are with their babies. How Aisha is. Even how Oz is with baby Eli. And Aubrey with Oz and Zed even though they're grownups now."

"Hyrum."

"Moms protect their babies no matter how old they are. You never protected me. You didn't even want me until you had to move out of Spencer's back yard."

"Hyrum," she repeated, angrily.

"Daddy *hurt* me. He hurt me all the time. You never stopped him, and you could have. You could have stopped him from hurting Aubrey, too."

Valerie got to her feet. "Stop the nonsense, Hyrum. You're leaving with me. Period."

"You knew what he was doing to Aubrey before I was even born and you could have stopped him. You never did *anything*. You could have told *your* daddy and he would have stopped it, but you didn't. When he started punishing me, you didn't do anything."

"I couldn't have."

"You changed the sheets on the bed under the stairs," he wailed. "You kept that little room clean. You *helped* him. Why didn't you stop him?"

"I was terrified of Levi," she said, still angry. "I wanted to stop him."

Hyrum placed his hands on the table. "Tell Aubrey how you could have stopped him. The very first time you knew Daddy touched her, you could have. Tell her!"

"Sweetie," Aubrey said, gently.

"No. You didn't have to get punished. Neither did I. And it *hurt*." Hyrum was sobbing hard now. "It hurt so much."

"I know." Aubrey's voice was soft, and only for him. "Mom couldn't have stopped him. Daddy was the head of the family. He was the head of everything in Florida, and there was no one for her to turn to. No one else would have listened to her."

She wanted to reach for him, to soothe him, but his hands and arms were turning red and little wisps of smoke curled around his fingers.

"Tell her, Mom. Tell her how you coulda done it. Tell her!"

Drew risked the burn and pulled Hyrum's hands off the table, ignoring the quarter-inch deep mark burned into the one-hundred-year-old wood. "It's all right, Hy. Aubrey is right."

Still red, Hyrum's hand shot forward and he grabbed his mother's wrist. "If you won't tell her, then show her."

When he let go, Valerie's wrist was bright red, with tiny blisters covering where he'd held onto her. Aubrey lunged for her mother, trying to drag her to the sink, ordering her to get cold water on the burn, but Hyrum barked, "No. She can fix it by herself."

"Hyrum, no," Drew whispered.

Valerie covered the burn with her other hand. "It's all right. It's not half as bad as it looks."

"Fix it," Hyrum growled.

"I'm not hurt."

"You're burned, and I did it on purpose," Hyrum said. "I'll do it again until you show them."

She jabbed her finger at him again. "Living here has turned you rude and disrespectful."

"Aubrey," Drew whispered. "Look at her wrist."

"All you had to do was put your hand on his chest when he was sleeping," Hyrum said. "You could have frozen his heart. That's how you do the thing. Your thing. You have a thing just like me."

She tried to deny it. While Aubrey inspected her wrist for blisters and found none, Valerie claimed Hyrum had been reading too many books and was only using his imagination. He hadn't hurt her.

"Nuh. I remember. When Lazybones was old and sick and

Daddy wouldn't let you take him to the vet on account of he was going to die anyway, you put him on the table and told him he was a good boy and you loved him. Then you put your hand on his chest, and he died. I picked him up to take him so Red could bury him, and he was so cold. His chest was frozen. And I saw you lots of times fix yourself when you burned your fingers cooking, but I didn't tell anyone. I didn't want Daddy to throw you away and he would have."

"Mom?" Aubrey choked.

"You coulda stopped his heart the same way you did Lazybones' the first time he touched Aubrey, but you didn't. You knew he punished her and you didn't do anything."

"You wouldn't have been born—"

"I don't care! Daddy hurt us. It hurt more than anything else, even when I broke my arm. You helped him!"

"I hated that man," Valerie seethed. "I hated him and wanted him dead. But the Lord—"

"Jesus woulda understood. He loves us. I know you hated Daddy but you coulda stopped him. You really hated him, so I don't know why you want me to live with you again on account of you don't much like me, either."

I felt his anguish punch the air. It was nearly percussive, slapping at everyone in the room, and it took the span of several heartbeats before anyone could even blink.

Valerie swallowed hard, and then croaked, "Hyrum, I love you."

"But you don't *like* me. You see him when you look at me. You think God did this to me to punish you for all the things Daddy was doing that you didn't stop. And you want me to be a little boy so you can tell me what to do, and I'd never have any fun and I'd never get to have a job, on account of keeping me stupid feels like hurting Daddy."

Valerie slapped at the table, her hand landing on the burn marks. "You're leaving. That's it. I am your mother—"

"Aubrey is more my mom than you," he said.

Spittle shot from Valerie's lips as she shouted, "Go to your room and get your things!"

Hyrum stood up straighter. "No."

He saw her hand shoot up and stepped out of the way, refusing to be hit.

"Hyrum Charles Munson."

"Nuh. I'm a Blackshear now."

"Goddammit, Hyrum, *do what I say*. I've had enough of this nonsense, and you're going home."

"*This* is my home."

Aubrey tried to say something, but she was crying and nothing came out. I heard the sofa creak of the sofa and footsteps on the carpet; Eli went to her, kissing her temple, whispering that it was all right.

"Eli," Valerie started.

I'd seen Eli stare like that before, at a meeting with the Russian president. He silently willed the man to push his agenda just a little harder, to get one toe over the line that led to war. Instead, he took a step back, because Eli meant it; he would rip Russia to shreds if he had to.

Valerie took a step back, as well, unsure that he wasn't about to let go of Aubrey and come after her.

He let her stand there, fear percolating, with no one to comfort her.

"Valerie." Eli's voice was calm and even. "You are no longer welcome in this home. I want you gone by noon."

His voice cut through the fear. "I'll leave when Hyrum has gathered a few things," she scoffed.

"No. He's given you his choice, and his choice is to remain here."

"He's a ward of the King," Drew added. "Only Jax gets to say where he goes."

Eli shook his head. "Hyrum is a ward of the King, but he's free to go at his choosing." He glared at Valerie. "However, by the rules of your own culture, I have the final word."

"Jax," she sputtered.

"Jax is King and rules over the United Kingdom, but *I* am the eldest male Blackshear. I find your traditions repulsive and archaic, but I will use them as I damn well please, and Hyrum is a member of this family. He stays."

"Ask Red," Hyrum started.

"Oh, to hell with that useless, pretentious prophet. Hyrum Charles Munson—"

Eli cut her off again. "No. Son, you are not obligated to your father's name."

"I don't know what that means," he admitted.

Eli said he was tired of the nonsense, and it hurt him every time Hyrum was upset by the burden of his mother's whims and his father's legacy. "You are a Blackshear in everything but name, and I'd like to change that." Hyrum blinked, trying to understand. "If there are no legal roadblocks, I want to give you my name, officially. To adopt you."

Will's voice drifted from the entryway. "If he cannot, I will."

"Or I will," Drew said. "There's nothing to stop me if Jax or his lawyers think either of them can't."

Hyrum ignored Valerie's strangled cry. "You mean you would adopt me like you did Will?" he asked Eli. "Can I keep my mom even though you would be my new daddy? Could Red still be my brother? And Spencer and Joe?"

"My parents are still my parents," Will reminded Hyrum.

"I want you to have my name," Eli told him. "With that, I want you to have the title I would have given you at birth and all the protections that come with being a member of the House of Blackshear. Your siblings are still your family."

"This is ridiculous," Valerie said. "He's an adult."

"Then damn well start treating him like it!" Aubrey shouted. "And shut up. Just…shut up."

"Would I have to move downstairs with you?" Hyrum asked.

"You would break my heart if you did," Aubrey said. "Nothing has to change, sweetheart."

"Could I still go visit mom sometimes?"

"Of course," Eli said.

"I love you, Mom," Hyrum said. "But I really want Eli to be my dad. I never had a daddy that loved me before and Eli loves me."

"Always," Eli said.

Tears spilled over her lashes, but she nodded. There was no victory, no remote chance that Hyrum would ever leave Pacifica with her, and she felt the weight of that press her into a chair at the table.

"Show Aubrey your thing," Hyrum said. "You don't gotta be afraid of it anymore. I'm not afraid of mine."

She was at a loss about how she could demonstrate her gift. Hyrum plucked an orange from the fruit basket and handed it to her. She wrapped frail fingers around it and squeezed, and within seconds it was withered and frozen solid.

She handed the orange to Aubrey. "I could have killed him while he slept. I was terrified. They would have found out, and my father— I swore to him I would never tell anyone."

Aubrey turned it over in her hand, squeezing, the peel not yielding to pressure. She blinked, finally understanding what Hyrum meant, then set the orange on the table and pushed past everyone, disappearing into the guest room. A minute later, she was on her way out, shoving things into the bag Valerie had brought with her. She handed it to Will, determined to not look at her mother.

"Take her home. Just—deposit her into her living room and come right back. Don't give her the courtesy of listening to any more explanations."

Without a word, Will reached for Valerie's arm, tapped at his jump bracelet, and they vanished.

~

Hyrum stood by the table, staring at the marks he'd made, eyes filling with tears. He didn't hear the tiny feet on the stairs, nor did he turn when Rhys ran into the apartment, looking for Will. Rhys felt the tension, though, and he ran to Hyrum, climbing on the chair to get his attention. When Hyrum still didn't look at him, Rhys climbed on the table and stood where he couldn't be ignored.

"Let me kiss your head," Rhys whispered. With a sniff, Hyrum looked up, and Rhys placed a slow, gentle kiss in the center of his forehead. "It's okay. Your mommy loves you. She's just...sick."

"She was okay," Hyrum murmured.

"No, she's a different kind of sick. She's got herself in a hole. Inside herself. And she's stuck."

"I don't know what that means," Hyrum whispered.

"Rhys is describing depression, I think," Eli explained. "I wouldn't be surprised to learn that she suffers from chronic depression."

"Yeah, but she's also a bitch," Rhys said sincerely. "Joe said so. Joe doesn't lie."

That made Aubrey snicker. She lifted Rhys from the table and kissed him, then kissed Hyrum on the cheek. "You were very brave today. I know how hard it was for you to stand up to her."

"She coulda stopped Daddy," he said, still whispering.

Aubrey admitted that she'd often wondered why their mother had never done anything in their defense. Jacob Keats would have killed Levi where he stood and not cared about the consequences, but now, knowing Valerie's gift, she was angry. "I'm not sure I can see her again."

"She's still our mom," Hyrum said. "We don't have to like her, but Jesus wants us to be nice to her and give her a chance to say sorry."

"You," she said, kissing him again, "are a good man, Hyrum Munson."

"Nuh."

"You are, and you know it."

"No, I'm a Blackshear. I'm never gonna be a Munson again. I'm glad you ran away when you were fourteen, Aubrey. You woulda tried to stop him from punishing me, and he woulda killed you."

"I would have taken that chance if I'd known he would turn on you." Her voice trembled, barely above a whisper. "And I would have stayed and taken his abuse as long as it took. I wouldn't trade you for anything, Hyrum."

She had to run, he argued. If she hadn't, she wouldn't have married Jax, and Jax is the one who finally stopped their father from ever hurting anyone again. "I know he hurt Oz, too. But..."

"Oz would take it every time, too," Drew said. "He didn't

hurt her as badly as he did you. He didn't...punish her. Not like that."

Rhys sighed dramatically. "Stop being sad. I can't kiss everyone, you know."

"You can if you try hard enough," Drew teased him. He was about to grab Rhys into a giant hug, but Will popped back into the living room, and Rhys lost interest in everyone else.

"Daddy! Where did you go? Was it fun?"

"I gave Hyrum's mother a ride home," he said, looking at Aubrey. "She had things to do today."

"Okay. Are you sad, too? Do I need to kiss you?"

Will bent over to look at his son. "I'm fine. In fact, I'm happy."

"Why? Did you get cookies? It's not Sunday, but you can have a cookie if you want."

"It's not cookies."

"Then why are you happy? Sunday cookies always make me happy."

"I'm happy because before I took Valerie home, Grandpa Eli had some good news. How would you like it if Hyrum became your uncle?"

"For real?"

"For real. Eli is going to adopt him, the way he adopted me, and that makes us brothers."

Hyrum brightened considerably. "Really? We'll be real brothers?"

"Real brothers," Will said. "You might even be my favorite, but don't tell Jax."

"Hell, might be my favorite, too," Eli snorted.

"I like that," Hyrum said. "You would be my brother, and Jax would be my brother. You can't have too many brothers unless they're like David."

"David's a dick," Rhys said solemnly.

Hyrum still had tears in his eyes. Drew stepped over and whispered to him, "We have time before we need to be at work. Do you need to do something to calm down? We can cuddle on the sofa for a while."

He wanted to. He twitched in that direction, and a week ago, if he'd been this upset, he would have. A week ago, he had cuddled up on the sofa in Oz's bedroom with Drew because he was tired and anxious and didn't know what else to do. This day, however, he pulled his shoulders back and sniffed one more time.

"We got important things to do at work. If we don't get it right, Oz is gonna kill you."

"Only if I die," Drew said.

Will nodded toward the door. "Go on. I'll be there later. I imagine Eli has things for me to do this morning."

Hyrum reached for Drew's hand, and as they descended the stairs, I heard him ask, "Can we cuddle later? I think tonight I'll want to."

Drew promised they would cuddle in front of the TV, with baby Eli sleeping in his bassinette, even if they had to kick Oz out of the room. Aubrey allowed herself a bit of a smile and then dropped into her chair in the living room, struggling to not cry again.

"Valerie's terror was not misplaced," Eli said. "If she'd tried to kill Levi and failed, he would have publicly executed her."

"Eli, I would have risked that a thousand times over for my children," she said. "She had the means. She had a gift she could have used, and she didn't. I'm not sure I can forgive her for this."

"No one would blame you," Will said.

"I hear a 'but' in there."

Will ruffled Rhys's hair. "Go upstairs, cowboy. Jay will be there soon, and he's bringing finger paints. You don't want to miss that."

He took off, clearly not wanting to miss that.

"Your time to make peace with her is limited," Will said when he was sure Rhys was upstairs.

"How long?"

"Aubrey—"

"How long?" she repeated sternly. "I've had a bitch of a day, and it's not even eight in the morning. Goddammit, Will, I need to know if I have time to wade through the absolute shit pile my mother just dumped here."

Eli barked out a laugh, which made Aubrey sigh.

"Presuming the timeline holds?" Will said. "A little over three months. In my history, Valerie Munson died from cardiac arrest in her sleep while living in Kansas. Levi moved her from Florida a week before the bomb that ended the war was delivered. Your mother, this Valerie, never escaped Florida. We have no way of knowing if anything else about her changed."

"Surely her heart didn't," Aubrey said. "Should we warn her?"

Will's hands went into his pockets, but he didn't say anything.

"You already told her, didn't you?"

He thought it was fair. He let her know her days were limited, and sincere amends would need to be made soon. "She knows that her death in my history is not a guarantee of her death in this timeline, but she was quite accepting of the notion and thinks she's lived long enough."

"She surely knows you can change this for her," Eli said.

Will nodded. "I offered to take her forward. She refused, citing religious objections."

With a sigh, Aubrey got back up. "Get the ball rolling, Will," she told him. "I don't care if it's Eli, you, or Drew, but I want that adoption sewn up as soon as possible. If Jax thinks there's a legal block to Eli, move down the line until Hyrum is legally a Blackshear. I don't care if you invent a damned family member, but I want it done."

Aisha came in just in time to hear Aubrey issue Will an order. She had Alex on one hip, Charlie by the hand, and Rhys trailed behind her. "All right, you apparently have other things to do today. Jay had to back out. Navi called. God knows why, but she wants to talk."

Aubrey held her arms out to Charlie. "I can watch them."

Aisha set Alex down. "Oh, I'm not working today. I was just planning on fobbing the kids off on Will to grab a couple hours."

"Good," Eli said. "Then they're mine today." He bent over to speak to Rhys. "What would you rather do today? Stay at home with Mommy, or go to the Exploratorium with me?"

"Can we?" He looked up at Aisha. "I like the exploring place."

"Take one, take all three," Aisha teased.

"Perfect. While we send Will to do our bidding, I'll grab Finn, and we'll have fun with the munchkins and you two" —he pointed to both Aubrey and Aisha— "go do something. Anything. Jump forward and play with old man Finn. Or just go spend his money. He has more than anyone needs and won't even miss it."

"Two hundred years," Aisha said. "We can go get loud and sloppy drunk and not make the news."

"Booze," Aubrey sighed. "Absolutely. Let's get there around five this afternoon. I need a drink."

~

Ten minutes later, the apartment was quiet. Will headed off to speak with Jax, and then the lawyer. Eli grabbed the diaper bag, called Finn, and then ushered the three kids into the elevator. Aubrey and Aisha went upstairs to the portal and headed for Will's birth When, laughing about shameful head-sized drinks and the possibility of running into someone who needed their tits tied together.

I stepped into the entryway and listened.

Oz must have already left with the baby.

Jay wasn't downstairs.

I didn't hear Zed or Sophia or any of their kids.

Other than guards, I was alone in the building.

I didn't like it, not one bit.

I could go upstairs and get my hover cart, then chase some of the guards around. Or I could curl up on someone's bed and sleep the rest of the morning away. I could even, if I made sure no one was looking, sneak out the cat flap near the front door and wander around Union Square.

None of it sounded fun.

I could go get Lux, and either spend the day there or bring him here to surprise everyone.

I'd promised to not sneak into the simulator, so that was out.

Maybe it was time to ask Will for a kitten that I could name Bob. But that sounded like work.

I was about to go into Oz's room to take a nap on the window seat. At least I'd be able to watch people down on the Square if I wanted, until sleep overtook me. But then the elevator pinged, and Will stuck his head out.

"Come on, Wick. I just realized you were probably alone. You can help me sort out the paperwork and put your official paw stamp on Hyrum's adoption papers."

I scrambled in before he could change his mind and climbed his leg to get to his shoulder.

Are we having lunch out today?

"We can. Is there something you would like?"

Not really. But I'd like to spend some of my allowance if you don't mind going into the paper store before we eat.

"I don't mind. What sort of paper do you need?"

Not for me. For Hyrum. There's a tablet cover I want to get for him. I can have his name put on it. Hyrum Charles Blackshear, Esquire.

"Esquire, Wick?"

Important people have titles, Will.

"Esquire implies he's training for knighthood. Perhaps use 'Prince' instead."

Prince Hyrum Charles Blackshear, Esquire.

"Drop the esquire, Wick."

I can't even pick him up, Will. I'm kind of small, if you hadn't noticed.

"You're a smartass, you know."

So you admit it, I'm smart.

It's about time, Will.

I've only waited four hundred years to hear that.

I flicked my tail around his neck and tickled his ear. *Onward, noble steed. We have a prince to adopt, and we need to get it done before the old King gets home. And then we'll have a party because that's what you do when you adopt someone. Oh, and we need to stop and get some cinnamon whiskey, so we can toast Hyrum and then get him toasted. Because that's what you do when you adopt a grown man.*

Will sighed, steadied me with his hand, and sped up.

By the end of the day, Hyrum would be ours.

GIFTS

Flat on my back with my paws stretched out, the sun warming my bacon-filled belly, I was on the fuzzy side of my third catnap of the day when I heard the jangling of a dog's ID tags. It was distant enough that I didn't immediately scramble to safety, but instead rolled over and stretched, then looked to see if Will had heard it and if Rhys was close to him.

Rhys stood on his father's feet, death grip on his fingers, as Will stomped in a circle with him. The three-year-old's head was thrown back, and he squinted against the sunlight, giggling with each step Will took.

I sat up and cocked my head to listen. The dog was on the steps to the right, and with the sound of his tags came the soft thud of someone's shoes. So, not alone.

Dog approaching.

Sounds like a big one, too.

Will stopped. "Hey." He bent over to speak to Rhys, his voice soft. "How about some chocolate milk? Just for you."

"But I had a cibbamom roll. Cinnabom. Cinnamon."

"I know. I also know you wanted the chocolate milk but didn't ask for it."

"'Cause you don't like it when I eats lots of sugar and that has lots of sugar. Hyrum said so."

"Just this—"

Dude.

Too late.

The dog was on Union Square, and Rhys had spotted it. He slid from Will's feet and grabbed onto his leg, the fabric of his father's jeans caught up in one miniature fist. When he was certain the dog was coming his way, Rhys jammed his free thumb into his mouth, but he didn't try to hide behind Will's legs; instead, he kept a wary eye on it.

At the human end of the obnoxiously bright orange leash was a man named Scotty; he was a lawyer who represented the shelter system and had been Aisha's first real boyfriend. Will didn't hold that against him. The familiarity, however, meant that Scotty was going to come over and greet Will, not knowing that Rhys's lone experience with dogs had been painted in terror. He'd been trapped up a tree, a small pack yapping and growling beneath him, and he was sure they were going to eat him.

When Scotty was ten feet away, Will held up a hand to stop him.

He stopped, and with a gentle tug on the leash, his dog sat down.

"He's a bit wary of dogs," Will explained. "Perhaps not frightened, but unsure of what to expect."

"Ah." Scotty crouched next to the golden retriever and ruffled the fur on his head. "This is Strider, Rhys. He's very friendly and doesn't bite, but he might try to lick you."

The thumb came out of Rhys's mouth. "He's a nice puppy?"

"Very nice."

"He won't eat Wick?"

I moved to sit by Rhys's feet, where Strider could get a good look at me while Scotty had the leash firmly in hand.

"We have a cat at home, and they're best friends. He might want to sniff Wick, but he won't hurt him."

"Promise?"

Scotty nodded. "Promise. Would you like to pet him?"

Strider opened his mouth to pant, and his giant pink tongue flopped out.

"That's a big tongue," Rhys said, taking a few tentative steps closer.

"He's a big dog."

Rhys stopped a few feet away and squatted, trying to decide if he trusted the big, hairy beast and if he wanted to get close enough to touch him.

"You don't have to if you don't want to," Will said to Rhys, gently.

He wanted to; I could feel it. If he didn't, he would be upset with himself for the rest of the day. There was a puppy, albeit a fully grown one, right in front of him, and he wanted to pet it more than he wanted the chocolate milk Will had offered.

I absolutely did not want to get too close to the dog with the now-dripping tongue. It didn't matter if he had a cat at home. I was not that cat, and he might not like me nearly as much. Still, Scotty had a firm grip on him, and I didn't think he would be able to catch me even if he wanted to lunge.

I inched my way to him and didn't stop when I heard Will suck in a worried breath.

Strider looked down at me, but he didn't move. The tongue went back into his mouth, and his head pushed back a bit so he could see me down near his front foot, but he didn't make a move toward me.

Dude, up close, you're humungous.

Strider looked up at Scotty, and a tiny whine escaped him. He had no intention of grabbing me with his mouth but wanted a little slack on his leash so he could get a better look at the tiny cat near his feet.

Rhys scooted a bit closer but was watching warily. I wasn't sure what he hoped to see, other than Strider not biting my head off, but I had an idea and went with it.

I rubbed up against Strider's leg.

See? He really is friendly.

He whined again, and Scotty let out a few inches on the leash, giving him enough space to lay down. I was nose-to-nose with the biggest dog I'd ever been remotely close to and endured his loud sniffing as he took in my scent.

Okay, so you really are friendly. How annoyed will you be if I climb on you? Just so Rhys can see that everything will be okay.

Strider nudged me with his nose and rolled onto his side.

Do you understand me? Know what I'm saying?

He grunted in return.

Carefully, after rubbing my head on him a few more times, I jumped onto his side and laid there. I didn't want to use my claws to hang on, but I flexed my paws and hoped for the best. Rhys smiled and came within reach of Strider and squatted next to him.

"Wick likes you!" He looked up at Scotty. "Is he a boy puppy or a girl puppy?"

Really? Pronouns, kiddo. Pay attention to them.

"Boy. And he likes kids. His favorite thing is to play with them at the park."

"Don't bite me, okay?" he said to Strider. "Can I pet you? I'll be nice."

Strider answered by jutting his snout toward Rhys. He went to his knees and carefully reached out, setting a few fingers on his head.

"Daddy, he's soft. Like Fluffy."

Fluffy is a cat. Don't take it personally.

Strider did not take it personally. He remained as still as a chronically happy dog can; his tail thumped, and he kept trying to wedge his head under Rhys's hand, but he did nothing to frighten the little boy. I jumped off and went to stand by Will; Rhys had inched as close as he could and was scratching Strider between his ears.

You might want to remind him that Strider isn't a cat. He might not like head skritches.

"He's used to petting Wick," Will said. "If he touches Strider in a way—"

"He's fine. This dog thinks he's a cat. A lap cat. There's nothing like seventy pounds of dog leaping at you before you're even all the way into your chair."

Will had an idea what that was like. Hyrum often ran and jumped at him, counting on Will to catch all one hundred eighteen pounds of him.

"Daddy, can I have a puppy for my birthday? I wanted one since forever."

He's not exaggerating. He's been asking for once since he learned to talk.

"We talked about this, Rhys."

Rhys got up and stood in front of his father, craning his neck to look up. He clasped his hands at his chest—something he'd picked up from Hyrum—and knotted his eyebrows together. "But Wick likes Strider and Strider didn't try to eat him."

"That's not my concern. I can see that Wick is fine with Strider, but there are other people to consider. And I don't want this to be a whim. If you still want a puppy when you're ten, you will absolutely be allowed to get one. But not until then."

"But that's years and years away."

"Six years. And by then, your brother and sister will be old enough to help care for one, as well."

Dude, you had me when you were his age, and you cared for me just fine.

"But—"

"This isn't a negotiation, Rhys."

Killjoy.

I can talk Drew into getting a dog and letting Rhys play with it all day, you know.

"Rhys," Scotty said, tugging a bit on the leash to get Strider to sit up, "I'm a lawyer. Your dad is now contractually obligated to get you a dog when you turn ten. It's a guarantee."

"Yeah," Rhys grunted. "I have a witness."

I bet Drew likes dogs.

"Does Uncle Drew like dogs?"

Will and I both twitched. "I don't know," Will said, evenly.

"I bet he does. Can you take a picture of me and Strider so I can show it to him?"

Right now, I really wish I could laugh out loud because you're gonna get so played.

~

"Jax seemed certain that Rhys's gifts included everything everyone in the family already had," Aisha reminded Will that night. They were at the dining room table with Jo and Finn, the kids in bed and supposedly asleep, though I heard whispers and quiet giggles drifting down the hall. "He might not be aware that he understands Wick."

Hyrum catches words, and he doesn't realize it.

Hell, the dog understood me today.

"Are you sure Strider understood you?" Will asked me.

He rolled onto his side when I asked if I could climb on him. And then grunted when I asked if he understood.

"That could be a coincidence."

Jo wanted to know if Will remembered at what point he was certain he understood me. "I know you were around Rhys's age when we finally admitted that you and Wick were having honest conversations, but it had to have been going on a while."

He was pretty quick on the uptake. I don't remember him not understanding me.

"Rhys is also intelligent enough to mask his understanding of Wick," Finn said. "He's aware that you and Drew speak to Wick, but he's smart enough to grasp that other people shouldn't know."

"Wick," Aisha said, "do *you* think he understands what you say?"

I think he's where Hyrum is at. But it would be easy to test. I can do that if you want.

"Just pay closer attention," Will said. "He's a little boy, not an experiment."

Jo nearly flinched at that, and he noticed.

"I didn't mean anything by that, Mom."

"I tested you," she said. "There's a difference between testing and experimenting. And frankly, I'd like to repeat those tests on you to see if there are noticeable differences in your brain now."

"And Rhys?" he asked.

"If you'll allow it."

You thought it was a game when you were little. Just tell him the truth, that Grandma wants to see how his brain lights up, and then show him it doesn't hurt.

He repeated what I'd said and added, "I honestly did consider it to be a game, and I enjoyed the interaction with your technicians. That my brain created more colors on the monitor than theirs was a victory. Aisha?"

On our first visit to Saint Francis, before we knew that we were locked into a simulation, Will and Aisha found a tablet with the data Jo had collected from him. Aisha hadn't met Jo, knew little about her, but the idea that she had turned her little boy into an experiment angered her. Will braced himself for a stern "Oh, *hell* no," but that upset had long faded. She understood Jo now.

"As long as he's told the truth and understands you're collecting data because you're interested in his brain, it's all right. But I swear, he will never be made to feel like there's something wrong with him—"

"I never felt that, Enzo," Will said.

You go first and let him watch.

Or I'll go first and let him watch. My brain was never peeked at, was it?

Jo wasn't sure she could extrapolate useful data from me, but if she could get it to work, it would be worth a try. Will had ideas about connecting me to the computer without shaving my fur and was about to share that when Drew came in, waving his phone at them.

"Why do I want a dog?" he asked.

"Good lord," Aisha sighed.

Rhys had Will's phone and was texting Drew from the bedroom. "At first, I thought you were the one suggesting it," Drew said. "It was a true 'what the hell?' moment. But then you asked if I had any strawberries and would I share them? So."

Told you he was going to try to play you.

Start a betting pool. I have a month's allowance on Rhys.

~

Because the underground spaces of Finn's lab—once Will's playground—were fireproof, Jo moved her equipment there, on the third level where Finn had built the gates he used in his quest to invent personal transporters. Those had been moved to the lab in the Wastelands, leaving the entire level open for Jo's use.

It looked every bit as it had when she originally designed her workspace; the only difference was the people. A trip forward and a few phone calls could fix that if she wanted. There were a dozen or more former employees who would happily jump here to help; some already were here, working with Mass. But for now, it was family, with the doctor ready to join them should an emergency arise.

"Rhys can't start a fire here," Jo mused. "What about his percussive abilities? How strong are they?"

We had only seen Rhys use that ability once. Instead of sending a surge of electricity from the tips of his fingers—his most prominent gift—he sent a blast of explosive air, knocking a knife from the hand of a woman intent on burying it in Jax. It had also sent her sprawling to the ground, and Will had no idea how strong Rhys would become if allowed to develop the skill.

He wasn't worried about Rhys bringing the entire lab down on them. "After the last major earthquake, this was built to withstand one of the magnitude that nearly leveled the city, and then some. I think it's safe to presume that one little boy does not contain that much power."

"It's wiser to not presume," she said.

"Your other option is to wait and allow me time to build a new facility for you. Perhaps retrofitting one of the buildings at the Wastelands complex or a new build at Ozoo headquarters."

She waved him off. His confidence in the structure of the lab space was good enough.

He wanted to argue. After all, she would eventually lease space at Ozoo, and she knew it, she knew what the future likely held for baby Eli and herself—absent ending her marriage to Finn and moving to a new When to live out her final days. Will presumed that Eli would be himself, still interested in the same things, curious about how Finn built his original time machine, and he would want to play around with it.

"I'm not sure this Eli is the same as Finn's father," Aisha confided one night, as they cuddled in bed with the lights off. "What if he's not?"

"Why wouldn't he be?"

"Will. The Eli we first met, the one who cared for your sick mother, could have been your twin. And his eyes—that was the first thing I really noticed about him. They were as green as yours, just not quite as bright. The baby's eyes are so blue they're nearly violet."

He'd noticed, too, and wasn't sure how it was even possible.

"It doesn't matter," he said. "We have the Old Mint—"

"It doesn't matter as far as the end of the world," she said. "But it matters to me. There's a timeline coming up behind us, and I damn well want that Aisha to end up right here, basking in the afterglow, listening while you complain about Wick offering suggestions to you."

That Aisha would never know the difference. Her life could take a new trajectory, with an unbroken heart. "The fact that we're together now, when every other timeline registered in the old Mint suggests otherwise, might be an anomaly. We might be the lucky ones. It might never happen again."

She told him to bite his tongue. "I swear, I'll run through a portal myself and find the younger me and warn her what's about to come, and I'll make sure she knows that she just needs to be patient."

Oh, tell her what you did.

Go on. Tell her.

If you don't, I'll go tell Drew and tell him to tell her. So start talking.

"Is it enough if the young Emperor has been spurred to make certain decisions that will get us right back here?"

"Will, what did you do?"

He'd told teenaged Will that his life wouldn't end at 42, as expected. He would get the girl, start a family, and have—no matter how long or short it was—his happily ever after. "Once he was asleep, I suppressed the things I'd told him, and I implanted timed suggestions, information that would create a path to get him here and help him survive. He's still going to break her heart, but he'll make decisions along the way that will yield the same results. That includes allowing Aubrey to host the birthday party that brought you back to me."

"Eli has to be born to make that happen. If this isn't the same—"

"It is. He is. We just have to get him in the right place at the right time so that he meets my grandmother."

Plant the idea in his head now so that by the time he's nineteen, he's ready to go.

"I am not playing with an infant's mind, Wick."

So wait until he's three or four.

"He needs Jo's cooperation, too, doesn't he?" Aisha asked. "She's why he left."

He needed more than her want of leaving this When for another. Eli drew close to her because of her grief in losing Will. If they weren't as close this time, he might not have a reason to go.

"Drew has assured me that they'll do everything they can to cultivate that closeness. He and Oz intend for her to be his third grandmother. And before you protest about the unfairness to Aubrey, she agrees. She understands the stakes, and it matters to her that Eli has Finn, and Finn has me."

"This is the first When that Jo has her own grandchildren," Aisha reminded him. "Their feelings—"

"I know. We'll find the balance."

I hear tiny feet in the hallway. At least pull a sheet up, cripes.

Aisha covered; Will did not.

Rhys shuffled into the bedroom, clutching the stuffed bear Hyrum had given him. He squinted against the light and rubbed one eye, sniffing.

"Can't sleep, sweetheart?" Aisha asked.

"I had a bad dream. The puppies were gonna eat me. Daddy kept saying they were only gonna lick me, but I was still scared."

Will patted the mattress and told him to crawl up, and as Rhys wedged himself between them, he finally grabbed the sheet and tossed it over his lower half.

"Were you dreaming about being stuck in the tree?" he asked.

"Huh-uh. We were outside by the donuts, and they were running and jumping and trying to bark. But they could only go 'yip yip yip!'"

"Big dogs or little dogs?" Will pressed.

"Little but they were bigger than Wick. There was three."

Just about every dog is bigger than I am. Except maybe Chihuahua puppies.

"Rhys, dogs generally don't eat people. Those puppies truly wanted to play with you, and puppies like licking little boys."

"Wick said they were tasting me."

"Wick."

Hey, I was not present for his dream. I wasn't even in there peeking.

"The Wick in your dream was teasing," Will said. "I promise, puppies don't want to eat you. They won't behave as nicely as Scott's dog because they're not trained yet, but the worst one might do is lick you."

"And you'll laugh when they do," Aisha said. "It tickles."

"Maybe it hurts in my dreams," Rhys said.

Will leaned over and kissed him. "All right, that's fair. But it was just a dream."

"What if I have it again?"

"Then you'll come back here and tell us, and maybe we can make you feel better," Aisha said.

"Can I stay here until I fall asleep? Then Daddy can take me back to bed?"

Will reached over and turned the bedside lamp off. "No kicking or squirming, all right? Your feet are within reach of things I prefer to not have kicked."

"Okay." He closed his eyes and tucked the bear in tight. "Why are you naked?"

"Sometimes I enjoy sleeping this way," Will said. "Your mother often radiates an uncomfortable amount of heat at night."

"Can I sleep naked sometimes?"

"If you like."

"Not until you decide you want your own bedroom," Aisha added. "Examples, Will."

"Alex and Charlie are free—"

"Not until they're completely out of diapers."

"I won't pee on you," Rhys sighed.

"This," Will whispered, "is not a conversation I ever would have guessed I would have even as recently as six years ago."

"Oh, hon," Aisha snickered, "we've had far better conversations in the last five years that you never would have imagined then. Once he's asleep, we might even have another one."

Softly, Will placed a finger on Rhys's forehead, sending him into deep sleep.

"I am not above this." His fingers lingered a bit, and when her eyebrow went up, he said, "I'm also not above nudging a bad dream into a decent one. I promised him a dog when he turns ten. I want—"

"You don't need an excuse, Will. Except for that promise."

"I'm obligated. He has a witness. A lawyer, even."

I was witness, too. I'll even remind him.

"Why would you remind him, Wick? You realize it means a dog in the building, which might be measurably worse for you than if a flock of pigeons wound up inside."

You'll train the dog and I have a hover cart. I'll get used to it.

"Puppies are not predictable," he warned.

But they stop being puppies. I'll be fine. You don't even have to wait until he's ten.

"We'll wait until he's ten because that's what I told him."

We'll see.

Even Aisha laughed at him.

~

Hyrum skipped over the notion that Will and Rhys were there to play games and asked Jo to include him in her testing. He understood he'd suffered brain damage from his father repeatedly beating and shoving his mother down the stairs before his birth, and he wanted to see it. He wanted Jo to see it. She knew more about brain things than anyone he knew—more, he suspected, than even Dr. Brian—and he hoped she could explain to him what was wrong.

Jo felt an unexpected surge of reluctance. Ideally, she wanted to include him—she'd wanted a look at his brain since she'd met him, a want that doubled when she learned about his ability to throw electricity—but she also worried he would ask her to fix the damage. Her concern was amplified by knowing that she *could* do that; she could take him through a portal, stick him in a surgical tank, and allow the nanobots to carefully repair much of the damage done to him. What she didn't know, what none of them knew, was how that would affect his personality. No one knew if it would change him, better or worse.

No one wanted to risk infantilizing him, and especially no one wanted to turn him into another Levi.

Hyrum just wanted to see. There had been other scans of his brain, but he'd never paid attention to the images displayed for his mother to fret over, nor to the scans done when he arrived in Pacifica. All he'd wanted then was a cheeseburger, a bath, and to deliver his message to Aubrey, though not in that order.

"We're treating this as a game," Will reminded Hyrum while Jo accessed her old test files. "Rhys is here to play, and we don't want him to think he's doing anything more than getting to do something fun that his little brother and sister don't."

Hyrum understood. "Can we tell him he wins a lot? It'll be more fun if he wins a lot. I know Drew lets me win games sometimes and it's fun."

"Drew doesn't let you win as often as you think," Will chuckled.

"We're gonna learn how to play poker. Drew says people play for money, but we'll play for pieces of candy. That way everyone wins, on account of the winner will share."

"Hyrum, I've played poker with him. He wants to play for candy because he's afraid you'll win all his money."

When Jo was ready, they gathered around the cluster of monitors set up in a semi-circle on the right side of the room. She'd pulled up old footage of Will when he was a little older than Rhys. He played video games with a young Brian Massimo, and Jo was off to the side, monitoring the influx of data. Will's brain lit up like twinkling Christmas lights, pops of color here and there, moving around as the game progressed.

Mass gave off the air of someone losing intentionally to a child, but his brain told the truth: Will was faster, strategized better, and was a step ahead throughout the game.

She then switched to footage of him at twelve. In one test, he had placed a hand on Finn's bare forearm; Jo pointed to the spot in his brain that had flared bright red as he listened to a specific thought Finn shared. In another, he ran on a treadmill, competing against a male technician. In a third, unintended data capture, Will's brain went haywire as a younger female tech walked past. There was nothing salacious about it, but he was twelve and had only recently started humping things around the house.

"You did what?" Drew asked, snorting.

"Shut up."

"Do we get to play video games?" Rhys didn't care about his father's hormonal impulses. He wanted to get started. "Hyrum and me wanted to play Word Wizard."

"Hyrum and I," Will corrected.

Rhys frowned. "Well, you can play, too, but it was my idea, so I get to go first, okay? Can we play it?"

"It's not free," Hyrum said. "I forgot to ask if I could buy it."

"You don't need permission." Will turned to the closest computer terminal and began searching for the game. "You only need to ask if something is appropriate before allowing Rhys access."

"That's what I meant," Hyrum sighed.

I want to see what Rhys's brain does when you correct his grammar. I bet it's not a happy color.

"Wick."

You know what he meant, and he tries hard. He's not even four yet. And think about what always being wrong made Hyrum feel like when he was little.

Will hesitated before finishing the game purchase. "Point made and understood."

Jo explained how they would be hooked up to the computer; they would have fewer wires than Will had been forced to tolerate, but their brain scans would light up the same way. "We'll use the game as a baseline, and then move on, all right? Half an hour or so."

"That's not very long," Rhys grumbled.

"I know, but we have a lot of games to play today."

He still thought it wasn't enough time, not until Will promised that he and Hyrum could play again after lunch. "We won't be doing this all day. And if you decide you're not having fun, we'll stop. All right?"

The game, which involved earning imaginary points and trinkets for spelling words correctly, went on longer than Jo intended. She fell prey to Rhys's requests for "just a couple more minutes because we're almost done with this level" until they had completed it, their score nearly identical. Will sat back and watched, saying nothing when Rhys pressed for playing a little bit longer; his attention was largely focused on the monitors, watching the pops of color as they played, and the increasing intensity in vibrancy as they went deeper into the game.

"Fascinating," he mumbled to himself. Hyrum had clearly intentionally misspelled a word to give Rhys the edge at the end of the level, and his brain flared. "Pleasure," he said to Finn, who leaned close to see what Will was looking at. "Rhys was pleased to edge ahead, but allowing it to happen made Hyrum truly happy."

"We need to get Hyrum to play one of us," Finn suggested. "See how he feels if he's earnestly playing."

That could happen later, without Rhys present. Hyrum wouldn't want Rhys to see him struggle for victory, nor if he gave up.

Get Drew here. Have him play against Hyrum. Tell him to let Hyrum win at first and compare how he feels about being allowed to win against how he feels about letting Rhys win.

Will whispered to Finn, who nodded.

"Hyrum knows Drew often lets him win. Make it obvious."

"That feels a bit manipulative," Will said.

Hyrum already agreed that he might not like some of the tests. He understands what Jo is doing.

"Somewhat," Will said. "He understands she's looking at areas of his brain that were damaged before birth. He doesn't know she's also using him as a contrast between the results I had as a child and Rhys's results now."

She's also hooking you up, you know.

"I am aware."

She should compare your sparky sponge ability against Hyrum's. Last person to light up loses.

"Very funny."

After the game ended, Will was the next one hooked up to the computer. He repeated games played when he was Rhys's age, and others from when he was older. Jo stood back, eyes darting between Will and the displays, eyebrows furrowed. When he'd run through them all, she added Rhys and Hyrum, watching the monitors carefully.

"Will is obviously faster than he was when he was young," she said to Finn, softly as to not disrupt the testing. "His sense of reasoning is obviously more age-appropriate than it was, but this—" she gestured to a particularly bright area on the monitor "—is vastly different."

It suggested that as a child, he'd had a heightened sense of fight-or-flight; he'd nearly always chosen to fight, awash in cortisol, not aware that the edginess he felt was somewhat internal. Finn wanted to know what it meant in a broader sense.

"It means our son was a terrified little boy. Even at play."

Rhys, on the other hand, was evenly tempered and immersed in the joy of playing a game with no rules. To him, it was a video game in which he had to hit the big red button as quickly as he could when a new color flashed on the screen in front of him, and his goal was to beat Daddy to it. He mimicked Will, sometimes standing on one foot, sometimes running in place. Finn mused that data might be lost or skewed because Rhys and Hyrum both were having fun and, unlike young Will, were not competing for a clear win.

The Word Wizard game was forgotten. When Rhys slapped his button at the end of the test, he squealed and asked if they could play it again.

There were several games still to be played. Jo wanted to move onto their most basic of gifts, sparks dancing above fingertips. She quickly ran them through increasing skill levels; there was a metal target on the farthest wall of the massive room, and they spent fifteen minutes shooting ropes of electricity at it.

Neither was fatigued by the prolonged use of their gifts, but Will called a stop to it. Finn needed to check the temperature of the floor surrounding the metal target, concerned that the concrete was too cold for the amount of heat being generated.

"How come?" Hyrum asked, not ready to quit.

"Cold concrete, when placed under extreme heat, tends to expand," Will explained. "Given that there is no place for it to expand, the result is potentially explosive."

"Huh?"

"It could burst. Not something we wish, given that we're so far underground."

Wide-eyed, Hyrum blurted, "We'd get *buried* here?"

"No. We're safe here. But the floor surrounding the metal plate could explode and send fragments through the air. So we'll be careful, all right? I only want to make certain."

Rhys remained unconcerned. "Can we make a jump rope? A pretend one. Like we made when we were playing at Quinn's. It won't touch anything."

"Grandma hasn't seen that, has she?" Will mused. "You'll appreciate this, Mom. They've developed an interactive method for their abilities. This is the safest place for them to show you."

As they had in Shivan's Saint Francis back yard, Hyrum and Rhys stood close together, white light crackling between their outstretched hands. When they had enough energy moving between them, they began taking backward steps until they were ten feet apart. Each moved their hands in circles until they had a thick rope of white electricity and began turning it like a jump rope.

"Make a ball!" Rhys squealed.

The rope shot back into their hands, and Hyrum created a soft ball of light, carefully tossing it to Rhys.

"Get a little closer," Will said. "Let's limit the possibility that one of you might miss and catch it in the face."

"That won't hurt me," Hyrum said.

"But it might hurt Rhys. He clearly has some of your absorption capabilities, but we don't know about impact, and I'm not willing to test that."

"I wouldn't hurt him! I promise!"

Jo's head snapped to the monitor. Hyrum's brain was flaring red.

"I know you would never intentionally hurt him," Will said. "But he's still developing and might not catch the ball."

The ball disappeared.

"I'm not doing this if it might hurt him. I'm sorry, Rhys. You're so smart that I forgot that you're so little."

"It's all right—" Will wanted to soothe Hyrum's feelings before he ramped up, but Rhys ran to him and threw his arms around Hyrum's legs. He didn't say anything but reached up to take his hand, and Jo watched as the flaring red in Hyrum's brain rapidly settled.

"Curious," she muttered.

Will didn't care what she was curious about. He punched through the tension and announced that it was time for lunch, and they could play their video game while waiting for the pizza to arrive.

Hyrum perked up. "Can we have root beer, too?"

They were getting anything they wanted, whether Will realized it or not.

~

"So far," Will told Aisha a week later, "I have fed them more junk food than I would care to see in six months. Worse, Hyrum seems to know where every greasy cheeseburger and pizza is on this side of town, and they all know him by name and what he prefers to order."

Stick to delivery, then. Order from BlahBlahBlech Healthy Food-like Products. Maybe you can get a giant box of Cleaner Colon and a side of Looks Like Barf.

"Wick, stop," he sighed.

"They'll survive on the junk for a bit. How much longer is Jo going to do this?"

"Two weeks, no more than three."

"I want it over by his birthday."

"I want it over before he starts school," Will said.

Jo had promised to end the testing in plenty of time for the start of pre-school. She had already run through most of their known abilities, discovering that along with Rhys's ability to generate percussive energy and his empathic traits, he also clearly had Jax and Oz's ability to see color in sound, but it came with control. He could choose to see the colors or not, depending on what he wanted to know.

Where concussive noises in large cities, with traffic and the hum of thousands of people gave Oz a headache for all the colors that slapped at her, Rhys could simply choose to not see them. But if he sensed a lie, he could sniff that out. If he wanted to see the beauty in the music he listened to, one blink and it was there in front of him.

"He also has Zed's ability to smell emotions and other things about people," Will told her. "I am not, however, willing to test against Zed's ability to hear the final thoughts of the newly dead."

Can you test to see if he really does understand me? Sometimes I think he does.

That was next. After lunch, we were all connecting to the system and having a conversation. Jo wasn't sure it would reveal anything, but she'd never peeked at my brain and had only measured Will's when he spoke to me.

I was willing to let her shave me if it meant finding out that in time, Hyrum and Rhys would be able to understand me.

"If you tell her that," Will said, "she *will* shave you."

Only parts of my head. Can I have a mohawk? I would rock a mohawk.

"She doesn't need to shave your head, Wick. We have leads small enough to adhere to your skin, even with your fur intact."

Are you sure they'll work?

"Why wouldn't they?"

Well, given the massive range of my intelligence, she might need something a little sturdier.

"Trust me, that's not an issue."

I think he insulted me, but it was time for lunch, and there was real live fresh dead shrimp, so I let it go.

~

Rhys and Hyrum were already hooked into the system when Jo pulled up video footage of Will at five and then at twelve as he carried on conversations with me. She grabbed still shots of some of the images of his brain, times when it was most active, to have a ready comparison of the real-time conversation we were about to have.

I kept my eyes on the monitor that would display the mapping of my brain as she placed the tiny leads on my head, watching as the picture popped up section by section until there was a full-screen rainbow visual of how my brain worked. Everyone but Rhys was silent as they examined it. Hyrum got closer to see better—making me wonder if he needed to have his eyes checked—and then glanced at the monitor with his data.

"Wick's brain has more colors," he said. "Does that mean he's smarter?"

No. Tell him no.

"This doesn't measure intelligence," Jo said before Will had a chance to. "Wick has less mass to work with, so his images will appear brighter than yours or Will's. This is a matter of having similar numbers of electrical impulses in a smaller space."

"Like sparks in a box," Hyrum mused. "A hundred sparks in a tiny box is brighter than a thousand sparks in a big room."

"Exactly."

Damn, dude, that was creative.

Jo directed Will to sit with me on the floor, as he had when he was a child. She'd replicated as much as she could. There was a plush piece of carpeting on the floor, along with a tiny table he'd often used for drawing pictures. Will didn't need the table now, but when he was five, there was an assortment of small toys nearby, things he could grab when he felt anxious, things he could use as a distraction. Now there were graham crackers on a plate, snacks for Rhys and Hyrum when they sat down to talk to me.

What did we talk about before? I don't remember.

"Initially, how boring this was. Though truthfully, I was at a loss as to the topic we should begin with. A conversation that occurs naturally is much easier than one contrived for data."

We managed, though. But we also had a lot to talk about then. I think we were trying to figure out if cracking open one of the plasma batteries and licking it would give us superpowers.

Jo was not prompting us by reminding me of the things we'd discussed. Her eyes were on the data, particularly mine.

"Did we ever resolve that?" he wondered.

Mass guessed at what we were talking about and said the only thing it would get us was dead. I suppose we should pick something else. Maybe we can bitch at each other this time.

That made him chuckle. "Fine. What's on your mind, Wick? What list of complaints do you have for me?"

That could take a long time.

"We have enough time."

I don't really have any complaints. I have suggestions, though.

"Do I really want to hear them?"

Does it matter? We're here to talk. So I'm talking. First suggestion. Take the stick out of your asterisk. Making Rhys wait until he's ten for a dog seems...arbitrary. Why wait?

He hesitated, not wanting Rhys to know what I'd said.

"It seems appropriate in terms of his ability to handle the duty of care required."

You're gonna get stuck with most of that no matter how old he is. The point isn't being able to do all the work.

"Then what is the point?"

Unconditional love.

"He has that."

But he won't always grasp that. He needs someone who will be happy to see him no matter what, even if he's been a little shit all day and had a dozen temper tantrums. He needs someone who won't see the little boy with the big brain, someone who won't treat him like he should be fourteen when he's still just four.

"I hear you."

You had that. You had me. Finn didn't find me and say, well, Will isn't ten yet, and he's not ready to deal with scooping poop and regular feeding, so I'll leave this cat right here. He picked me up and said he had a little boy who would love me.

"He did, didn't he?"

That's all that really mattered. I needed someone, and he knew you would love me. You did. Your mother did most of the work in caring for me until you were older. And I know you're going to wonder how Alex and Charlie will feel, and what if they want their own pets, too.

"Well, I'm certainly wondering about that now."

It doesn't matter. It's not math, so they're not part of the equation. Besides, I don't think they'll need a pet as much as Rhys does. But even if they do, cross that bridge when you get to it. Maybe they'll just want hamsters or fish.

"Is there a particular reason you're bringing this up now?"

Glance over my head at his monitor. He's listening, isn't he?

"You believe he understands you."

When he wants to. But he's only a couple of weeks short of turning four, Will. I don't think he has the restraint to hold back if something goes his way. And we both know, it's an issue you'll fold on. Because you had me, and you needed me. You know how that feels. You know how he feels.

"Indeed."

So just admit, he gets to have a dog, and he gets it soon. Like, for his birthday.

He glanced at Rhys's monitor.

"I have to discuss it with Aisha, but I understand your reasoning. He should have this sooner rather than later, though I'm wholly against that sort obligation as a gift."

But you agree, he would benefit from getting a dog.

"I do now."

Rhys's hands went to his chest, and he sucked in a tiny breath.

He's listening.

"I believe you're right," Will said. "Though I'm less sure of his awareness in the matter."

I'll settle for his lack of awareness right now. It just means that someday he'll be able to talk to me. And I might need that, Will. You and Drew aren't going to live forever.

"Not something I wish to contemplate."

I know, but the truth is that I might be like Finn, and he's going to live longer than anyone thinks is possible. If Rhys has your life span, then I'll have nearly two centuries more of someone to talk to.

"And you do need that," Will mused.

As much as Rhys needs a dog. And I'll be okay with it, I swear.

"You'll tease it with your hover cart, chasing it up and down the hall."

Of course, I will.

If he had any doubt before, Rhys's quiet giggle convinced him. *The boy understood me.*

~

"Just talk to him," Will told Hyrum and Rhys. "When he meows, give him a chance to finish before saying something else."

The three of them sat in a little circle on the rug, and I perched on Will's legs, where I could easily see both Rhys and Hyrum. They asked questions—what's your favorite food, do you like being a cat, who owns you—and as instructed, they waited for my answers before moving on, glancing at Will's face to be sure it was all right to ask something else. We established that being a cat was fine, though there were times I wished I had thumbs and access to an infinite number of food cans in a wide variety of choices, and that I had never considered myself owned so much as cared for. I enjoyed having free reign in the building, and I slept with whomever I felt needed the company most, or whomever I wanted to pester just for the fun of pestering them. Sometimes that was Will, sometimes Jax, often it was Drew, but many nights I spent an hour or two on each of their beds, making sure they weren't having bad dreams.

Rhys was curious about my ability to perceive human language. Did I hear words, or did my brain turn them into meows? Did I know what Daddy hears? His head tilted as he considered my answers—I understood English as spoken but no other languages, and I knew that Will heard both words and meows. The meows he heard with his ears; the words settled into his brain.

My turn.

"Wick wants to ask you things now," Will said. "I'll be his translator, but when you answer, be sure to talk to him, not me."

Do you still want to be a scientist and a wizard when you grow up? I asked Rhys.

"Uh-huh. But they're the same thing. Kinda. I want to go to space like Drew's gonna, or work on his tiny robots and make them tinier. Oh! Or maybe invent a new spaceship that can get to the moon in five minutes or maybe an hour."

What about you? I asked Hyrum. *If you could do any job in the world, what would it be?*

I thought he would need time to consider it, but it rolled off his tongue without hesitation. "A pastor, I think. But not the way it works in Florida where any man can be a priest or bishop or talk in church about his testimony. I think I'd like to be one more like Father Dan. But maybe not just Catholic. A pastor for everyone."

You could do that, you know.

"Nuh. You gotta go to school for that."

Rhys perked up. "I'm going to school soon. You can go, too."

"I'm too old. And besides, that kind of school is probably really hard."

There has to be something that would let you share your faith with people and minister to them without getting a degree.

"Maybe, but I don't know how."

Will probably knew but stayed out of the conversation.

"You could start your own place for people to go," Rhys said. "If you open your own place, no one can make you go to school."

"You can't just start a church, Rhys."

Why not? That's basically how religion starts, right?

"God has to tell you to do that, I think."

Maybe God just did, and that's why it occurred to you.

"I dunno. I have two jobs already. If I did more, that would be selfish."

You don't have to keep those jobs forever, you know.

Hyrum was horrified at the idea he would ever be willing to leave Ozoo or stop helping Zed at Alcatraz. "They need me!"

"You should do what you wanna and not what they wanna," Rhys told him.

You can quit a job when something better presents itself, People do it all the time.

"I like my jobs, though. I don't want to quit."

Even if you could one hundred percent be a minister?

"No, I really want to keep working with Drew and Zed. They make me think a lot."

There you go, then. That's what you truly want to do.

"If you were a person, what would you do, Wick?" Rhys asked.

King of the World, kiddo. I'd run it all.

"Jax says being king is hard work," Hyrum said. "You'd miss lots of naps."

This is true.

"You should be a doctor like Doctor Cheshire. You listen good, just like him."

"Who's he?" Rhys asked.

"He's my special doctor. He helps me feel better about my daddy."

With that, Will declared the conversation over. Surely Jo had gotten what she needed, and he didn't want Rhys to learn any more about Levi Munson than necessary. "It's time for lunch. What do you want?"

Waffles.

Waffles.

Waffles.

"Waffles," they said at the same time.

"Lots of butter and syrup," Rhys added.

I'm a benevolent dictator, Will. I give the people what they want. And they wanted the suggestion of waffles. You're welcome.

~

Years earlier, Will held his mother as she died. He'd gone forward thirty-five years on Drew's request, to let the people who had loved him and lost him know that this time, he'd lived. While that wouldn't change their loss or the grief they'd suffered, Drew hoped it would give them a sense of relief. He knew he would want to know; the idea that there was a version of himself that had existed and lost Will ate at him, and he wanted that man to know that his Emperor had not died in the next loop of time.

He was right. The Andrew who had been Midlam's King was happy; Oz was happy. Jax and Aubrey were thrilled, and Finn was a scattered mix of overjoyed and curious, wanting all the details. But lost in the settling dust was his mother. Jo had left that When for one in which she hoped she would be able to live without an anchor, and it was there he next visited, hoping to bring some peace into their relationship.

Will was angry and at odds with the mother waiting at home; she'd known he could learn to control his gifts when he was young, yet never hinted that he could have the normal life he craved. But the woman who laid in bed with a Nightwatch switch plugged into her arm, ready to end her own life, deserved to see that her son would eventually live. He wanted that for her and wanted to give her hope.

She'd spent the years after his death trying to understand how he came to be, hoping to pinpoint why her son could touch someone and read their thoughts. She played with miniature versions of Finn's egg-shaped time machine, sending small animals into null space, then animals that had been bred, and those offspring had unusual gifts of their own.

Her conclusion: she'd exposed Will to null space in utero, and she was the reason he was afflicted with his abilities. Comforted by his forgiveness, she died in his arms, believing the gifts would end with him.

She hadn't known about Hyrum, who had never been exposed to null space, nor any of his family members who each had quiet gifts of their own.

She hadn't realized that I was the product of her experimentation, offspring of one of the cats she'd sent off, nor that I was later stuck in null space for the same 400 years as Finn.

That Jo died believing Will could safely have children and not pass anything on.

Our Jo had listened to Will's retelling of the experimentation, was appropriately horrified that she had ever, in any lifetime, risked the lives of innocent animals to quench her curiosities. She accepted her counterpart's theory as truth until Hyrum came along, and after Will had spoken to older Hyrum thirty-five years in the future and learned of his siblings' abilities, dismissed it and mourned the things done to me.

"That never had to happen," she told Will as they set up for the next round of testing. "I suppose if she had known more about Aubrey's empathic abilities, she never would have considered it."

Will didn't know if future Jo had been aware of the things Aubrey could do; he accepted that he had, after all, passed something along to Rhys, and was certain that those abilities came from Aubrey's side of the family. He was also certain that there was some component of exposure to null space involved; there was nothing else to account for me, and nothing in the Munson line to explain how long Finn would live, and he would live for a very long time.

Maybe it's not genetic. Maybe it's evolution.

"If that were the case, I would have expected far more people such as myself when I was growing up," Will said.

Who says people would be open about it?

I still think they're here, now, and just hiding.

And maybe it's not in your brains. Maybe there's something different about your DNA. Or kidneys. Who knows?

"That might be next," Jo surmised. "But for now, we're playing with brains, and using Drew as a control."

I thought you wanted to look at functioning brains.

"Hey," he barked from across the room. "I heard that."

Will flipped some switches on the computer console. "Ignore the sarcastic feline. And be ready. I'm turning this on in three seconds."

Drew's brain was an explosion of color. Even when he wasn't talking or interacting with Jo's tests, it fired off as if he were playing games with Rhys and Hyrum, and when he spoke with me, the brightest was a thin line that Finn traced on the monitor with his pointy finger.

There were dozens of lines in Drew's brain, threads that had set after his initial transponder was placed, and there were smaller, newer lines from the secondary transponder he'd gotten that was specifically programmed to operate his nanosuit. It was a bright line emanating from the original that intrigued Finn. He compared it to images of Will's brain and of his own, and when he was positive about what he saw, he turned to Will and said, "He's the only one with this path. It specifically attached to the language centers of his brain."

"Capture a static image," Will said to Jo as he stepped closer to look at it. "We were reasonably certain that the simulator's computer had given him a way to understand Wick, though I was never certain how."

Jo wanted to know if the simulator's system had access to the computers used to program the transponders. It was a program designed to learn, to accommodate anyone inside the simulation, and could have—theoretically—drawn on the original program to create this neural pathway.

She grabbed an image of Rhys's brain and displayed it next to Drew's. "He has a transponder," she said. "Just curious if it created the same pathway."

It had not.

"Rhys's abilities are organic," Will said. "This does mean—" he pointed at Drew's picture "—that if we can find the code within the simulator's programming, we might be able to replicate it. Anyone's transponder could be programmed to understand Wick."

"Or any animal, really," Jo mused.

No.

"No?" Will repeated.

I'd like to be able to talk to everyone in the family, but I don't want to risk anyone. Drew's brain is unique. It might damage someone else. Let it happen naturally.

"Or," Drew said, "we can replicate the code into an external translator. Piggyback off an existing universal translator and see if that would allow family to communicate with him."

"Well?" Will asked me.

I had no ready answer for him. Until that moment, I had deeply wished that everyone could understand me. It would make my life easier.

I looked over at Rhys and Hyrum, who were playing on the rug. Hyrum was on his back, and Rhys ran a toy car up and down his legs and chest, giggling wildly when Hyrum stuck out his stomach and flicked the car off.

They were both close to understanding everything I said, and I wanted it to happen. Every word I thought they heard excited me. It was as close to understanding why they looked forward to Christmas and Santa as I was probably going to get: the hope, the thrill of expectation, knowing something good would happen, even if it wasn't exactly what was imagined.

Yet, I suddenly felt as if I needed to guard that gift.

When something special is given to everyone, it stops being special.

Drew opened his mouth to argue, but Will nodded and said he understood. "Perhaps later, when we know if the other kids can understand you on their own. There's no hurry and no obligation to allow this to happen."

"But the data—"

"No, Andrew. Wick is right. For the same reason we don't share the portals with the world, nor with every family member, we won't intrude on Wick's wish that this gift be organic. If he changes his mind, we can pursue it then."

And no doing it behind my back, all right?

Reluctantly, Drew nodded. "I won't, but I don't get it, Wick."

"Think about it," Will said. "When you realized that you understood him, didn't that make you feel a bit, well, special? Pride undefined, perhaps. But you could do something that only one other person could."

Drew's concern wasn't how special he was, but how improved my life might become.

I asked him to pick me up and hold me close to his face.

My life is fine as it is. But if everyone can understand me, Hyrum and Rhys might stop sharing their secrets with me.

"They know you'd never tell."

But they'll think twice, and right now, Hyrum especially needs a sounding board. The only people I can tell are you and Will. If I can talk to everyone, if I slip up and let something out, then everyone will know.

"And they know neither Will nor I would ever tell."

Not unless it was an emergency.

"All right. We'll leave it alone. But, damn, Wick...if Oz could understand you?"

She'd kick me out of the room at night. She doesn't really want to hear the things I tell you. Not everyone wants suggestions. And you really don't want her to know you've done some things I've told you to.

"True."

Next time I tell you to lick an armpit, dude, don't listen.

Will snorted, but Hyrum giggled. Drew set me down and groaned, and then wholly agreed: the entire world did not need to know what I was thinking.

~

It was another week before Jo was ready to continue. She had agreed to several of Hyrum's requests, specifically testing what went on in his head while he did "sparky-sponge things." He wanted to know what happened when he pushed his own limits, when he handled electricity that didn't come from himself, and to do that she needed to protect everyone else.

While she combed through the data of everything done during the previous week, Will supervised the construction of an insulated chamber in which Hyrum could play with increasing voltage without risking anyone else. He made sure that there was a giant window so that Hyrum could see and be seen, and thick enough that no matter how hard Hyrum went, it wouldn't break.

"It's not glass," Will said when I asked about flying shards. "It's a composite. Fireproof, electric proof, percussive proof, and for good measure, it's four inches thick. The flooring inside is similar."

What about exploding cement?

"Accounted for."

I hopped onto the desk and sat next to the keyboard, so I could see inside the chamber.

Is that glass? Or is it like those giant aquarium walls?

"Similar composition, but a much higher grade."

It looks heavy. It's heavy, right?

"Indeed. The chamber will remain here unless we need it elsewhere. Moving it would be more difficult than its construction."

Then Hyrum and Rhys will have a place to test their abilities. Leaving it is probably a good thing, and you can build another somewhere else.

"Indeed."

Inside, the chamber only contained two small Hyrum-waist-high tables with curved metal pieces pointed toward each other, a foot apart. Thick cables went down the sides of each table and across the floor, bolted down with brackets and covered with wide pieces of heavy tape. It took up nearly a quarter of the floor space, which was enough real estate to install an apartment for six people.

The buffer zone was probably unnecessary given the control Hyrum typically displayed, but there was no reason to take any chances.

What's that? The two tables with the cable thingies.

"Conduits. Electricity will arc from one side to the other, and Hyrum can do with it as he sees fit."

Hyrum sat on the throw rug with Drew. He had a pencil dangling from his lips and another in hand, drawing a picture of dragons flying over water. Rhys was not present for this test; Will left him at home with Aubrey, placating his upset over being left behind with the promise that he could spend the morning playing with his brother and sister, and that Marco would come upstairs to play, too. When Aisha was done with her classes for the day, and he was done here, they would go to the park to play and then out for pizza.

"Just pizza?" Finn asked after Will explained where Rhys was.

"We'll see," Will sighed. "Ice cream may have been implied."

"Can I go?" Hyrum asked. "I know where the best pizza is. And Sean works there."

Drew looked up from his drawing. "Hell, I want to go, too. The pizza there is amazing. Super thin and crunchy crust and the pepperoni bites back."

"Maybe we should take Oz on a date," Hyrum said. "I can drive. Then you can drink. Will can drink, too. Even Aisha."

Just what the kids need to see. All of you drunk off your asterisks.

"Perhaps the two of you should take Oz on that date," Will said. "We'll take the kids on a less adult outing."

"Hey, we can make Oz drive," Drew said to Hyrum. "She can't drink right now, but you can."

"Aubrey might get mad if I drink. She says things to Jax when he takes me to Fuzzy's."

"She's not really upset when we go to Fuzzy's, Hyrum.

You know how she sighs and rolls her eyes a little? She's more amused than anything."

"Truly," Will said.

"Will Rhys's feelings get hurt if I go out with Drew instead?" Hyrum asked Will.

It didn't matter if it bothered Rhys, but Will wouldn't risk upsetting Hyrum by leaving room for any doubt. He assured him that Rhys would be fine because he was getting an afternoon in the park; instead, he suggested that they take me along because my life would be incomplete if I missed seeing Drew throw up after just a few shots.

Hyrum's eyes went wide. "We're getting shots?"

"Not those kinds of shots. Little glasses of booze." Drew got up from the floor and then held out a hand to help Hyrum. "It'll be your reward for letting Jo peek inside your head. She really digs stuff like this."

"I do," she agreed and then gestured to the chamber. "We're ready when you are."

He jumped up and skipped to the entrance, eager to begin, yet hesitated before stepping inside. "Promise no one can get hurt?"

"No one will be hurt," Will said.

"That's not a promise," Hyrum sighed. "You have to promise."

The baby Jesus will cry if someone gets hurt.

"You'll make the baby Jesus cry—"

Will held up a hand. "I promise. This chamber was built to withstand more energy than even you can handle, Hyrum." When he seemed doubtful, Will added, "I designed it personally. We could set off a bomb in there, and everyone outside the chamber would be safe."

Sure about that? I asked after Hyrum was inside, while Finn pulled the massive door shut.

He was sure. The chamber could hold up to the amount of power he'd harnessed from the old solar farm years earlier, when he needed more electricity than the city could afford to spare to send Finn through a gate built on the Bay Bridge, just to get him home. Finn's time machine didn't have a problem with that much power, and neither, he swore, would this.

"Well, the ship was a bit on the crispy side when it stopped," Finn said. "Still functional, though I was never able to rid it of the stench of burning polymers, even after the hull was replaced."

"*You* didn't melt," Will said as he flicked a switch that opened the communications system between the chamber and lab. "Can you hear me, Hyrum?"

"Uh-huh. What do I do?"

He instructed Hyrum to carefully examine the conduits and the control panel in front of it. Will had built it with simplicity in mind; he didn't want Hyrum to have to stop to ask questions and wanted it to be as intuitive as possible. There were only three controls: start, pause, and stop. Everything else was in Will's hands. He controlled the flow of energy, and if he felt that Hyrum was pushing limits that he didn't understand, he could stop everything.

"The green switch means 'start,'" he said to Hyrum. "The yellow switch means 'pause.' If you need a break, flip it, and the conduit will power down but not shut off. If you need to stop completely, use the red switch. That will stop everything, and the unit won't turn on again until it's cooled down."

"Okay. When do you want me to turn it on?"

"When you're ready. Take your time."

Hyrum flicked the green switch and then wrapped his fingers around each conduit. He giggled when the electricity began to move through him—it tickled—and then asked if he was doing it right.

"You've got it," Will said. "I'll gradually increase the power. Tell me if it begins to bother you."

He and Drew had seen Hyrum absorb a fair amount of power. When we followed him on his trek across Midlam, he'd run into the shell of a wrecked air car that buzzed with power leeching from sheared cables, and none of it affected him. One foot on an active cable would have killed either Will or Drew, but for Hyrum, it was merely an obstacle to avoid tripping over when he had a crash victim in his arms.

"What about the leads attached to his scalp?" Drew asked Will. "If he really gets cooking, will they melt?"

The wires Will had attached to Hyrum were wrapped in the same material Drew created for his spacesuit. Enmeshed with nanobots programmed to activate under stress, they would spread out enough to keep the heat from destroying the leads, and if necessary, would slide under the spots where the leads adhered to Hyrum's skin and force the wires to detach.

"The bases are covered, Andrew. However—" he pointed to the big red button on the secondary control panel "—I want you near that at all times. If Hyrum is clearly in distress and my attention is diverted, hit it."

"What if I hit it prematurely? Will that screw things up?"

"The worst that will happen is that we wait for the system to reboot. The conduits will need to cool, but if Hyrum chooses to, we can resume."

"So, no harm, no foul. Got it."

Jo and Finn sat in front of the cluster of display panels, monitoring data and imaging while Will focused on Hyrum, who now looked bored, waiting for something fun to happen. Slowly, Will increased the amount of power fed through the conduit, until Hyrum giggled again. He lifted a finger on each hand and sent threads of electricity from one finger to the other until there was a short, thick rope running between them.

Will asked him to pull the conduits closer together without taking his hands off, and then span the distance between them with one hand. "Little finger from your left hand on the left one, index finger on the right."

"Huh?"

Pointy finger.

"Pointy finger," Will repeated. "Then let go with your right hand."

He did as he was told, then wondered what he was supposed to do. Will left it open to his whims. Create sparks. Balls of light. Whatever he wanted to play with, as long as he kept a hand on the conduits.

Hyrum began with a short cascade of sparks that spilled

over his hand to the floor, and as Will increased the power, it became a shower that shot several feet into the air.

"He's like a human sparkler," Drew mused.

Hyrum rubbed his fingers together, working the light into a ball. We'd seen this before; he taught Rhys to create small balls of light that he could then throw, but he worked longer, and the ball grew large enough that Will and Drew squinted against the brightness of it.

"Hyrum," Drew said, "have you ever let power seep out from anything other than your hands?"

"Sometimes. But I'm not allowed on account of I set fire to my pants once."

"Can you get your shirt off without letting go? And then limit it to your torso?"

The ball disappeared, and Hyrum yanked his shirt off over his head, letting it dangle from his left arm. "No making fun of me," Hyrum said. "I know I'm skinny."

"I would never," Drew said.

"Joe used to. 'Eat a cheeseburger, Hyrum. *God.*' I can't help it. I eat a lot, but I stay skinny."

"Your metabolism is very high," Will said. "We know that. And we will not shame you for it."

"Promise?"

In unison, they all said, "Promise."

I like Joe, but that's a dick kind of thing.

"Joe just teases. He don't know about it hurting my feelings."

Hyrum grabbed the conduits with his free hand, let go with his left to let the shirt fall, and then took hold with both hands. He closed his eyes, and twenty seconds later his skin began to glow. He shimmered at first, tiny sparks of light dancing across his chest and shoulders until he was enveloped in white light that ended half an inch from the waistband of his jeans.

"Will," Jo murmured, "look."

He glanced at the monitor. "Keep it up, Hyrum," he said. "Are you comfortable?"

"Uh-huh. My nipples got pointy."

He gestured for Drew to keep an eye on Hyrum while he turned his attention to the monitors. Hyrum's entire brain was lit, including the areas most damaged.

"Ask him a series of questions," Jo said. "I don't care about what but make them a bit more complicated than things you normally would."

Will wanted to know why.

"Just a hunch."

Finn reminded Will of the memory stick he'd once used to jar Finn's amnesia loose. It was fake; he'd wired a battery to a metal pipe, but Finn didn't know any better, and it worked. "Ask those kinds of questions first," he said. "Work up to the hard ones."

"Am I okay?" Hyrum asked.

"You're doing fine," Will said. "Jo is getting excellent information from you. Do you mind if I ask questions?"

"Like a test?"

"Essentially. There are no right or wrong answers, all right?"

"Okay."

"What's your full name?"

"Hyrum Charles Blackshear. On account of I'm not a Munson anymore."

"Where were you born?"

"In Florida."

"Specifically. What region?"

"North Carolina."

"Did you live near the ocean?"

"Nuh. We were on the other side. But Red took me to the ocean a few times even when it wasn't my birthday. We had fun. Daddy took us, too. He liked the ocean."

"What's your favorite color?"

"Red. Sometimes pink, though."

"Favorite food?"

"Cheeseburgers. Or pizza. I can't choose. I like them both."

"Who's King of Midlam?"

"Jax."

"Who's King of Pacifica?"

"Duh, Jax."

"In which direction is Canada?"

"North."

"How many things are in a dozen?"

"Twelve."

"What's two times eight?"

"Sixteen."

"What's point-five plus point-five?"

"One."

"One-eighth times three-quarters?"

Hyrum hesitated. "That's minuses and you know I can do minuses."

Jo gestured to the monitor and mouthed, "He knows."

"Six times twelve times four, divided by nine."

"Lots," Hyrum sighed.

Drew tapped Will's arm; he wanted to ask questions.

"Hy, do you remember when we were working on the hoses that run air from canisters to my helmet on the spacesuit?"

"Uh-huh."

"You had an idea on how to improve it but said you couldn't find the right words and needed to think about it. Do you know what you wanted to tell me?"

"Oh, yeah! You need a second set because the way it is now, if the tubes rip, you're not gonna be able to breathe."

"It's pretty sturdy material."

"But the tubes are on the outside and things might hit you or you might snag on something like my shirt snagged on my bike and tore when I was cleaning the chain. You need another tube that goes under the suit right to your nose. And the nanobots need to plug your air tank if it cracks or something so the air goes into the tube under your suit. Like the tubes that give air to fishes in tanks but maybe flatter, so they don't poke you funny under your tights. Maybe a special thin thing that holds the air against your chest instead of your back on account of you'll already have stuff on your back."

"I'll be damned," Drew muttered. "That's a terrific idea."

"Can we do it?"

"Damn straight. It won't add much weight. I can almost see it in my head already. Let's sketch it out and run it by the tech heads."

"Engineers," Hyrum sighed. "They don't like me."

"They don't have to. They just have to make it work."

I jumped from Will's shoulder to the desk to get closer to the microphone. Will's eyes flicked from Hyrum to me and then back, and he nodded.

What kind of pizza is your favorite?

"Pepperoni."

Do you know that you can understand me?

"Sometimes. I always try but sometimes you just meow."

I just wanted to talk to you. And I wanted to be sure that you know I love you.

"I know. I love you too, Wick."

You look like a glowstick right now, dude. You want Drew to take a picture? It's kind of awesome.

"I never seen myself like this. Yeah!"

While Drew stepped back to get the entire chamber in the shot, Will began scaling back on the power, until it was just a trickle, and then he shut it off. Hyrum still glowed, but he let go and played with ropes of light and sparks until Will told him that they were done, and he could come out when he was ready.

Jo reached over and turned the microphone off. "He knew the answer to that math problem. Whatever you tell him—"

"I know, Mom."

"Wait." Drew shoved the phone into his pocket. "Hyrum, you still up for a few more questions?"

He lobbed a golf-ball-sized wad of light against the window. "Yeah. You want me to keep doing this, too?"

Hyrum could do anything he wanted; light ropes, balls, sparklers, anything that came to him as he listened to the questions.

"More like a conversation," Drew said. "Like we did with Wick."

"Okay. What do you wanna talk about?"

"Well, remember that girl who was flirting with you last week, when we went for burgers?"

"Nuh. She wasn't flirting. She was just being nice."

"She was flirting, Hy. Oz and I went back, and she asked about you. She wanted to know if you were single."

"Okay."

Drew pressed on, knowing how Hyrum felt. "So, do you think you might want to go out with her? Give dating a try?"

He lobbed another wad of light at the window, harder. "Nuh. I don't want a girlfriend. Or a boyfriend."

"But you like girls."

"Girls are nice. But only for friends."

"Tread carefully," Will whispered.

"Hy, how will you ever know if you want a girlfriend or not, if you never give one a chance?"

"I just know."

"Girls are nice. They're soft and fun to kiss—"

Sparks began to flit across Hyrum's chest and stomach. "So?"

"You might like that."

"So?" he asked, a bit more forcefully.

"And then there's sex."

The sparks flattened and became a thin sheet that pulled around him, and began to pulse, while he worked up balls of light with his fingers.

"Sex is fun," Drew went on. "But if you don't give a girl a chance—"

"I'm never doing kissing things!"

"I mean, it's *really* fun."

"No! I don't want a girlfriend and I'm never doing kissing things! I don't want to hurt anyone, Drew. I like girls but it would hurt, okay?"

"It doesn't hurt," Drew said, but Hyrum wasn't listening. He was surrounded by pulsing white and red light, and when it sounded as if Drew was going to continue speaking, Hyrum flung his arms wide, sending a wave of power that shook the floor and caused the monitors to jiggle.

"Stop it!" Hyrum shouted. "I won't do it! I won't!"

"All right," Drew said calmly. "Are you okay?"

"No, it hurts. It never didn't hurt. I don't know why everyone likes it."

"I'm sorry I upset you," Drew said. "Remember, we told you that we might do things to make you mad? I went too far, and I'm very sorry."

The light faded. Hyrum stood in the center of the chamber, sweat pouring from his skin, trying hard to not cry.

"I promise I will never do that again."

Hyrum swallowed hard. "Did it work? Did Jo get good stuff? I'm okay if Jo got good stuff."

Will looked to his mother, who nodded. "Indeed, she did. Are you ready to come out now?"

"Uh-huh. Can I have a root beer? I'm really thirsty now."

Drew shoved the massive door open, promising him he could have anything he wanted. If he wanted to stop at Fuzzy's and get a real beer, Drew was buying.

Hyrum stepped out, shrugging his shirt over his head. "Maybe not beer. But I'm hungry again. Can we get something to eat?"

"Anything you want. And after, we can go to the office and sketch out details on your idea for the spacesuit."

Dude, you can get Drew to do just about anything right now. Ask him for a raise. And a pony.

"I don't want a pony," he snickered. "Just a cheeseburger." He went over to Jo and looked at the monitor. "Did you get good stuff?"

"The best stuff," Jo said as she shifted the image on the monitor to a stream of data that probably made sense only to her. "Thank you, Hyrum. I have more information now than I can go through in a month."

"Did I sponge up a lot?"

Will nodded. "The amount of energy you absorbed could power an entire city block for the afternoon."

"Oh. Should I give it back? I can do that."

"Wait, you still have it?" Drew asked. "You can store it?"

"He's a sparky sponge, Andrew," Will said, sparing Hyrum the mental gymnastics required to explain it.

"I'm kind of a battery, too," Hyrum said. "I bet if you stick a plug in my mouth, I can turn on a lamp."

"We will not," Will said when it looked as if Drew were hoping he'd try it. "Hyrum is not a toy."

"We can try it later," Hyrum whispered to Drew, loudly. He turned to Jo and asked, "Did I pass the test?"

"You did wonderfully."

"I can still answer questions if you want. I'm still hooked up, right?"

"You've given me more than enough." She gave him a short hug. "Thank you, Hyrum. I appreciate all the time you've given me."

He wanted to know how long it would before she could tell them anything about the games they'd played and what it meant. He wanted to know what his brain had told her and knew she wanted to see how Rhys's looked against Will's.

"It could take a month or two," she told him.

"That's okay. Drew says you can't be in a hurry when it's science. Even though he's in a hurry to finish his space suit on account of he needs it so he can go to Elysium."

They left to get cheeseburgers and root beer, and on their way out, Hyrum excitedly reminded Drew to call Oz for their date, but even if she didn't want to go he still wanted to get pizza on account of he'd get hungry again, and Drew could drink, but if he threw up, he was cleaning it up his own self.

There was a stretch of silence after the door clicked shut. Will and Jo stood there, staring at static images of Hyrum's brain activity, while Finn scrolled through the data they'd collected.

"You know," Finn finally said, breaking the quiet, "give him a transponder, and it can reach those parts of his brain that aren't firing off."

"At what cost?" Will said. "We don't know the long-term effects. How his personality might change. I'm already concerned about his life span, if we change anything, what will we truly be doing to him?"

"Why his life span?" Finn asked.

"He burns, Dad. His metabolism—"

Old Hyrum is old. You know how long he lives, right?

"I know how much longer he *could* have lived, Wick. His body gave out before his spirit."

You can say the same for most people. No one is really ready to die.

From the accounts Will had recently read, the Hyrum of his history was perfectly healthy and happy but went to bed one night and simply didn't wake the next morning. There was nothing about his body to suggest why he had died. No cardiac event, no disease, nothing. He was old even for the average life of people in Pacifica at the time, but given his spryness and activity level, he should have lived longer.

"I have hopes that some of the things we learn now will help us keep him alive longer."

Even old Hyrum?

Will nodded. "I will do what I can to extend his life, as well."

"Shame on you, playing with the timelines," Jo chided.

Finn chuckled. "His playing with the timelines is why another you didn't die and has offered to go forward to hump old, old, old Liam Finnegan."

"She's not having sex with him," Jo sighed. "She's offering her DNA. And if hers fails—"

"You will," he finished for her. "I'm not sure why you're waiting. Why he's waiting. Go spit in a cup and get on with things."

"He's looking for the ideal host," Will said.

"Incubator," Jo said. "He prefers a human host. And no, I will not be that host."

"I wouldn't object," Finn said. "If you wanted to—"

"No. If I give birth again, it will be yours, and we'll raise him together. I don't care if Liam's DNA is identical to yours, he's not you. There will be no physical contact with that cranky, contentious old lech, and I won't have his child."

Are they really still thinking about having another kid?

"Apparently," Will sighed.

They're kind of old.

"We're not that old," Jo said to me, even though Will hadn't translated. "And quit looking at me like that. I don't understand him, but I know him."

You're pushing eighty.

"Middle age, Wick," Will said. "They're not even over the halfway mark in terms of expected life span."

For there. They live here.

"Then we better get to it," Finn said. "Go home, Will. We have things to do."

Bounce, bounce, bounce. Done.

"Wick," Will chuckled.

Jo tapped the top of my head and then planted a soft slap on the back of Finn's. "Stop. Pull up the images of Will, Rhys, and Hyrum speaking with Wick. I'm oddly curious about those."

Will wanted to see the more current images; why had Hyrum hesitated, and why did Jo think he knew the answer?

She pointed to a bright spot on the picture. "He did the computation and did it quickly. But the answer simply wouldn't form well enough for him to express it. He doesn't know that he could have answered correctly."

Will traced a finger over fine lines on the image and then asked Finn to magnify it. "Here," he said, tapping on the monitor. "Call it a misfire, if you will. Perhaps fractions are truly beyond his ability to articulate."

Then ask Aubrey to stop.

"She no longer attempts to teach him those, Wick. But this explains his frustration and why he's so quick to anger when presented with them. Somehow, he understands that the answers are right there. He simply can't access that information."

Like, it's on the tip of his brain's tongue?

"Indeed. That's frustrating for anyone."

They spent the next hour poring over Hyrum's brain. Jo needed time to compare the data, but on the surface, she believed Hyrum's brain had mostly compensated for the damage, though there were spots that went, for lack of a better way to express it, haywire.

"Those are spots that can be repaired," Finn said. "Just those, nothing else. I know you're worried about his personality and what treatment might do—"

"It's more than that," Will said.

"His abilities?" Jo guessed. "I don't think he'd lose them."

"But we don't know, and he truly understands them to be gifts. Losing those would devastate him."

Ask him what he wants.

"Wick?"

Ask Hyrum what he wants to do. Explain the risks, but you need to let him decide what to do for himself. It's his life. His choice.

"That's not much different than giving Rhys a choice between an extra serving of vegetables and dessert. You know what he would choose, despite it not being the best thing for him."

And sometimes, dessert is the right answer. The difference is that Hyrum isn't a child.

"Regardless, this may be an instance where his guardians need to choose for him."

After work today, Hyrum is going out drinking with Drew. Like an adult. He has two jobs, like an adult. He's trusted to roam all of San Francisco, like an adult. Either he is, or he isn't. It's not your choice.

"All right," Will said. "Consider this. The typical eighteen-year-old male, an adult, presented with two options. One is a woman who will, without question, engage in coitus absent prophylactics, something he desperately wants to try. The other is a woman who will, with reservation, engage with a prophylactic. If he chooses the first woman, he's warned there will be a fifty percent chance he will contract an STD. If he chooses the second, that chance drops to less than one percent, but the condom will break. Which do you think he would choose?"

"What the hell, Will?" Jo sputtered.

"The point is that each situation carries a risk that no eighteen-year-old wants."

"Needs more data," Finn said. "Where's the second woman, cycle-wise?"

"And does this hypothetical eighteen-year-old understand treatment protocols for sexually transmitted disease?" Jo asked. "His actual risk is low—"

"Don't complicate this," Will said, sighing. "The point is that with that information, a young adult might roll the dice, so to speak, and engage with the first woman. Those are the surface odds for Hyrum. Fifty-fifty. His gains versus losses."

"It's a poor analogy," Jo said.

"But it illustrates my point."

You're the one complicating things, Will.

"How so?"

Hyrum only wants two things, really. To be good and to be smart. Start there. Just ask him. If he had to choose, would he want to be good, or would he want to be smart?

"He'll want both."

He might surprise you.

It's his choice, Will. Give him the information in terms he can understand, and then get out of his way.

~

Instead of sending me out with Drew and Hyrum, Will scooped me up with the proclamation that I was going to the park and then out for pizza somewhere other than where they would be. He was afraid I would inadvertently push Drew into telling Hyrum about the things he had discussed with his parents, and he wasn't ready to defend his position. He wanted to discuss it with Aubrey and Jax first, and he especially wanted to give Jo a chance to comb through everything.

I could have stayed home, you know. There are other people with opposable thumbs willing to cater to my needs.

"Aubrey and Jax have a previous engagement," Will said. "You'd have been disappointed come dinner time."

Who's watching baby Eli?

"The old King."

He can feed me.

"I can't believe you still call him that," Aisha snickered.

"Habit. I avoided his name for years, not wanting to influence Oz and Drew. In hindsight, I understand it was ridiculous. To the seventeen-year-old who made that decision, it seemed terribly wise."

To be fair, that's also what you heard growing up. Finn and Jo always referred to him as the old King when you were little.

"True. Though my mother referred to Finn's mother as 'the snowflake' but that didn't stick."

"Snowflake," Aisha repeated.

Will half-shrugged. "Charlie gets it from somewhere, you know. My grandmother was filled with joy and wonder, and quite a bit of...specialness."

Quirky. She was quirky.

"Indeed. Quirky, in a fun way."

"Nudist at heart?" Aisha asked, looking at Charlie as he chased his sister across the park grass.

"I have no idea. But she had the same earnest sincerity Charlie does, as well as his penchant for stating the obvious."

He'd caught up to Alex, poking her with a finger. Tag, you're it.

Giggling wildly, they turned on Rhys and began chasing him, and the air was thick with the mist of toddler joy.

"I can't believe he turns four next week," Aisha sighed. "And he starts pre-school. Where did my babies go?"

Have another one.

"Bite your tongue," she told me. "I turn fifty next year."

"Your age has little to do with the decision to have another child," Will said.

"You got snipped, mister."

"Which can be undone."

She scooted a few inches on the bench and turned toward him. "You want another baby?"

"I am not opposed to having another child. That said, if you don't, I'm not opposed to that, either."

"I really don't," she said. "It's not the number of kids, Will. But being pregnant again? No, thank you. My body may never recover from the damage those little shits inflicted on it."

Grow one in an incubator.

Will ignored me. "I'm content with the size of our family. If Jay has children, we can borrow them every now and then."

Jay was still nursing a broken heart. That wasn't happening any time soon.

Rhys ran around the merry-go-round, Alex close behind.

He kept circling it, round and round, until Charlie was dizzy and Alex was close enough to touch him. "Get on!" he shouted. "I'll push."

Charlie's gonna hurl.

Rhys pushed slowly enough that no one's stomach was at serious risk. There were high-pitched squeals of laughter, loud enough to draw other children out of the sandbox and off swings to join them.

"Jo's done with testing him now, right?" Aisha asked.

"She is. It will be weeks before she has data ready to share."

"But?"

"But there was no doubt. That little boy has a myriad of gifts, and I don't think he's scratched the surface. And while I refuse to isolate him because of it all, we need to nurture those gifts with extreme caution and care."

"No idea what else might be coming at us?"

"All we know is that he's suppressing some things, subconsciously or not."

Tell her about the dog.

"We've discussed a dog," Will said.

"Changing your mind about waiting until he's ten?" she asked.

He admitted to serious consideration of the idea, and then repeated the conversation we'd had. "Wick is right. I suspect Rhys will have issues that are quite similar to mine when it comes to relating to children his own age. Friendships might be difficult. A pet will afford him the unconditional love he will surely crave."

"He has siblings. You didn't have that."

He didn't think it would have been enough. "Having Wick helped keep me stable, I think. Being able to talk to him and play with him gave me a slice of childhood I otherwise would have missed. Siblings fight. Rhys is sensitive enough to absorb childish bickering and feel it as a personal attack."

And even though I'm still here, I'm not his. He'll feel that.

"Are you sure you'll be all right if we bring home a dog?" she asked me. "This won't happen if you feel like you have to avoid our apartment. We want you there."

A dog is not a pigeon. I'll be fine.

"I still don't want to grant this wish for his birthday," Will said. "He'll be stressed and excited because of the start of school, and we've already purchased his bicycle. If we decide to proceed, perhaps in a few weeks."

Give him an IOU. A birthday card with a puppy on it that promises he'll get one in three weeks.

"Three weeks," Will repeated, softly. Rhys was now running toward the swing set, and he laid across the seat on his stomach, slowly rocking back and forth, fingers digging in the dirt. "I'm not sure we can be that specific. When we're able to get one for him depends on the animal rescue, and typically there's a waiting list."

It needed to be young, Aisha said. She appreciated the idea of rescuing an older dog, but she wanted him to grow with it. His experience with the feral dogs in the simulator made her think he would trust a puppy more. They would deal with the issues a puppy brought. They had Charlie; she was used to cleaning up messes.

"I've never had a dog," Will said. "We'll need a trainer. Someone who can teach me to teach Rhys how to handle one, and who can handle the thousands of questions that little boy will ask."

Talk to Scotty.

"Scotty?"

He has a dog that Rhys likes. Start there. He might even know where you can find a puppy that needs a home.

"Sure. Consult with my wife's old boyfriend."

"You like Scott. Stop pretending it's an issue."

It's only an issue when he thinks about the bouncy parts.

"Let's get through his birthday and the start of school before we contemplate this again," Will said.

What happens if he starts sparking at school?

"He knows to close his fists to snuff them out."

If he notices. He doesn't always.

"Will?" Aisha scooted closer to him. "What *do* we do? We've been so focused on not isolating him and giving him the chance to have friends, but Wick's not wrong. He doesn't always realize when there are sparks and light at his fingertips."

It's a bunch of little kids. Somewhere in that mix is another George.

Will looked past the swings, where the kids had congregated. "Rhys will have what I did not. George's sister."

Vicat was on the far side of the playground, watching everyone within sprinting distance of Rhys. Other guards were hiding in plain sight, eyes on the children around Alex and Charlie, but Vicat's primary responsibility was the young prince who could, if he wanted, set the entire park on fire.

~

Just as Will finished paying for dinner, we felt the ground rumble. No one panicked—if it was an earthquake, it was a baby quake—though the chatter in the restaurant increased and a man in the booth behind us cracked, "See, I made the earth move for you."

Neither Alex nor Charlie noticed the sensation, but it made Rhys giggle.

That wasn't an earthquake.

"How so, Wick?"

It didn't feel like one. It was more...boomy. The earth didn't just shift. It vibrated.

He glanced at the people around us. No one else upset, and there was no damage, nothing falling off the walls or table. He was less certain about my assumption than I was, until his phone pinged. Then Aisha's phone pinged. She grabbed hers before he could; it was Jay, texting in bold letters WHERE ARE YOU?

Will lifted his phone from the table while she answered him. MARKET & MONTGOMERY, EXPLOSION, DAD & GEORGE HERE SOMEWHERE.

'Are you all right?' she texted back.

FINE BUT I CAN'T FIND THEM. IT'S A MESS. PLZ TELL ME YOU'RE NOT HERE.

Will was on his feet and had snatched up Alex and Charlie

before Aisha could hit send on her next text. We were two blocks away and could run there. Vicat raced in and grabbed Rhys, I jumped onto Will's shoulder, and we took off.

The smoke hit us half a block down; Will thrust the twins at another guard and ordered him to take them home if it was safe, and if not, hunker down in the lab. He told Rhys to go with the guard, run behind and keep up; he wasn't sure what we were heading into and thought Vicat might be needed.

He should have been more specific about the guard Rhys was supposed to follow.

~

Smoke was indistinguishable from dust; it hung in the air, stinging my eyes and nose, and Aisha covered her mouth with her hand. As we turned onto Market, the chaos thundered around us in frantic voices and agonized wailing. Half a block from the Market Street portal, the entire front of the Burger Bash restaurant and everything above it, the wall from ten feet all the way up, was fractured and crumbled, chunks of building materials and blackened pieces of artwork that had hung inside spilled onto the sidewalk and across the street. The tree that had already broken, the one Hyrum rescued a woman from when a branch fell, was completely down. Its crown was sprawled across the sidewalk with the trunk blocking all the bike lanes.

Sirens screamed from all directions, overhead and on the ground. A blanket of desperation layered over panicked voices calling out names, and Jay's voice rode the highest. He yelled for James and George, his voice insistent but not yet thinned by fear.

To the left. Jay's near the tree.

Will barked out his name, and Jay turned. His eyes went wide and he ran to us, confusion blurring with anger.

"You brought *Rhys* here? Are you fucking nuts?"

Rhys stood a few feet behind his parents and several feet behind Vicat.

Will snatched up his young son. "What did I tell you to do?"

"You said to run and keep up with my guard," he answered, puzzled by Will's ire. "I keeped up."

He couldn't ask Vicat to take him home. She scanned the detritus for her brother, focused on the voices around her, the sights and smells, anything that would point her to George. If she was aware of Rhys, it was peripherally.

"What happened?" Rhys asked.

"We don't know, sweetheart," Will said, his voice soft. "I don't want you to look. Lay your head on my shoulder and close your eyes, all right?"

Rhys scrunched his nose. "I can help. It's okay."

"It's not—"

"Rhys." Jay's hand went to his little brother's back. "You know what my dad's voice sounds like, right? Can you listen very hard? Listen for him, even if he's whispering?"

Rhys nodded and cocked his head. After a few seconds, he pointed to a decorative cement lamp post that was strewn across the ground in massive, broken chunks. "Over there. I hear Isaac's daddy telling Jay's daddy to wake up."

Will handed Rhys over to Aisha. "Stay here with Mommy," he ordered. He set me on her other shoulder and told me to keep an eye on things. "Don't get down unless you see something important. You could get trampled in the chaos."

"Is Isaac here, too?" Rhys asked Aisha. "Is he okay?"

Zed and Sophia were supposed to watch him tonight. He's probably with them.

He heard me. "Okay. He's playing with Marco. Why was Daddy mad? I did what he said."

Aisha heaved out a sigh and wrapped her arms around him a little tighter. "He meant for you to go with the guard taking Alex and Charlie home, sweetie. He's not mad. You're not in trouble."

"Okay." He squinted, trying to see what Will and Jay were doing. "I can help, Mommy. You need to put me down."

"You need to stay put."

"No." Eerily calm and evenly, he said, "Put me down. I can help."

Aisha twitched, but she didn't argue. He slid from her arms and took her hand as he led us toward the bulky end of the lamp post. It was cracked in half, the heaviest part of it resting on

George's pelvis. James was next to him, unconscious, pinned by his legs. One arm was bent at an unnatural angle, and his face was bloodied.

Jay was on his knees near James's head, bent over, pushing hair out of his eyes. He pleaded with his father to wake up, and George's voice rumbled, begging Will to save James. Vicat crept alongside them on her belly, sliding her hand under the space between them, checking for blood and taking a quick measurement of the distance between the post and the ground. After checking the space between James and George, she sat up, giving a slight shake of her head before grabbing her comm unit to call for an emergency tech with pressure equipment and a trauma kit.

One of the guards was there before she ended the call. He threaded a cable under the post, a tiny camera, examining the damage. There was a beat of quiet while we waited for him to say everything was fine, we just needed to roll it off them or find someone with giant muscles to pick it up. But, with a glance at the monitor in his hand, he told Vicat to call for additional medical personnel.

"Tell me," George grunted, focused on Will. "Come on. I know I'm a dead man. I can feel it."

"No." Jay shifted, his face directly over George's. "We'll get you out of this."

An EMT began strapping pressure cuffs onto both George and James, arms and legs, and a police officer ran another cable between them, measuring the pressure they suffered under. Will went to the far side of the post and looked at the images and pressure measurements, whispering to the EMTs.

"The truth, Emperor," George demanded. "I won't live through this. You can save James, though. Right? Please tell me you can save him."

Will went back to him, kneeling by his head. "They have to lift this to get James out," Will explained. "It has essentially crushed your lower torso and severed...everything. Once they lift it—"

"I die," George said. "Blood pressure tanks, I bleed out, and

I'll be dead in under a second. Two if I'm lucky. What a fucking way to go."

"No," Jay barked. "We are *not* letting this happen."

"Save your dad," George whispered to him. "Please. And listen to me. *Listen.*"

Jay began pleading with Will. "Find a way. You can do it. You can do damn near anything. Save them both."

"The time it would take to work this out would be the time your father needs in order to survive." Will reached out, a hand on the back of Jay's neck. "If we wait, they'll both die. Allow George these moments. This is a gift."

"Listen to him." Vicat choked on the words but was still defiant. "Start talking, George."

Jay gasped, fighting tears, but nodded.

"I love you," George said, voice already tiring. "I've always loved you. From the moment James allowed us to meet...and I'm sorry. For everything. You were the light in my life... My will names you as Isaac's legal guardian, but James—" his voice broke "—James is his other daddy. In both Whens. Please, take care of them."

Jay sniffed his promise through his tears.

"Vicat," George whispered, weakening. "I knew you'd want to stay with the Guard. Otherwise—"

"Shut up. I know that. I'm still his aunt. Goddamn you, George."

"Emperor." George's eyes fluttered. "I'm sorry. So damned sorry."

"I am aware," Will said.

George managed a chuckle. "Still with that stick up your ass. A friend in the end despite it all. Fuck you, you know it."

"I am aware of that, as well."

"Jesus..."

Rhys let go of Aisha's hand and moved close to Will. "Daddy, I can help. Let me help."

Don't get mad. He did...something. Aisha had no choice.

"Rhys, there's no time," Will whispered.

"But I can make time." He turned his face to the dust-choked sky, held his arms out from his sides, middle fingers curled to his palms, and then flicked them upward. Quiet snapped around us like a wet towel. The world stopped. Dust hung in the air. The EMT's stood in mid-step like statues. The only other people moving and aware were Jay, Vicat, Will, and Aisha. No hearts were beating around us; I heard no jagged, terrified breaths, no tears of anguish.

"Dr. Brian is coming," Rhys announced calmly.

The screaming silence turned the footsteps coming toward us into drumbeats. Will stood and turned, not at all surprised to see Brian Massimo sprinting around the corner.

"I was almost here when I heard Rhys's voice in my head, urging me to hurry," he explained. "What the hell?"

"We have to help Isaac's daddy," Rhys said simply. "You can save him."

Will explained the situation as Mass absorbed the picture in front of him. He didn't ask why the rest of the world was frozen; he'd learned a long time ago that nothing was ever simple with Will's family.

Instead of telling Rhys it was impossible, he asked him how he thought it could be done.

"Daddy can jump him to your swimming pool," Rhys said. "I can make him frozen, and then when you're ready, you can save him. Okay?"

"I would need the exact coordinates," Will told Mass. "From here to the tank."

"Both of them," Jay said. "Two tanks."

Aisha wasn't sure how long Rhys could hold everything still. "He's just a little boy—"

"Time is stopped, Mommy," Rhys said. "It won't go again 'til I say so."

Will directed Mass to the portal on Market, just a few feet away. Once through, he could send someone with the coordinates; he would jump George first, and then James, and hope to hell that the post didn't settle once George was no longer under it.

This is freaking eerie.

"Understatement of the century." Will scooted on his knees to Rhys. "Is this hard? Don't hurt yourself."

Rhys stuck out his pointy finger on both hands and poked Will's cheeks until he was puckering. "It's okay, Daddy. It's not hard."

"Do you know how you're doing it?"

"Nope."

Will had a hundred questions spinning through his head, but Rod bolted from the portal, computer tablet in hand. He had the exact coordinates for two life support tanks two hundred years in the future; they expected George first, and Will needed to be prepared to wind up in the tank with him.

"Take a deep breath and then hold it before you jump," he told Will. "These are massive tanks, so there will be room. But you'll be under the gel, so try to not breathe."

He tapped the coordinates into his jump bracelet, told Vicat to head through the portal with Rod, and he would see her there.

"Make it quick, Bilbo," Aisha said. "It might be harder than he thinks."

He grabbed George's hand, tapped the bracelet, and was gone.

"One Mississippi, two Mississippi, three Mississippi," Rhys muttered. Before he got to four, Will was back, coated in orange surgical goo. He grabbed James by the foot, and in a blink was gone again.

"Okay. JayJay, you gotta come over here. I'm gonna start everything again."

Jay did as he was told. He got up and stood near Rhys, who again had his arms out, fingers curled over his palms. "No one's gonna remember they were here, okay?"

Before they answered, he flicked his fingers, and the world began to breathe again.

~

Aisha wasn't sure where to go. Once time restarted, the lamp post settled to the ground, and the EMTs went about their business as if nothing were missing. The police officer asked Jay if there was someone he was looking for, if we needed help, and once assured that all was fine and we'd been mistaken about friends in the area, he sighed and said, "Damndest thing. Near as we can tell, it was a buildup of natural gas under the building. Who uses gas these days? Never heard of it in my lifetime. This is old-movie kind of stuff. Go figure."

Or someone was cooking drugs in the burger joint.

My money is on the drugs.

He shrugged and wandered off to help someone else, far calmer than the situation called for.

"I have no idea if I should go through the portal or if I should take Rhys home," Aisha said to Jay, who was clearly going to run through the portal when no one was looking. "Both? Take him home, then—"

Will, hair wet, barefoot, and dressed in a borrowed set of Mass's professional pajamas, was suddenly there. He picked Rhys up and told him to hold on, grabbed Jay by the wrist, then Aisha, and answered her question for her. In the time it took to draw a breath, we were in the hallway by Mass's office door, bathed in blueish light that bounced off the brushed metal walls.

"How long?" Aisha asked before Will let go of them.

"Half an hour," he answered. "I wanted them both intubated and well under before bringing you here. Their hearts aren't beating yet. They're still...frozen."

Rhys flicked his fingers and then reached for Will. "They're unsticked now. Did we save them, Daddy?"

"I think so." Will hugged him, then leaned his head back to get a better look at Rhys. "How did you know about the tanks, cowboy? We've never discussed them."

Rhys pointed at Jay. "I saw them in his head." Before anyone could chastise him for snooping, he added, "I didn't mean to. He told Navi about getting a surgery and I was on his lap and I just see'd it."

Jay exhaled hard. "Damn. Rhys, do you understand what the surgery was?"

Rhys whispered, "You had to get your wiener fixed."

"Kind of. When I was your age, I was a girl—"

"Nuh-uh."

"I was—"

Rhys shook his head sharply. "Hyrum says people aren't always the same inside as they are outside and it's the inside that counts."

"Fuck, I love Hyrum," Jay murmured.

Rhys leaned away from Will and whispered to Jay, "He loves you, too, he telled that to me."

"Sweetheart, did you tell Hyrum about Jay's surgery?" Aisha asked.

"Nuh-uh. He doesn't want to see anyone's wiener so he pro'lly doesn't wanna talk about it either." He stretched to look over Will's shoulder. "Is Isaac's daddy in there? Is he okay now?"

"Isaac's father is in that room." Will pointed to the closest door. "And Jay's father is in the one next to it. They're going to be in there for a while, so you won't be able to see them until they're at home."

"Days and days?" Rhys asked.

"Probably."

"Where's Isaac going to sleep?"

Aisha reached for him and then passed me over to Will. "Isaac will sleep in your room until his daddy is ready to come home, all right?" When Jay opened his mouth to protest—he could move back into his apartment, Isaac was his responsibility—she wagged her pointy finger at him. "I love that little boy, Jay. He's welcome in our home for as long as it takes, and he'll need to be surrounded by people who care about him."

"But George—"

"Was truthful," Will said. "We've become friends, of a sort. He won't mind if his son stays with us."

"You need to tell him where Isaac is, Daddy," Rhys said. "So he doesn't worry."

"I'll find a way," he promised.

Just stick your arm in the tank and plant it in his head.

"Stay as long as you need," Aisha said to Jay and Will. "I'll get Isaac from Zed's."

Rhys wanted to know about the cats. There were three waiting at home, probably hungry, and they'd be lonely, too. Will didn't want to bring them over; he wasn't sure how well they would fare if taken from their home, but he promised Rhys someone would see to them several times a day.

Once she was through the portal, Will led Jay into the surgical suite where James floated in the tank. He was surrounded by orange surgical gel, thousands of nanobots scurrying over his skin, and he twinkled under the bright lights. There was a medical technician seated near the head of the tank, and she glanced up when she heard the door open.

"Heart started a minute ago," she said. "Everything looks good. Slight delay in starting the procedure but progressing as usual now."

"What caused the delay?" Jay asked.

"He was frozen in time," Will reminded him. "They were able to intubate and then inject the nano-serum, but once in his body, they froze as well."

"Bit of a traffic jam at the insertion point," the tech said, pointing to a monitor over the tank. "It resolved quickly."

James's injuries were, Will said, significant though not life-threatening. His legs had been crushed. His left arm badly broken. There was minor internal bleeding and a ruptured organ or two. He needed to stay in the tank for five to seven days, and this time Will didn't think Mass had fudged on the estimate. It would be a week, and he would require physical therapy once the surgery was done.

"Why? I thought the way things were done here, it would be fine."

"You endured significant pain following your surgery," Will reminded him. "His knee and hip joints are being rebuilt. He'll be weak."

Before we went in to see George, Will warned him that he was worse off than James; even his face was bruised. Vicat was already there with her toes at the blue line, back ramrod straight, hands clasped behind her, and she didn't budge when she heard the door slide open.

There was a surgical sheet covering most of the front of the tank, hiding the worst of George's injuries.

"I wasn't sure if Rhys needed to be in here to restart things," Will explained. "I didn't want him to see how badly George is injured."

"Or you, for that matter," Vicat said. "It's brutal. I'm not sure how he didn't bleed to death, even with Rhys freezing him."

"Nanoplugs," the tech at George's head said. "Frozen or not, the second he was in the tank, they formed a film that prevented the worst from happening and had half an hour to cover the tips of blood vessels before his heart started beating again."

"How bad?" Jay asked.

The tech looked to Will first. "He was basically torn in half. The only thing holding his lower half onto his upper half was a crushed spine and a few ligaments."

It would take, Mass had told Will before we got there, several weeks to repair George's body. Because of his own schedule, cases here and there, this would be a linear time hop. If it took a month, that meant George would not return home until a month had passed.

"Their jobs—" Jay blurted.

Will nodded. "I'll take care of it."

Vicat finally moved. She took a step back and turned to Will, folding her arms at her stomach. "I need—"

"Consider yourself on leave for the duration," Will said. "I'll handle that, as well."

"Rhys begins school soon. He'll need his guard on hand, and frankly, I don't trust anyone else to be as careful with him. George told me about the things he did to you, Emperor. He also worried that Rhys would suffer from someone just like him. His other guards won't understand."

With that, Will let out a deep breath. "I'm no longer certain he'll enter preschool this year."

"No, Will. He'll be crushed," Jay said.

"I am aware," Will said, looking at George.

Zed needs to finish building the castle and open his school. Not just for Rhys, but all the kids. Because Rhys might just be the beginning.

~

"Homeschooling." Aubrey made the declaration while Rhys, Isaac, and Marco rolled back and forth on her living room floor. There was a purpose to their action, a winner would be declared, but after five minutes, I was still unsure what the point was or how victory would be decided. "There's no hard and fast rule about the starting age for preschool, and no reason we can't begin here instead of sending him into the public school system."

"Between the four us, we have the bases covered," Aisha said. "Rhys and Isaac already read far beyond the average four-year-old. Marco lags behind them a bit, but he's still ahead for his age. They're at least a year ahead of anything they would learn in a formal setting."

Will's concerns weren't about how well they could be taught at home. He worried that they would feel slighted and worried more about losing the social aspects of school.

Aubrey held firm. "Half the children in San Francisco are homeschooled through grade six, and there are social groups specifically tailored to their needs. The boys will get over the disappointment of not going to school once they see how much fun we'll make it for them."

"Zed and Sophia might not want Marco to stay home," Jax said.

"What won't I want?" Zed asked from the kitchen.

"If we homeschool all the kids," Jax said.

Zed came into the living room carrying Jonathan and a baby bottle. "Yeah, sure, it would be awful to send Marco upstairs to Grandma's instead of having to get up early and go halfway across town for a freaking total of four hours a day. Homeschooling will make my life a lot easier if it's really what you want to do."

"How disappointed will he be?" Will asked.

"Don't know. Don't care. He'll get over it."

Ask them. Stop assuming and ask them.

"This isn't a choice to be given, Wick," Will said. "The issues are complex—"

I didn't care. I pounced from the coffee table to the middle of the mayhem and landed near Rhys.

Dude, do you want to have school here at home with Marco and Isaac, or go to preschool where no one but you can read big books like Harry Potter? With Aubrey as your teacher?

"We can do school here?" He sat up and looked at Will. "Really?"

"We're discussing it."

"Can Isaac do school with us?"

"Until his father comes home, yes."

"Can we have a classroom like on TV? With desks and tablets on them and a big board that Aunt Aubrey writes on?"

There was plenty of space to create one, Aubrey pointed out. They could turn the old staff kitchen into a classroom, and the filled bookcases Will had stored there could be lined along the back wall. It was only a matter of getting some appropriately sized tables and chairs, an interactive monitor, tablets, and a copy of the state-approved multi-grade curriculum.

"I'm still a licensed teacher," she reminded Will. "I'm damned good at what I do. Jax never let his license lapse and misses teaching. This is doable."

"Drew has a valid license," Aisha pointed out. "I could brush up on teaching math to children, and I know of a dozen professors who would proctor any testing required by the state."

Will reminded her of Rhys's excitement over attending school with others his own age. He needed friends and needed to learn to deal with others.

"And that's what the social groups are for," Aubrey said. "We'll have trips to the museums, the science center, playgroups in the park—"

"Daddy, please?" Rhys stepped over Isaac and put his hands on Will's knees. "I like it when I get to sit with Hyrum when Aunt Aubrey teaches him stuff. Last week was rhyming words. It was fun."

"What about meeting new kids?" Will asked him.

Rhys held a hand up, sparks dancing at his fingertips. "What if they see? I don't know how to stop it sometimes. Marco and Isaac already know but they don't care. Other kids might make fun of me or be mean to me. I get tummy aches when I think about it." He leaned closer and whispered, "I don't want to wear gloves, Daddy."

He grasps why this is necessary, Will.

He'll make friends when it's time.

He still wasn't convinced, not until Aisha leaned against him and said, "Bilbo, do we really want him discovering a new gift during naptime at school? You saw what he did today. No one saw that coming."

It matters more to you than it does to him. You want him to have the childhood you didn't, but dude, it's not possible.

"Wick—"

He openly understands me now, Will. Did you notice that? I don't think he has yet. He can root around in someone's head. What if he doesn't realize when he's hearing someone's private thoughts?

"He has control."

He's four. He doesn't. And what if there's a George in his future? A more ruthless George. The George that finishes what he couldn't. Even George worried about that.

"Perhaps, but—"

The boy at the bottom of the pool, Will.

Aisha patted Will's knee. "Listen to the cat, Bilbo. Whatever he's telling you, he's usually right."

He sighed and then looked to Zed. "Get that castle finished. These kids? They may be the first graduating class of Blackshear Academy."

~

They lingered in the doorway of the children's bedroom, listening to soft sounds of sleep, resisting the urge to pick Rhys up from where he slept on an air mattress with Isaac to place him in his own bed. Isaac had woken up crying; Rhys wanted to comfort him. Charlie's legs jutted through the slats of his crib, and Alex had turned around on the mattress, her feet on her pillow.

"Time for real beds," Aisha whispered.

"So we keep telling ourselves, yet neither of us has done anything about it."

They didn't want to. They wanted their babies but instead had full-fledged toddlers.

She tugged him away from the door and led him into the living room, not letting his hand go until they were cuddled together on the sofa. He was still uncertain, still wanted to send Rhys to school, and the conflict was drawn in tight lines at the corners of his mouth and his eyes. Aisha let him wallow in the feeling; nothing she said would change it, and he was entitled to want for Rhys what he hadn't had.

"Every parent wants more for their children," she'd said earlier. "His life will be better, Will. He won't be isolated. We'll make sure of it."

It wasn't just the isolation. It was the overwhelming sense of being Other, something different, something others were afraid of once they discovered what he could do.

He acknowledged, though, that by allowing him to stay home and to be educated by his aunt that he would never be the little boy wrapped in plastic at the bottom of a swimming pool, using what few breaths he had left crying out for his mother.

Rhys would not suffer at the hands of another George.

They sat in silence until Jay came home. Vicat was staying there for the duration; she would keep watch over her brother, the same way Will and Aisha had kept watch over Jay. She waged her own internal battle, the regret of years lost that could have been spent with him, and she wondered out loud if their parents should know that he was there and so profoundly injured. There was no guarantee that he would survive the overall shock once removed from the tank, and she knew her aunt had made sure they were aware he was alive and lived part-time in his birth When.

She was far less certain that they knew she'd reunited with the brother who had been told she was dead and that he was responsible.

"I might do it just to see if one of them drops from the heart attack they deserve when they realize who I am," she told Jay.

"Yeah, she's not leaving the hospital," Jay said. "Mass set up a bed for her in the lounge attached to his office. But she's worried about Rhys. I think she feels like she's leaving him to the wolves by not being here."

"There are other guards," Aisha said. "How's your dad?"

Mass assured Jay that James was already progressing nicely and had then practically shoved him through the portal. If anything went wrong, he would send word. "He knows he can't do anything about Vicat but doesn't really want me there all the time. And there's Isaac. I promised I would watch him."

"Isaac is fine," Will said.

"Does he know?"

"He is aware that George and James were injured and needed to return home to recover. He does not, however, realize how badly they were hurt. As far as he's concerned, he's staying here to play with Rhys and be with you while his parents enjoy their recovery."

"He has nightmares every now and then," Jay said. "I—"

Aisha knew about his nightmares and promised Jay that if he had one, he would either crawl into bed with him, or he would wake Rhys up. If that happened, Wick would get someone.

"I do know a thing or two about caring for little boys," she reminded him.

"I know. He's just so...fragile. I know that's why George named me as his guardian. Isaac feels broken so much of the time, and Dad would eventually fall back into old habits."

Isaac did not need to live with someone whose bedroom had a revolving door. Jay knew that; he didn't want that for his little brother. If it meant stepping up and raising him, he was ready to do that.

Aisha wanted to know why Jay had been there on Market Street, and if he had been there when the building exploded.

"I was meeting them for dinner," he answered. "I was late. Like five fucking minutes late, so they waited outside for me. If I had gotten there on time...Jesus."

"You might have been inside, seated near the windows, which took the brunt of the explosion," Will said. "You might all be dead."

"Lots of might haves," Jay sighed. "But no, I don't blame myself. I'm just damned grateful that Rhys discovered that particular gift when we needed it. George had no time left, did he?"

"Literally only seconds," Will said.

"To think that just a few years ago, we would have let him die."

"You would not have," Will said. "No matter what he did and said throughout your life, you would have done whatever you could have to help him."

"I just wish I'd understood better when I was younger. George wasn't deliberately mean. He was terrified."

"But you did grasp that." Will reminded him of his post-surgical musings. Late one night, in pain and unable to sleep, he'd sleepily told Will that George was scared all the time, from the moment he woke up until he closed his eyes at night. "You knew it, but there wasn't anything you could have done about it. For that matter, had I known when George and I were children, I couldn't have done anything, either."

"Yeah, but I keep thinking if I had known it when I was little, and known how much he loved me, it would have made a difference, you know? I see how he is with Isaac. He's gentle and affectionate, and sometimes I catch glimpses of him being that way with me. He wasn't a dick twenty-four hours a day."

"He's less of one now," Aisha said, "but don't diminish the damage he did."

"I don't. Hell, he won't let me. He admits what an asshole he can be. Wait, what about the cats? Was anyone able to go over to feed them?"

The cats were downstairs in Eli's apartment. Will had not wanted to move them, concerned for their comfort and stress, but upon hearing that Isaac had pets that functioned as his anchor, Eli declared they would stay with him, where the little boy could visit and play with them however many times a day he needed. The cat flap by the door was secured to keep them inside, and I was banned from entering, lest I upset them. He sent his administrative assistant to buy food and fresh litter and declared he was working from home for the duration.

"If Isaac needs to go forward for a bit, we'll take him," Will said.

"Yeah, I don't think it's an issue. Isaac doesn't get sick, not like that. He only gets sick when it's time for George to go back for a while. He prefers living here, in this When."

Here, Isaac had his big brother. He also had Rhys, whom Jay was certain was his only friend.

"No little brothers and sisters and cousins running around George's apartment," Jay said. "When they go forward, Isaac is lonely. When they stay here, I see him, I bring him over to play. He'd stay here forever if he could."

Rhys would like that, too.

He has a friend, Will. That's what you wanted for him the most, right?

"I was hoping for friends that weren't family," Will said. "Isaac is, through Jay."

"Well," Jay snorted. "I'm not really related to him. He is George's clone, after all. It's not like he and Dad managed to figure out a way to reproduce."

Your best friend is your great, great grandfather. Family. So maybe Rhys never has a George. Maybe he already has a Jax.

"Indeed," Will said softly.

He's going to be all right.

"I know."

And maybe Jo will compile all that data and figure out what other gifts he might have, so you can be prepared for it.

"I don't think it works that way," Will said. "All she can do is see what parts of his brain activate when he does things, and predict future activities based on those patterns."

Too bad. I was hoping for a warning when he figures out how to levitate.

"Wick."

That would make Jax wet himself. Who doesn't want to see that happen?

"That would defy physics."

And stopping time doesn't? Face it, Will, your kids might redefine the whole thing and change how we understand the universe.

I might have been wrong, but at least now he was thinking about something other than Rhys not going to school and missing out on forming social groups.

No, now he could worry that his kids might fly off the balcony without the aid of a jetpack.

You're welcome.

~

The things Jo most wanted Will to see were side-by-side-by-side comparisons of his brain, Drew's brain, and Rhys's brain. She had tracked specific sections of each, over-laid one on top of the other, and had re-sized each image to scale so that their brains were the same size, lobes aligning as closely as she could get them.

There were hundreds of pictures to look at, but the most prominent ones were taken during conversations with me.

"Right here." She used a laser pointer to track a specific line she wanted him to see and warned me to not attack the monitor. "This is Drew. There's a line running from his transponder that goes right to the language center of his brain. Neither you nor Rhys has that."

"As previously noted," Will said.

"You have an affinity for languages," she said, not asking. "You've always been able to at least discern intent, if not what others are saying."

"To a degree," he said. "My understanding follows a considerable amount of study, but you wouldn't want me to attempt to speak with any degree of eloquence."

I've heard you speak German. Totally not eloquent.

His brain and Rhys's were active in the same areas, and she suspected he would have the same aptitude to pick a language apart and learn it well enough to get by. "My gut says that if not for your resistance to your abilities, you might have a wider range of understanding. This isn't simply grasping the language." She circled other spots in their brains. "This area highlights when you're searching someone else's mind. It's much like watching a computer-generated animation of data exchange. Drew doesn't have this, and neither does Hyrum."

"Then, it's genetic."

She didn't know if it was genetics or chance. No one else in the family had that gift; Will was the first. "It could simply be an evolution of sorts, building on Aubrey's empathy. It would help if I knew more about baby Eli and his siblings."

"I will inquire when I visit his parents."

She had one more for him to see, imaging obtained while Rhys was sitting on Hyrum's lap, half asleep, waiting for the next test to begin. While relaxed but fighting slumber, his brain was lit, and there were few quiet spots.

"Does he resist bedtime?" she asked. "And naps?"

"No more than the average four-year-old."

He's scared a lot when he's alone in the dark. After Charlie and Alex are asleep, he fidgets and tosses and turns.

Will thought he simply needed a later bedtime and his own room.

Maybe. But maybe he can't get his brain to shut up. You were like that sometimes. You couldn't sleep because of all the things spinning in your head, and then when you grew up?

"I could barely sleep at all," he said with a sigh.

"What fixed it?" Jo asked.

With a snort, he answered, "Sex."

"Oh. Well, that won't work for a few more years."

It wasn't the sex. It was Aisha. That connection you couldn't have with anyone else. You know what you have to do, Will. And do it before he really does levitate right off the balcony.

~

Rhys turned four with all the fanfare that stepping out of toddlerdom and into boyhood deserves. There was chocolate cake and ice cream, balloons and streamers and noisy things that made the kids all giggle and had Jax reaching for the scotch. He played with Isaac, Marco, and his little brother and sister most of the day, and after he'd been presented with his shiny new blue bicycle, he solemnly passed along his trike to Charlie and Alex with the reminder that they had to share. At least, he added in a loud whisper intended to be overheard, until Mommy got fed up and bought a second one.

No one floated away during his day-long party, and no stray sparks set anything on fire.

During a lull, when the toddlers were napping and the older boys were hanging on every word of a story Hyrum read to them, Will slipped away for an hour. He would only say that he had an errand to run, which wouldn't have raised an eyebrow until Aisha told him to play nice. After that, Jax wanted to know, but she refused to say anything.

"Later, after the kids are in bed for the night."

Bed turned out to be a blanket fort in the living room, with Hyrum teasing them with a flashlight. There was also scotch to be sipped on the balcony; Hyrum promised to watch them and not scare anyone too much, and then warned them against getting drunk. No one likes a hangover when excited kids get up at six in the morning.

I sat on Will's lap, wanting to see Jax's face when Will explained why he'd left his own son's birthday celebration. I'd hoped to see confusion and then a bit of upset, but he dropped my hopes over the side of the balcony like pigeons torturing a cat. Up, over, and then *splat*.

Sometimes, you people are too reasonable.

Will then waited a week, long enough for the rush of having a big-boy bike and officially no longer being a toddler had worn off. On a warm afternoon, he and Aisha took Rhys to the bakery on Union Square with the promise of a donut and chocolate milk, and they waited in anxious quiet until Scotty came up the steps with Strider by his side and a puppy in his arms.

Rhys squealed when he spotted them, and jumped up, wiping chocolate from his face with his arm. "Strider had a puppy! I thought he was a boy!"

Scotty set the wiggling ball of fur down carefully and let the leash out enough that he could sniff Rhys's feet and knees. "Strider *is* a boy," he said. "He's also a daddy, and this is one of his sons."

"What's his name?" Rhys sat down to allow the puppy to crawl onto his lap. "He's soft."

"He doesn't have a name yet."

"Everyone needs a name."

Will crouched next to Rhys. "Perhaps you could think of one."

Rhys grunted. "Dogs and cats come with names. They have to tell you."

"So far, he hasn't said a word," Scotty chuckled.

"Wick?" Rhys asked. "Can he tell you?"

The puppy wasn't going to tell me a thing. I rubbed against Strider's leg and asked him if he knew what his son wanted to be called.

Strider pushed his nose against the puppy's backside and let loose a gentle woof.

Thor. His name is Thor.

"Thor," Rhys repeated. "That's a nice name. I like that."

"God of lightning," Will said softly.

They led Rhys and the puppy back to the table, but he wanted to stay on the ground with Thor, forgetting about the chocolate milk and half-eaten donut. Rhys paid no attention to the adults and their discussion about puppy food and Thor's training. Instead, he collected puppy kisses and giggled loudly.

I'm surprised you answered me. I wasn't sure we could communicate.

Strider grunted, with no clear answer.

Does Thor speak yet? Can he understand me, too?

He was a baby; he might come to understand me someday, but for now, his brain was occupied with the little boy who already loved him.

Do you know what's happening? Did they tell you he would go live with Rhys?

Strider understood. All his puppies moved away when it was time. If he showed any hesitation about the potential forever home his litters were headed for, Scotty would pick the puppy up, wish his friends well, and take Thor home. But Strider could already tell, Rhys was meant for this boy.

What came next was what Strider enjoyed the most, and he'd looked forward to it all morning.

"Rhys," Will said, touching his shoulder to get his attention. "Do you think he likes you?"

"He's the best! I hope he likes me. He's too little to eat me, too."

"He needs a good home," Scotty said. "He doesn't have a little boy of his own yet, and I think that's what he wants more than anything."

Rhys looked up at Will and Aisha with wide eyes. "I'm a little boy."

"Really?" Will teased. "I thought you were a big boy now."

"No, I'm not. I'm little. I'm puppy-sized."

Aisha nudged Will. "Stop teasing him."

Will slid from the chair and crouched next to Rhys. "Puppies are a lot of work. They have to be fed and brushed and need to be taken for walks. Every day. Someone has to pick up their poop, and they don't use a litter box."

"That's why puppies need little boys," Rhys said, as if Will were missing the obvious.

"Wick? Are you sure?" Aisha asked.

I wiggled onto Rhys's lap and got nose to nose with Thor. I wasn't thrilled with his puppy breath and was especially unhappy with the tongue that lapped up the side of my head, but Rhys was overjoyed, and I felt the calm that settled and wrapped around him.

I can train a puppy.

Hell, I can make this work for me. He can be my noble steed and learn to carry me around. This could be fun.

Will tucked his hand under Rhys's chin and tilted his head a touch. "You are Thor's little boy, Rhys. He clearly needs you. There will be rules about keeping your toys off the floor and helping to care for him, but I think you two belong together."

"You mean it? You promise? I'm not ten."

"I promise."

"He won't eat Wick?"

"Wick can take care of himself." Will leaned close and whispered, "He swore to me that this was all right. Wick wants you to have a puppy as much as you want one, and he was the one who made me understand you shouldn't wait until you're ten. This is truly his gift to you."

Whispering back, Rhys asked, "Wick? For real?"

"He knows you'll love Thor as much as he loves you. And I wanted you to have the kind of friend Wick was to me when I was your age."

While he and Rhys continued to whisper to each other, Scotty gave Aisha a list of the foods Thor was used to, his walk schedule, and medical information. He slipped off when Rhys burst into tears, burying his face against his new best friend, and Strider trotted beside him, not looking back.

He's okay, I told Thor, hoping he would understand. *He's crying because he's happy. He's never been this happy. You got yourself the best boy ever.*

He must have agreed because he wet himself with joy.

Right on Will's foot.

Good boy.

"Disney wants the Wastelands project."

Oz was half out of breath, having run from a meeting in her Ozoo Enterprises office to Drew's personal workshop on the other side of the complex. He was crouched near his desk, trying to reach a wayward cable that had slid between it and the wall, his tongue half out from the effort stretching his arm required.

His forehead slammed into the edge of the desktop when she tossed her bag onto the desk.

Smooth move, dude.

"Disney," he repeated. "Your meeting was with *Disney?* Holy hell, Ozzy!"

Aren't there already giant mice in the Wastelands?

He ignored me.

"It was one hell of an offer, too." She dug into her bag and pulled out a thick red folder. "We have to run it by the board, but they'd be insane to not jump on it. This offer was everything we hoped for, and a few years earlier than expected."

Drew flipped open to the front page of the offer and let out a low whistle. "Damn. They have a hard-on for it. They do know it's not finished, right?"

"It's operational, doing better than breaking even, and they're keenly aware that we're sharing a pool of customers. It hasn't been quite the tourist triangle between Vegas and Disneyland I'd hoped for, but there's a definite path being worn between them and us. As far as Vegas? They could open that triangle." She reached over and flipped a few pages for him. "This is what they want to do. They'd maintain what we've already built, and then quadruple the size of the surrounding amusement venue. They already have ideas for several venues within the park, complete with mockups."

"Expanded old west," Drew muttered. "Americana. Woodstock. The early space race." He looked up. "They've taken your idea of history as fun and really run with it."

"The fun *and* the ugly bits. And they have the money to do it. Expansion, several more resort hotels, and shuttles that will run between the parks—ours and theirs. People can spend the night in a resort hotel there, hop on a shuttle in the morning, and spend the day here. They can go back and forth—they have the Interstate corridor to play with and can run shuttles twenty-four hours a day."

"But do you want to sell?" he asked. "This was your idea, and you've done all the work to build its foundation. You're nearly five years into it. Do you want to give it up?"

She flipped back to the first page. "I'd still be on the board. And there's Eli. He's crawling and getting into everything, and I don't want to miss any more of it than I have to. Expansion requires so much more time and effort, and I'm not sure I have enough personal reserves for that."

He set the folder on the desk. "You'd go a little bit nuts without work, Oz."

"I didn't say I'd stop working. Just not *this*. Dad has a million things for me to get to, and I'd free Will's schedule up a bit."

"I didn't mean that the way it sounded. I just meant—"

"I know what you meant, Drew. But this offer...it's more than selling the park. It means I damn well did what I set out to do. It's a success. It *works*. People are visiting and spending money, so much that it hit Disney's radar. If the board approves the sale?"

"You could do anything you wanted."

She snickered. "Ozoo's capital would skyrocket. It's company money, Drew. We've paid out all the initial investors.

This is billions that go right into Ozoo's coffers. The enhanced shuttle program you've been thinking about? Selling off the Wastelands could underwrite that. Daily shuttles to Elysium instead of weekly. That means commuter traffic. Businesses. Residents."

"*If* the board approves."

The board was Will, Jax, Drew, Finn, a few significant investors, and Anthony Meyers, who was close to reluctant retirement from military service. None of them would block the sale, and Oz knew it; they would vote it through without much discussion. Aside from the sale itself being important, their current focus for the company was aimed at Elysium, and Drew's upcoming trip to install a new satellite computer on the space station, along with his side project of testing a new spacesuit.

It's not the board you need to worry about. It's the lawyers. They have to say whether it's a good offer or one written to just look good.

"There may be some further negotiations," Oz admitted. "But my gut says we'll make the sale by the end of the year."

"In time for our fifth?"

"Wow. Our fifth. We need to celebrate. By the time the end of the year rolls around, we'll have had a baby, sold a major property, and you'll have gone to Elysium."

"Damn. Yeah. Huge year. And now I'm nauseated."

"Nervous?"

"So nervous. I mean, excited, but I still want to hork up my toenails. I can't believe this is happening so soon."

"People go to Elysium every week now," she reminded him. "They worked out the kinks months ago."

"I know. And people head for Mars all the time. And beyond."

People traveling beyond Mars was part of what Drew was doing on his trip to Elysium. His main task was the installation of a new computer that could run just a little warmer than the others, and he planned on testing out a new suit while he was at it. It was lighter than the standard-issue suit and allowed for more delicate work. If it worked as well as he hoped, they could bring new systems to Mars, which in turn would enable more ships to launch into deep space, with people in suits that were more comfortable and significantly more flexible.

Oz grabbed him by the waist and tugged him closer. "I'm nervous, too. None of those people are you."

"I don't have to go, Ozzy. I can send someone else."

"No, you can't. You'd be so disappointed."

"And I'd get over it."

"Childhood dream?" She shook her head. "No, you'd chew on that. And I want it for you. We'll just have to live with the nerves."

It's too late for anyone else. The suit only fits you.

"There's that, too," he said.

General Myers is about your size, though. Can he install stuff?

He would be a tight fit in Drew's slim nanosuit, and the helmet might not seal properly, which rendered his lack of installation skills a moot point. Still, he had the training for space travel and would be in the seat next to Drew on the shuttle ride there. Once on the station, he was in charge of Drew's security, controlling who was allowed near him and monitoring the communications system that would be open between Drew and Ozoo.

"He'll have access to a standard suit," Drew said to Oz. "Even if he could install the equipment, it wouldn't give us the data we need."

"Seriously not trying to get you to stay home." Oz wagged her pointy finger at me. "Stop trying to help. I knew a long time ago that this day was coming."

"We're not there yet. We dunk today if you want to watch me sink to the bottom of a very deep pool."

"Is that the royal we?" she asked, snickering.

"Myers," he said with a sigh. "We get to practice maneuvering in as weightless an environment as we can. It's just covering the bases, in case the gravitational engines on Elysium hiccup."

"And you're hoping they will."

He gave a light shrug. "That would be wrong of me, Ozzy. Right? Right."

"Dork."

The pod will be weightless, won't it?

"Essentially, but I'll be held to the floor anyway. That's a lot of what the dunk will simulate. Trying to walk with my feet weighed down and my body trying to float the hell away."

~

Standing side by side, Drew and General Myers looked as if they were from centuries separated by several other centuries. Drew's suit was form-fitting and seemed more appropriate to gymnastics than space exploration. The only parts that suggested he was wearing anything more than athletic wear were the joints for his helmet and the connections for his air supply harness and life sign indicators. Under it was the nanosuit he had developed, created from a base layer typically worn with an exoskeleton, part of the uniform worn by Pacifica's elite military members.

In between the nanosuit and spacesuit was a flexible chest and abdominal plate, molded to fit his torso, and it was filled with oxygen. Flat tubes were connected to it; if his external air supply was damaged, the nanobots in his base layer would seal everything off and create a nasal canula that would tuck behind his ears, cross his cheeks, and seat under his nose. This was the prototype for Hyrum's secondary air system: air-filled man boobs. AFMB, officially.

In comparison, General Myers' suit was clunky and added considerable girth to his otherwise slender frame. The boots gave him an additional two inches in height, and he towered over Drew.

"I look like I'm about to launch on an Apollo rocket," he grumbled, tugging at the band around his throat. "How the hell does your skimpy suit pressurize?"

"Layers," Drew said. "If I leave the safety of the station or shuttle, the base layer activates and provides all the pressure I need."

Myers' twirled his pointy finger, indicating for Drew to turn around. "Duration of air supply?" he asked, tapping at a polymer-alloy canister on Drew's back.

"Three hours external, an hour internal."

"Internal. How the hell?"

Drew nodded toward Hyrum, who was perched on a stool with a computer on a portable desk. "His idea. Long, thin air packets that nestle between the outer and inner suits. Tubing runs air under the base layer from a chest plate and will auto-connect with my nasal frenulum if it activates."

The general's eyes flicked toward Will, and then back to Drew's air canisters. "Any plans for this to become standard issue? And can it be outfitted with larger tanks?"

"That depends on NASA's needs and the King's willingness to spend the money," Will said. "But yes, it can be fitted with tanks triple in size. The suit you occupy is older technology. The suits assigned to those who work on the outside of Elysium are newer and fit individually. They're sufficient for current needs."

"Great, I really am in an old Apollo suit."

"The Apollo astronauts would have killed to have the suit you're in," Drew said.

He knew. His need for a functional suit was minimal, and the odds he would put one on while at the space station were practically nil. This was an exercise everyone assigned to Elysium was required to endure, and despite his grumbling, he was excited to be there.

Will set me on Hyrum's portable desk. "There will be splashing, Wick. You're far less likely to get wet here."

I thought they were going to sink.

He gestured to the dozen men and women sitting at the pool's edge. They were outfitted with breathing apparatuses, masks, and flippers, and would be in the water with Drew and the general. Will had diving gear of his own; he had no intention of going into the water with them, but if something went wrong, he would carry an extra tank of oxygen down.

The pool was built for dive training. There were staggered levels, from fifteen feet to sixty feet deep, but Drew wouldn't go any further than the twenty-foot level. His equipment would function at the pool's deepest level, but if something did go wrong, getting him—and more likely the general—out would be difficult. At twenty feet, they could peel the general's suit off, and it would require only one person to drag him up. Any deeper, and time became an issue.

"I hope they'll be okay," Hyrum whispered as Drew connected his helmet to his suit.

Zed once said that Drew was like a freaking fish. He's a strong swimmer. He'll be okay.

"Heart rate?" Will called out.

"Drew is sixty-two, and General Myers is eighty," Hyrum replied. "And it says blood oxygen is ninety-eight and ninety-nine."

Will pointed to the pool, and everyone put their masks on and slid in. Drew jumped, but Myers sat on the edge first and then slipped under.

"You've been quiet," Will said to Oz. "Are you all right?"

"Scattered brain today. But I'm not worried about him in there, at least not about his safety."

"Then about what?"

Oz leaned forward to look into the water. "His levels of frustration if he can't maneuver the way he hopes. I know this is just a lot of tying ropes onto rings and jumping through hoops, but if he doesn't do every little thing exactly right?"

"He'll be upset for a few minutes, and then he'll move on. Truly, my only concern today is whether Anthony can climb the ladder to get out or not. He's carrying a considerable amount more weight than Drew."

He's not a big dude.

"I didn't mean that, Wick. His suit is far heavier than Drew's."

"Does he know what Drew's base layer can do?" Oz asked.

Will nodded. "One of the few who do."

"Their heart rates are up a little," Hyrum said. "Drew's is ninety-three and the general is one hundred and ten."

"That's fine. I expect those to elevate as they move more."

"How high before I have to say stop?"

"Drew's heart rate can safely reach into the one-nineties. If the General's goes above one-fifty, let me know."

"How come Drew gets more beats?" Hyrum asked.

"Because he's young, and Anthony is not."

"That doesn't seem fair," Hyrum said. "Old people should get more beats on account of it takes them longer to do stuff."

"That would seem to be the fairer thing, but biology doesn't work that way," Will said.

Hyrum scrunched his nose. "That's blood and guts stuff. I'm glad Aubrey didn't make me learn too much about it."

She had tried. Hyrum was content to learn external anatomy and functions of some internal organs. He vehemently shook his head when offered a more in-depth view of the human machine, citing his lack of interest in becoming a doctor, and what was the point unless he wanted to be a doctor?

He understood basics about digestion and his stomach, and he could name the major internal organs and point their general location on himself, but he refused to consider that it was perfectly all right to view images or drawings of the inside of a body. Aubrey reminded him that he had cleaned a chicken by himself and was well acquainted with the blood and guts of a formerly living creature, but that wasn't the same.

"Those guts are tiny and make good food for the garden and the cat. People guts are gross."

She let it go. A large part of biology became the same as fractions; he was aware they existed, but he didn't want to hear anything about them.

"And yet," Will said, "you'll change the worst diaper without flinching."

Hyrum shrugged. "For babies. When you get really old I probably won't change yours."

"When I'm really old, so will you be, Hyrum."

"Well, then you won't change mine, either."

Oz sighed and gestured to the pool. "Focus. Drew's trying to thread string through tiny hoops. We're here to watch."

"If I weren't aware of the order of his exercises, I wouldn't be able to tell from here. This won't be a spectator event."

"Yes, but we need to pay attention so we can clap for him when he surfaces."

Did anyone bring cookies? He'll expect a cookie if he does well.

"Can I have a cookie?" Hyrum asked.

"There are no cookies." Will turned from the pool to see if Hyrum was upset by that. "Wick was teasing. But I think if all goes well, we should stop at the bakery on the way home for a celebratory treat."

Three years ago, Hyrum would have been upset. If someone mentions cookies, there should be cookies, and getting his hopes up wasn't fair. After all, he was being good, too, and that deserved a cookie. Now he considered it and shrugged. "If the babies look out the window and see us there, they'll be mad."

"No, they'll simply pester Aunt Aubrey to bring them outside, which she will either do or allow Rhys to call me with a delivery request for chocolate-frosted donuts."

Oz leaned forward a bit, trying to see what Drew was doing. "Dammit, now I want a donut. See what you started, Wick?"

I'm here to serve.

Will someone take me closer so that I can see, too? But promise you won't drop me in.

"You should learn to swim, Wick," Hyrum said. "Will's been teaching me. It's not hard."

I can swim. I choose not to.

"Who taught you to swim?"

Will. When he was five. I still have nightmares about it.

"Stop. You were in the water for fifteen seconds, and dropping you in was unintentional."

So you say. I think you wanted to see the kitty swim.

"I had not considered that you could. Even at five, I wouldn't have risked it."

Well, you found out that I can swim if I have to. Still, don't drop me.

Hyrum laughed at my misery. "Did he holler? Lazybones fell in the bathtub and boy did he holler."

"He had a few choice words for me."

And that was long before there was a Bad Word list.

Will kept me tucked close, one hand supporting me from underneath, the other pressing me close to his chest. I stretched my neck to see past the edge of the pool and tried to make sense of the watery blobs below. Drew's arms were moving, and he kept bending over, but there was no telling what it was he was doing.

"Simulation of small parts installation." Will stepped back from the edge of the pool and set me back on the table next to Hyrum. "There are cameras below if you'd like a better look."

He reached across the table and tapped at Hyrum's computer, and half the screen filled with two live feeds of the exercises happening in the pool. General Myers was, apparently, dancing, and Drew was passing small things through a small hoop, trying to get them to land in tiny boxes.

The general needs dance lessons. He's really bad.

"It's an exercise in movement, designed to test how well he can negotiate physical space without full gravity."

"He's dancing," Oz said.

"He was not given specific instructions regarding *how* to move. However, I think he's leaping."

Hyrum giggled. "Can I try that on our next swim lesson? I can hold my breath a long time now. I want to dance on the bottom of the pool."

The look on Will's face suggested 'knock yourself out,' but he bit back the sarcasm and told Hyrum he didn't need to wait for a swim lesson. He only needed to be sure there was someone with him because the number one pool rule was that no one was allowed to swim alone.

He refrained from mentioning that he swam alone often, typically at three in the morning when he was unable to sleep or when he wanted time in the pool without his children. Drew sometimes swam alone, too, but he always informed the desk guard that he would be in the pool, and they could keep an eye on him through the security cameras.

I did not mention that in case it upset Hyrum that he was held to the same rules as the children.

He was focused on his task at hand, monitoring Drew's and the general's vital signs as well as the amount of oxygen in their tanks. At the one-hour mark, he looked up and told Will that they only had five minutes of air left, and they should probably come out soon. "They have lots of heartbeats left and their blood thinks it has enough air inside, but if they run out in the tanks that might change."

On the right side of the screen, there was a red bar. Will told Hyrum to click on it, which would flash a light underwater. That was the signal to come out, and a few seconds after he clicked on it, a diver was guiding Anthony Myers to the surface, and Drew was right behind him. Myers had no difficulty hauling himself up the ladder, and Drew pushed himself up over the edge.

"Showoff," Myers muttered when his helmet was off. "I'd give a year's pay to be that young again."

"That could be arranged," Will said. "Well, truly, you would only gain twenty to thirty years, but it's possible."

"Don't tempt me, Emperor. If you take me home, I might not want to leave."

"That could be arranged, too."

"He might even get you your own jet pack," Drew said. "There's your retirement plans, General. Move two hundred years away and spend it playing with all the toys you ever wanted but just don't exist yet."

"Let's just get your scrawny ass to Elysium."

Did you see the way his jaw twitched? He wants to. And nothing is holding him here.

Will scooped me up but didn't say anything. If General Myers wanted to retire to the future, all he needed to do was ask.

I wondered if he would work up the nerve.

~

To justify the expense of sending the husband of Pacifica's crown princess into space, Jax spoke about the trip during an interview that was originally intended to cover the progress of integrating Florida, and to a lesser degree, Midlam, into Pacifica. The data points on that were brief and didn't really need his input. Shazia Van Hoff, former Queen and current Prime Minister of Midlam, had their government well in hand, and they had surpassed estimates in how long it would take to rebuild. His input amounted to, "Yes, going well, we're far ahead of the anticipated timeframe, Chicago is looking spiffy, go visit. Florida might take a bit longer because we scare the bejeezus out of them, and they're not quite ready to accept air cars and food that hasn't had the crap processed out of it."

Florida's Prime Minister was hamstrung by petulant old men not ready to allow equality into their lives, but Redmond Munson, head of the Church of Florida, kept poking them in that direction and was satisfied with the progress already made. Jax expressed an interest in incentivizing immigration to Florida, to expand its pool of intellectual resources, but so far, few shared his interest.

Drew's launch was a week away, and that was the thing the media focused on. Florida and Midlam would sort themselves out or not, but Andrew Blackshear heading for the space station that his work had turned from lost hope into a functioning reality was deemed newsworthy and something the people wanted to know about. The people themselves, Will thought, were less interested in the justifications for the trip than were the media, but Jax humored the reporter who sat with him in his city hall office, with the official throne and the display stand with his ill-fitting crown looming behind him.

"The computers on Elysium are largely Andrew's conception," Jax said. "His unique approach eliminated the overheating issues that initially ended the Elysium project, and his drone designs have made ongoing maintenance significantly easier. What he's doing now is installing a computer in a new satellite pod that runs just a little bit warmer, which will allow for an increase in the time human workers can spend in the pods."

"That's it? He's hooking up a computer?"

"That's a small part of it. He will also reconfigure several of the drones working in a tethered satellite to maximize their productivity while increasing throughput on the main computer system. He's testing a new suit design that may go into production if it works well, and given that it's his invention, we didn't see a reason why he shouldn't go. Someone has to. He could send someone else to do this, yes, but why would he? Who else knows the system and the suit better? The cost is the same, regardless."

"But he's the crown princess's husband. Why risk him?"

"Because he's not the crown prince, and he chooses to do this. Truthfully, he would go even if he were still the crown prince. Titles don't absolve us from risks, and don't absolve us from work."

"You want him to go."

Jax didn't hesitate when he answered, "No." He sucked in a deep breath and added, "I say that as his father-in-law, not his King. I would prefer he stay home, safe, playing with my grandson and irritating my daughter with his endless musings over the books he's recently read and the million ideas spinning in his brain. I would prefer to see him at the dinner table every night and prefer to watch as he and my daughter wash dishes and fling soap bubbles at each other. I would prefer he go to work, the same as he does every day, and then greet him at home in the evening. However...I was not consulted."

"You could forbid it."

"And that would be an abuse of power. Drew knows what he's doing, and he's trained well for this. If he hadn't, Oz would stand in his way."

"She would restrain him."

"Restrain? Hell, she would tie his ass to a chair, and then for good measure, staple him to it."

~

Hyrum had one final idea before Drew left for the launch pad. His entire trip would be monitored, with data and images streaming to the workspace near Will's office, and we would be able to hear him—so why not attach a camera to his suit so that we could see him, too?

"It can be stuck in a box thingy on your chest until you poke at it and let it go, and then it will be on a rope, pointed at you. Or you could point it around so we can see what you see."

It was a simple addition, a small harness often worn by air

bike racers, procured and clipped to the suit the night before he left.

Drew opted to not turn it on until he had reached the space station. He knew three levels of anxiety would be painted on his face in a lovely shade of pink and green, and he really didn't want video of him horking up his toenails to live online for the rest of forever. We settled for tuning into the official launch channel and waited at Ozoo, where a dozen monitors on the wall gave us a close-up view of Drew's experience, and we listened to audio of a monotone voice relating all the details of the future Prince Consort's inaugural trip into space.

"Someone needs to tell that talking drone that he has a name, and it isn't 'future Prince Consort,'" Oz grumbled after the fourth mention of the title that he might not even use. "Seriously. He'd hate that."

After a nod from Jax, Will pulled his phone out and tapped away. For the rest of the pre-launch coverage, Drew was referred to only as Prince Andrew, though at one point, the drone tacked on, "husband of our Crown Princess."

"The world knows that," Oz sighed. "Why else would you be covering this?"

"On account of Drew is important anyway," Hyrum answered. "Even if he was just Drew Blackshear, he's important to everyone."

Van Hoff, but you make a fair point.

"Huh?" Hyrum scrunched his nose. "What's a Van Hoff?"

Will replied before Oz could. "Andrew's given surname. He took Oz's when they married."

"Boys can do that?"

"Indeed."

"Why didn't you use Aisha's name then?"

Aisha laughed at the idea. "Sweetie, he would have been taking my ex-husband's name, and no one wanted that. And I sure as hell didn't want to keep it."

"James is nice, though. And Jay has his name."

Before Aisha could explain—which was good because she clearly didn't want to—the monitors clicked on and began streaming video of the media coverage, cameras pointed at a shuttle waiting for the final order to take off. It was a large shuttle, three times the size of an airbus, and was painted in Pacifica's royal colors. That was not because Drew was on board; the shuttles that headed weekly to Elysium were all painted red and blue, a reminder that no matter who traveled there or from which country, the space station belonged to Pacifica and we controlled its population.

Oz stood close to the center monitor, half holding her breath, half hoping someone would call the whole thing off. Aubrey and Jax watched from just behind her, though Oz was Aubrey's focal point, waiting for clues that she needed comforting.

Will and Aisha were off to the side, where Will had a good view of everything and a keyboard within reach. Finn and Jo stood near the center of the room where they could see the launch coverage as well as the other monitors displaying data coming directly from Drew, and Hyrum—as much as he wanted to watch the launch—bounced his way along a line of powered-down drones, resisting the urge to touch. He'd been in the room while Will and Drew worked on them but had only observed, and right now, he wanted to play with one.

He shoved his hands into his pockets to stop himself from touching anything.

"What's the ET on his spacewalk?" Finn asked.

"Nine tomorrow morning," Oz answered without looking at him. "Today is arrival and a tour of Elysium, and if he doesn't experience disorientation or start throwing up during the night, he'll take a hopper out, and he'll exit before it docks with the pod. It's a short walk but will hopefully be enough to collect information on the suit."

Will was not as happy about it as Drew. "It's an unnecessary exercise, scheduled only to suit his whims."

"It's a childhood dream," Oz said.

"And because of that, I did not object strenuously. But it's not necessary. The hopper could dock with the pod and save the wish-fulfillment for another time when we have additional data about the suit. I understand he feels this is the time to test that suit, but—"

"What if he never gets another shot at it?" Jax asked.

"He will."

Oz didn't like it any more than Will, but she still felt pressed to defend it. "Just because old man Drew did, doesn't mean he will."

"Old man Drew doesn't enjoy the venture," Finn snorted. "If he can send someone in his place, he does."

"Something happened?" Aubrey asked.

Finn hesitated. "It was work. It was never for fun. He was always heavily guarded and rarely alone." He pointed his hand at the monitor. "His visits were carefully choreographed, and that sucked the joy out of it."

"How come?" Hyrum bounded over from the drone line. "It's supposed to be fun."

"He was the former King of Midlam," Will said. "At the time of his first launch, he was the Prince Consort of Pacifica and considered far too valuable to lose."

"By whom?" Jax asked.

"The Queen."

That made Oz laugh. "I'm guessing he went later than my Drew. We probably had more kids, and she wasn't about to raise the little shits alone. There's no doubt who's in control in that marriage."

"Give it a few years," Jax said.

"Not a chance. She had a reason to be firm. There was a lot at stake. Drew and me? I think we'll be on more equal footing no matter what else happens."

Jax chuckled. He didn't believe that, and I don't think Aubrey did, either. She hid a smile behind her hand and refrained from reminding Oz how headstrong she could be compared to how easygoing Drew was. She also refrained from pointing out that Drew was where Finn inherited his ability to get lost in work, and at some point, she would need to grab the reins just to keep him focused.

For the moment, they agreed with her.

"Here we go," Will murmured when the shuttle engines fired up. There was a tight whine that bled through the speakers, and a few of the images jiggled as cameramen readied themselves to track the shuttle as it streaked through the sky.

The front end lifted first, hesitated, and in the time it took to blink, it rocketed upward. There was a streak of bright light in its wake and was gone within five seconds, leaving everyone in the room staring at shots of the empty sky, with only the trail pointing to where Drew was.

~

I knew before Oz opened the private video feed what Drew was going to say.

Amazing.

Elysium is amazing.

Everything here is amazing.

She sat on the sofa in their room with Eli perched on her lap—the baby, not the old king, because that would be several degrees of weird and uncomfortable—with their entertainment monitor set up to receive video sent over satellite. Drew had configured the feed before he left, reasoning that waiting to share the space station with her was not something he could stand, and besides, he wanted her to be the last thing he saw before falling asleep on a cold, hard, unfamiliar bed three hundred miles up and away.

It turned out that the bed was quite comfortable and heat-adaptable based on his own body temps, and the room he'd been assigned was cozy and warm. General Myers was across the wide corridor in a room that felt less cozy to Drew but was still nice enough for someone of the General's stature. Myers proclaimed it wonderful, far better than his tiny apartment at home with its gray walls and kitchen that had little more than a sink, a mini-fridge, and a stove that functioned no better than a hotplate.

Drew showed her snippets of the video he'd shot throughout the day—much of it she had already seen, while it streamed live to the workshop—but she humored him and shared his excitement. She didn't laugh when he gushed about the circular geometry of the station, yet how walking in the corridors it felt perfectly flat, and she pointedly did not remind him about the gravity engines and that from her vantage point he just might be hanging upside down in his room.

He'd seen most of the station, absent personal quarters and dining halls that were identical to the one in which he and the general had dinner. All the things they'd envisioned when pondering the possibilities of Elysium were in various stages of development, including a massive business and education sector. There were large gardens on each level where fruit and vegetables were grown. Within a year, two at most, families would live on the station, and businesses had the potential to thrive. Huge sections had been mapped out to house schools that ran from preschool through the early years of college. He'd spoken with men and women who had been on-site the first day Elysium went online and were ready to rotate home and some who were planning on a career there, waiting for permission to send for their spouses and children.

"The views, Oz," he breathed. "Remember when Will took us to that park in his When? It's like that, only better because it's real."

"I do remember where we spent our wedding night," she teased. "Did you get a room with a view?"

"Oh, hell, yes." He slid off the bed and went to the giant window, turning the camera so that she had a view of Earth from above, with all the swirling clouds and long swaths of blue and green that she'd seen in countless pictures. He reached out with his free hand and tapped on the window with his pointy finger and said, "You are right about here."

"Great, you just squished me. Can you really see landmarks from there?"

"Nah. I can see a lot of light pollution, though. It's weirdly pretty, especially in spots where the lights look like a fine net stretched across the continent."

Turn the camera back around and bend over. Maybe we can see Uranus.

"Oh my god, Wick," Drew snorted.

He turned the camera around but didn't bend over. "Someday, Ozzy. Seriously, someday we're coming here together."

Her expression—it sounds like a business trip and not a vacation—came and went quickly. She humored him and agreed, when Eli was older, it would be nice to take him someplace unique, even though we all knew the first place Drew would take him was Disneyland. He'd been talking about that since Eli was born, waiting for the day when he was tall enough for the kiddie rides and old enough to not be frightened by giant, walking rodents and other inhuman creatures come to life.

They talked while Oz fed Eli and then put him to bed, talked while I left to get some food, and were still talking when I came back half an hour later.

Morning comes awfully early.

Drew sighed. "I know, Wick. I should at least try to get some sleep. So should you, Oz."

"The bed's going to be awfully cold without you there."

Oh, barf. Tell her if she needs a heater, I'm happy to lay across her face.

"Yeah, suck the romance out of it," he grumbled.

Happy to help. Say goodnight. Go to bed.

"Goodnight. Go to bed."

See, that wasn't so hard.

For some reason, they didn't appreciate my help.

~

Cameras followed Drew from the moment he stepped from his quarters, clad in the nanosuit that would function as a base layer for his space gear. There was a nonstop stream of video available to the world, and it began with him refusing to eat breakfast. If he'd had gills, they would have been a lovely shade of green and fluttering as he tried to not hyperventilate. Instead of eating, he sat at a cafeteria table and watched Anthony Myers destroy a meal of fried eggs, potatoes, bacon, and toast.

"You should eat," the general told him.

"Not hungry." He probably was hungry but didn't want to throw up in the hopper. Or worse, inside his helmet while he floated around in outer space. He sipped at a glass of water because the general insisted on that much, and then carefully slid it away when the hopper pilot walked up to them.

The pilot stood at attention and greeted them formally and didn't move until Myers pointed at a chair and said, "Sit down, Major Gaff. We're at ease until the Prince steps into the hopper."

"Yes, sir." He turned to Drew. "I understand this is your inaugural visit to Elysium?"

Drew nodded.

"What's the projected time frame to get from here to the pod, his walk, and then back?" the general asked, even though he knew better than Drew what the schedule was.

"Five minutes to the pod, and he has twenty to play outside while I dock and engage a pressurization exchange. He's estimated to require an hour inside, so we've accounted for ninety minutes. Give us five minutes after that to get back into the pod and belted up, then five minutes back."

"How long have you been a pilot?" Drew asked.

"Twenty years. Ten earthbound, a few trips to Mars, and I've been piloting hoppers to the pods since Elysium went online. A dozen trips a day, Prince Andrew, and no hiccups."

"There was one death," Myers reminded him.

"Natural causes. A colonist leaving Mars died on the way home. Nothing I could have done about that."

"Jesus, what happened?" Drew reached out for his discarded glass of water and took a sip.

"Ninety-year-old man. His heart gave out. Felt bad for the guy, I really did. He wanted to go home and see some of the world before he died. All he got to see was Earth from a distance."

Drew thought that didn't sound awful. If the last thing you ever saw was the view he'd had from his quarters the night before, it would be a beautiful final sight.

"No sight is that good when you feel like you have a lot of living still to do," the Major said. "When I retire? I'm getting a small long-distance shuttle, and I'm seeing the world close-up. Space is just darkness with freckles of light, but home is a million different things, and none of them look alike."

"How long until retirement?" Drew asked.

"Six months. I imagine those will be both the longest and shortest months of my life."

Myers wiped up the remnants of his eggs with a piece of toast and then nodded at Drew. "Showtime. Let's get you suited up and out the door, and when you get back, you are fucking going to eat."

~

I heard Aubrey behind me, sighing. Hyrum giggled at the same time Finn snorted, but Jax shrugged it off.

"So he dropped an f-bomb that was heard around the world. If Drew had eaten breakfast, no one's sensibilities would have been offended. He might regret skipping it once he's doing somersaults outside the hopper."

"He's nervous, Dad," Oz said. "He doesn't want to throw up."

"Still needs fuel."

Will stood with his arms crossed, watching as Drew and the General marched down a long corridor. "Anthony enjoyed poking at him. It won't harm Andrew to delay breakfast a few hours. I've put him through stressful workouts on an empty stomach, and he doesn't have a tendency toward blood sugar issues. He'll be fine."

The General isn't nervous? He scarfed down his food.

"He has no need to be nervous," Will said. "He'll remain on Elysium, watching from the observation deck."

"Myers would be able to eat even if bombs were going off around him," Jax said. "Hell, he *has* eaten with bombs going off around him. You don't get to where he is without nerves of steel."

Drew had nerves of steel, or he was at least good at hiding it when he wanted to fold. I'd seen him in combat. He got the job done and worried about it after.

The cameras continued to follow him and his pilot, with General Myers walking right next to him, occasionally resting an assuring hand on Drew's shoulder, until they reached the access port for the hopper. At that point, Myers reached over and tapped the camera on Drew's chest harness, reminded him there was a release switch if he wanted to float it to allow his family—and a good part of the world—watch him work.

Our viewpoint changed. The media cameras, which were operated by Elysium staff for the sake of security—clicked off, and Drew's camera went live. Once he turned to the hopper port, General Myers was gone, and the only other person we saw was the pilot, who guided him down the ramp to the hopper's entry.

The inside of that looks like a mini-shuttle.

"Essentially, it is," Will said.

Designed for three passengers and the pilot, one of the rear seats had been removed and a track installed, which allowed the front passenger seat to slide back, giving him access to the side door. From there, Drew would leap into space, held by a tether that connected to the lower half of his harness, right at his ribs. Hyrum had argued against the placement; he wanted it lower on Drew's body, around his hips or even his waist, because it was too close to everything that kept Drew alive outside of the hopper.

It was the most secure connecting point, though, and he was outvoted.

Major Gaff went in first and scooped Drew's helmet off the seat and handed it to him. He didn't need it yet; he wouldn't need it until he was about to exit the hopper.

"Strap in," the Major said, pointing at the front seat. "When I disengage from the port, you'll feel a few seconds of tightness, like you're being pushed back into your seat, but it'll be over with before it can bother you. I'll flip this bird around, head for the pod, and we'll be there before you can begin worrying over the details."

Once Drew was strapped in, all we saw was the control panel, a bright, flat display with sensors that a kitty could activate with one well-placed swish of a tail.

I presumed I would never be allowed in a hopper, just for that reason.

"The computer is on board?" Drew asked.

"Strapped to the seat just behind me. Component parts are in the bin bolted to the floor behind it. Don't worry, Prince Andrew. Everything you need is on board."

"Drew. Just Drew."

"Major. Just Major," Gaff said, chuckling. "Or Don. Just not Donald. Not even my mother uses that, no matter how mad she is."

"Oh yeah, the mad mom voice. I got called Andrew a lot. Still do, thinking about it."

He pointed out the various controls to Drew; steering, acceleration, deceleration, stopping, even how to dock in an emergency. It was a quick, just-in-case lesson in getting the hopper back to the station, in the unlikely event that the Major dropped dead or became incapacitated.

"Hasn't happened yet. But you need to know."

"Cripes, I didn't even want to learn to drive a car."

"Way easier. No traffic to bump into out here."

Drew leaned forward, which gave us a nice view of the floor. "Yeah, but you have a wicked awesome commute. Even if it is a short one."

The sound of an engine coming online peppered the audio feed. "I haul a lot of ass to the pods every day," the Major told Drew. "Haven't seen this pod, though. It was just tethered and released last week."

"It's a testing facility," Drew said. "It felt safer to experiment with the new system a little further away from the station. Once we're sure that this works, they'll either haul it back in or leave it as a testing site."

"Seems cheaper to leave it. Nothing in it but drones right now, and I don't think any of them are powered up."

Drew leaned back. "I'll power two of them once I've installed the computer. All I need to do is get it online and running, and someone else will come out to check on it in a few days."

"Data sent on auto?"

There was a loud clunk as the hopper disengaged from its dock.

"Auto seemed prudent. I don't want to leave a person in there until we know how efficient the heating and cooling will be. But once it's on spec, people will be able to spend more time in it than the other pods. If the oxygen exchange system functions well, they can do it without having to remain helmeted."

"You'll remain helmeted, I presume."

"Definitely. We'll flood the pod with oxygen and then create a stable breathing environment, but today is only for data collection. No one is breathing in that air until we're certain the suit is sufficiently protective."

"Fewer runs for me, I imagine. Now hold onto your nuts, I'm about to turn this puppy around and head out."

"Please do not actually grab your nuts," Oz murmured.

"I heard that, Ozzy," Drew snickered. "Audio is two-way. Video, too, if I float the camera."

"Wait, they can hear us?" the Major asked.

"Yep."

"Hello from Elysium!" he called out. "If I'd known we had company, I would have cleaned up a bit."

Will cleared his throat and said, "Please bear in mind that your audience includes the King and Queen of Pacifica, as well as the Crown Princess."

"Sure, scare the guy who has Drew's life in his hands," Jax said.

"Can we not?" Oz sounded pained. "Not right now."

"I'm fine, Oz," Drew said.

She nodded, which he couldn't see, which was just as well because she wasn't fine. She wanted to cry and wanted to tell him to go back to the space station and then come home where he was safe, and then she could yell at him for making her worry.

Hyrum inched closer to the monitor. "Drew, take your camera off your chest and hold it up so we can see!"

There was the sound of fumbling, and then the image began to move. Drew held the camera near his head, giving us a nice, wide view of Elysium sliding out of view as the hopper turned. Our field filled with stars, and then one red-twinkling orb, the pod Drew was headed for.

"Brace," the Major said., which prompted Hyrum to shout, "Grab your nuts, Drew!"

The room went silent, and everyone save Hyrum sucked in and held a deep breath. Hyrum bounced on his toes, fists held at his chest, and the grin on his face was Christmas-worthy.

The hopper hesitated, clunked again, and without another warning, it shot forward, pressing Drew into his seat. He fumbled the camera but caught it before it floated far enough away to get in the Major's way, and as the ride settled, he began moving it around, so that we had a glimpse of everything he saw.

The pod was tethered to the internal hub of Elysium by a several-miles-long cable made of braided metal cased around millions of heavy wires. On screen, it looked thin, no bigger than the cable Drew used to connect his phone to his computer, but I knew it was larger around than a human. The wire was packed around hundreds of thousands of smaller cables that carried data and communications, and while it also appeared to be ramrod straight, it was flexible.

After a minute, Hyrum cut through the tension. "What's it like, Drew? Does it feel fast? Is it like a roller coaster?"

"Hy, it's *so* fast," Drew answered. "It feels like riding on the straightaway of a coaster. I feel the buzzing and humming coming up through my legs, but there's no up and down sensation."

"That's too bad. The loops are the best part."

"I can do a loop," Gaff said.

"You will not," Will said.

"Buzzkill," Drew snorted. "Hyrum, when I get back, I'll take you out to the Wasteland facility, and we can get on the test sled. It's a lot like that, but dark."

"I can close my eyes! That's like dark!"

"There's a simulator in Alameda," Gaff said. "Real enough that you'll grab your nuts."

Hyrum giggled, but Will sighed. "The simulator is for military use only."

"Man, you're just itching to suck the fun out of today, aren't you?" Drew grumbled. "Tell me General Myers wouldn't get us in if we asked nicely and bought him a few drinks."

"You presume we can get Anthony off that station," Jax said.

"Thus sayeth the King, who has more influence than anyone else," Drew said.

"Please," Oz said softly. "Pay attention to what you're doing."

The only thing Drew was occupied with was sitting in the passenger seat, staring out the window, watching the pod loom larger. The port that had looked like a tiny red smudge just a minute earlier now clearly resembled an access point, and its doors slowly slid open. A corrugated duct inched its way out, and metal spikes lined the circular opening, the pieces to which the hopper would dock.

"Thirty seconds," Gaff said. "Get your helmet on."

Drew snapped the camera into his chest harness, and we listened as they fumbled for their gear. His helmet clicked into place with a series of loud pops; it sounded broken, and Oz flinched, but Will assured her it had connected in all the right places. "You heard the connections and the seal forming. His nanosuit is now activated and working with the suit to provide oxygen and will fully engage when he orders it to."

The pod came into view as Drew stood.

"All right, Prince Space Cadet Blackshear," Gaff said. "You'll exit to the right when the door opens, and I'll slide to the left and dock."

"Last chance Ozzy," Drew said. "I don't have to do this. I can go straight into the pod."

We all turned to look at her. She swallowed against the fear and shook her head. "There is no way you're not doing this, Drew. You'd regret it for the rest of your life."

"I just want to be sure you're okay with it."

"You're walking," Finn said firmly. "That's a large part of testing that suit. It's not just for you to have fun."

"You've been oddly quiet," Drew said, the tamper of his voice changing as his voice filtered through the microphone in his helmet.

"Jo and I are watching the data." Finn's attention was glued to a side monitor, where Drew's and the Major's personal stats were displayed, along with information about the hopper and the pod. He had everything from heart rate and blood oxygen levels to the temperature of the interior of the hopper and of the pod. "I can watch a video of the whole thing later."

"Fair enough."

The hopper's door lifted open as Drew hooked his tether into place. He pressed his hands into the roof and stood quietly, taking in the sight of an endless stretch of stars. I wasn't sure if he was hesitating or appreciating, and apparently, neither was the Major because we heard the sound of a hand slapping Drew's back, and then, "Take a walk, sunshine. I have work to do."

Drew grunted, but was free of the hopper, hanging weightless outside. "Fuck you, too, Major."

Aubrey sighed audibly.

Hyrum giggled again.

Will made a clicking sound but turned his attention to the stream of information that scrolled past on the same screen that displayed the feed from Drew's camera. "Increase your distance from the hopper, Andrew. Try to stop just shy of the tether reaching full tension."

"Moving now."

As Drew moved away from the hopper, there was audible clicking as the Major inched it toward the pod. It connected into the spiked duct opening with a clunk, and there was a hiss as the pressure inside the hopper changed and oxygen flowed into the pod; Drew turned to watch it dock and grunted approvingly when the Major gave him a thumbs up from the pilot's seat.

"Engage the nanosuit," Will said.

Nothing in our view changed. By thinking a single word, "engage," Drew activated the hundreds of thousands of nanobots embedded in the fabric of his base layer. They spun and interlocked, creating a barrier between him and the universe, covering his head and face, though he still had a clear view of everything in front of him. Testing of the suit had proven that someone could shoot at him or even try to stab him, and he would be completely protected, but this was the first time it had been used in space, and its protection there was theoretical.

"Pulse and oxygen are fine," Finn said, not taking his eyes off the screen. "Body temperature normal."

You can still change your mind, Drew. You can still go back inside.

"I'm fine."

But you're about to open your suit. You don't have to.

"Even if the nanosuit doesn't provide complete protection, I'll have time to close it up before any damage is done."

How will you know?

"I'll feel it. You know, people have been exposed to space for tiny periods and have done just fine. I'm only opening a one-inch section on my arm, and only for a minute. It'll be all right."

"You better be," Oz muttered.

I turned to look at Will. Is it going to sound wrong to people watching that he's responding to a bunch of meowing? Because that's all they'll hear.

"Yeah, guys, I can hear the cat in there," Drew said before Will could answer. "And yes, I'm talking to the cat. It beats talking to myself, which is what I'll probably start doing soon, because this is amazing, and I want to seal every detail in my brain."

"Wick is watching you, Drew!" Hyrum squealed.

"Good boy, Wick," Drew chuckled.

I am going to pee on everything you love.

"Peel back the seal," Will said to Drew. "In three, two, one—open it up."

There was no sound as he carefully pulled back the flap on the left arm of his spacesuit. I'd thought it would have that scratchy sound that hook and loop fabric made, but there was only the sound of Drew's breathing. All we could see were chunks of his arms as they crossed in front of the camera; I wanted him to release it from his chest harness, but it seemed like a poor time to make the request.

"Heart rate increased by three beats per minute," Finn reported.

There was nothing wrong with that, but Finn lived by data and was going to report anything different.

"Drew?" Oz's voice cracked. "Well?"

"I don't feel a thing. Is my temperature stable?"

Finn nodded.

"No changes," Will said. "Forty seconds more, and seal it up regardless."

"It's working." Drew sounded a bit surprised. "Damn. I don't feel anything on my arm, and I'm still comfortable all over."

Will asked him to consider carefully, and to perform a mental check on anything that felt wrong. He was looking for spots where there was insufficient coverage, a pinch of metal, or pressure from the suit where he normally felt none. Under the spacesuit, a thin spot wouldn't make a difference, but if someone needed to rely on it without cover, there could be no errors.

To Drew, it felt no different than the hundreds of times he'd put on a nanosuit and tested various things with it in the lab. Nothing poked his skin. He flexed his back, checking for spots where his oxygen tubes lay, and then ran his hands up and down his legs, feeling from the outside.

"I can feel the flat tubes, that's all. And we expected that."

"You can breathe okay?" Hyrum asked. "You remember where the switch is, right? In case you need your inside air?"

"Right here on my helmet, Hyrum. I didn't forget."

"Say it so I know for sure."

"It's on the right rear of my helmet, just behind my ear. All I have to do is tap it twice."

"Okay."

"Thank you for reminding me, Hy. I feel better knowing you have my back."

Drew didn't need any reminders; everyone in the room knew that. Hyrum knew that. But everyone equally knew that regardless of his high level of excitement, Hyrum was terrified for Drew's safety and had fixated on how much air he would have available. The under-layer air system was Hyrum's contribution to the project, and it had been labeled as the HCB-1 Reserve Oxygen Delivery System with AFMB.

Will suggested it be named the Hyrum Blackshear System, which initially excited him, but he then scrunched his nose and decided that sounded vain. But he liked using his initials and thought Jesus would be okay with that.

While Drew went through the planned checks of the new spacesuit and base layer, Major Gaff began removing the security straps from the container that held the new computer

Drew intended to install in the pod. That was all he needed to do: remove the straps and store them, then loosen the bolts that held it to the floor. After that, he was free to stand and watch Drew or sit and stare out at the stars.

Instead, Gaff pulled the computer from its container and hauled it into the pod. While Finn tried to make sense of the shift in data displayed—Gaff's heart rate and oxygen use spiked, and there were clear signs of unexpected movement—General Myers' voice cracked through the speakers.

"Major, return to your position."

Gaff grunted. "Just helping the kid out. If I move this for him, he has more time to play."

"Major," Myers repeated, "return to your position. That is not a suggestion."

"It's already in place, General. Just let me plug it in, and I'll go back to the hopper."

While the General and Will both shouted, "No!" Finn bellowed, "Andrew, cut your tether! Cut it now!"

Drew hesitated for only a fraction of a second. He'd trained just enough to obey orders that made no sense to him and reacted out of a thin layer of instinct. As he let go of the tether, pushing it away from him, the pod and the hopper were enveloped in a ball of white light that expanded and then contracted, and the tether vibrated with the electricity that shot through it.

Layer upon layer of the tether peeled away from its core, fracturing into shuttle length razor blades.

Fewer than five seconds later, Drew floated in space, and the pod and the hopper were gone, with only a small section of the tether left, neatly sliced into sharp angles.

"What the actual fu—"

General Myers was shouting, "Move, move, move!" and the sound of footsteps thundered around him. Jax had his phone in hand and immediately began barking into it, demanding that a shuttle be ready to launch as soon as possible, with a rescue floater ready to be deployed. Chaos erupted in shouts of concern, but Will and Oz were eerily quiet, staring at the monitor, looking for signs of Drew's level of distress.

"Don't panic," Will said evenly. "You have plenty of oxygen, and we'll get someone out to you soon."

"What the hell, Will? What happened?"

"Gaff took the computer into the pod," he answered. "He plugged it in."

"What the hell?" Drew repeated. "Why?"

"He wanted to help," Oz said.

The pod had been free of air until Gaff docked the hopper. Once connected, the air exchange system activated and flooded it with oxygen, and the stream of forced air moving through it was steady; the electrical system in the pod was not prepared for a direct connection with a computer that carried its own power supply.

"Between the sparks from plugging the computer in, the oxygen, and the materials stored in the pod—" Will started.

"Not even a bang," Drew murmured. "Just...whoosh."

"What kind of debris field is there?" Jo asked Drew. "What's coming at you?"

There was a pause. "Nothing. It's just gone. The hopper, the pod, and the head of the attachment cable. There are bits and pieces of cable, but I can't tell if any of it is moving. And let me tell you, Elysium looks about as far away from here as it does from home."

~

There was no shuttle available in Pacifica's United Kingdom that could reach Drew in time. Given twenty-four hours, a Mars-capable ship could be launched, but he didn't have even half that time. There were three other hoppers stationed at Elysium, all were on the far side, and none had enough fuel left to reach him. One would have to be pulled from the pod it was docked at and returned for refueling before it could be sent to Drew.

"Then do that," Jax said.

Quietly, turned away from the microphone that piped audio to Drew, Will said, "The hopper requires multiple hours to recharge. All three have made several trips since their first launch of the shift. Their reserves are drained."

"They were supposed to hold one back." Jax glanced at Oz and then turned to Will. "What the hell happened?"

Will didn't care if the station's commander overheard. "Incompetence."

They ran through all the options. There were drone repair crawlers that scurried along the cables that connected the pods to the station; Finn postulated that one could carry a secondary tether, let it loose, and then drag Drew back to the station. Jo did the math; after programming the drone, releasing it, waiting for it to reach the end of one cable, and then deploy the next, Drew would run out of air. She didn't bother accounting for the time back, because he wouldn't make it.

While they spoke quietly, Drew asked Hyrum to switch the audio feed from open to private, because there were things he wanted to say to his family, things only for them. Hyrum flipped the switch Oz pointed to, all while listening to the discussion going on.

"Is there another nanosuit?" Hyrum asked. "You could jump there and grab him and then jump back."

"Absolutely not," Aisha said before Will could answer. "You haven't tested it in space. We could lose both of you."

Will still didn't rule it out—he had tested those distances—but it would be a last-ditch effort for no reason other than the unknown of space. Finn insisted that if it came to that, Will was not going. He would. "I'm old, and you have small children to raise."

"For that matter," Jo said, "go get Liam Finnegan. He would go in a heartbeat, and the man is older than God."

Drew snickered. "You don't believe in God."

"We'll look for answers that don't require risking someone's life," Will said firmly.

But you will if it comes to it, won't you?

Finn gestured to Drew's oxygen supply numbers. He had three hours at most, more likely, two. That was longer than he had been expected to be away from Elysium. They'd accounted for delays, but not for an accident that removed the pod from the equation. It had been assumed that if necessary, the pod would serve as a life raft. If not the pod, then the hopper.

"Find the answer soon," Oz said. "Because if you don't, I'll grab one of the damned bracelets and get him myself."

"The suit won't fit you, Ozzy," Drew said. "It would be just a little too big, enough that it would get in your way. We'll think of something."

Send a drone.

"A drone," Will repeated.

I turned to the line of powered-down drones along the wall. There were five of them, all programmed to mimic human behaviors. It would take little coding to add to their capabilities, and all one needed to do was show up close to Drew and hand over the bracelet, and he could jump to the station.

"No," Oz said. "Aisha is right, it hasn't been tested in space, and he won't be the first."

Then send one with a crawler. It jumps, Drew gets the crawler, and he can make his way to the station on it. You'd lose the drone, but that seems okay.

Jax wanted clarity. "Explain the crawler. Didn't Jo just now say it wasn't possible?"

"That was a crawler drone," she said. "Cat-sized spider-like robots."

"The crawler we mean resembles a large hover cart," Will said. "There's a flat surface one can stand upon or handles at the rear one can hold onto as they're being pulled along. It's typically used to carry small loads by workers outside the station when repairs are necessary."

"Would that work?"

"We can program a drone to carry a cart. The weight isn't an issue. Our issues are whether the jump tech will work, and then how close to Drew we can get. He'll need to be able to reach the crawler and free it from the drone's grasp."

The drones were largely autonomous. They could easily do the work they were programmed to, and if the jump was successful, it would attempt to hand the crawler to Drew. The issue was the size of the crawler and the risk that the drone's attempt to release it would be rougher than necessary, resulting in injury to Drew, or that it would fall short and send the crawler out of reach.

"But first, we need to get it there."

"How many bracelets do you have now?" Jo asked.

"Hundreds. That's not an issue." He eyed the drones standing on the far side of the room. "An additional issue is that we're limited by the number of attempts we can make. We have five drones here. If necessary, I can have more brought in, but that takes time."

"The more you send out here, the more things I have to dodge," Drew said. "I mean, I will, but I'd prefer we don't turn this into a drone minefield."

"Send Shivan," Hyrum said.

Everyone turned to him. "Shivan?" Oz asked.

Hyrum nodded. "He's a computer program, isn't he? If we put a nanosuit onto the drone and then put Shivan into it, the whole thing will look like Shivan. And he can think and do things without being told to."

"Hy," Drew breathed, sounding amazed. "You know what Shivan is?"

"I didn't when you took me there, but I figured it out. I know he's not real like you and me are real. I mean, Tobias made himself look like my daddy, and real people can't do that. That's a pretend place, isn't it? That's why there are dragons and giant cats like Fluffy." He gasped and clasped his hands over his mouth. "Oh. Don't tell Rhys. He thinks it's real. I don't want to ruin it for him. Quinn is his friend."

"We won't tell Rhys," Will promised. "Explain your idea. Why Shivan?"

"On account of the drones—" he pointed to the line of five against the back wall "—only do what you tell them. So if it dropped the hover thingy on accident, it might not know to bend over to pick it up, and it might float away, and then we'd have to start over. But Shivan doesn't need to be told extra. If he drops it, he knows how to pick it up. And if Drew says to him, 'Shivan, you gotta reach more,' Shivan will reach more."

The drones could correct for mistakes, but Will's expression suggested he thought Hyrum was onto something.

"And if we send Shivan," Hyrum went on, "we only have to send him once. If you send a regular drone, you might have to send them all to get it right. Right?"

Will nodded. "And your logic for using the nanosuit? We could import his programming directly into the drone without it."

"On account of it needs to look like Shivan, and you can make the suit do that, right? It's all nanobots and light. If it looks like Shivan, then it *is* Shivan, and Drew won't be so scared out there. Because he is, even if he says no. If you were lost like that, you would want a friend, right?"

"The coding—" Will started, thinking of time lost to make it happen.

"The code already exists." Drew sucked in a deep breath. "It's buried in the files for the suit function. I was playing with the idea that we could bypass the AI laws and bring Shivan to our—"

Jo cut through his explanation. "I have the files, but I need the password, Drew."

He grunted, not wanting to share it. "Cripes. All right. I'm sorry, Oz." He took another deep breath and said, "'Ozzy's boobs are awesome.' All one word, no caps, no punctuation, and drop any 's' and replace it with a 'z.'"

Hyrum giggled, Aubrey sighed, but Oz said, "Thank you, hot stuff."

Without looking up, Jo said to Will, "I've got the code. You need to get to Saint Francis and get Shivan."

"Just move him," Jax said.

"Holographic or not, he deserves this to come as a request, and he deserves the right to refuse."

"Jesus, we don't have that kind of time," Jax grumbled.

"Under a minute." Will stepped away from the computer and to the other side of the room, just past the line of drones, and uttered, "Open portal," and was gone before Jax had a chance to refute.

"What the hell? How does he have a portal here that I can't see?"

"It's not on the tunnel line," Finn explained. "I added that sound so that you and Oz could see the portals, and others can hear to find them. Will doesn't need sound. He knows where his portal is."

"And why does he have one?"

Finn shrugged. "It's not like he needed my permission to open one."

"It's an escape hatch," Drew said. "If something horrendous happens at Ozoo, he can wipe the system and bolt. There's one in my lab, too. We can access the portal at home with these. Or anywhere, really."

Finn's portals were designed to move strictly through time. Enter at Union Square, exit at Union Square. To enter here and exit at home was adding the space parameter, something that excited Finn. He would have started blabbering about it, but the portal opened again, and Will was back.

"Did he say okay?" Hyrum asked.

"There was no question. I'd barely explained the issue before he volunteered. For that matter, so did Hagar, Krisf, and Tobias."

"Tobias?" both Drew and Oz blurted.

"He reasoned that he still has a debt of honor to pay. If this effort fails with Shivan, he's asked to be next. He wanted to be first, but…"

"Shivan wouldn't allow it," Oz guessed. "And his word is law in Saint Francis."

Will directed Hyrum to run to Drew's office and grab three of the nanosuits from storage while he powered up the drones. Once Jo was done with the coding, they would make the first attempt.

"Aisha, if you could go into my office and grab the red case sitting on the left bookshelf. There are several jump bracelets in it."

Once Will had the first drone powered and in the center of the room, Drew suggested they send one without Shivan in it first. "Test it. Send it to my last mapped location, but a few feet back. And then leave it."

"Why?" Oz asked him.

"In case I'm drifting. I feel like I haven't moved, but I probably have. Place the initial drone, and by the time you're ready to send Shivan, you'll have a better lock on my location."

"Send a crawler with it," Jax said. "If you can get the drone close enough, you save sending Shivan."

There was only one crawler to send. Granted, there were hundreds in production, but only one that Ozoo could get its metaphorical grubby little hands on, and it was still ten minutes away at best. Will wanted to send the drone within a couple of minutes because time was an issue, and Drew's oxygen was limited.

Hyrum ran back in with the nanosuits, but before he had a chance to set them down, Will asked him to fetch the blue box in the bottom drawer of the file cabinet. Oz took the suits—Hyrum looked confused, unsure if he was supposed to carry them along while he got the box—and he scurried off again. His confusion was the only off thing I sensed from him. He wasn't scared, he didn't feel in the way; he moved with purpose, a certainty that he was doing exactly what he was supposed to. There was no guesswork here. He knew where everything in Will's office and workspace was, he'd learned to not second-guess himself when he was working. If someone new came in, they would never guess that just three days before he'd needed to hold Will's hand on the way home, and then crawled onto Drew's lap to cuddle before bed.

"What is it?" he asked as he handed the small box to Will.

"This," Will answered as he clipped the contents into a port on the drone's shoulder, "is a sensor that will measure the distance between the drone and Drew, so that we know where to send Shivan."

"Oh. That seems smart. Won't Shivan know, though?"

Drew explained the plan to Hyrum while Will finished preparing the drone for transportation. Oz was torn; she wanted to watch Will work, but she also didn't want to divert attention from Drew. All she could see on the monitor was the black of space and a small sliver of Elysium, but that was Drew's view, and she was afraid to miss anything.

Dude, release the camera and turn it so Oz can see you. Distract her.

"I'd like this a lot more if I could see you, too," he said once the camera was in place. "I'm looking at myself, and I'm just not pretty enough. Hell, I can't even see my own face with the cowl activated."

"It will pull back partway," Will grunted. "It would be safe to do so."

Finn allowed himself a few seconds away from monitoring Drew's stats and stepped over to the keyboard. Fifteen seconds of typing later, and Drew's camera screen filled with the activity happening behind Oz. He asked her to take a step to the left so that she would be in front of the camera because the only thing he really wanted to see was her.

"I'm pretty, too," Hyrum called out.

That made Drew laugh. "You're busy, Hy."

Hyrum was carefully slipping a nanosuit onto the second drone, exercising a high level of caution about securing the top and bottom layer, making sure all the tiny connections matched and that it clipped into the controller that laid flat against its skin.

"There's not enough light to see you all that well," Oz told Drew. "But I'll take what I can get."

"Yeah, I don't imagine there's much to see beyond the face shield anyway. But I'm here. And I can see you. It's okay, Ozzy. I'm really okay."

Softly, voice breaking, "I'm not."

"I'm sorry. I know you had reservations about this whole trip."

She shook her head. "There's no way we could have envisioned this. Your pilot was supposed to get you there, that's all. How in the hell, Drew?"

"I suppose he thought he was helping."

"No, I get that. But the only thing he did was plug the computer in."

Gaff was supposed to dock the hopper, flip a switch, and then wait for Drew to re-enter the hopper. The pod was power and oxygen-free until that switch was flipped; once flipped, a very small amount of power was sent to the ventilation system, which flooded the pod with pure oxygen intended to stream into the corrugated connection port and then the hopper. By the time Drew was ready to take the computer inside, the environment would have stabilized, with breathable air if his own oxygen supply was running low.

"The computer had its own power supply," Drew explained. "When he plugged it in, it sparked. Oxygen and sparks are a horrible match."

"The pod's power was coming online as well," Will added. "Finn had you release the tether because of that."

"I figured," Drew said. "Funny thing is, when I was free from it and realized what was happening, I had the thought that Hyrum could have hung onto it. Not that it would have helped, but still. Just one of those thoughts."

Will plucked a jump bracelet from the storage case and clipped it onto the drone's wrist. "All right, just let me input the coordinates, and you'll have a drone in your face soon."

"If that thing lands on top of me…"

"We'll have words for Will," Hyrum said. "I'll say them first."

"If the drone appears within reach, take the jump bracelet," Will said to Drew. "Don't use it, but you'll have it just in case. Secondary targeting is to Elysium's sickbay."

"Eh." Drew sounded uncertain and cupped his hands around his face shield. "There's a bay door opening on this side of the exterior ring. I think."

Another voice cut in. "How much time does Prince Andrew have?" It was General Myers. "We have a hopper returning, but it's doubtful that it has enough fuel to reach him. In the meantime, we're running spider drones along a pinch cable. Best we can do is run a cable, have a drone drag another, and we'll stack them until we reach him."

"And then what?" Oz demanded. "He pulls himself along until he's inside? Do you have any idea how long that would take?"

"That's why I asked about the time frame," Myers responded.

Will glanced at the monitor with Drew's stats. "He has approximately two hours of oxygen left. Perhaps more effort could be placed into readying additional fuel cells for the hopper."

"That's covered, as well."

Will explained what he was doing and warned the General that in under thirty seconds, it would appear as if there were someone out there with Drew.

"Ready, Andrew?" he asked.

"Send it."

"Three...two...one." He tapped the bracelet, and the drone blinked away. "It should take five seconds."

Everyone began counting under their breath. Right at five seconds, the drone was there and Drew spun the camera around to show Will.

"It's maybe four feet away, facing in the opposite direction. Not quite close enough to reach, and I'm not sure how much effort I should put into it."

"None," Will said. "Let's just get the measurements, and then prepare Shivan to jump to you."

"Did I mention it's facing the wrong way?"

"Did I mention the sensor is multi-directional? It's fine."

"If I drift?"

"We'll measure again before we send him."

"Four feet, one inch," Finn reported as the data appeared on his monitor. "If you can get the next drone within the same general space, perhaps a foot closer, Drew should be able to reach for the crawler."

Hyrum put his arms around the drone's waist. "His name is Shivan. Don't call him a drone."

Will agreed that was a fair point. The moment Shivan's programming had transferred, the drone was not to be referred to as an 'it,' and his name would be used. Finn shot Will a 'what the hell?' look over his shoulder; he didn't share the same feelings about the citizens of St. Francis that we did—they weren't people to him, they were amusing lines of code—but he humored Will and generally went along with it.

If it were just Will this time, he would have snorted out loud and made his argument that Shivan was a drone while he occupied the space, but even though Hyrum understood what Shivan was, he was still real, and he loved Shivan.

"Do you need to tell Shivan it's time?" Hyrum asked Will.

"He understands that he'll be at home, blink, and then be here," Will said.

"Does his wife know?"

Will nodded. "She understands. For her, Shivan will only be gone for a very short time. I'll return him to his family just a minute or so after he's left."

Just don't hose it up. Otherwise, we get Tobias.

"I don't have a problem with that, Wick," Drew said. "Tobias's ego would push him toward getting the job done. He needs to feel like a hero, I imagine."

No one else was ready to give him that, though I thought that if Will had tapped him for this and something went wrong, we'd hate the outcome a bit less.

"Let's just get this done with Shivan," Will said. "Tobias can further his redemption another time."

~

Will activated the nanosuit, including the face cowl, and stepped back. He asked Finn for another estimate on Drew's oxygen and grunted when the answer Finn gave was less a number and more like, "Just hurry up."

He was hurrying as fast as he could. Once the suit was fully activated, he asked Jo if she was ready. She nodded and said she would transfer Shivan on his order.

"Do it."

The drone shifted a bit, and its hands and face quickly transformed into the closest version of Shivan that could be managed; the rest remained the shiny metallic blue of the nanosuit. His face was a bit flatter, and the color was not quite right, but he was recognizable, and Hyrum threw his arms around him, thanking him for coming.

"This feels...different," Shivan said. "As if I were standing in a glass box looking out. While wearing a suit of armor."

"Mom," Will said, "transfer the optics to the nanosuit. He's looking through the faceplate."

A few blinks later, and Shivan relaxed a bit.

"Better?" Will asked.

"Considerably."

"Practice moving!" Hyrum blurted. "I bet it feels different, too."

He only needed to adjust to the movements he would make once transported. Will instructed him to move his legs and arms and to reach forward as if he were reaching for Drew. He didn't need to worry about the weight of the crawler; the drone's structure allowed him to lift more weight than the average human, and he only needed to get it close enough for Drew to grab the handles.

Once he was confident with moving, Jo began adding to his programming. He was bombarded with information on using the jump bracelet and how to attach it to Drew's wrist without puncturing his suit. There were instructions on changing Drew's oxygen tank—he would be sent with a spare—and how to send himself back to the simulator once Drew was safely on his way to the space station. He was also given rudimentary direction on the operation of the crawler; it had been decided that Shivan would kneel on it during transport, and Hyrum mused that he probably needed to know how to make it move up, down, and side to side.

Somewhere in his programming, he already had that information. The drone was loaded with data, and the further along Shivan went, the easier it would be for him to access it all.

"You only need to do three things," Will said, despite knowing that Shivan was fully aware of the tasks at hand. "First, attach the fresh oxygen tank. Then place the bracelet on his wrist. Once those two things have been done, and Drew has a good hold on the crawler, shove him in the direction of the space station. Once he's on his way, flip the switch—" he tapped a spot just above the switch on Shivan's chest "—and you'll transfer back home."

"You'll let me know how this ends?" Shivan asked.

"Of course."

Hyrum handed Will a harness and camera, which he slipped over Shivan's head. Shivan turned to allow Will to cinch the harness a bit tighter, and when he did, he saw Drew on the main monitor for the first time.

"Incredible," he whispered.

"Gotta speak up, Shivan," Drew said. "I'm kind of far away and can hardly hear you."

Shivan took several awkward steps toward the screen. "How is this possible?"

Oz explained about the camera floating on a short tether in front of Drew. Once Shivan was there, Drew would clip it back onto his chest, and we would be able to see both of them on a split-screen. Shivan turned and began taking in everything around him.

"I knew this place existed. But seeing it..."

"You haven't seen anything yet," Drew said. "Come on, let's get this done, and when I'm home, we'll put you back in a drone and show you San Francisco."

Jax opened his mouth to refute that; AI was still illegal, and that's what Shivan was, but Aubrey touched his arm, a signal to stay quiet. Whatever Drew wanted, Drew was getting. And right now, he wanted the comfort of acting as if this were simply a social matter with a promise of more to come.

The crawler was placed on the floor, and Shivan kneeled on it. Will had him repeat the order of things, and when he reached the slipping of the switch, he reached up as if to touch it, and realized the camera was in his way. "How easy is the camera to remove?"

"You have to move it!" Hyrum blurted. "Otherwise the camera might jiggle it and send him home before he can do all the things. He has to do all the things first."

"We can code for a return," Jo said. "Send the signal from here."

There was no time to write the code. Will slipped the switch pack from its spot near the camera and moved it to the back of Shivan's shoulder, where it was less likely that anything would touch it. "Drew will have to flip the switch."

"You can't send the code later?" Shivan asked. "I can wait there."

The risk in that was leaving Shivan in the drone, and the signal being lost or degraded. There was a risk in sending him to begin with, but if something went wrong, his program could be restarted from a save point. If everything went right up until the point the recall code was transmitted, it would leave a conscious version of Shivan floating in space, potentially forever.

"But I would also be home?" he asked. "Two of me?"

"Essentially. That would be cruel to the one of you left out there."

Shivan deemed it an acceptable risk. If something happened and Drew couldn't reach the switch, he was willing to wait until someone recovered him.

"When you're ready, tap the bracelet, and you'll jump." Will pointed toward the activation tab on his own bracelet. "This one. Only touch it once. I haven't added any mapping other than getting you there. It won't know how to send you anywhere else."

With a nod, Shivan tapped the bracelet, and was gone.

"He would return here, wouldn't he?" Jo asked.

"I removed that parameter." When she frowned, he added, "Had I not, they might have attempted a jump from there."

"I'm not that stupid, Will," Drew said.

"Desperation often displaces intelligence, Andrew. Nevertheless, the bracelet is mapped to get you here from Elysium, if the situation warrants."

"Like hell." Oz was angry. "Test that jump on someone else."

"He meant in an emergency, Ozzy," Drew said. "Like one more emergent than—" He suddenly flinched, his arms covering his face and head protectively. "Son of a bitch. Yeah, Shivan made it, and he just decapitated the other drone."

Drew grabbed the camera and pointed it at the head now drifting away.

"I'm fine, thanks for asking," Shivan said. "I come bearing gifts of fresh air and a ride back."

The side of the oxygen tank filled the screen until Drew took it from him. "Damn. Will, the indicator reads empty."

"What?"

He held the end of the canister up to Shivan's chest so we could see. The level line had been green—full—when Will set it on the crawler near Shivan. It was now red, indicating that it was empty.

"Air doesn't jump?" Hyrum asked.

"It should," Will grumbled.

"Test it," Jo said. "Jump another canister across the room."

Hyrum sprinted for the office, where there was a smaller oxygen tank. After making sure it was loaded, Will set in on the floor, wrapped a bracelet around the end of it, and sent it across the room.

"Empty," he groaned. "Goddammit."

Take a deep breath and jump yourself. Don't ask, just do it.

He sucked in hard, tapped the bracelet, and appeared five feet away.

You just inhaled again.

You were holding your breath, and you inhaled.

There was no time to figure it out. He was sure he had accounted for every minute thing in a living body; he remembered considering blood oxygen content. He accounted for water content. He asked Jo to make a note, they could tackle the issue later, but for now, the main thing was that Drew no longer had the extra air they'd hope he would, and he had less than two hours.

"Will." Finn beckoned him over to look at the monitor displaying Drew's stats. Speaking softly, so that no one else would hear, he said, "His main tank is depleted. He's running on the secondary system now."

"How?"

"The tank emptied immediately after Shivan jumped. I suspect pieces from the other drone pierced a hose."

The nanosuit immediately sensed it and closed off the opening and began feeding air to Drew directly.

"All right, no talking behind my back. Or my front." Drew bent over so that his face was close to Shivan's camera. "What gives?"

"Math," Will lied, hoping the colors surrounding him didn't change because Oz and Jax would know. "Finn is calculating the distance you need to traverse and the speed the crawler is capable of. You'll be cutting it close, but you'll make it."

"Of course, I'll make it. Oz will kill me if I don't."

His bravado was eclipsed by the paleness of his face. It might have been the lighting; Shivan only had a couple of small lights aimed at Drew, and Drew only had one clipped to his harness. It might have been the helmet and how difficult it was to see past the face shield. It might have been a lot of things, but I thought reality was settling with him. There was a holograph-filled drone in front of him, while General Myers tried desperately to string cable out of a shuttle port, hoping to get to his prince.

Will re-opened the line to the general to check his progress.

"The spider crawlers are a waste of effort," he grunted, sounding almost out of breath. "They can't haul more than quarter-inch line. So we're going another direction."

"I still see movement," Drew said.

"Well, I wasn't giving up. See how close that crawler can get you, Prince Andrew. I'll see how close I can get with the tethers. Maybe we can meet in the middle."

"Exactly what are you doing?" Jax asked.

"My ass is hauling cable," he grunted. "Somewhere behind me is an engineering specialist hauling boosters. When he catches up, he'll slap those onto my feet."

"For?" Jax prompted.

"For the hell of it," Meyers answered in a way that suggested no one ask anything else about it.

He was outside of Elysium, attached to a half-inch cable, being propelled along with additional cable connected to each ankle, each calf, each thigh, and two on each arm. His plan was to move along until he reached the end of the first cable, connect another, and to keep going until he had connected all that he could carry. If the crawler could just get Drew to him, he could attach a pincher to Drew's harness, and they would be pulled in.

"I know he can ride the crawler all the way," Myers said, "but if it shuts down, I want to be ready."

Drew chuckled. "You just wanted to play outside, old man."

"No reason you should have all the fun."

He needed to do something. I empathized; if there was any possibility that I could jump out there and find a way home for him, I would do it without consideration to the likely end of my already lengthy life. I felt paralyzed and assumed everyone else did, too.

Shivan had placed the jump bracelet on Drew's wrist, and he slid off the crawler, patting the surface. "Time to get moving. You can either hop on or grab on, but it's time."

Drew didn't move. He stared at the space station, then squinted, trying to see the shuttle bay port. "That's a long way to go," he finally whispered.

"So the sooner you get started, the sooner you get there," Shivan said.

"How fast does this thing go?"

"Fast enough," Will said. "Get on or grab on, Andrew."

He still didn't move.

Will stepped over to check his stats and let loose a deep sigh. Every minute he delayed placed Drew short of the shuttle bay, and if he kept delaying, he wouldn't have enough power to reach the general either. But he was frozen, unable to make himself grab the handles on the crawler.

Oz was trembling, waiting for him to move, but when he didn't, she took a step closer to the microphone and barked, "Get on the goddamned crawler, Drew, or I swear to God I will jump out there and shove the entire thing up your ass. Don't make the story I tell your son one day be about the day daddy fucking split in half because mommy lost her shit and jammed that damned thing up there so hard—"

Drew grabbed the handle before she could finish describing his potentially painful demise in space. "We wouldn't want that," he mumbled. "You know, they can hear you in China. Literally."

"I wasn't yelling," she said.

"Kinda were, sunshine. And I swear, I'm trying. It's just—"

"Switch near your right hand," Will said. "Flip it, and the crawler will begin to move."

Shivan let go, ready for Drew to also flip the switch just behind his shoulder. Instead, Drew grabbed him by the wrist and set his hand on the other grip.

"Not yet, Shivan. I can't do this alone."

"You're not alone. You have your family, and they'll make this trip with you."

"I can't."

Will stood next to Oz. "You *must*, Andrew. If you drag the weight of Shivan's drone, you'll lose power before you reach Elysium."

"And maybe Myers will be there. Maybe, maybe, maybe."

"Do it the way we planned," Oz ordered. "Don't risk anything. We have a baby at home, Drew. He needs you. The world needs you."

"Don't ask me to leave Shivan hanging here," Drew said softly.

"That drone is not Shivan," she said. "Shivan is in that little box attached to its back, and as soon as you flip the switch, he'll be back home with his family."

"I see Shivan, right here. My friend. And in all the maybes crushing me, he's the only sure thing I've got right now." He turned the crawler on, and as it began to move, he added, "Just give me a minute or two. Because I can't..."

Aubrey slipped her arm around Oz's shoulder and tugged her close. "Give him this."

Will glanced at Finn, who nodded. Drew's heart rate had climbed and was nearly 190, and his breathing rate had increased. If he panicked, he would run out of air long before reaching the general, and he would definitely not reach the station.

"Proceed, Andrew," he said. "When the time comes, if you're concerned about Shivan, flip his switch, and then shove the drone toward the station. We'll send someone out later to rescue his drone."

"By then, it will be a shell," Shivan said. "Don't risk someone's life on pieces of metal."

"Stop fighting!" Hyrum wailed. "Drew, just go and send Shivan home when it's time. If you do it, I promise I'll bake some wiener cookies when you get back. Okay?"

Drew huffed out a bit of a chuckle. "All right, Hy."

"Wiener cookies?" Shivan asked.

"Snickerdoodles. Long story. Well, not long, but not important."

"Apparently, I have time."

Rhys, to his frustration, had a hard time saying 'snickerdoodles.' It often rolled off his tongue as 'dickerdoodles' and to soften his upset when he couldn't get the word right, Hyrum had used Hyrum logic. He latched onto the obvious slang, pared the word down, and told Rhys that just between them—the two of them and Drew—they would call them wiener cookies.

"Yet dickerdoodles sounds more fun," Shivan mused. "Does it matter what he calls them as long as you know what he means?"

"It doesn't, but try telling him that."

"Rhys is sensitive," Will said. "He simply wants to get everything correct."

"I told him kid mistakes are the best mistakes but he doesn't believe me," Hyrum said. "And he's smarter than me so what does it matter if he can't say some words right?"

"Stop that," Drew said. "We're not comparing intelligence."

Hyrum folded his arms and huffed. "I'm not. But he's smarter and I know it. I never said that was a bad thing."

"No, you did not," Drew conceded.

Oz's breath hiccupped, and Hyrum twitched toward her, but she whispered to him to keep Drew talking.

"We need him and Eli and the other babies to be smarter than us," Hyrum went on. "When we're old they'll be in charge. They have to be smarter for that."

"Are you suggesting I'm not smart enough?" Drew snickered.

"I'm not suggesting it, Drew. I'm saying it. Rhys is smarter than you, too, you know."

Shivan's voice cut in. "Hyrum, maybe you can explain to me why Drew is kicking his feet as we move along?"

"I'm what?" Drew asked. He turned to look at his legs. "Really?"

"He probably thinks he's in the pool with a kickboard," Hyrum said.

"Well, I can't help it."

Finn called out, "You need to help it, Drew. Move less. Let the crawler pull you. You can't swim your way in."

"Are you sure about that? Because I'm moving and I don't feel the cart doing much. If I can swim in, I'm breaking out my killer backstroke."

"You mean you're gonna bonk your head on things," Hyrum said. "You don't go straight most of the time."

Will went over to check Drew's oxygen level, which was steadily going down. He set his hand on his father's shoulder, normally a warm gesture, but I saw his finger slide onto Finn's skin, and he tapped twice, which meant he wanted Finn to listen inside his head and not with his ears.

They didn't speak out loud, but I guessed that Will wanted the bigger picture: *does Drew have enough air to breathe? Does he need to send Shivan home now? Will he?* It was quicker to converse inside their heads than with their mouths, and the benefit was that they wouldn't frighten Oz or Drew.

"He's still doing it," Shivan reported.

"I can't help it!" Drew shot back.

"Cross your ankles," Hyrum said. "Like you do when you want to swim with just your arms."

"Or starfish," Oz said. "Hold on with one hand and spread everything. You won't kick that way."

"Isn't that your thing, Ozzy?" Drew chuckled.

"I can still shove that crawler up your ass," she warned.

"She's still formidable," Shivan mused. "Still the warrior I met when I was fifteen and full of myself. You know, Tobias has spoken about you, Oz. Regardless of the circumstances, he's still impressed by your nerve and bravery. If he has his way, his daughters will be much like you."

"So he's honoring his promises?" Drew asked.

"He's still an arrogant ass," Shivan said. "But he's also

willing to do whatever needs to get done. He and his wife live away from the village, yet he's there every day, doing as much of the manual labor as he can."

"Is his wife still angry with me?" Jax asked.

"That's putting it mildly."

"Hyrum knows what you are," Drew said to Shivan. "Doing this? It was his idea. And part of that was thinking I would be less afraid if you were here."

"Is it working?" Hyrum asked.

"Yeah, I think it is."

"But you're still kinda scared?"

"I can't help it, Hyrum. The space station is still so far away, and I'm getting low on air."

Jax touched Will on his arm and stepped closer to Jo. "Is he close enough for us to use the cameras on Elysium to get a better look? All we have now are flashes of the crawler and each other's sides. And I don't want to ask Drew to unclip his camera again."

"We have a line to the bridge," Jo said softly.

Will opened the channel and asked for the captain, who was waiting nearby. They were watching from the bridge; he was ready to give the orders to send more men out to assist the general with tethering cables together, and there was a hopper inside and fueling up, but it currently did not have enough charge to get to Andrew and then bring him back.

"Another half an hour, we can send it out and get him."

Jax stepped close enough to join the conversation. "We'll discuss your inadequate equipment manifest and how to fix that at a later date, Captain. Just give us control of the cameras for now."

"Yes, sir."

Fifteen seconds later, the view on the main monitor shifted, and we were looking at a four-way split screen, all views on Drew and Shivan. Will added the captain to the audio feed, and Jax reminded him that the conversations heard by the bridge crew were covered under the highest level of security. If anyone present didn't have that clearance, they needed to leave.

Why?

"Because of Shivan," Will whispered to me. "And Drew might mention the jump technology. Bases need to be covered."

"Elysium command crew is cleared," General Myers said. "Third cable is secure. I should have the fourth one in about five minutes."

"How many cables?" Drew asked him.

"Three more. I'm moving quicker now. Not sure why."

"Still pretty freaking far away."

"We'll get there. Just keep heading this way."

The captain's voice cut in. "Captain Gardner here, Prince Andrew. Heads up. There's a debris field headed your way."

Drew swore under his breath. "How bad?"

It didn't matter how bad. Shivan inched closer and crawled onto Drew's back, reasoning that it was better if he were hit than if Drew were. It appeared to be a wide swath of particle matter, dust-sized pieces of the destroyed pod, and segments of the tether Drew had cut loose from his harness.

"Damn, Shivan," Drew breathed. "I like you, but come on."

"This may be the biggest thrill you have all day," Shivan chortled. "Enjoy."

"Cover his head!" General Myers shouted. "Now!"

Without hesitation, Shivan shimmied up Drew's back a bit further and used his arms and chest to protect Drew's head as the debris began pelting them. The only sound we heard was Drew's breathing, which was hard and fast, and swearing riding between each breath.

Hyrum clamped his hands over his mouth, and from behind them shouted, "Drew, look out! There's big things!"

There was nothing Drew could do. The head of the decapitated drone bounced off Shivan's backside, but the worst of it, the thing Hyrum saw speeding at them, was a section of the cable that had attached the pod to Elysium. It was flayed open, with internal cables and wires exposed, and the casing had split in sharp angles.

They had no way to dodge it.

Shivan doubled down on his grip, one leg wrapped around Drew's torso, and he held Drew's head as tightly to his chest as he could while telling Drew to grip hard, to not let the impact tear his hands off the crawler.

When it hit, smashing into their legs, the crawler began to spin. Drew yelled out, "Shit, shit, shit, shit, shit!" and Hyrum dropped into a squat, covering his own head with his arms to avoid seeing whatever might happen to them. Oz gritted her teeth together and took a step closer, and then very calmly said, "You're all right, Drew. Ride it out. You can reorient when it stops."

He was still saying *shit* on repeat, but his breathing began to slow. "Reorient," he grunted. "I'm dizzy as hell."

"I'm not human," Shivan reminded him. "I'm unaffected. She's right. Ride it out, and then we'll get you headed in the right direction."

"Sure," Drew said, sounding doubtful.

"The Emperor made sure I understood everything necessary about this crawler. There's nothing to worry about."

It began to slow, but having seen the impact and the result, Oz jammed the side of her fist into her mouth to keep from crying out.

"Dude," Drew said, "nothing to worry about? Is that your leg or mine floating toward the planet?"

Shivan slid off Drew's back and looked down. "I have both."

"Fuck."

"The nanosuit will seal off the wound," Oz said between sharp breaths. "Just keep going. I'll buy you a new one when you get home."

"Foot, too? Because I see a boot floating past, and it looks a lot like mine."

"Just get pointed the right way again." Oz's voice cracked. "Move."

"I'm charging you for damages to the suit," Will said dryly. "Shivan, turn him twenty-three degrees to the right."

Shivan held Drew by his hips and turned him so that he was facing the shuttle bay again. "This is where you send me home, Drew," he said gently.

"What? No. I need you here. I would have died—"

"I'm draining power from the sled, and that incident caused you to use far more of your available air that you would have otherwise. You need to flip the switch for me. I can't reach it."

"But what if it doesn't work? What if you're stuck here?"

"It will work."

"You don't *know* that," Drew snapped. "I'm not leaving you here to float forever in space. Or maybe worse, fall into the atmosphere and burn."

"If that happens, I won't feel anything. Will considered that possibility and will send a signal that turns off my ability to feel."

He was lying and counting on Drew not knowing that.

"And if I wind up floating around out here, aware, they'll send someone to get me later."

"Presuming another debris field doesn't damage your transmitter."

"Save points," Shivan said. "He'll roll the program back. I'll wake up in my yard, where I left, and my wife will be right there. I just won't remember this."

"But *you'll* still be out here."

"I'll be fine, I swear. But you have to do this, and now. Send me home to my family, Andrew, for no reason other than it will allow you to return to yours. Please. We both need our families."

Drew nodded, and Shivan began to turn so he could reach the switch.

"Andrew. I hope that whatever creator you believe in, whichever God it is, that he protects you the rest of the way. I am certain that mine will."

"When did you start believing?"

"I have met my creator. It's not religion, it's just…fact."

"Your creator is probably sitting there, staring at Jo, thinking up kinky things to do to her."

"Still. God be with you."

Choking on his breath, Drew flipped the switch. He watched as the suit deactivated, and he stared at the shiny blue fabric now devoid of anything resembling Shivan. After a moment, he reached over and gave the drone a gentle shove toward Earth, where it would enter the atmosphere and burn.

"Hyrum." Drew's voice was soft. "What's that song you sing to the kids? The one Aubrey used to sing to you? Will you sing it for me?"

Reluctantly, Hyrum stood up and swallowed the rest of his tears. He began singing, quietly, until he heard Aubrey join him. His voice rode over hers, strong and sweet, until they reached the end of *You Are My Sunshine*.

"I really dig how you sing that, buddy. I hope you sing it for Eli, too."

He was quiet over the next five minutes, until he pulled himself onto the surface of the crawler. "I can't hold on anymore," he said softly, "I'm running out of air."

"You're almost there," Will said. "Five more minutes."

"I have three."

"No more talking," Oz said. "Save your breath. Not another word."

For the next two minutes, no one moved. No one spoke. Static popped from the speakers, but otherwise, there was silence. General Myers kept working on the cable, ignoring the person who was creeping along the cable behind him, now close enough to touch and almost close enough to clip the boosters onto his boots. Captain Gardner left the line silent out of respect.

I heard Hyrum sniff, trying to not cry loudly, and from the corner of my eye saw him wipe tears off his face. He wanted to wail but refused to have that be the last thing Drew ever heard from him.

At two minutes, ten seconds, Drew breathed out, "Ozzy, I love you."

Oz was sobbing but managed to croak, "I love you, too, you big jerk."

~

She refused to crumble. Oz stood stiffly, her jaw grinding, hands clasped tightly behind her back, and she watched as Drew floated slowly toward the open shuttle bay on Elysium. Tears poured down her face, but she refused to sob out loud again.

There was a chance that Drew could still hear, but she'd said the last thing she wanted him to hear and ground her teeth together to keep another word from slipping out.

Anthony Myers continued to work feverishly, scrambling along the cables he had tethered together. He'd connected the final one and rushed to reach the end of it, which left Will with a puzzled look of his face. His job was done. There was nothing else he could do. When the crawler was within reach, the cable pinchers would grab him, and a security tech on the other end would engage the recoil, and the cable would begin to rewind inside the shuttle bay.

When he reached the pincher, Myers stood on the thin cable, balancing, giving a slight bounce to test its rigidity. Jax cut through the tense silence, causing Hyrum and Aubrey to flinch when he asked loudly, "Anthony, what the hell are you doing?"

"Mental measurements. I don't have traction, but I have a minion with me, and he can generate a little ballistic force, I think. He'll help me reach him and what his push doesn't do, the boosters will."

"Don't."

"I have no doubt that I can reach that crawler, sir."

"I imagine you can, General, but that doesn't mean you can bring it in. It's low on power, and Drew is out of air. Don't make this worse."

"My risk to take."

"Do not do this," Jax said. "That's an order."

"What are you going to do, Your Majesty? Fire me?" He crouched, tested the line again, and then gestured to his new companion. His unnamed helper grabbed the cable with both hands, tucked his feet to his chest, and shoved against Myers' backside, hard. "Go ahead. Fire away."

The line wobbled. He didn't have the push-off he'd hoped for, but he had movement and was heading toward Drew at almost the same speed the crawler was moving.

"Son of a bitch," Jax spat.

"I don't care if I die out here, Your Majesty. I care if he does."

"You'll fucking slow him down!"

"I'll fucking push him harder. And I have something he needs."

"It'd better be good," Will said.

Myers' hand twitched toward his back. "Spare tank. I have air. I'd intended on waiting until we'd snagged him, but I don't imagine he has that kind of time. And you know what? I do. I can swap his tank out, push him closer to the pinch cable, and hang right here until that damned hopper is topped off enough to come for me."

Jax turned to Will. "Will that work?"

Will gave a light shrug. "It's not as if we can stop him now. He's already moving. You'll drift, Anthony."

"Then I drift. Just get someone to me before I enter the atmosphere, and we're good."

Oz finally turned. "If he gets air to Drew, you'll give him a goddamned raise and a parade on top of it."

"No parade," Myers grunted. "I'm kind of shy."

"You're a crazy old man, that's what you are," Aubrey said. "And forgive these cranky boys. Anthony...thank you. Thank you for trying."

He gets a dozen wiener cookies, too.

"Eh, what's the cat saying?" Myers asked.

"He wants you to eat a dick." When Hyrum realized what he'd said, he clamped his hands over his mouth. "I'm sorry! I didn't mean it like that."

"You've been hanging around Jay too much," Aisha sighed.

"Cookies," Will explained. "He means the aforementioned wiener cookies."

"Sure, he did. I've always suspected that cat didn't like me." Myers chuckled. "Can't say as to how I blame him. And son of a bitch, how the hell do I stop when I reach the prince?"

"Grab the edge of the crawler," Will said. "Curve your body so that you move in a circle. You'll spin him, but you'll slow and mitigate loss of any forward progress he's made."

The general did exactly as Will said. The moment his fingertips touched the side of the crawler, he curled and spun Drew around several times until he'd stopped. Before he changed the air tank, he made sure Drew was pointed in the right direction, and once he'd connected it to Drew's system, he activated the boosters. Bright light exploded from his heels, and they sped up; as the boosters sputtered fifteen seconds later, Myers shoved as hard as he could, aiming the crawler for the cable.

The man who had kicked the General into space was responsible for snatching the crawler. If needed, the pincher would catch Drew without the crawler and drag him in at high speed, coming to a stop before he reached the bay.

A soft sound echoed in the workshop. It was somewhere between a gurgle and a whine, as an unconscious Drew struggled to begin breathing again.

Hyrum began bouncing on his toes, his hands clutched to his chest. Jo left the computer she had been at, and Finn abandoned his scrutiny of all the data Drew's suit sent. We watched, collective breaths held, as Drew slipped toward the station, and as the pincher grabbed him by the stump of his leg and began pulling him in. He sped toward the shuttle bay and two people floating outside. They waited, ready to snatch him when the pincher released his leg, ready for momentum to push them inside.

He looked like a ragdoll. He hung there in the clutch of the pincher the way toys did from Thor's mouth, and the only thing missing was drool dripping from his fingers.

The tension didn't abate when he was inside.

Hyrum bounced harder. Oz fought the impulse to collapse onto the floor in a massive, wailing lump. Aubrey reached for her, trying to soothe, while Will stepped over to the computer, looking for signs of life.

"Mom," he said softly, "change the camera view to Drew's." He turned his head a bit and motioned for Finn to join them. "Send a signal to Drew's suit. I want him to draw a sharp breath if he can."

"He's breathing, right?" Hyrum asked. "He got air."

"He is, but not deeply enough." Will didn't look at him. "I want to hear a hard, sharp breath. Captain Gardner, if you will."

The captain's voice came through the speaker. "Listening."

"The prince has a camera tethered to his chest. I want it freed and turned so that we can see him."

Three seconds later, the view on the monitor changed. The cowl of his suit obscured his face, but it was clear that he was inside, on the floor, though he wasn't moving. Will ordered his helmet removed and indicated to Jo to send a signal to Drew's suit to lower the cowl.

The nanobots separated and fell to the back of his head, where they would then pool to his shoulders. The camera moved around too much to get a good look at his face; there were too many people grabbing at him, trying to get his harness off so that he could lay flat on his back. With his oxygen system attached to his back, it wasn't possible to do much of anything to rouse him. They were treating him as they would any injured crew member, ready to jump-start his heart if needed, ready to breathe for him.

"Step back from the Prince," Will ordered.

There was confusion, and they kept working.

"Step back," Captain Gardner bellowed.

Will nodded to Jo. She sent a signal, which in turn activated a command in his external suit's controller, which sent another signal to his nanosuit to shock him.

Drew's eyes flew open, and he sucked in the deep, hard breath Will hoped for. I wanted to hear him yell, to swear at the pain of it, but he slumped back again, and his eyes closed.

"He's breathing," Will said, looking at the monitor. "Heartbeat is slow but increasing. Blood oxygen is climbing."

"Anthony," Jax said, "how much of a raise do you want?"

"Screw that. I want a wiener cookie."

"I'll make bunches!" Hyrum shouted. "I promise!"

"What's the word, Prince Andrew?" Myers asked. "Are you with us?"

There was a grunt, then a groan, and one thinly spoken, exhaustion-laden whispered word. "Oz."

~

Anthony Myers waited in space, alone, for forty-five minutes. A new power cell was inserted into the crawler and sent back using the newly tethered cables at a speed that, when it was released, reached him in two minutes. He turned it around, grabbed on, and returned to the station just fifteen minutes later.

The first thing he did after shedding his protective suit was to head for the medical unit. As he stomped through the corridors, he ordered security cameras turned on and streamed to Will's workshop and demanded a direct audio line to the station's physician, reminding him to not remove Drew's inner suit.

"That shit is the only thing keeping him alive right now, and it'll do a better job of addressing his wounds than you can."

Myers didn't worry about playing nice. If the doctor took offense, he didn't care.

Captain Gardner met him at the door; he began uttering his congratulations on a successful rescue, but Myers cut him off. "You had the son-in-law of our King under your command, were fully aware that he would be outside the hopper, and you had nothing in place to rescue him should an accident occur. Your orders included a directive for backup. You paired him with a pilot who refused to obey a direct order, and the result is that the Prince very nearly died and has lost half of one leg and his foot from the other."

"Sir, I—"

"I don't want to hear it right now. I don't want you in sickbay with him. You'll get me Major Gaff's service record, you'll find out where in your chain of directives the order for backup failed, and you damn well start contemplating life outside the military. If I have my way, you're done."

"Is he done?" Hyrum asked Jax, whispering.

Jax nodded.

"What does that mean? Is he gonna be dead?"

"We will not execute the captain," Will said. "Anthony, can you still hear us?"

"Affirmative," he answered. "I'm bringing a mic pack to Andrew so that you can communicate with him as well."

Drew was propped up on a padded medical bed, drink cup in hand. Standing near was a medical technician with a tablet in one hand as he gestured with the other, seemingly inquiring about the nanosuit, and how much of it could be peeled back. They wanted to place a data patch on his chest; the information from Finn's data stream was readily available, but they wanted their own. Drew gave a slight shrug, though I wasn't sure if that was because he didn't care or because he didn't know.

He was the pinkest I had ever seen him. His hair was sweat-slicked, and tiny drops were clinging to the stubble above his upper lip. Fatigue burned in his eyes. Myers entered the frame of the video feed, stood at the foot of the bed, and he crossed his arms as he did a quick assessment of Drew's condition.

"You look like shit, son," he said.

"You look a little too happy about that."

"I am. You're not dead."

Drew grunted and set the cup aside. "You're just excited because you got to play outside in outer space and then got to be the hero."

"I'd be lying if I didn't admit that leaving the station was a thrill. But I'm not the hero. I did my job. Nothing heroic about that." He unfolded his arms and leaned against the footboard. "We both know who the hero in this is."

"Hyrum," Drew said, voice stronger. "Can he still hear me?"

"I hear you, Drew!" Hyrum called out. "But I didn't do anything!"

Myers moved to the head of the bed and slipped a micro-speaker into Drew's ear. "Hyrum can hear you, but you can't hear him. He doesn't think he did anything."

"Not long ago," Drew said once the speaker was in place. "Do you remember when you said something might happen to my air supply, and you wanted to add to it? Every technician in the room said you were wrong, that what you wanted to do wouldn't work. But it worked, Hyrum. It worked, and it saved my life."

"But it was just air. Shivan saved you."

"Listen to me carefully, Hy. Shivan might have been the one to bring me the crawler, and General Myers might have been the one who was brave enough to leap after me, but if you hadn't insisted on adding another layer of oxygen, and hadn't thought of a clever way to do it, I wouldn't have lived long enough for the general to get me. I would have died after the debris cloud hit me. And putting Shivan in the drone was your idea. I needed him. You were right. I was scared, and I needed him."

"But you lost a leg. I'm really sorry about that, Drew. Can you get it back?"

"Damn, dude, you are way too sweet. All I want you to hear right now is this: you saved my life. All those days ago, without even knowing it, you saved my life."

Oz put her arms around Hyrum, hugging him tightly. "He's right, you know. We'll get Drew's leg and foot fixed, but you really are the hero here. My hero, Hyrum. I'll never be able to thank you enough."

He tolerated it when she kissed his cheek, pretending that it was gross and that he hated it.

"I'm telling the whole world, Hy," Drew said. "When they ask, I'm telling them that I'm alive because Hyrum Blackshear, maybe the most important person at Ozoo, invented the system that saved my life."

"Oh, don't do that," Hyrum said. "If you tell the world, then girls will want to kiss me, and maybe be my girlfriend, and I don't want that."

"All right." Drew struggled to sit a bit more upright and looked annoyed when the med tech tried to help. "But I need to ask you something. Don't tell anyone about my leg and foot, okay? We can only talk about it with family."

"Okay."

"He means family that lives in the building," Oz said. "I know you'll want to tell your mom and your brothers, but it has to stay a secret."

"On account of how Dr. Brian will fix it?"

"Exactly."

"Then you better make that guy playing with your pillow pinkie swear."

Drew promised he would elicit a time-honored pinkie swear out of everyone who saw him, and then asked if he could have time alone to talk to Oz. Reluctantly, one by one, they filtered out of the room until it was just Oz and Will, and Will was only there because he was trying to pick me up and I kept running from him.

I need to stay. Just go.

Scottish ire reared its head. "I will no' leave you here to eavesdrop."

I really need to stay. If I leave, I'll throw up. I'm upset. I mean it, I'm more upset than I've ever been. And you dropped your 't' again.

"Give up, Will," Drew said. "You know he's going to win."

"They deserve privacy," Will chastised.

I've seen them do things to each other. Privacy left the station several years ago.

"Fine." He directed Oz to his office, where she could curl up in the comfy corner chair and then ran the feed from Elysium's sickbay to her phone. He wagged his pointy finger at me—respect their conversation, or I'll turn you inside out—and then left.

I'm not sure what he was worried about.

It's not like I ever repeated anything.

~

"How much pain are you in?" Oz had made herself comfortable in Will's oversized corner chair, the first time she had sat down since Drew's hopper left Elysium. She hadn't eaten anything, had nothing to drink, her boobs were leaking a little bit, and I could hear her stomach growling.

"Not feeling anything," Drew said sleepily. "The moment they yanked my helmet off, someone slapped a couple of patches on my neck. Pain control and shock prevention. I might be a little bit high right now."

I jumped onto the arm of the chair and stuck my head over Oz's arm.

"Wick," Drew snorted. "Let me talk to Oz."

I will after you tell her where Will's little fridge is. She needs something to eat and drink. Tell her, and then I'll leave her alone.

"Just show her. Oz, Wick is going to show you where there's sad, disappointing food and equally sad bottles of water."

I ran across the office and pawed at the mini-fridge, which was easily overlooked because it blended in with the file cabinets. After she grabbed water and a veggie box, I pawed at the cabinet to the left, where Will kept crackers for times when the kids were with him.

"You're a good man, Wick," Oz said, rubbing my head.

I didn't answer, because I had promised to be quiet after that. I stretched out on the back of the chair, where I could see Drew on her phone's screen, and tried to give them as much privacy as I could while they talked about Eli and missing him. Drew wanted to take him and Oz somewhere, anywhere, when he was back home and healed.

"No work for a while," he said quietly. "Ozoo can run fine without me, and maybe you can carve out some time."

"We're selling the Wastelands park," she said. "I'll leave it to the board to deal with the sale. We'll have time. We'll go anywhere you want."

"Except Elysium." He'd meant it as a joke, but the humor faded before it passed his lips. "Ozzy, I'm sorry. All of this...all because I wanted to be the one to test out the damned suit. Anyone could have done it. Someone with training—"

"You made that offer," she reminded him. "I told you to go. No regrets, Drew. And I know it's going to eat at you for a while. We'll get through it."

He swallowed hard, giving a slight nod of his head. "I choked. I was fine until I had the crawler in front of me. But then the station seemed so far away, and I couldn't..."

A deep voice cracked through the speaker. "You couldn't fathom covering the distance. When the pod blew, you sucked it up because you had to and there was nothing you could do. When the crawler showed up, you'd drifted so far that getting back felt like it would be the hardest thing you've ever done. And I bet it was."

Drew's eyes widened. "Carter."

Oz twitched. "*Carter?* Your brother is there?"

"What the hell?" Drew looked as puzzled as he was fatigued. "How?"

Carter leaned over the edge of the bed and smiled at the camera. "Hey, Oz. How's that nephew of mine?"

"Probably less confused than I am right now."

"Cross-trained a year ago," he said. "I'm here on a temporary assignment as a comms specialist. I keep the magic talky boxes talking to each other. Or not, as the case warrants. You know, in case someone here needs to talk to someone there. Privately. Desperately."

"You kept the lines open?" Oz asked. "When Drew was...out there?"

"They'd have stayed open. I just sat on top of it and made sure there was no lag and no bleed into a public transmission. When General Myers entered the bridge a few minutes ago, he recognized me and sent me on my merry way. Tough son of a bitch, that one."

"You're here," Drew breathed.

"I knew you would be on Elysium. I asked for the assignment." Carter shrugged. "I wanted a chance to hang with you here before I move onto the next one. I'd really hoped I would surprise you by showing up at your quarters tonight with pizza and beer."

"What's next?" Drew asked.

"Mars. I wanted to see you before I left."

"*Mars?* Does Mom know?"

Carefully, Carter sat on the edge of the bed. "She knows. Dad knows. I asked them to keep it quiet because I don't want the media sniffing me out before I leave. But they're still looking for Carter Van Hoff, not Sergeant Hamid Mor."

"Dammit. They're hauling me home in the morning."

Carter shook his head. "They're hauling you home in about three hours. Canada is sending a shuttle."

"Dammit."

"Hey." Carter set his hand on Drew's shoulder. "I'm going with you. It's been squared away with my commander. I'll take a couple days and then hop on the next shuttle back. Mom and Dad will be there, too."

Drew's eyes closed, and he moaned about how much they didn't know and how awful it had to be for them to get snippets of information.

"I've talked to Mom. Aubrey kept her apprised, and the Emperor kept the video and audio streamed to the war room at home. They know. And they know you're basically okay. But they still want to see you before you get whisked away to fix all this shit. So it'll be a short visit."

"Your mother is tougher than you think," Oz said. "Even if she's breaking inside, she'll hold it together."

Drew's eyes filled. "I didn't want them to see that. I didn't want anyone to see it. I choked, Carter. If I had let Shivan go when I was told to, if I had gotten moving when I was told to… the General could have died out there because of me."

"You think he cared about that?" Carter asked. "He's been prepared to die for the last fifty, sixty years. You don't get to where he is without having a steel spine. General Myers is a true solider, Drew. He decided when he was younger than you are that he was willing to die for King and country. That includes you."

"Yeah, but—"

"But nothing. You didn't choke. You hesitated at your own mortality like anyone else would have. And I guarantee that if you'd been out there trying to save Oz, or save your son, or just about anyone else, you would have taken off like a shot and not considered the worst possibilities until it was over."

Drew couldn't speak but was able to give a slight nod.

"Truth, little bro? I would have died if it had been me. When you were told to cut your harness? I would have hesitated then. Just for a second, but that's all it would have taken. I would have lost my shit when I realized my leg was flying away. And that's if I even got that far."

"You would have. And don't lie to me to make me feel better. I saw you fight in Chicago. I watched you fight hand to hand and win. You're a tough bastard."

"All right. I'll give you that one. But for as big of an asshole as I am, and the front I always put up? I got my eye-opening lesson about my core a couple months before you got there. I was not a tough bastard. Just a bastard."

He set his hand on Drew's chest. "All right, bro. You're half in the bag and about to fall asleep. Let yourself. And while you drift off, I'm going to tell you a story, and I want you to remember it. But if you fall asleep, Oz will tell it to you again."

As far as Queen Shazia of Midlam knew, her eldest son had stuffed a backpack with enough clothing to get by for a week, retrieved his passport under the name Hamid Mor from security lockup, and hopped on a trans-Atlantic shuttle to spend the summer wandering around Europe.

It was his last blast after having graduated from Northwestern with a degree in political science. Upon his return home, he was expected to fulfill a range of royal duties for a year and then enter law school. It was a career she thought he would be especially good at; she sent him on his way with her blessings, because he'd found his footing and wanted to learn enough of the law to help serve his country.

Carter did wish to serve his country. He also recognized that he was a selfish, senseless, borderline misogynistic twatwaddle and that if he took off on that summer trip, he might not return for several years. He had no real interest in law school. He felt no direction in life calling to him and realized that he would do no good in the world if he didn't, as he told Drew, get his shit together.

He took his passport and other ID supporting his identity as Hamid Mor and headed for the closest military recruitment center. He hoped that by not being Prince Carter, by having lived as much out of the public eye as was possible for a member of the royal family, that he could slide through basic training without anyone realizing who he was.

He was wrong.

The recruiter knew who he was but accepted his passport and ID as proof enough. His drill instructors knew who he was; that bought him a slim margin of leeway during training, something which he both appreciated and resented. His squad knew who he was, but that earned him no respect; they resented the bit of leeway he was given, too.

They made life difficult during basic training and treated him the way he had treated so many others before, but they honored his wish to remain as anonymous as possible. They appreciated that he was not there as a prince, but as just another recruit. There was no teasing when he came straight out and asked at the end of the first week: don't tell anyone who would tell my mother.

Carter floundered at first but found his footing before basic training ended, and assumed that everything that came after would be easier. But then Florida attacked, flying ancient bombers over Chicago, destroying much of the city before anyone comprehended what was going on.

"Two weeks after they attacked, I graduated basic. My first assignment—I was a security grunt at the time—was patrolling Chicago to protect survivors, the people who didn't leave the city. There weren't many, and the ones who stayed were generally parents who had lost children and were basically walking zombies at that point. But damn, Drew. They dropped me into Chicago, and it was like walking into hell."

The city was still on fire. Flames and smoke rose from the crumbled remains of Carter's childhood. Broken bodies of the dead littered smoldering streets, and as his squad marched toward city center, someone behind him remarked that the aroma cutting through the air was too much like a church barbeque gone wrong.

No one laughed.

They skirted wide cuts caused by Pacifica's defensive burn runs as they headed for shelter that was no longer there. A dozen times during that march, they were attacked by Floridian fighters they had presumed were long gone. Their squad was well armed but small, and it was small because they had been assured that they were only there to protect Chicago's few remaining citizens.

"Their fighters? Fuck. Initially, most of them were kids. Thirteen, maybe fourteen years old. They attacked with hunting rifles and knives, and they were too damned successful. We just hadn't expected them. By the time we reached our post, half of our men and women were dead. Most of those kids were dead. And my lieutenant was screaming into his comms system, blasting some major on the other end who hadn't thought those little bastard fighters were worth mentioning."

The post has been blown to bits in the initial bombing. They were down half their squad, had little food and water, and no place to dig in.

Carter scouted the skyline, wishing more than ever that he had gone on the trip to Europe, and spotted the Hancock building. It was standing tall, there was clearly electricity running, and he expected that its residents had evacuated. His gut told him that his parents were in San Francisco, and anyone else would have been ordered out. At best, there were a handful of guards still roaming the halls.

"There," he said to the lieutenant. "We can set up a base there. We'll have food, water, beds, and access to the Queen's war room."

"What is it?"

"Home, sir."

From the Hancock, they were able to survey the city. They knew where electricity was still running—buildings not entirely on the grid, with self-sustaining solar—and had made sure that Pacifica's military would leave the building out of its sights. They began patrolling the city, battling the remaining young men from Florida, and then members of Florida's army.

"They could fight, too. I knew these were soldiers trained by someone else. They were too well-honed to be a product of Florida. They came out at night, all-black uniforms, and picked us off one by one. And that was just the first few days. Our lieutenant was a casualty before the third day was over."

His certainty in serving Midlam by way of the military faltered. In half a week, he'd seen more than half of his squad dead. He'd seen the intestines of the soldier next to him spill out and hit the ground. He'd seen an arm sliced off. Throats slit. An eye exploded when a bullet went through it.

"Day five," he said softly. "We heard the whine of a Pacifican burner cutting through the city. I dove into the closest trench, one probably created by the same burner a day earlier. I pushed myself as hard as I could into the wall of that thing, trying to make myself smaller, less visible. I heard fighting on the ground, fists and feet pummeling into someone's body, and I wasn't sure what I should do. I mean, I'd done what I was supposed to do, I took cover, but one of my squad was still up there fighting for his life. But I was frozen. I couldn't make myself move. And then his head flew into the trench and landed at my feet.

"I lost it. Like, full-on, toddler-level lost it. I wanted to go home, even though I *was* home, and home was broken and burned. I wanted my mom. I wanted everyone's mom. I curled up and cried like a goddamned baby and was probably ten seconds away from pissing myself when I heard someone else wailing even harder."

Ten feet from him, curled up on the blackened, burned ground, was a Floridian soldier. He was dressed in a dirt-encrusted white dress shirt, torn black slacks, and beat-up high-top sneakers. He was crying loudly, giving voice to what Carter had wanted: *Mom. Mommy. I want to go home.*

"Couldn't have been more than thirteen. No rifle, he'd lost it before running for the trench. The head had rolled onto its side, and its open eyes were staring at him. That boy was *done.* He'd also gotten to the point I was almost at and had peed like a fucking racehorse. I scrambled to get an aim on him, but he didn't move once he realized I was there. He just, fuck, sat there with tears and snot streaming down his face, my gun pointed at him. I could have shot, probably should have, but I wasn't looking at some trained soldier. I was looking at my baby brother, *someone's* baby brother, and couldn't do it. I lowered the gun and told him to sit tight. We'd wait it out until the burner was out of the area, and then I'd get him to safety."

Carter inched over, putting himself between the boy and the head of Jaron Hightower. He calmed himself by asking the boy questions—what's your name, where are you from—and in the half-hour they spent there, he found the resolve he needed.

Boys like Colin Kimball from Pensacola, Florida, were only there because of old men too afraid to fight for themselves. They were there as fore fodder for the trained soldiers who were also there on behalf of those old men. His targets would not be the boys like Colin; he would protect them when he could, he would take prisoners and not create more grief for their mothers, but he would fight like hell when faced with the soldiers in black.

"I took that kid in, and yeah, we held him as prisoner. We took a lot of kids as prisoners and shipped them to Canada to wait out the war. But Colin Kimball? Man, that kid was my real wake up call. I was just as scared as he was, but I was there by choice. And I made the choice again. I would do whatever the hell necessary to grow up and be a man for the first time in my life. And I'd be lying if I didn't admit that I wanted to be the man my baby brother already was.

"You've had your shit together since you were fourteen of fifteen. You knew the path you would set out on, the girl you wanted to walk it with, and you were patient enough to make it happen. I sat in that trench and realized that the only thing I had done with my life is hurt other people. I knew what you probably thought about me. And I just wanted my brother to be proud of me.

"So yeah, I get it. You were out there alone, and it was scary as hell. You thought you were going to die. I sat in that trench and thought I was going to die, and I cried like a goddamned baby. You saw the distance from the crawler to safety and hesitated. You *just* hesitated. And when you started running out of air, you didn't start crying. You used what you thought was your last breath to make sure Oz knew she was what you were thinking about, and that you loved her.

"You didn't choke, Drew. You had a moment, that's all. And that's fine. No one that matters will even think about it. What we're going to remember is that you did something the rest of us don't have the balls to do and survived what we wouldn't have. Cry about it for a while because it hurts, cry as hard as you need to, but then fucking get over it. And let Oz help you. If anyone can empathize, it's Oz."

By the time Carter finished, Drew was asleep. He took the phone out of Drew's still-tense fingers and turned it so that he could see Oz.

"He'll probably sleep until it's time to move him to the shuttle," Carter told her, almost whispering. "I'll stay with him. Maybe it's time for you to go home and tell your son that Daddy's coming home soon."

"Carter." Oz's breath hiccupped. "After this, if you ever call yourself an asshole again, I'll rip you a new one."

"Still am," he chuckled. "I have a lot to make up for. Some of it to him. I wish I had more time."

"You can go with him when he gets his legs taken care of. He'll be out of it for the whole thing, but you'd have the hours before and a few days after."

Carter shook his head. "I can take three days, tops. And it's not that I wouldn't wait until the next Mars cycle if I could. I'm one of only half a dozen people who can deal with the colony's communications problems right now. This shit is the one thing I'm good at."

"Trust me," she said, a slight grin tugging at the corners of her mouth, "we can make it happen, and you'll get to Mars on time."

~

On Drew's 25th birthday, we sat on the roof and watched as Elysium went live. On his 26th, we sat at the kitchen table with the remnants of pepperoni pizza that had been delivered from Sean McAllister's restaurant, keeping an eye on the children playing in the living room. His parents had gone home in the afternoon, reluctantly, and only because Shazia had business that could not wait. Carter lingered for two more hours, until the taxi taking him to the launch site in Marin had arrived.

Drew wanted to go with him to watch the shuttle depart. Carter wanted him to stay home to celebrate his life with his wife and son, promising that he would call from Mars as soon as he'd fixed their communications lag. So Drew stayed, enjoying the pizza and the noise. He opened gifts from the kids—a bell for his bicycle that played an obnoxious tune at an equally obnoxious decibel, bathtub toys that he could enjoy with Eli—and from Hyrum, a rare print copy of short stories by some of Drew's favorite authors. Mostly, he tried to smile and appreciate the effort put into his birthday, but there was no hiding the pain behind his smile.

I could see his teeth, the upturn at the corners of his mouth; what I missed was the twinkle in his eyes.

He'd spent several days in Will's birth When, sedated to unconsciousness as he floated in a surgical tank. The first few hours kept him alive; the next few he spent just above the surface as Mass carefully attached a bio-printed leg and foot to his body, after which he was lowered back into the gel to allow the surgical nanobots to finish the job, creating new nerve pathways and blood vessels, sculpting tendons and ligaments, strengthening muscle. When he was awakened at the end of the surgery, Mass reminded him that he would be weak and needed physical therapy, but no one warned him about the sadness that would wrap around him like a wet, itchy blanket.

The pain, the physical pain, the angry tingling and itchiness of nerve growth, hadn't surprised him. That would go away in time. Every night until then, Oz rubbed his legs, starting at his toes, working up to the faint scar on his thigh, trying to soothe the fire with an ointment that only took the edge off. He knew he would recover from that.

The melancholy, the lurking sense of impotence, was something he wasn't sure about.

The night of his birthday, he pretended. He smiled when it was expected and laughed when he was able; his gratitude over the gifts the children had picked was genuine, and he was able to make them understand that he was, after all, happy.

After the kids had smeared cake and frosting all over the table and exhausted themselves into bedtime unprotested, he went out onto the balcony with Will and Aisha, Jax and Aubrey, and a bottle of cinnamon whiskey. Will wasn't fooled, though he kept it to himself. I don't think Aubrey was fooled, either, because she found every reason she could to touch him and for her hand to linger on his skin.

Oz was the least fooled. Just before midnight, she whispered to him that he had one more thing waiting and pulled him toward their room. He tried to object; he didn't feel like it, it would suck for her, his heart wasn't into it, not yet. She promised it wasn't what he thought, and he needed to follow her.

I followed, too, because she'd asked that of me earlier.

Instead of leading him where he assumed, she told him to sit on the window seat and get comfortable. I stretched out on his lap, careful to stay above his scar, and when Oz handed her phone to him, I wiggled up a little higher so that I could see better.

"You fell asleep when Carter was telling you about his first couple of weeks in Chicago," she explained. "I know he said I should repeat the story for him, but I think you need to hear it in his voice."

I stayed as still as I could while he watched and listened and didn't look as she quietly left the room. His breath hitched twice, and I heard him swallow against the lump in his throat; when he set the phone aside, I started purring.

"Is that why you're here, Wick? Purr therapy?"

That's why Oz wanted me here. It's not why I came, though.

"Ah. You're here to tell me to stop being stupid. Suck it up and move on."

No. You'll get to that.

"Then?"

I'm here because I can't cry, Drew. I want to, but I can't.

He lifted me from his lap and held me close to his face. "I never considered that. But why would you want to?"

Because I thought you were going to die, too.

"Wick."

And now you're here, and I think you keep chewing on how you could have done more to save yourself.

"I think you're right."

All those years ago, when Levi Munson took Oz and tortured her, do you think she could have done more to save herself?

"What? No. She *did* save herself. She did everything she could have."

Yet she felt like she should have done more. She thought she should have fought sooner and harder.

"If she had, they would have killed her. She lived, and that's all—"

Let the lightbulb go off, sunshine.

"Wick, I *am* grateful that I'm alive. I'm grateful for everything done to save me. I really am."

So was Oz. Yet it took her time to heal emotionally. Longer than it took physically. You were super patient with her then, and she'll be patient with you now.

"I can't help how I feel."

I know. Neither could she. There's nothing wrong with how you feel, but you'll get from feeling this to feeling better a lot sooner if you stop pretending and just ask for help. Don't wait until we meet a boy with a sword and his cranky wizard. Don't wait for a dragon named Jeff and a cat named Fluffy.

"Don't wait for my own Tobias to jerk me into acceptance," he murmured.

Carter was right when he said that Oz can empathize the most. So let her help. Be honest with her. Be honest with everyone. Let them help, too. And when you're really recovered, dude, we're rocketing your asterisk back to Elysium.

"Why?"

So you can do what Oz wasn't able to. Face your demon. She never had the chance to face Levi, not really. But if you don't go back, you'll be afraid of Elysium for the rest of your life. Build another computer and go back. Just get a better pilot.

"Learn to fly, furball."

I'll enroll in flight school first thing in the morning.

"And I'll get started on your tiny, tiny flight suit."

Wait. Did you pee in your spacesuit? You were out there for a while, you know.

"I did not pee in my suit."

Yeah, I bet you did. How does that work? Like, you go, and it fills your boots, or what?

He might have been willing to tell me, but Oz came back in and saw the one thing she hoped for.

He was laughing.

And that was good enough for now.

There's something else you need to do. Before you start creating my tiny, tiny spacesuit. There's someone else who needs to see you. I know he's sent messages to the Emperor through the communications system in Jax's office. Don't wait until you're healed. He needs to see you like you are right now.

"You're right. I need to see him, too."

I bet he peed in his suit. That seems like a Shivan thing to do.

~

Fluffy, the magnificent, Clydesdale-height, sleek feline created from a whim that rode on a wish, stretched out on the dirt that extended from the edge of the village's ongoing bonfire to the gate of Shivan's front yard. He'd come to life as a massive orange tabby with piercing green eyes, but tonight his multi-colored fur glowed in the firelight, and his now blue eyes shimmered.

"Jeff taught him how to experiment," Shivan explained. "He has seemed undecided about his primary fur color, so he settled on this. Every color he can conceive. Refrain from telling him how beautiful he is. He preens when he thinks he's gorgeous."

Jeff, the dragon, was perched on Shivan's roof, wearing his ruby-red skin. He continued to play with color, changing to suit his moods, but enjoyed red the most. Because he was happy to see us, he wore his best suit, and it glittered the same way Fluffy's eyes did.

We arrived in Saint Francis shortly after Drew's birthday, just after lunch, with the intent of returning home before dinner. Intentions vaporized by late afternoon, when it was clear that Rhys and Quinn had Things To Do, egged on by Hyrum, while Alex and Charlie—mostly stunned into silence on their first visit to the simulated city by the sight of Jeff and Fluffy—tagged along.

Shivan and Lani were appropriately awed by the baby and took turns holding him; when he pulled Shivan's collar away from his chest in search of a food source, Oz was confident that Eli was comfortable enough to take a bottle from him, and she also wondered what Shivan had going under that itchy green tunic.

"Males in Saint Francis nurse the young," he said with a straight face. "Eli knows. He's a wise little man."

There was scotch—after the baby bottle was empty—enjoyed by firelight, until it was clear that everyone under ten needed to go to bed. Will and Aisha disappeared into the guest house with their children, followed a few minutes later by Oz, who asked Hyrum to help her get Eli ready for bed.

He protested; she always got Eli ready for bed and didn't need help. And he wanted to stay outside to pet Fluffy because he missed the giant cat.

Dude, she really means that Will and Aisha probably need help. The kids will wind down quicker if you're there to tell them a bedtime story. Your stories are better than Will's.

"Will tells good stories."

Will's stories are almost always educational. They like yours because you tell them just for fun. And this isn't school. We're here for fun.

"Oh. Is that like when Jax says Will needs to pull the stick out of his ass because he sounds like a teacher sometimes?"

Exactly like that. And Jax would know. He was a teacher for a while.

After Hyrum went inside, the villagers began vacating their seats near the fire. I wondered if that was coincidence or because Shivan willed it; within five minutes, the only people left were him and Drew, and he picked up another bottle from his front porch, Drew's preferred alcohol.

I felt the vibrations from Fluffy's gentle purring rise up from the ground, and he stuck his tail through the gate, winding it around Drew's ankle.

"You're not well," Shivan said after some time, as he poured another drink for Drew. "You're laughing at all the right moments. You smile for your son. You're amenable...but you're not well."

"And you are?"

Shivan set the bottle on the table where Drew could reach it. "No."

"You did everything right, though. Hell, you were *there*. You didn't have to be."

Shivan thought he'd done everything he could, yet it didn't feel like enough. He thought he could have shoved Drew toward the space station right from the start; it didn't matter if he couldn't reach the switch on his shoulder that sent him home. Someone on Earth could have written the code that recalled him, or they could have simply sent a signal to shut him down and restart his life in Saint Francis from the second after he left. He had one job; get the crawler to Drew. Instead, he indulged his own wants and stayed too long.

"Your life was at stake. Your human life. I am, and I embrace this, merely a compilation of finely crafted data."

Data with feelings, dude.

"But I needed you there," Drew said. "I needed to not be alone because I didn't honestly think I would make it back."

"Is that your source of guilt? Surviving when you felt you shouldn't? Because it makes no sense, Prince Andrew. You are alive because everyone else wished you to be."

"I didn't need to be out there in the first place."

"So? I don't *need* to be here, alive, right now. I exist because of the wishes of others. Finn could turn the entire program off, and we would vanish. And for those who have asked him to leave us be, I am grateful."

"I *am* grateful. But that spacewalk was selfish. If not for that, Major Gaff would be alive, General Myers wouldn't have taken such a huge risk—"

Gaff's death is on him. He broke the order of things. He refused to obey an order. That's not on you.

"But Gaff is still dead, Wick, and wouldn't be if I'd let someone trained to do the damned job do it."

Shivan exhaled hard. "So, someone else goes in your place. They take the same walk in space. Major Gaff does the exact same thing because he thinks he's helping. His intentions were good and that wouldn't likely change. It wasn't because it was *you* on that spacewalk, he did it was because he thought he was saving you a few minutes of work. He's dead either way. And in that scenario, the man hanging in space is not Prince Andrew, does not have the Emperor and the Princess Oz and the King Jackson fighting for his life. The Emperor would not have exposed his jump technology for anyone else. Which means the other man dies, too."

Listen to the Prince Regent.

Someone else would be dead where you're not.

Someone else might not have severed the tether in time.

Jeff grunted, sending tiny puffs of smoke to blanket the table, filling in the spaces of quiet that formed while Drew contemplated the mortality of an imaginary substitute.

"I have nightmares," Shivan said after a time, quietly. "Until now, I hadn't even considered that I sleep. Not really. I go to bed, close my eyes, open them, and it's morning. But now? I dream, Andrew. I have visions of spinning out of control, I feel all those things that pounded into us, and the helplessness of not knowing when or if it would stop. I often wake with a jolt, because in that dream I am hurtling toward the planet, where I know I will burn."

"You said Will turned off your ability to feel."

Shivan picked up his glass and stared into it. "I lied."

Drew has nightmares, too. But he doesn't tell them to Oz.

Drew glanced at me but didn't repeat it.

I creep into his dreams when I think they're bad. Sometimes, he dreams about spinning on the crawler, never slowing down, never getting closer to the station. Other times he dreams about the General shooting past him, getting lost in the atmosphere. He can never breathe in his dreams, yet at the same time, he's heaving giant sobs. I can feel him struggling to breathe, and I can't breathe for him. I sit on his chest and beg him to wake up while he struggles to breathe. I don't know how to help him. And he won't tell anyone.

"I never tell anyone my nightmares, either," Shivan said.

Drew jerked, then sat up straight. "How? And when?"

Shivan turned his arm over, looking at an imaginary watch on his wrist. "I began hearing words from him about fifteen minutes ago."

The computer. It sensed a need.

"And a wish," Shivan said. "I imagine this is transient. But I needed to hear what Wick has to say."

Why don't you tell the people you love about the things that haunt you at night? Let them help you.

"Because they can't," Shivan said simply. "And to expect them to try places an unfair burden upon them."

"You could ask Will to take the nightmares away," Drew pointed out. "Ten minutes, a few lines of code. He could temper them at the very least."

"He could. Yet, I won't. This might be the most human experience I ever have. I refuse to rid myself of it. Eventually, the dreams will fade."

You both need to talk to someone.

"I promised Oz I would," Drew said. "And I will, once we figure out someone safe."

Maybe someone who understands regret. Someone who understands what it's like to live with having inflicted decisions on other people. Worse than anything you can imagine.

"I don't think that person exists."

Not the way you're thinking of.

Fluffy let loose a low growl at the sound of footsteps crunching the dirt nearby, but he didn't move. Jeff also huffed again, but this time it was a warning.

"I felt compelled to be here." Tobias stood with his hands on the gate. "I don't know why."

"Wick?" Drew asked. "You called him here?"

I wished him here.

Shivan sighed again. "I am not sharing my innermost thoughts—"

He has new data. Everything ever written about human psychology, in theory and in practice. He knows what torture feels like from both sides. He knows how it feels to make the wrong decisions, even when he thinks they're the right ones. He gets that sometimes all you have are bad choices, but you still have to choose.

"I don't believe the worst of mine were ever right," Tobias said after Drew translated. "But I do understand the pain of it all, and the angst of chasing redemption."

"You've done well with that," Shivan admitted.

"But neither of you have done anything for which redemption is required." Tobias's eyebrows knotted, and with a grunt, he looked at me. "How are you doing that, cat? Even at my most powerful, I could not access information in that manner."

The computer likes me. And the game is over. You were a giant douche because Finn wrote you that way. Now you're not. I'm adding to his storyline with my own, and in my story, you know shit, and you help people.

"You know shit," Shivan repeated. "Wonderful."

Tobias would have gone into space to save Drew and died without regret. And he would have done it if you'd let him, just to keep you from dying. He's not the dark wizard anymore, Shivan. His going would have been more for you than Drew. To save his Prince Regent.

Drew reached for me, rubbing the top of my head with his fingers. "I know you mean well, Wick."

Then do it.

Drew, you can't talk to Hyrum's doctor. There's no one at home you can talk to because of everything about our family. You can't explain about Shivan or how he got there. Tobias can listen. And he can do it without judging you. He can explain things. He—

"I will help in any way I can," Tobias said, opening the gate when Shivan gestured for him to enter.

"I believe that, but…"

You have to let him help.

"Why, Wick?"

I told you before, Drew. I can't cry. You have to let him help because I can't cry, and it's going to break me. I can't change your dreams, I can only crawl inside and watch them, and I can't help you because you're so scared in them that you can't hear me, and I CAN'T CRY and I want to. I want to cry.

He reached for me again, but this time he picked me up and held me close. "I'm sorry, Wick."

Everyone else can break down and sob like babies, and they have someone to talk to in the middle of the night, but I don't, and if you don't do something about your bad dreams, it's going to kill me, Drew. I really think it will kill me. I can't fix anything, and I just can't...

"All right. I promise."

There were more footsteps, and then Will opened the gate. He didn't seem surprised to find Tobias there but didn't greet him, instead focusing on me.

"I heard you from the hut," he said softly, taking me from Drew. "You're not all right, are you?"

I am not all right.

"What can I do?"

I didn't know. Tobias reached over and tucked a finger under my chin, turning my face so he could look at me, tilting his head as he considered my pain.

"You are a tiny, mighty soul and carry the weight of your entire family, Wick. Do as you've ordered Prince Andrew to do. Talk. Perhaps not to me, as I am unfamiliar with the feline psyche, but perhaps to someone who understands pain that no one else can feel."

"I will help him any way I can," Will started, but Tobias shook his head.

"Hyrum."

Hyrum?

"The Emperor will feel your pain and cry because of it. Hyrum will empathize with your pain and cry for *you*."

He sees things no one else does.

I changed Tobias, Will. I made the computer teach him things Finn maybe never wanted him to know, so Drew would have someone to talk to.

"Finn will forgive you for that."

Will Oz?

"Will the things you allowed Tobias to learn end Andrew's pain?"

No. But maybe learn to live with it. Enough to let him sleep at night. Enough to get him to go back to Elysium.

"Then, she'll forgive you."

I feel lost, Will. Like I was on the right path but wandered off, and no matter which way I turn, I don't know where to go. The only road I was sure I should follow was getting Drew here to see Shivan and Tobias. Now he's here and I'm still scared. Because he almost died and I thought he was going to, and I know I have to take another step toward something, but I don't know what or who to go to—

His breath was warm against my ears. "You go to Hyrum. Tobias is right. Hyrum knows what it's like to look down a road and not be sure it's the right one."

Why can't I cry, Will? Everyone else gets to. I don't know how.

He was about to explain why, I think, but Fluffy flicked his tail and then got up. He sat in front of the gate with his face turned upward, looking past Jeff, and with his mouth slightly parted, he began to moan softly, which then turned into a sad, plaintive wail.

"Sometimes," Will whispered, just for me, "tears don't come, no matter how badly you need them to. But you can still cry. Follow Fluffy."

Follow him.

Fluffy stopped, and then looked to the path that cut between Shivan's house and the guest hut.

"Not everyone wants an audience to their pain, Wick. Perhaps you need to be by yourself for a bit and yell at the moon. Fluffy will show you how."

Dogs howl at the moon, Will.

Drew reached for the bottle. "You go yell at a thing or two, and I promise, I'll sit here and talk to Tobias. I'll even share the booze."

Will followed Fluffy and me, but before he went back to the hut, he hesitated. "Wick. We'll all be fine, I hope you know that. But that path, right there, that's the one you need to be on."

Where does it lead? Is this more a giant metaphor that I'll have to think about harder than I want to?

"No metaphors. When you're ready, it leads right back to here. Take all the time you need. We'll wait for you."

Fluffy led me into the woods; he wound through the trees in the dark as if their location had been tattooed on his brain. Jeff waited for us in a clearing, his face already turned to the sky, moonlight twinkling off his scales. Fluffy's colorful new fur blew back a tiny bit in the breeze, and he looked up, too.

I don't know if I can do this.

They waited.

Drew hadn't known he could walk in space; he was afraid and did it anyway. It didn't matter that he now wondered if he should have sent someone else. It was new, and he faced it. Now he was back at Shivan's facing a man who had been an enemy, trusting him to help him shed layers of agony that might otherwise choke him. Layers that would let him take a breath or two, even when stuck in a nightmare.

Breathing lessons.

I inhaled deeply and then looked up.

It didn't matter that this moon was only thirty feet above me, embedded in projectors and monitors, and filled in with nanobits that gave it texture and made everything feel real. It didn't matter that the breeze was simply coming from a series of fans in a wall that I couldn't see. Jeff and Fluffy were products of wishes, bits and pieces of me that came from parts of my mind I could barely reach and rarely gave much consideration.

I opened my mouth and allowed myself a tiny yowl, and then a little more. They joined in because they couldn't help it and because they were a part of me; I stopped worrying about the people who loved me hearing any of this, and I let go.

There were no tears, but I cried.

I cried for people I had loved and lost, I cried for the things I couldn't change but desperately wanted to, and I cried for tiny me who had wound up in San Francisco just before the earthquake that changed the city forever. I cried for all the names I'd had and the lives I'd endured as Seven and Merlin, the pain of those years seared into my soul from starvation and loneliness and terror. I cried for a dead Emperor who lived, the people who existed thirty-five years in the future who had grieved for him and felt cheated out of the time lost. I cried for the existence of

Levi Munson and the horrors he'd inflicted on Hyrum and then Oz, and then for the guilt I felt at that tiny taste of victory when he was murdered in his jail cell.

I cried for Will's happiness, the joy that he lived, that he deserved all the wonderful things life was giving him now. For Hyrum, that he was as unbroken as a shattered soul could be.

I howled for everything bad and everything good, every scar on my soul and every blessing I'd been gifted.

And when we were spent, when I could barely breathe and I had nothing left to wail over, Fluffy guided me back, down the path to here, where there was an open door and a hut filled with the quiet sounds of children sleeping, where the Emperor Will waited by the fire, his feet up and book in hand. He didn't look up, didn't say anything, but patted his lap, an invitation to join him.

I pushed Drew to Saint Francis because I thought he needed to see Shivan, to thank him, and to commiserate.

Did you know why I wanted to come here? I asked Will after a while.

"I was not certain," he admitted. "I was aware you needed something and hoped you'd find it here."

Drew has to go back. Otherwise—

"I know. And he will, eventually. But we will not push him, all right?"

Not for a few more years. He still has babies to make. They'll be the same babies, won't they?

"One would think. But I cannot guarantee that."

When I was out there with Fluffy and Jeff, I had a want. A wish.

"You didn't—"

I didn't create another giant creature. I didn't create anything. I just wished that the old Queen was still alive. There's this little voice in my brain that says she would have made everything all right, somehow.

He set the book aside.

"She would have tried. Though placing that expectation upon her would be as burdensome as the weight you've felt lately. We rely on you perhaps a bit too much, Wick. You truly don't need to take on every need this family has. I know you've taken to spending time with each of us at night, making sure we're all right."

But I do.

I do that as much for me as for you.

Will you bring me back here if I ask? Without asking why?

"I will."

Will you make Drew come back here, even if he says he doesn't want to or need to?

"I will."

Thank you.

And that was like vows, so I think that makes us a little bit married now.

He snorted and picked the book up, flipping it open to the page he'd left off. "Wick, you stood on my shoulder at my wedding, and you kissed the bride. I think we've been a little bit married for a very long time now."

For better or for worse, dude. But not richer or poorer.

I expect richer.

And a raise in my allowance.

"A raise."

I'm gonna have to pay Hyrum for services rendered. And I am gonna do that, talk with him. Because Hyrum? He'll understand, even if he doesn't.

Smart man that he is, he didn't argue.

I totally got that raise.

Also by Max Thompson

The Emperor of San Francisco: The Wick Chronicles, Book One
Ozoo: The Wick Chronicles, Book Two
Forked: The Wick Chronicles, Book Three

The Space Between Whens: Wick After Dark, Book One
The Blessings of Saint Wick: Wick After Dark, Book Two

The Whens of Wick: Return of the Wick Chronicles, Book One
The Book of Hyrum:Retrun of the Wick Chronicles, Book Two
JUMP: Return of the Wick Chronicles Book Three
The King of Saint Francis: Return of the Wick Chronicles Book Four

The Psychokitty Speaks Out: Diary of a Mad Housecat
The Psychokitty Speaks Out: Something of Yours Will Meet A Toothy Death
The Rules: A Guide For People Owned By Cats
Bite Me: A Memoir (Of Sorts)
Epistle: A Love Letter
There Once Was a Cat From Nantucket

Visit Max online at his blog, The Psychokitty Speaks Out
http://psychokitty.blogspot.com
or on Facebook
http://facebook.com/thepsychokittyspeaksout

Books one of his people (K.A. Thompson) wrote

The Charybdis Novels:
Charybdis
As Simple As That
Finding Father Rabbit
The King and Queen of Perfect Normal
The Flipside of Here

It's Not About the Cookies
Rock the Pink

Visit K.A. Thompson online at her blog,
Thumper Thinks Out Loud
http://kathompson.blogspot.com